Sympathy for the Devil

CHRISTINE POPE

DARK VALENTINE PRESS

SYMPATHY FOR THE DEVIL
ISBN: 978-0-9883348-6-1

Copyright © 2014 by Christine Pope
Published by Dark Valentine Press

Revised 2014 edition. Originally published by Pink Petal Books, December 2010.

Cover design and print layout by Indie Author Services.

Go to www.christinepope.com to learn more about this author.

And now these three remain: faith, hope, and love.
But the greatest of these is love.

Sympathy for the Devil

Prologue

Chartres, France, twenty-eight years ago

THE DEVIL PAUSED ON THE STREET outside a café and glanced in the window. God already sat at a table inside, blowing on a cup of café au lait. After stopping to brush some snow from the shoulder of his coat, the Devil entered the building.

"You're late," God remarked, not looking up from His coffee.

"An unavoidable delay, I assure you." The Devil waved a waiter over and ordered a double espresso.

"Sticking to the dark side, I see," said God.

"That stuff," the Devil retorted, pointing a gloved finger at God's café au lait, "is entirely too frilly for me."

God didn't bother to reply, but instead took a small sip from His maligned coffee and then shut His eyes momentarily. "You don't know what you're missing," He said. "But no matter. We're not here to discuss coffee, are we?"

"Hardly." The Devil drew off his gloves and laid them on the scuffed tabletop. The waiter reappeared and placed an espresso at the Devil's elbow, then retreated toward the kitchen. Without bothering to blow on the steaming liquid to cool it, the Devil tossed back a healthy swallow, after which he set the cup down on the table and said, "I want out."

"Out?" God inquired, in a tone of mild curiosity.

"Out of Hell. I'm done. Eternity's gotten to be too long."

For a moment God regarded the Devil over the rim of His coffee cup. He sipped again, then put down the café au lait. "Any reason for this change of heart?"

"The world doesn't need the Devil anymore. These people can manage quite well enough on their own."

God considered that statement for a moment, then said, "Any other explanations for this sudden onset of angst?"

The Devil drained the rest of his espresso and signaled the waiter for another. "Does it matter? Isn't this what you've wanted all along—for me to come crawling back on my hands and knees?"

"Penitence is laudable, of course, but balance must be maintained. Hell must have its guardian."

"So promote Beelzebub," the Devil growled. "He's been grousing about 'glass ceilings' and all that lately. I knew I should have canceled that subscription to *Inc.* magazine."

God smiled. "Very well. But I'm afraid it's not quite that simple."

The Devil made a sound of muffled anger in his throat. "What, then?"

Still smiling, God waited until the waiter had placed another espresso on the table and moved off to take an order from a portly gentleman a few tables away. "To re-enter the Kingdom of Heaven, you must prove that you're worthy of it."

"And how the hell—if you'll pardon the expression—am I supposed to do that?"

"Love."

"Excuse me?"

God finished off the rest of His café au lait. "Ah, excellent. Truly the best on Earth. Anyhow, if you can prove that you're capable of love—*true* love, not simple lust or infatuation—then you may become mortal, live out a span of years, and die. At that point you should have redeemed yourself sufficiently to return to Heaven."

"I have to die to do it?"

"I'm afraid so."

The Devil let out an exasperated sigh. "It's never easy with You, is it?"

God lifted His shoulders. "How badly do you want to be quit of Hell?"

"I see your point." There was a pause as the Devil took a more modest sip of espresso. Frowning, he asked, "Who is this person I'm supposed to love?"

"Ah, that." God traced a finger along a particularly deep scar on the tabletop. "She's just been born, as a matter of fact."

"Is she pretty?"

God lifted an eyebrow. "Typical. If I wanted to make this particularly difficult, I could have made her plain, but—yes, she will be pretty. Not," God added, giving the Devil a stern look, "outstandingly beautiful."

"I suppose it would have been too much to request another Marilyn Monroe or Sophia Loren."

"Some of My best work," God said modestly. "But yes, of course. Nothing like that. Still, she should be pleasing enough."

"All right," said the Devil, after drinking more espresso. "What else?"

"She must love you for yourself. This means she must know who you are."

"I have to tell her I'm the Devil?"

"Yes."

The Devil frowned but said nothing.

"You will retain all your powers, but you may know nothing of her—nothing more than you would learn from observing her as any mortal man might. It would give you an unfair advantage for you to know everything of her life as you do with other mortals." God picked up a sugar packet and considered it, then put it back in the wire rack that held its companions. "And you must accomplish your goal in thirty days."

"Why thirty?"

God raised an eyebrow. "It seems a good round number."

The Devil looked away, gazing through the window at the town square outside and the bulk of the cathedral that loomed up through the twilight. He asked, "But I am allowed to keep my powers?"

"Up until the time you meet the strictures of our agreement. Then, of course, you will be as mortal as anyone else. Oh, you won't be cut off completely," God went on, His voice somewhat amused. "If nothing else, you've earned a very good retirement package, but how can you expect to live out your life as a regular man if I allow you to retain your powers?"

The Devil tapped his fingers on the table, considering. "All right," he said. "I suppose You have a valid point. So I simply have to fall in love with her, and have her fall in love with me? Then I live my life, go to Heaven, and am finished with Hell forever?"

"The fact that you used the word 'simply' in that sentence proves how little you know about love."

"Hmph." The Devil set his empty espresso cup down on the battered tabletop. "We'll see about that."

"Yes," God said mildly. "I suppose We shall."

CHAPTER ONE

I FIRST SAW THE DEVIL when I was six years old.

Of course, at the time I didn't actually know he was the Devil. When you're six, if you notice adults at all, it's mostly to make sure they're not about to tell you to stop doing whatever it is that you're doing. Or maybe you're reassuring yourself that the adult off on the sidelines isn't the Evil Stranger in the trench coat who does horrible but unexplained things to small children—you know, the ones who aren't smart enough to remember that they're not supposed to talk to anyone outside a small, well-defined circle of family and friends.

The strange man stood quietly off to one side of the park, watching as I played with Ashley, my then–best friend. I didn't notice anything particular about him, except that he wasn't any of my friends' fathers, as far as I could tell. Ashley and I were playing on the swings, taunting each other to see who could go the highest, and when I was able to focus on the ground once again, he was gone.

At the time, I didn't think anything much of it.

But then he turned up again seven years later. I was at my junior high school's graduation and had just picked up the fake little diploma they gave out to all the eighth-graders. After I took the piece of paper from the principal's hand and turned to walk off the platform, I saw the Devil again. I didn't know who he was then, either, just that he looked vaguely familiar, a dark-haired man, tall, whose features nagged at my memory. By then I'd become aware enough of the opposite sex that I was able to decide I thought he was sort of cute—for an old guy.

Of course, I had no idea how very, very old he actually was.

By the time I turned twenty-one, I'd almost forgotten about those two odd little encounters. I'd managed to escape what I saw as the smothering suburbia of Orange County (although UCLA wasn't exactly Outer Mongolia or anything), and it was on the campus at UCLA that I saw the Devil for the last time. Let me rephrase that—it was the last time I saw him as just an observer.

I was hurrying to class, late because I'd stayed up most of the night finishing a paper on German Expressionism. Exactly how an in-depth analysis of Murnau's *Faust* was supposed to help me with my future as a productive member of society hadn't been fully explained to me, but at the time getting a good grade on that paper seemed like the most important thing in my world. I almost didn't see the stranger as I staggered toward the Humanities building, lugging a bulging backpack that was destined to send me to the chiropractor.

But there the man was, a flicker at the corner of my peripheral vision. I paused—I think I told myself it was to hitch the pack a little farther up on my shoulder before it slid down and dislocated my elbow. Really, though, I stopped so I could get a closer look at him.

He hadn't changed. Now, I know there are people in the world who age extraordinarily well. In fact, my mother still looks pretty damn good for her age. But she still looks older than she did when I was six, or thirteen, or even twenty-one. This man looked exactly the same that day at UCLA as the first time I'd seen him some fifteen years earlier.

My brain churned away at the improbability and then did the most logical thing it could: It told me I was mistaken. *He just looks like the person you saw when you were a kid*, it told me. *How could it possibly be the same man?*

How indeed?

So I re-shouldered my backpack and continued on my way. Right before I ducked inside the building, I glanced back at the spot where he had been standing, just to prove to myself that my eyes had been playing tricks on me. By then he was gone.

I felt a little shiver touch the back of my neck, despite the warm spring day. But I had a class to get to and was late, and so I shook my head at myself and hurried on. I didn't have the time to deal with impossible conundrums.

Sometimes I wonder what would have happened if I'd gone up and spoken to him then.

Fast-forward another seven years. During my senior year of college my parents went through a typically messy divorce, and rather than deal with the fallout of the situation, I decided to stay up in L.A. and look for work there. I was lucky enough to land a job as an editorial assistant at a glossy regional magazine. A few years later, the magazine's copyeditor got an offer he couldn't refuse from a big-time investment firm downtown that needed someone to oversee the company's publications and website. So I got promoted to copyeditor and actually had my own office. I was also finally making enough money that I could bail out on my less-than-optimal roommate situation and find an apartment of my own.

Contrary to popular belief, working at a magazine isn't all that glamorous. All right, maybe some magazines are glamorous. My editor does get some pretty good perks, but believe me, when the invites come in for movie premieres or store openings, it's not the copyeditor who gets to walk down the red carpet. No, sir. The copyeditor gets to wait for the editorial staff to write about their glam evenings and then make sure all the commas are in the right place.

Still, it wasn't a bad life. My apartment wasn't anything special, but I liked it because, unlike a lot of places in Southern California (and especially in Irvine, where I'd grown up), it had a bit of history. It was built sometime in the '40s and had a cute little faux fireplace with a molded plaster mantel, actual crown moldings in the living room, and even a tiny laundry area that allowed me to have my own stackable washer and dryer so I wouldn't have to suffer the indignity of dragging my unmentionables to the laundromat. Unlike most other Angelenos, I didn't have much of a commute; I'd chosen this apartment partially because it was exactly 2.3 miles from the office, which meant I could get to work in five minutes most days, barring the unforeseen accident or unscheduled "street improvement." (Which I think is Caltrans code for shutting down lanes on random streets because they feel like it.)

My love life, on the other hand—well, let's just say the 500-thread-count sheets I'd bought on clearance the previous summer hadn't been getting much action.

I'd been dating this one guy, Danny Koslowski, on and off for about six months. He didn't seem that interested in having things progress any further, and I didn't know if I even cared all that much. For one thing, I had a problem with a guy who was staring down the barrel of the big 3-0 but who still went by "Danny." It made him sound like a five-year-old who should be calling me about play dates, not real dates. Also, he was a computer geek. Now, I don't have a problem with geeks, per se. I mean, I'd rather have that than a guy who's sports-obsessed. But after the third or fourth date canceled because he got wrapped up in playing Warcrack—excuse me, War*craft*—I'd begun to seriously reconsider where our relationship was going. If we even had a relationship.

Unfortunately, I didn't have much of an alternative, and he was so obsessively casual about the whole thing that he made it almost impossible for me to break up with him. Go two weeks without a phone call? No problem. Inquire innocently whether our relationship was "exclusive"? His only answer was a shrug and, "I don't know—do you want it to be?"

I think I answered yes. But what immediately depressed me was that I didn't have anyone to be non-exclusive with, even if I had told him I wanted to see other people. I almost signed up for an online dating service in a fit of pique, but I came to my senses after recalling some of my friends' horror stories on that subject.

"You should do what I did," my friend Nina told me at lunch one day. We were roommates during college, and we still saw each other a good deal on the weekends. She'd moved back to Brentwood, where she was living in her parents' guest house rent-free. It was a pretty cushy setup that allowed her to use her salary for important things, like shopping. Also, Nina's father was a plastic surgeon. It wasn't as if he needed her rent money to make his mortgage.

And Nina, irony of ironies, sure as hell didn't need any plastic surgery. She was part Irish, part African-American, part Japanese, and all gorgeous. I considered myself a moderately attractive person, but if I entered a room with Nina I might as well be invisible for all the attention I got. Despite this, I really did like her.

"So what did you do?" I asked her, pushing a crouton off to one side of my plate. Damn those carbs anyway.

"I went bi," she replied blithely.

I almost choked on a piece of arugula. "You what?"

She shrugged. "Hey, it doubles the size of the playing field."

But—but—I stared at her for a few seconds, then asked, "So when did this momentous change take place? I mean, I don't remember you being into anyone except guys during college."

"Oh, a few months ago." Her green eyes, startling against their surrounding milk-and-coffee skin, laughed at me. "I met someone."

She met someone? I had to infer that someone was female, or there wouldn't have been any reason for this sudden switch to the Dark Side. Feeling more than a little uncomfortable, I said, "So all that time we were roommates…." I let the words trail off, not knowing exactly what I had meant to say.

Nina burst out laughing at that comment. "Oh, don't worry, Christa. I wasn't attracted to *you*."

"Gee, thanks."

"I didn't mean it that way." She took a bite of her burger; besides being gorgeous, she had one of those metabolisms where she could eat anything she wanted and never gain an ounce. I wasn't quite as fanatical about my weight as a lot of people I knew, but more than two or three cheeseburgers in a month, and my pants started to get a little tight. "I hadn't really started to explore that side of my sexuality back then, and besides, you're my friend. I just wouldn't look at you that way."

If you say so, I thought, but somehow Nina's words depressed me even more. I mean, I'd certainly never been interested in women and wouldn't go that route no matter how desperate I got, but still it would have been nice to know that at least she found me attractive. "Well, I'm pretty sure your solution isn't an option for me," I said, setting down my salad fork. The field greens and vinaigrette had suddenly lost their charms. "Do your parents know?"

"Are you kidding? The doctor would freak. Gina and I get together at her place off Montana Avenue."

"What? You tell your parents you're going over there to help her with her homework?"

"They think Gina's an artist we represent who needs a lot of hand-holding," she said with a smirk.

Was she serious? Nina and Gina? I could just see them getting matching Juicy Couture track suits with their names embroidered across their butts. I shook my head to rid it of that frightening image. "My father would probably say you were just going through a phase."

She snorted. "Like he would know. How's your stepmom? Has she gone through all the Botox in Newport Beach yet?"

"I think they had to send out to Beverly Hills for a restock," I replied.

If it hadn't all happened to me, it would have been funny, in a clichéd sort of way. Successful psychologist has midlife crisis, dumps his wife, and trades up for a newer model. At least my stepmother wasn't younger than I—I'd been spared that indignity—but Traci was still almost twenty years younger than my mother. Of course, that didn't stop her from exploiting every cosmeceutical means necessary to prolong her late-thirties status for as long as possible.

Maybe she was worried that my father would end up doing the same thing to her that he'd done to my mother. I think I read somewhere that off-loading wives got progressively easier as you moved up the food chain.

At any rate, I'd tried to play nice as much as I could. Luckily I was already out of the house when my parents split up for good; my younger brother didn't fare so well, since he was almost eight years younger than I am. I had to say this for my father, though: He never tried to get out of paying alimony, and he kept on sending my mother child support even though Jeff was twenty-one at that point and well past dependent age as far as the courts were concerned. My father said he'd pay for Jeff as long as he was in school. Since my younger brother seemed to be on the ten-year plan at Irvine Valley College, I wasn't going to hold my breath on the child support going away any time soon.

Lisa, my older sister, claimed that Jeff was just having a tough time because of the divorce, but seriously, when she made that remark it had been almost seven years since the final papers were signed, and five since Traci officially became our stepmother. After a while things stop being reasons and start becoming excuses.

Then again, Lisa had always babied Jeff because he was the youngest and the only boy. She and I squabbled a lot as kids, probably because we were barely two years apart, but as we got older we didn't so much make up and become friends as we just got on with our own lives. We never had much in common, since she was this uber-organized mega-sales real estate agent in south Orange County, and I'd always done all right for myself but never accomplished anything that extraordinary.

Frankly, I was the stereotypical middle child— never causing much trouble, never wanting to make waves. Pretty, but not the sort who would stop a guy in his tracks. Straight brown hair, brown eyes, a shade taller than average, slender but not thin, the girl next door. *Boring,* I thought for the millionth time, as I looked across the table and took in Nina's perfect curls and five-foot-ten-inch frame. Even the damned busboy was loitering as he cleared the table next to ours so he could get an eyeful.

"Children of shrinks are always messed up," Nina said. "You're lucky you got out with just a few minor neuroses."

"Lucky," I repeated, thinking of Danny, who seemed to care more about his computer and his online gaming than he did me, of my bleached stepmother and my stoner brother and especially my mother. The breakup with my father had made her go all New Age-y and spiritual as some sort of Zen coping mechanism, and lately it had been driving me nuts.

Giving me a stern look, Nina reached for her water glass. "I smell a pity party coming on," she said, after taking a drink. "Which I definitely will not allow. Especially with your birthday coming up next week. What do you want to do, anyway?"

"Nothing. It's on a Tuesday—how much partying can I do on a Tuesday?"

"We could still go out to dinner or something." Her eyes narrowed. "Unless Danny's taking you out?"

"Danny?" I laughed, but I didn't sound very amused, even to myself. "If he actually remembers that it's my birthday, I'll probably fall down dead of a heart attack."

"Well, did you tell him it was?"

"I might have mentioned it once or twice." And I had, even though the last comment had been almost a month ago. Still, the guy was practically glued to his iPhone. He could have written it down and put an alarm on the entry or something so he wouldn't forget. Unfortunately, that assumed a level of concern I was pretty certain didn't exist.

"So if he forgets, are you going to dump him?"

"I might," I said evasively. "Look, something is better than nothing, isn't it?"

Nina sighed. "That's bullshit, and you know it. You were doing fine before Danny came along, and you'll be fine when he's gone. I think he's more of a distraction than anything else. If you've got a relationship going on, even a half-assed one, you're not going to work very hard to find someone else."

"Maybe there isn't anyone else," I argued.

"There's always someone else," she said calmly. "All this stuff about there being only one perfect person for everybody is crap. Don't tell me you've started reading romance novels in your spare time, 'cause that's the only way I can see you starting to think that's how the world works."

"No romance novels." I held up a hand in a mocking imitation of the Girl Scout salute. "I solemnly swear that there are no Nora Roberts or Barbara Michaels books lurking under my bed."

"I'm serious."

"So am I."

The conversation drifted off into other matters after that, and then it was time to head out and get in a little more shopping before the early dark of a January afternoon fell. Rather, I got to watch Nina create havoc with her platinum card as we wended our way down the Third Street Promenade. She'd landed a cushy gig as the manager of an extremely high-end art gallery in Santa Monica, and her paychecks were a lot fatter than mine. But I didn't mind watching as she shopped; at least it kept me occupied and away from my apartment for a few more hours. I didn't even have a cat to go home to. My apartment building didn't allow pets, and besides, I had a mortal fear of turning into the crazy cat lady. Anything but that.

Eventually, though, I had to go home. Once there, I shoved my iPod in its dock and turned up the volume on my stereo to drown out the silence. Then I got to work on laundry and bills and all the other fun stuff I inevitably put off until the weekend. It worked a little; I actually had stretches of a half-hour or so where I didn't feel completely alone.

As it turned out, my birthday ended up sucking even more than I thought it would. Not only did Danny completely forget that Tuesday, January 23, held any special significance, but Nina came down with a nasty cold that was making the rounds and couldn't possibly be expected to go anywhere except maybe the local drugstore to pick up more tissues and Nyquil.

"Sorry," she told me. I winced as a particularly piercing sneeze came through the earpiece of the hands-free unit on my cell phone. "I've been sucking zinc lozenges like there's no tomorrow. I haven't noticed much of a difference."

"It's all right," I said miserably. Someone behind me honked, and I realized the light I'd been sitting at had finally turned green. I took my foot off the brake and slowly moved forward. "I'll figure out something."

"What about Jennifer or Micaela?" Nina asked, naming the only two from our group of friends at UCLA that we'd continued to hang out with after graduation.

"Jennifer's up skiing in Mammoth, and Micaela's production schedule just got bumped ten days. She'll be lucky if she gets home before midnight." A film major, Micaela was actually doing what so many people only dreamed of—she was a production assistant at Warner Brothers. Unfortunately, her dream job meant her schedule was beyond screwy. I repressed the urge to heave a world-weary sigh and said, "It's all right. My dad sent me a huge check— guilt money for being in Hawaii on my birthday, I guess—so I'm going shopping."

"Good girl." Nina sneezed again. "Don't spend it all in one place."

"I won't," I promised. "You go lie down. You sound terrible."

"You should see how I look. It's even worse."

Somehow I doubted that, since even with a head cold Nina always managed to look fabulous, but I didn't argue. I just made some more sympathetic noises into the phone, assured her I was fine, and hung up.

My father really had sent me a birthday card with a check for five hundred dollars in it. While I had no intention of blowing even a third of that money tonight, I thought a little shopping at The

Grove might make me feel better about being completely abandoned on my birthday. Oh, I supposed
if I had really wanted to I could have driven down
to Orange County to see my mother, but the traffic
was so bad by the time I got off work at five that
it would have taken me at least two hours to get
there. Besides, we already had plans to get together
on Saturday. No doubt she'd take me to some "fabulous" new organic place she'd found in Laguna
Beach, and I'd have to pretend I was happy eating
something covered in sprouts and suspiciously lacking in meat. But if it made her happy, I'd survive. I
figured I could always get a burger on the way home
if I felt particularly starved afterward.

The Grove was located near the old Farmer's
Market at the corner of Third and Fairfax. While it
had considerably expanded the shopping possibilities in the area, its presence also increased traffic to
the point where it was practically gridlocked during
peak drive times. Although my company's offices
were a scant mile and a half from the shopping center, it took me almost fifteen minutes to get there,
crawl up to the top level of the parking structure,
and finally drag myself out of my Mercedes C-class,
feeling vaguely homicidal. I reflected it was a good
thing I didn't have to do much driving. For some
reason, being in a car really brought home to me
how overpopulated Southern California actually
was. When you start to sympathize with serial killers

because at least they're reducing the surplus population, you know you've got a problem.

By the way, the car was a graduation present
from my father. I sure as hell couldn't have afforded
it on my salary. I had to give him that—he definitely
wasn't stingy. And in L.A., where what you drive is
just as important as what you do, having something
better than the tired Honda Accord I'd been pilot-
ing since tenth grade was a definite relief.

Intellectually I knew that you shouldn't have
your identity wrapped up in your car, and I didn't
(mostly), but the change in people's attitudes after
I started driving the Mercedes told me there was a
very good reason why people here were so car-obsessed. Besides, I felt safe in it, the gas mileage was
fairly decent, and it hadn't given me a moment's
trouble in the almost four years that I'd been driving
it. I couldn't say that much for my Honda, which
by the end was making piteous groaning noises and
leaking oil. It had practically been begging to be
taken out behind the barn and shot. Not knowing
what else to do with it, I'd donated it to charity. The
tax write-off was helpful at least, although I came
out of the transaction feeling as if I'd done something vaguely illegal.

I pulled my coat more closely around me as I
hurried over to the elevator and pushed the button.
Some people might claim that Southern California
doesn't have seasons, but they must not have ever

lived here. Sure, it doesn't snow in L.A., but it can get pretty darn cold during the winter. Okay, maybe not cold compared to say, Quebec or something, but certainly cold enough to require a warm coat if you're going to spend any more time outdoors than simply walking to your car.

It had rained the night before, but at least by the time I got to The Grove it was dry. Shoving my chilled fingers into my pockets, I stepped out of the elevator and moved into the open plaza in the center of the mall. The Grove was always fairly crowded, but that night it was more maneuverable than usual. January was sort of a dead season for retail sales, and the cold weather wasn't helping much.

I didn't have a real game plan; I just wandered in and out of several stores, thinking something would catch my eye. Having that much spare money burning a hole in my pocket certainly wasn't my normal experience. Usually I had to budget and figure out if I'd really have enough extra cash to buy that great pair of shoes I'd been lusting after, or whether it would be better to just put it away in case of any real financial emergencies. I'd say my better nature won out only about half the time, but at least I had some killer shoes.

Eventually I came to Victoria's Secret. Part of my brain tried to instruct me in the futility of buying fancy underwear when I didn't have anyone around to give a damn about how I looked in it, but I'd always had a weakness for girly stuff. Besides, they were having a sale, and damn it, it was my birthday.

I suppose it was my musing over the matching red satin bra and panties I'd just purchased that made me a little absentminded. Then again, maybe that was just what he wanted me to think.

Whatever the reason, I was peering into the bag as I left the store (I tended to get paranoid about dropping a store receipt and having someone somehow steal my identity from the four digits of my Visa number printed on it), and I walked right into him.

"Sorry!" I said automatically. Then I looked up to see who I had collided with.

It was *him*.

He smiled at me.

"Hello, Christa," he said.

CHAPTER TWO

FOR A SECOND, I just goggled at him. Then I remembered to shut my mouth. At first I wanted to demand how the hell he could possibly know my name, and then that thought got twisted up in bemusement at the fact that he still looked exactly the same.

My tongue tripped over itself, and all that came out was a strangled, "Wha—who—"

Again that smile. "Call me Luke."

If someone asks you to "call them" something, then you can be pretty damn sure it's not their real name. I clutched my Victoria's Secret shopping bag against my chest like a shield and tried to gather whatever shreds of my dignity might be left. Not knowing what else to say, I asked, "I've seen you before, haven't I?"

"Perhaps."

Perhaps? Who says "perhaps" these days? "I know I saw you," I said firmly. "About seven years ago, on the campus at UCLA. Or maybe we should go a little further back...say, to my eighth-grade graduation?"

"You are observant, aren't you, Christa?" He glanced around us, at the people hurrying in and out of shops and restaurants. "Not a very private place for a conversation, is it?"

I narrowed my eyes at him. "Why would we need to have a private conversation?"

"You'll see." He stuck his hands in his coat pockets, still smiling that enigmatic smile, and then suddenly we were someplace else.

The whole world seemed to tilt around me, and I let out a little shriek. Not very dignified, I know, but you try standing in the middle of a shopping center one second and then being—well, I didn't know exactly where I was, but it certainly wasn't The Grove.

My first impression was of a panorama that glittered in the darkness, and then I realized I stood in the living room of a house that must have been built up against the Hollywood Hills or someplace like that. Los Angeles lay spread out beneath me, a moving carpet of light. After I caught my breath and looked around a little more, I realized the place looked oddly familiar.

What the hell? "Is this the *Charlie's Angels* house?" I demanded. I was kind of obsessed with that movie back in high school. Kicking ass while wearing a progression of crazy disguises looked like a lot of fun.

"The what?" he asked.

"In the first *Charlie's Angels* movie, the computer genius who turns out to be the bad guy had one of those houses up on stilts in the hills. This one looks just like it."

The stranger appeared nonplused. "Aren't you even going to ask how we got here?"

Well, my brain had sort of skipped over that part, probably because if I'd stopped to think about it, my head would have exploded. But the rationalizing had already kicked in. Maybe he'd injected something in my arm when we bumped into each other, and he'd dragged me up here while I was in a drugged state. Or maybe I only thought I was here, while in reality I'd actually fallen down and was now lying on the ground, still at The Grove, with a concussion and possibly worse.

I shot him a wary look. "Are you going to tell me if I ask?"

He gave me the last answer I expected. "Of course."

That took me off-guard, so I had to digest his reply for a few seconds before saying, "Okay, then... how did we get here?"

"I brought us here."

"You...brought...us here."

He shrugged. "It's a little thing I do."

"You…*do?*"

Up until that moment I thought he had dark eyes, since his hair and brows were such a deep brown, but as his eyes glinted at me I suddenly realized they were a very dark blue. A corner of his mouth lifted slightly. "It's because I'm the Devil."

Again, I could only stand there and stare at him, feeling as if somehow I had been made the butt of a colossal joke. Finally I managed, "The *what?*"

He moved across the living room, which was decorated with museum-quality '60s-vintage modern furniture, and paused at the bar that separated the kitchen and dining room. "Cosmo?"

"Yes," I said automatically. Right then the only thing in the universe I thought I had a firm grasp on was that I needed a stiff drink.

As if by magic a cocktail shaker appeared on the bar before him; he busied himself with pouring a measure of Grey Goose vodka into it, followed by the necessary cranberry juice and Cointreau. He transferred the resulting concoction into a martini glass, then came back around the bar and handed the drink to me.

I looked at it with some suspicion, but need won out over caution. I took a sip, then another. It was good.

"So you're the Devil," I said, in what I hoped was an off-hand conversational tone. He didn't look particularly crazy, but that didn't mean much. The evening news was full of people saying, *But he seemed like such a normal person....*

"Yes," he said.

"And so you're visiting L.A.?" I asked, thinking, *Just don't make any sudden movements, and you'll be fine.*

"You don't believe me."

"I didn't say that," I said hastily. Nutcases hated having their psychoses thrown back at them.

"This isn't evidence enough?" He gestured toward the oddly familiar room in which we stood.

I hesitated. While I wanted to point out that he could have drugged me and brought me here, or that he could be another element in some elaborate hallucination, I didn't want to upset him, either. Just because I couldn't see any sharp pointy objects in the vicinity didn't mean he couldn't get his hands on something if necessary.

Realizing I still held the Victoria's Secret bag, I wadded it up and shoved it inside my purse. There were just so many blows to my dignity I could take in one evening, and every time his eyes went to the shopping bag I wondered if he were imagining what sorts of unmentionables I had hidden inside.

"All right," I said at last. "If you're really the Devil, why go for something so—so—"

"So what?" he asked softly.

"So typical," I replied. "I mean, wow, you're the Devil, and now you've got the ultimate L.A.

bachelor pad from the movies or whatever. Do you really think this sort of thing impresses women?"

Dead silence. I swallowed, and wondered where the front door was and whether I could get to it quickly enough before he decided my rudeness deserved a quick evisceration.

Then he threw back his head and laughed. It wasn't crazy hysterical laughter—he just sounded like someone who'd heard a friend tell a particularly funny bar joke. "I begin to see what He meant," he murmured.

"Excuse me?"

"Nothing." For the first time I noticed he held a martini of his own. I hadn't seen him mix it, but maybe he had a second cocktail shaker hidden somewhere on the bar.

Or maybe he really is the Devil, I thought, and he just conjured it out of thin air...because he can.

"Let's try this again, shall we?" he asked. Lifting his glass, he took a swallow of his own drink. Then he winked at me.

And the scene changed again. Somehow I managed to retain enough presence of mind to maintain a death grip on my martini glass. I blinked, and we were no longer standing in that overly retro-cool living room. Instead, my surroundings reminded me of a Tuscan villa—dark wood floors with faded but still costly oriental rugs, antiques in simple woods that matched the floors. At one end of the chamber in which we stood, a fire burned softly in an enormous fireplace with a surround of glazed red tiles.

"Let me guess," I said. "Italy?"

"Hancock Park."

Hancock Park was an extremely upscale part of Los Angeles approximately five miles east of where I lived in the Fairfax District. A hell of a lot closer than Tuscany, that was for sure, but still there was no way we could have gotten there in the blink of an eye, especially with rush hour crawling toward seven o'clock on the streets outside.

"I think I need to sit down." I spotted a couch a few yards away and stumbled over to it, feeling as if someone had smacked me upside the head a few times with a baseball bat.

"Good idea." He followed me but remained standing while I sank down onto the sofa. I felt the warmth of down-filled cushions support my outraged muscles.

Not knowing what else to do, I sipped at my drink again. Devil or not, he made a hell of a Cosmo.

"Better?" he asked.

"Nice house," I said cautiously. "Is it yours?"

"It is now."

I hated it when people made me feel stupid. Frowning a little, I asked, "What does that mean?"

"I mean that it was on the market, but with after-holiday sales sluggish as they are, the realtor had despaired and dropped the price. Lo and behold!

She'll come into the office tomorrow and find the offers all signed and countersigned, and the owners paid with a cashier's check for the full asking price."

"You can do that?"

He smiled at me. If it had been anyone else, that sort of smile would have made my knees melt. As it was….

"I can do anything I want," he replied.

"Anything?" I asked. It came out more as a squeak. So much for the whole dignity thing.

"Well, almost." The smile faded slightly. "I do have a few rules I have to follow."

I wondered who would set rules the Devil had to follow, came to the immediate conclusion that it had to be someone Very Important, and gulped. In what I hoped were airy tones I commented, "But obviously they don't prevent you from making real estate deals."

"No, not that."

Feeling a little braver—after all, he might be the Devil, but he certainly hadn't done anything threatening so far—I asked, "So why are you here? And what does any of this have to do with me?"

For a moment he didn't say anything. He turned away from me slightly and appeared to watch the movement of the fire in the hearth. Finally he said, "I needed to ask you something."

That sounded ominous. Maybe he was under his soul-collection quota for the month. With nervous fingers I tucked a strand of hair back behind one ear. "Um—what did you need to ask me?"

The blue eyes met mine. If he were just a regular guy I'd met on the street, I would have killed to hear the question he asked next.

"Would you have dinner with me?"

Again I found myself momentarily struck dumb. Possibly I wasn't acquitting myself too well—I, who had always prided myself on being good with words if nothing else—but then again, how many people can handle a dinner invitation from the Devil without feeling just a little over-balanced?

Eventually, however, my vocal chords decided to function again. "Why?"

He definitely had a smile that made you think maybe Hell had gotten a bad rap all those years. "It's your birthday," he replied.

"Well, when you put it that way," I said. Then I thought, Oh, the hell with it...literally. "Dinner sounds great."

The smile deepened. "I thought you might say that."

It was too late to back out now. I just smiled back at him and hoped I hadn't done something really, really stupid.

For some reason I'd thought he would simply whisk me away to a restaurant by the same precipitous eye-blink method he'd used earlier. Instead, he instructed me to wait for him at a side entrance of the house under a porte-cochere (which was something I'd read about but had never actually seen in real life). Then he pulled up in a massive hunk of impressively gleaming metal.

"What is that?" I asked, staring at the car. I'd never seen anything like it before in my life.

"Bentley Arnage," he replied, opening the passenger door for me.

Well, damn. I was sure my car-obsessed father would have a fit if he could see me riding around in something like this. He drove an AMG-tuned Mercedes S-class and thought it was just about the pinnacle of automotive perfection, but this behemoth made my father's Mercedes look like a Yugo.

"Nice," I said, sliding carefully onto the diamond-upholstered leather seat. "Being the Devil must pay well."

"It has its perks." He shut the door after I seated myself; it closed with the sort of soft, solid thunk that only a very, very expensive car can make.

I sat there, taking in the scent of finely burnished leather upholstery, as he made his way back over to the driver's side and buckled himself in. Then I said, "So you do get around like a normal person." Pausing, I took in the opulent interior and added, "At least like a normal oil sheik or something."

He chuckled, then put the car in drive. The only reason I could tell we were moving was that I saw the manicured front yard slipping past us as he pulled out of the driveway. "Although people do tend to be notoriously unobservant, after a while too much inexplicable appearing and disappearing can get one noticed." He leaned over and touched a knob on the dashboard; the delicate sound of a string quartet began to play in the background. "Besides, I like to drive."

Who wouldn't, with a car like that? I thought that even being stuck in traffic on the 405 Freeway could be made bearable by sitting in a mobile Ritz like this mammoth piece of machinery. The gas mileage must suck, I thought, then, as if that makes a difference for anyone who can afford a car like this.

"I thought we'd go to Campanile," he went on, pulling out of the exclusive subdivision where his home was located and onto Beverly Boulevard. "If that's all right with you."

It was more than a little all right. Although the restaurant wasn't that far from where I lived, it certainly wasn't the sort of place where I could afford to eat on a whim, and none of the guys I'd dated had the means (or the taste, I had to admit) to take me someplace like that. "Sounds great," I managed.

He nodded, then pulled into the left lane so he could turn south on La Brea. Everything in his manner suggested that he'd done this a hundred times before, and maybe he had. Who knew how long he'd been loitering in the Los Angeles area, driving around in his luxo-mobile and observing the doings of lesser mortals?

That led me to wonder exactly what he was doing here and, more importantly, what on earth he wanted with me. I wasn't anyone special, that was for sure. The fate of the planet didn't rest on my shoulders; I wasn't an activist or a politician or anyone with any real influence. There were probably a hundred thousand other young women of my age and basic physical type in Southern California, so what led him to hone in on me?

I shot a quick sideways glance at him as he expertly maneuvered the enormous car through the intersection just as the light turned all the way to red. One of the things that irritated me the most about Los Angeles was its complete lack of dedicated left-hand turn signals; you invariably had to wait until the last few seconds of the yellow and then floor it and hope no one who was waiting for the green light in the other direction had a trigger foot. But the Bentley obviously had an engine to match its impressive sheet metal, and I barely felt the acceleration as the car turned south, heading toward the intersection with Wilshire and the restaurant itself.

He didn't look like the Devil. Then again, who knows what the Devil is supposed to look like? No horns, no tail, no pitchfork here. Even though a part of my brain kept protesting this must be either an elaborate hoax or some sort of drug-induced hallucination, that interior voice was growing fainter and fainter. For one thing, I'd experienced those unbelievable jumps in scene, and there hadn't been any "lost moments" or breaks in continuity. One minute I was at The Grove, and the next I was standing in that flying saucer of a house in the Hollywood Hills. That didn't meet my approval, and bam! I was planted in the living room of a gracious Mediterranean-style mansion miles away.

So I decided to go with it. Okay, he was the Devil, or at least some sort of being with powers so advanced they might as well be supernatural. He hadn't given me one word of explanation as to why he'd sought me out in particular. I knew he had to be after me for some reason, or else why would I recall seeing him at various points in my life? That if nothing else clinched it; the first time I'd seen him had been more than twenty years ago, and yet he still looked to be the same age, late thirties, maybe forty at the most. The best plastic surgeons on the planet couldn't accomplish such a dramatic preser-vation. Besides, people who've had a lot of work done have a particular look about them. I lived in Los Angeles, cosmetic procedure capital of the planet, and believe me, I'd seen more than my share of facelifts and Botox injections. You could just tell, no matter how good the plastic surgeon might be.

I didn't see any of those tells in this man's face, however. Oh, he was good-looking, no doubt about that. Not picture-perfect—his nose was too long, his mouth on the thin side, and you could even quibble that his eyes were set a little too close together. He had a good set of laugh lines around his eyes, and his skin looked lightly browned from the sun. It didn't have that smooth, almost burnished look you get when you've been dermabraded and injected to within an inch of your life.

Eternal youth, or at least eternal prime of life? It didn't exist, no matter what the cosmetics and pharmaceutical companies wanted you to believe. The man who sat next to me was the only person I'd ever seen who had achieved it…which meant he probably wasn't a man at all.

I think I shivered. He must have noticed, because he asked, "Are you cold? Do you want me to turn on the heater?"

Shaking my head, I replied, "No, I'm fine. Besides, we're almost there, aren't we?"

"As a matter of fact, yes." He pulled the car into the suicide lane and waited for an opening in traffic, then turned into the driveway to the restaurant's parking lot. A valet hurried over, looking a little wide-eyed. I supposed even at an upscale place like Campanile they didn't see a lot of Bentleys.

The Devil tossed the keys to the valet as if he were handing over a Hyundai, then came around the back of the car to help me out. I wasn't used to such gallantry; Danny invariably pulled his truck into a space, got out, and was halfway to our destination without checking to see whether I was following or not. A little awkwardly, I put my hand in the Devil's, wondering if I were going to notice a spark or an odd rush of heat. Nothing like that, though—his hand felt human enough, although warm compared to my cold fingers.

And then he let go of my hand and led me out of the parking lot and into the restaurant proper. It was an amazing space, old brick that boasted a two-story atrium in the center and cozier side rooms furnished with intimate-looking tables. Even on a Tuesday night the place was crowded, but no waiting for the Devil and his companion—we were whisked away almost immediately to a booth off in a corner where we could be safely shielded from the noisier, more open parts of the building.

The hostess handed us our menus and departed, and I opened mine, forcing myself not to look at the prices.

"Wine?" he asked me.

"Oh...sure," I said. I wasn't sure what wine would do on top of the Cosmo I'd hastily gulped down a few minutes earlier, but what the heck.

"I'm partial to reds, but that depends on what you're ordering—"

"I'm going to get the prime rib," I said hastily before I lost my nerve. Normally I would scan a menu and then pick one of the two least expensive entrées so I wouldn't be overburdening my date, but I didn't think that sort of discretion was necessary here.

"Excellent." He folded his menu shut; as if in answer, a waiter appeared from nowhere, notepad in hand. Without looking up, the Devil said, "A bottle of the Chateau Neuf-de-Pape. We'll both be having the prime rib." He smiled slightly. "Medium rare, correct, Christa?"

I could only nod mutely.

"And rare for me," the Devil added.

"Very good." The waiter (who had to be an out-of-work actor, considering the perfection of his hair and teeth) jotted a few things down on his pad, then asked, "Any salad or soup?"

"Caesar," I said recklessly. Normally I avoided that stuff like the plague, since the dressing was loaded with calories, but how often do you have the Devil treating you to dinner on your birthday?

Another knowing smile. "For me as well." He handed the waiter his menu, and I did the same.

Then one of those awkward little silences fell, the type that inevitably crop up on a first date when you've gotten the business of ordering out of the way and aren't sure where to go next. Of course, was this really a first date, or a date at all? Calling something a first date seemed to imply there would be more to follow at some point, and that concept was a little too strange for me to deal with at this stage of the game.

We were saved from making conversation by the return of the waiter, who set a pair of over-sized wine glasses on the table and then struggled a bit with the cork before finally extracting it intact. After this procedure, he had a look of triumph on his face that led me to wonder exactly how long he'd been working as a waiter.

But finally the wine was poured, and the Devil and I were left to sit there and look at one another. I didn't know what he saw in my face—I was just glad that I'd had the presence of mind to touch up my makeup before leaving the office that afternoon.

Clearing my throat, I asked, "So did you have this all planned? Or do you just keep a standing reservation here in case you find some random female you want to take out to dinner?"

"Oh, I didn't have a reservation." He lifted his wine glass and held it under his nose for a few seconds, eyes half-shut as if he were concentrating on analyzing the bouquet or whatever it is that people smell when they sniff at their wine before drinking it.

"But we walked right in—"

His eyes opened all the way then, and again I was startled by their blueness under the straight dark brows. "I have a way of opening doors."

"Apparently," I remarked, and lifted my own wine glass and took a sip without bothering to inhale it or breathe it first. I didn't know much about wine, except that I either liked it or I didn't. This particular one tasted interesting, with a strong earthy underlay to it that was unfamiliar to me. Then again, I didn't drink much French wine. The cheaper house pours were invariably from California.

Statements like the one he had just made didn't do much to put me at ease. If he were up to no good, you'd think that he'd be doing everything in his power to conceal his true identity. Yet he'd told me he was the Devil the way another guy might have told me he was a stockbroker or a lawyer. Maybe to him it was just a matter of degree.

"You still haven't told me what you want with me," I said, although I made sure to keep my voice fairly low. The people around us didn't seem to be paying much attention, but I still didn't want anyone overhearing something that would either land me in a rubber room or on the front page of the *Star* with a headline screaming, "I Had a Date With the Devil!"

"I wanted you to have a good birthday," he replied. "You did seem to have been somewhat... abandoned."

Well, that was certainly true, although in Nina's case it certainly wasn't her fault. Danny, on the other hand....

Like he'd have taken you anyplace half this nice, my mind scoffed at me. You would've been lucky to get taken to California Pizza Kitchen, so shut up already.

"How altruistic of you," I remarked. "You certainly aren't living up to your reputation. Since when is the Devil moonlighting as the Birthday Fairy?"

Once again he laughed, and, unlike me, he didn't bother to keep his voice down. The woman at the next table, who looked as if she probably hadn't eaten a carb in five years, gave us an irritated glance. I groaned inwardly. Great. All I needed was for her to start eavesdropping....

But he apparently noticed my discomfort and quieted down quickly enough. After sipping at his wine once more, he said, "Reputations are very rarely built on fact, I find."

"So you've just been misunderstood and misrepresented all these years, is that it?"

"Something like that."

I lifted a skeptical eyebrow at him but was prevented from further comment by the arrival of our salads. After assuring the waiter that no, I didn't want any pepper, I waited a few seconds, then said, "So I shouldn't find anything at all out of the ordinary about this?"

"No, of course you should. I just wanted to reassure you that I certainly don't mean you any harm."

I let his comment settle in for a few seconds. The funny thing was that I really didn't feel any sort of threat coming from him. I didn't pretend to have supernatural instincts about people or anything like that, but you'd think the Devil would give off some fairly strong evil vibes, and I wasn't getting anything. Pathetic as it might seem, so far this was the best date I'd been on in months. Years, even.

I lifted my fork and ate a few mouthfuls of salad before saying, "Somehow I get the feeling you're not going to really tell me why you're here."

"And why must I necessarily have ulterior motives?"

"Everyone has ulterior motives," I replied. "Sometimes it doesn't matter, because you both have the same ulterior motives. Maybe I just agreed to have dinner with you because I didn't want to spend the night alone."

"A good enough reason for me," he agreed. "More wine?"

I nodded, then waited as he poured a few more inches of Bordeaux into my glass. He had nice hands, I noticed, with long, strong fingers. I suddenly recalled the feel of his hand on mine. This time, though I was able to repress a shiver. It would have been a lot easier if he hadn't been so damn good-looking.

Or was he? Maybe he was doing something to my mind that made me think he looked like an attractive man, and underneath he was all horns and tail and huge pointy teeth….

I lifted my wine glass and helped myself to a steadying drink. He watched me, and I saw him frown slightly.

"You look troubled."

Great. So much for my poker face. I met his gaze squarely and said, "Is that"—and I pointed toward him—"really you? Sorry, but you don't look much like who you say you are."

"So that's what's bothering you?"

"Partly."

"This is how I choose to manifest myself." He leaned forward, smiling slightly. "I assure you, however, that if you're worried I'm going to turn into some horrific lizard creature at the stroke of midnight, it won't happen."

I got the impression he was teasing me, but I thought it was a valid concern. It was sort of difficult to discard an entire lifetime's worth of preconceptions in just one evening. "All right," I sighed. "I guess I'll have to take your word for it."

"Excellent idea."

At that moment our entrées arrived, and we spent a few moments eating in silence. He'd managed to neatly dodge my questions about his presence here, or why he would have singled me out in particular. The millennium was long gone, as well as the significant date of June 6, 2006, so if he'd been angling for some sort of *Rosemary's Baby* or *End of Days* action with me as the mother of the Antichrist, he'd sort of missed the boat. That thought reminded me of the time I'd watched *End of Days* with Nina, and how she'd remarked that if the Devil really did look like Gabriel Byrne, she sure as hell wouldn't be running away from him. At the time I'd agreed.

The man who faced me was certainly just as attractive, if in a different way. Realizing that I seemed to actually be enjoying myself as I sat there with him worried me a little. Okay, it worried me a lot. I was beginning to wonder whether some freak-out circuit in my brain had been disconnected. Otherwise, shouldn't I have been putting on my running shoes and getting the heck out of there?

My friend Micaela, who was naturally jaded and had become even more so after working in the entertainment industry for the past five years, once told me I was way too trusting of people. "Expect the worst, and you won't be disappointed," she'd remarked. Then again, she hadn't been on a real date in almost two years.

So was the fact that I hadn't yet gone running off screaming into the night evidence that I really did tend to think the best of people, sometimes to my detriment? Or was it something more?

Even without the whole supernatural component, the man who sat across the table calmly eating prime rib and garlic mashed potatoes would have fascinated me. Once you got beyond the good looks, there was something oddly charming about him. And he'd certainly acted like a gentleman so far.

Whoa, there's some rationalization, I told myself. *It's easy to play at being the nice guy when you have the powers of the universe at your command.*

"So do you know everything about me?" I asked, hoping I sounded casual. "I mean, powers of heaven and hell and all that?"

"No," he replied. "I know no more of you than what anyone else observing you might have seen. Well, that, and what others know and think about you. But you, the real you" —and he tapped a finger against his temple as if to indicate one's mind or thoughts— "I don't know any more about that than anyone else."

"Ah," I said. "Let me guess. The rules?"

"Precisely." His eyes met mine then, and I made myself return his gaze for a moment before I looked down. I hadn't been expecting to see such approval.

Blood rushed to my cheeks, and I hoped the dim lighting in the restaurant hid my blush. It would have been so easy to let myself fall prey to his charm, and I knew I couldn't do that. Not until I knew what he was really up to.

"Well, that's a relief," I said lightly. "No girl likes to have all her mystery taken away."

"God forbid," he said.

"Did He?" I asked, and this time the Devil's laugh sounded a little forced.

"How's your prime rib?" he returned, and I knew I had scored a point.

The conversation wandered to commonplaces after that—for some reason he wanted to know about my job, about how I liked living in Los Angeles—all the typical things a man might ask on a first date. He continued to expertly steer the conversation away from anything involving him, and I let him do that for the time being. It was fairly obvious he didn't look on this evening as a one-time affair, and for now I was willing to go along with that. If nothing else, trying to discover his real purpose in seeking me out sounded like a challenge.

After dinner he began to head toward my apartment, and I protested that we had to go back to The Grove so I could retrieve my car from the parking structure. He shook his head and said, "Your car is already safely tucked away in the garage at your home."

"It—what?" I shifted in my seat so I could see his profile. "How could you do that?"

"The same way I do everything else." The laugh lines at the corner of the one eye I could see crinkled slightly in amusement. "It would have been tedious to have to retrieve your vehicle, so I…moved it."

Damn. Nice trick to have, especially in L.A. I was very lucky to even have the garage; there were more apartments than garages in my complex, and getting one involved seniority in the building. Well, technically, that was how it was supposed to work.

But one came vacant at the same time the apartment I occupied did, and although Lucille downstairs was next in line to get the garage, Rudy, the apartment manager, had been waging guerrilla warfare with her over her many cats even though the building was supposed to be pet-free. So his revenge was giving me the garage. I needed it more, anyway; my Mercedes deserved the protection a lot more than her ancient Taurus, which looked as if it should have been recalled years ago.

At any rate, after the Devil parked the Bentley at the curb in front of the building, I had to go around to the back to make sure my car really was safely inside the garage. Sure enough, after I had undone the padlock and lifted the door, I saw the Mercedes gleaming inside.

"Satisfied?" he asked.

"Yes," I said. "And mildly freaked. But I suppose I'll get over it."

"I hope so."

My apartment was on the second floor, and he followed me up the stairs and waited as I fumbled in my purse for my keys. I had to remove the Victoria's Secret shopping bag and tuck it under one arm before my fingers finally found the key ring at the bottom of my purse.

Then I took a breath, looked up at him, and said, "By the way, I don't kiss on the first date."

"Very old-fashioned of you."

"Guess that's the Orange County in me," I replied.

He smiled, but I could see his glance lingering on my lips. "Good night, then, Christa."

"Good night." I faced the door and inserted the key in the lock. It turned, and I had one foot inside when I heard him say,

"By the way—"

I looked over my shoulder. "What?"

For some reason he was staring at the Victoria's Secret shopping bag I still had clenched under one arm. "Red's my favorite color."

And with that he strolled off down the staircase. I could hear him whistling as he descended the steps and made his way to his car.

I shut the door behind me, then leaned my head against it, heart pounding.

Damn....

Interlude

AN EMPTY GRAY PLAIN, so featureless it was difficult to tell where the ground ended and the sky began. A strong wind, neither hot nor cold, blew from an indeterminate direction, and smelled of sulfur and ash. Nothing grew. Nothing changed.

Beelzebub fought the urge to look at his watch. What was the point, in a place that had no notion of time?

But then Asmodeus was there, his dark suit and perfectly groomed hair incongruous notes in that soulless place. Well, Asmodeus always was a bit of a peacock.

"I've been hearing things," Beelzebub said.

"Maybe you should get that checked."

Beelzebub chose to ignore his compatriot's snarky comment and went on, "*He* has been indulging in some questionable behavior."

Asmodeus stopped fiddling with his cufflinks. "Questionable?"

"I'm fairly certain *he's* trying to make an end run."

"How do you mean?"

Sometimes Asmodeus' obtuseness could be downright annoying. On the other hand, at least he was trustworthy. Most of the time. "He's gone off and done some independent negotiations with Him." Beelzebub cast a significant glance upward.

After a second or two Asmodeus nodded, then frowned. "You think *he's* trying to make a break for it?"

"Yes."

"Without us?"

"Yes."

Asmodeus appeared to digest that information for a little while. "Well, that's not very…sporting, is it?"

"No."

A small silence fell. Beelzebub held his tongue, knowing the best thing to do was simply wait until the other demon came to the same conclusion Beelzebub already had formulated some time before.

"So what are we going to do about it?"

Beelzebub would not allow himself to smile at the use of the word "we." He replied, "Put a stop to it, of course."

"How?"

"*He* has been spending time in the company of a mortal woman. She must be part of the deal, whatever the details may be. So the most reasonable thing to do is somehow keep the two of them apart."

Asmodeus tapped a finger against his chin. "Possession?" he asked.

Beelzebub shook his head. "No. At least, not of her. It's too risky—*he* would probably be able to tell right away, and then we'd have a lot of explaining to do, wouldn't we?"

"I suppose so. Then who?"

Luckily, Beelzebub had had some time to figure this out. Once he'd zeroed in on Christa Simms as the unlikely target of *his* attentions, it had taken little effort to make a quick study of her acquaintances, of those who could do the most good—or ill, depending on how one looked at it—in foiling this underhanded plan. "She has a boyfriend," he said.

"So which one of us gets to possess the boyfriend?"

"Neither."

Asmodeus frowned. "Excuse me?"

Allowing himself a small smile, Beelzebub replied, "Too risky. The woman involved might notice something odd about his behavior, and might say something to *him*. We can't risk that. However, the boyfriend has two roommates."

This time it only took an instant for comprehension to flare in Asmodeus' eyes. "So we possess the roommates—"

"—and use them to manipulate the situation."

"It might work."

"Oh, it will work. The boyfriend is very close to these two, and tends to take their advice. It shouldn't be difficult at all to get him to do whatever we say."

"So who are these two?"

"A couple of computer geeks."

Asmodeus looked pained. "Geeks with substandard wardrobes, no doubt."

"Is there any other kind?"

"I suppose not. If there is no other way—"

"There isn't."

Asmodeus muttered something that sounded like, *The things I do for you*, but since it was obvious the words weren't meant to be heard, Beelzebub chose to ignore them.

"Very well, then," he said briskly. "I'll contact you when it's time to go."

"And *he* won't notice that we're gone?"

"I think *he's* sufficiently distracted by this woman that we have some room in which to maneuver."

With a nod, Asmodeus said, "I'll be hearing from you," and then disappeared as precipitously as he had arrived.

Excellent. Just a few more things to set in place, and then it would be off to Los Angeles to take over the hearts and minds of his intended victims. Beelzebub hoped the endeavor wouldn't require more than a few days; lengthy possessions tended to be an exhausting proposition at best. Still, he was willing to make the sacrifice.

Because he was damned if he was going to allow Lucifer to regain the Kingdom of Heaven if the rest of the angels who'd suffered the Fall had to stay down here in Hell....

CHAPTER THREE

I WAS STILL FEELING A BIT DISORIENTED—to say the least—when I went in to work the next morning. It actually hadn't been all much past ten when the Devil dropped me off the night before, but I hadn't been able to sleep for hours. I even wrote an entry about my experiences in my private blog, hoping it might help me to set down the evening's events.

To say I just had the craziest birthday ever is probably an understatement, but it was. I'm still trying to process what happened, to understand how someone like me, Christa Simms, Ms. Ordinary, could have had dinner with the Devil.

Wow, that looks even worse written out. I wanted to not believe him at first. But that trick of transporting us halfway across town in the blink of an eye? Not something I could easily ignore. And when I tried to come up with "plausible" explanations for what had occurred, they just didn't work.

When your explanations are so convoluted that they start to sound crazy, too, then it's generally easier to take something at face value, even if your brain really doesn't want to.

The really insane thing, though, is that I enjoyed myself. Maybe I shouldn't have, but who would have thought the Devil could be such a gentleman? And fun. And amazingly good-looking, and…

Uh-oh.

I have a feeling this is going to get complicated.

Then I went to bed and stared at the ceiling for what seemed like half the night before I finally dozed off.

It didn't help matters much when I got into my car the next morning and stared at the fuel gauge in bewilderment. I could have sworn that it was getting close to empty; in fact, I'd made a mental note a few days earlier that I'd probably have to get gas on Wednesday. But there it was, the needle just a hair past full.

Trying to win my affections with free gas? I thought, then shook my head and carefully backed the car out of the garage. There wasn't a lot of room between it and the building, so even though I'd been doing the same thing for almost two years now, I still took it easy. Then I climbed out of my car, and shut the garage door and locked it.

I was running a few minutes late, since my sleeplessness of the night before had led to some definite sluggishness this morning, but I doubted anyone would notice. Most of the magazine's staff tended to be late-morning people. I got in around eight-thirty most days, and the only one who arrived before me on a regular basis was Marta, the receptionist, who had to be there so she could answer the phones. It was a good morning if anyone else showed up much before nine o'clock.

I liked having that time to myself at the start of the day; it allowed me to attack whatever bits and pieces might have come in after I left the afternoon before. Besides, the one good thing about getting to work before my boss was that she didn't have a clue about what time I actually showed up.

The art department had produced a few layouts late in the day—they were waiting in my in-basket after I let myself into my office. Michael, the art director, and Jesus, his assistant, rarely appeared before 10 a.m., but they also usually stayed until at least six or seven, depending on what sorts of deadlines they had breathing down their necks.

Yeah, I know—Jesus—very funny. But I didn't name the guy.

Anyway, I logged the layouts as being turned in and then went to put them in the feature editor's inbox. As I was walking back from his office, Marta called out to me.

"Hey, Christa! Delivery for you!"

Mystified, I turned and made my way over to the receptionist's desk. An enormous bouquet of roses in a cut-crystal vase sat there, almost obscuring Marta's bright-red hair.

"These just came," she said.

Of course the roses were my favorites—the creamy ivory type with deep red edging along the petals. There had to be two dozen of them—no lightweight baby's breath helping to fill the vase here. Just glorious roses, so many I could smell them from a few feet away.

Marta was looking at me with a mixture of envy and curiosity. Certainly no one in my dating past had ever shown any evidence of being this extravagant.

I saw a cream-colored card almost obscured in the masses of flowers. I didn't want to open it in front of Marta—not when I was fairly certain who had sent the flowers—so I only smiled and said, "Thanks, Marta. I'll just get these back to my office." And I scooped up the vase and hurried away before she could start asking any questions.

Once I was safe within the confines of my own office, I plucked the card off the little plastic holder and sat down in my chair. With fingers that trembled just a little I ran a fingernail under the envelope's flap and opened it. The card inside was the same plain ivory stock, so the black writing on it stood out plainly.

Thank you for a wonderful evening. I'll call you soon.

The only signature was a scrawled "L." For Lucifer?

My phone rang. I jumped and dropped the card. Heart beating a little more quickly, I leaned over and looked at the display on the phone. All it said was that it was a wireless caller, with no number shown. Still, I had a pretty good idea of who it might be.

Strange how I could identify his voice right away after only one evening spent in his company. "Do you like the flowers?"

"They're—they're gorgeous." All the normal questions, such as "how did you know those were my favorites?" or "how did you get this number?" seemed superfluous. Instead I asked, "How did you find a florist that was open this early?"

"You have such a practical mind, Christa. I like that." He paused, and then said, sounding amused, "There's a place up on Crescent Heights that opens at eight."

"Oh."

Of course I couldn't see his face, but somehow I got the impression he was smiling. "I wanted to know if you were available this evening."

Well, he was persistent. I'd give him that. "I can't go out with you tonight," I said.

"Why not?"

Because you're the Devil, I thought, but I only replied, "I can't go out every single weeknight—"

"What about this weekend?"

"I'm going down to Orange County to see my mother on Saturday."

"Friday, then?"

Resistance was obviously futile. "Oh, all right," I said. Besides, it wasn't as if I had anything else going on.

"I'll pick you up at seven. Enjoy the flowers." And he hung up.

I sat there for a minute, holding the handset and looking at it blankly, then replaced it in the receiver. It figured that my social life required the Devil's intervention to bring it back from the dead.

Trying to force him out of my mind—and not succeeding very well, with those amazing roses staring me in the face—I booted up my computer, then checked my email for any articles that might have come in the evening before. Several of our contributing editors worked freelance and just emailed their Word files from home. I'd been expecting three and had only gotten one. Typical.

Still, it gave me something to work on. I opened the Internet radio client on my Mac and chose a classical music station; I needed something to calm my nerves. After a while, I got back into the rhythm of things, tightening the prose, fixing some egregious run-on sentences. Seriously, you'd think some people never paid attention during their high school English classes.

Then I heard the voice of Jacqui, my managing editor, inquire in disbelieving tones, "Do not tell me those came from Danny!"

"Um, no," I replied.

She came around the corner of the desk and looked from the roses to me and back again. "Spill," she said.

"Um…." I hedged. Luckily, I'd already hidden the card in my desk drawer, but still it was fairly obvious that Mr. On-Again, Off-Again Koslowski wouldn't have sent me anything so amazingly beautiful. Or expensive. "I sort of met someone."

"Oh, thank God!"

I wasn't sure that was who she should be thanking, but I managed a smile.

Jacqui was about fifteen years my senior and generally treated me less as an employee than as the long-lost little sister she never had. Most of the time I didn't mind—in a lot of ways we were closer than I was with my own sister. But it also made for some awkwardness in the workplace. For one thing, she'd never approved of me seeing Danny. It wasn't just that we were on the borderline of the whole "employees shouldn't date other employees" policy. The magazine I worked for didn't have a big enough staff to justify a full-time on-site IT person, so we contracted with an outside company to handle our computing issues. That's how I met Danny in the first place—he'd come in to handle the upgrade of my older-generation iMac to a dual-processor machine with a cinema display.

Maybe I was starry-eyed over my fancy new computer, and that was the reason I'd agreed to go out with Danny in the first place. But as time dragged on and it became patently obvious this was a relationship that was going nowhere fast, Jacqui had become more impatient with the situation.

"Dump him," she told me a few weeks earlier, after he'd blown off yet another date. "I'll just have IT Solutions send someone else over here when we need service."

I pondered the surreality of getting dating advice from my boss, then shook my head. "I don't mind," I said. "We always knew it was going to be casual."

She gave me a dubious look. "If I were you, I'd stop wasting my time," she said. "You think you have all the time in the world, and then *boom!* You're thirty-five and wondering where all the good men went."

Harsh experience motivated her, I knew; she'd spent almost ten years in one relationship, always thinking that eventually they were going to get married, and then one day he'd come home and told her he thought it wasn't working out.

Maybe Nina had the right idea. On the surface, women did seem to be a lot more reliable.

"So now you can dump Danny," Jacqui said, sounding very pleased with the universe.

"I don't know about that," I protested. "I've only been out on one date with this guy."

"One date, which just *happened* to be on your birthday?"

I didn't bother to reply. I knew she was going to read whatever significance she wanted into that particular fact.

"And he sends you flowers the next day?" She pushed her glasses back up on her head and gave me a piercing look. "Where did he take you?"

"Campanile," I said with a sigh.

"A-ha!" She looked like the cat that had swallowed the canary. "So what's this guy's name?"

"L–Luke," I replied. After all, he told me to call him that, even though I was having a hard time thinking of him as anything except the Devil.

"Luke what?"

Well, that was a good question. He'd never given me a last name. "I'd rather just leave it at Luke for now," I said.

For a minute I thought she was going to keep prying, but maybe something in my expression told her she wasn't going to have any luck. "That's all right—you can keep your secrets if you want. But he sounds like a keeper to me."

Her comment made me want to burst out laughing. Somehow I managed to maintain a straight face, though. "He's very thoughtful," I said after a brief hesitation. That much was the truth, at least.

Jacqui gave me another penetrating look, and shrugged. "Kick Mr. Koslowski to the curb," she said, then departed, leaving me to stare at the roses and wonder exactly what I'd gotten myself into.

It never rains but it pours. Well, that isn't exactly true in Los Angeles, where we get lots of drizzly, misty stuff and not a lot of downpours. But in terms of my personal life, the saying pretty much hit the nail on the head.

That afternoon, one of the sales guy's PCs went blooey. The editorial staff and art department used Macs, of course—they're pretty much the industry standard for anything on the creative side. But the sales and operations people used regular PCs, and they tended to crap out on a much more regular basis than the Macs did.

So who shows up to fix the temperamental PC? Why, the absent Mr. Koslowski, naturally.

After he was done with his business on the second floor, he slouched his way down to my office, where I was poring over a layout covering the opening of a new art gallery on the Westside.

"Where the hell did you get those?" he demanded from the safety of my door frame.

I looked up from the color laser printout occupying my attention. "Oh, hi, Danny. Anything leap to mind about yesterday?"

"It was Tuesday. Who sent you those flowers?"

"Tuesday—very good." I took off my glasses and rubbed the bridge of my nose. The glasses were just for close-up work; I had a mild astigmatism in my left eye and started to strain after a few hours of looking at ten-point type. "A Tuesday which just happened to be my birthday."

For a few seconds he didn't say anything. Then he muttered, "Oh."

"Exactly. Thanks for the call, by the way."

His sandy eyebrows drew together. "What call?"

"The one you were supposed to make wishing me a happy birthday."

"Okay—okay, I'm sorry. I blew it. I should have written it down in my phone."

God forbid he should have to think or remember anything on his own. I wondered if he needed the iPhone to tell him to wipe his ass.

Then his frown deepened, and he said, "That doesn't explain where the flowers came from."

"Well, actually, it does. It was my birthday, and someone sent me flowers. Mystery solved."

"Who sent them?"

"I don't have to tell you that," I replied, my tone a little snottier than I intended. But the contrast between Danny's adolescent behavior and Luke's— okay, *the Devil's*—was almost overwhelming, and I could feel myself rapidly losing my patience. I was sure Jacqui would have approved.

"But—but—we're dating!" Danny spluttered. "I thought you said we were exclusive!"

"Maybe I made a mistake," I said coolly. "I mean, what kind of a person in an 'exclusive' relationship forgets his girlfriend's birthday?"

"What kind of girl in an exclusive relationship goes out with someone else on her birthday?" he shot back.

"The kind who doesn't want to sit home alone," I said.

That sort of pulled the rug out from under him. He opened his mouth, then shut it, looking both angry and embarrassed.

"Sorry," he mumbled, his tone sulky in the extreme. "Let me make it up to you. Let's go out Friday night."

"I can't," I said, a little surprised at how good it felt to say the next sentence. Hell hath no fury and all that. "I have a date."

"With him?" Danny jerked a thumb toward the roses.

A little amazed at how calm I was, I replied, "Yes."

He crossed his arms. I noticed, as if I were look-ing at a stranger, how the tie his company forced him to wear had been knotted off-center, how the name tag pinned to his pocket was a little crooked.

He was still sort of cute, in a rumpled, geeky sort of way, but I really did wonder in that moment why I'd ever thought I was attracted to him in the first place.

"Are you dumping me?" he asked at last, as if it had taken a long time for the thought to occur to him.

"No," I said. I reached up to adjust one rose slightly, felt the velvet-soft petal brush against my thumb and forefinger. "Let's just say that we're no longer exclusive."

"Fine," he retorted, and jammed his hands into his pockets. He turned to go, then tossed an angry glance back over his shoulder. "But don't think I'm going to give up that easily."

I lifted my shoulders. What, had he suddenly decided to become the gallant knight, jousting for his lady love? Yeah, right. He might be angry right now, but I seriously doubted his emotions had been engaged enough for him to be upset for very long. No, probably all he was really suffering at that point was a case of hurt pride.

"Good luck with that," I said, then turned back to my layout.

"Right," he snapped, and slammed my office door behind him.

The feeling of elation I experienced after my emancipation proclamation lasted approximately thirty minutes. Then, as usual, guilt started to set in.

Maybe I'd been too hard on Danny. Some guys just couldn't remember dates to save their lives. And what the hell had I been thinking, flaunting my next date with the Devil…Luke…whoever…with him? I'd talked as if that relationship actually had some kind of future. How could Luke possibly be doing anything except amusing himself with me for some reason I'd probably never discover?

The door opened. "Stop that," Jacqui said.

"Stop what?"

She put her hands on her hips and raised an eye-brow. "I saw Mr. Koslowski storm out of here earlier, so I'm assuming you finally told him off."

"I didn't tell him off," I said. "I just told him I couldn't go out with him Friday night because I already had a date with someone else."

"Close enough. I'm sure that was sufficient to bruise his poor tender little ego."

Bruise, and possibly sprain. I didn't know for sure, because Danny had always been very good at not showing much of what he was feeling (if any-thing). Certainly he'd gotten a lot more excited about advancing his character a level in Warcraft than he ever seemed to be about spending time with me.

"Anyhow," she continued inexorably, "you put-ting him in his place is certainly no reason for you to be sitting in here and beating yourself up about it."

"I wasn't—"

"Oh, yes, you were. I saw the look on your face."

I began to wonder if I should start going around with a paper bag over my head. At least that way people wouldn't be able to tell what I was thinking all the time. I reflected that it was a good thing I had never gotten into playing poker, then said, "All right. I guess I do feel a teeny bit bad about it. But I suppose I gave him enough chances to shape up."

"More than enough," she said. "So you already have another date lined up for Friday night? I'm impressed. Where's he taking you this time?"

"I don't know," I confessed. "I think it's supposed to be sort of a surprise."

Jacqui pursed her lips. "That could be good or bad."

You have no idea, I thought, but I said only, "True, but at least I know it won't be dull."

"Thoughtful and interesting?" she replied. "Hang on to this one, kid." She shot me a grin and disappeared down the hallway.

Somehow I doubted she'd be quite so encouraging if she knew who Luke really was. Then again, considering the way men had treated her and so many other women I knew, maybe she would have thought the Devil was an step up.

The funny thing was that I'd never really thought all that much about God and the Devil, Heaven and Hell. My parents both ditched Christianity ("too much guilt," according to my father) during their hippie days, and Lisa, Jeff, and I were raised in a cheerfully agnostic family with some slight Buddhist overtones. My mother got more into the spiritual stuff (in a strictly nontraditional way) as she got older, but I'd never been brought up to believe in a fiery Hell or a fluffy Heaven with angels playing harps and all that. I didn't believe in reincarnation, either, even though my mother swore she'd experienced past-life regression in several sessions with a hypnotherapist. If it made her happy, great, but I wasn't buying into it.

But to go from that religiously neutral background to facing an entity who claimed he was the Devil and in fact exhibited all the powers that such a supernatural being might actually possess—well, that was enough for me to feel as if my world had been seriously upended. I spent a considerable amount of time when I should have been working that afternoon trying to read what I could on the Internet about Lucifer, Satan…whatever. Of course I got everything from nutcases who swore they'd been possessed by the Devil to scholarly discussions of the linguistic roots of his name, but most of what I read didn't particularly paint him as a nice guy.

Full of pride, he had rebelled against God and been cast down from Heaven. But if the Devil was supposed to be stuck down in Hell, watching Adolf Hitler roast on a spit or whatever else the Lord of the Underworld did to occupy his spare time, what was he doing buying mansions in Hancock Park and driving me around in a car worth more than a quarter-million dollars? (I looked up that little fact, too…curiosity had compelled me to see just how extravagant that Bentley really was.)

A cold, sick feeling started to grow in my stomach. I'd already agreed to see him again, and even if I thought I could summon up the courage to call things off, I had no way of reaching him. At any rate, he didn't strike me as the sort of person who would take no for an answer. He'd certainly maneuvered me easily enough into dinner and a promise to go out with him a second time.

All right, look at this logically, I told myself. *So you've dug up some information about him that's less than encouraging. It's all secondhand data as far as you know. He could just be the victim of some really bad press.*

Of course, that sort of thinking only made me sound as if I'd swung into serious Queen of Denial mode. Who was I to refute centuries—millennia, really—of folklore and religious beliefs? All I had to go on was the fact that he'd rescued me on my birthday, given me a much more pleasant evening than I could have expected, and then sent me flowers the next day. Not exactly the actions of the Ultimate Evil, but several of the entries I'd read about Lucifer mentioned that he was the father of deception. This could all just be a really big buildup to some kind of horrible fate.

Jesus—the art assistant—stuck his head in my office door. "Christa."

I must have jumped about a foot.

"Geez, are you okay?"

"Fine," I lied, forcing the air back into my lungs. "What's up?"

He gave me a quizzical look. "You seem a little jumpy."

"I guess I was thinking about something else."

"Something a million miles away, it looked like."

Maybe even farther than that, I thought. *Who knows how far away Heaven and Hell really are?*

"Michael wanted to know if you had the layout for the restaurant review in your office. He needs to swap out one of the images."

I shook my head. "I haven't gotten it back yet, so it must still be on Roger's desk somewhere. Good luck finding it."

Jesus sighed. "Great. If he's lost another layout—" And, still muttering to himself, he wandered off down the hallway toward Roger's office.

Roger McKinley was the executive editor of the magazine. He knew his stuff, and he was a great writer, but he was probably the least organized person I had ever met. Filing systems lasted about five minutes in his office. Story envelopes, layouts, even complete contacts notebooks had been known to disappear into his domain, never to be seen again. The staff had started calling his office the "Bermuda

Triangle." Of course, since the workflow was mostly electronic, we could always print things out again if necessary. But that meant whatever markups the feature editors might have put on those layouts were lost and would have to be done all over again—not the sort of thing you want to be faced with at the end of the day when you're just trying to get the hell out of Dodge. Still, somehow we managed to get the magazine out without killing Roger. If it weren't that he was actually a fairly likable guy, he would have been marked for death after his first week on the job.

At least Jesus' interruption had gotten my mind off whatever torments Luke might or might not have planned for me. In fact, somehow I managed to summon a sort of fatalistic approach to the whole thing. If he really had an inventive and cruel plot in place for my imminent demise, there probably wasn't much I could do about it. Mortals tended to get the short end of the stick when going up against higher powers, no matter what the movies might say to the contrary.

On the other hand, I didn't see anything wrong with trying to get a little divine help on my side….

Don't ask me why I immediately thought of going to a Catholic church. Maybe it was just more influence from the movies; whenever you saw people fighting the Devil, they tended to be Catholic. I mean, the Exorcist sure wasn't a Southern Baptist.

Danny happened to be a practicing Catholic, which was strike one against the Church in my book. In this day and age, he managed to be one of the few young men left on the planet who still believed that premarital sex was a quick ticket to Hell. That actually worked for me in a weird way, since if we'd gone to bed together I would have had an even tougher time writing him off. Frustrated libido or not, avoiding physical intimacy did keep a relationship on a certain level.

But because of Danny I knew there was a Catholic church not too far from where I worked, and also because of him I knew that it was open for confession between five and six on Mondays, Wednesdays, and Fridays. I didn't know if having the Devil buy me dinner was grounds for confession, but if nothing else it would give me direct contact with a priest without having to make an appointment.

I felt more than a little strange pulling into the parking lot. After all, the only times in my life I'd even been in a church were at weddings and funerals, and not many of those, either. My mother was born in Southern California, so her family all still lived here, but my dad was originally from Baltimore, and we didn't have much interaction with that side of the family.

At any rate, the last time I'd actually been inside a church was for my cousin Marissa's wedding, and that had been almost two years ago. Since she and I were the same age, I'd been the recipient of numerous pitying stares and the ever-popular "so when are you going to get married?" questions. I'd ended up drinking way too much champagne to blot out the ignominy of the whole situation and finally barfed in the women's bathroom. Luckily, no one had seen me, and I managed to escape without anyone knowing what I'd done, but I'd taken a dim view of weddings—and churches—ever since.

At least this building's architecture was beautiful; as with so many other churches in Southern California, it was constructed in the Mediterranean style, with a red tile roof and clean white stucco exterior. Since by that time of day the sun had long since set, I could see the stained-glass windows lit up from within, glowing blue and red and gold in the dark. I welcomed the coming of evening because it made distinguishing facial features that much more difficult. I didn't really expect to see anyone I knew, but anything that reduced my risk of discovery was all right by me.

Trying to move as if I actually knew what I was doing, I walked from the parking lot into the main church building. One other woman entered just ahead of me and made her way to a set of three dark wood cubicles off to one side. I assumed those must be the confession booths, and hung back to watch as she pushed the curtain on the center one aside and went in.

All right. That seemed simple enough. I chose the one to the left and then sat down on the little bench inside. It was close and dark and smelled faintly of incense; good thing I wasn't claustrophobic.

I thought I heard movement on the other side of the little carved grille that separated priest and penitent, but since I had absolutely no idea what to do, I just sat there, waiting, until someone cleared his throat and said, "Bless you, my child. Are you here to confess?" His voice sounded quiet and kind, with a faint accent I couldn't place.

Well, there was a good question. What did I actually have to confess? That I'd spoken with the Devil, allowed him to buy me dinner and apparently fill my gas tank? Were those mortal sins? I knew there was some sort of ritual involved here, and I racked my brains, trying to recall what I'd seen or read about confessions in the various films and books I'd absorbed over the years.

"Um…." I hedged. Finally some bits and pieces started to come back to me. "Bless me, Father, for I have sinned…." I knew something else was supposed to come after that, but for the life of me I couldn't recall what.

A few seconds of silence. Then the priest asked, "How long has it been since your last confession?"

Oh, right. I should have remembered that. The only problem was that of course I'd never been to confession before. Would he throw me out if I told him I wasn't even Catholic? "I don't remember," I replied, feeling more and more as if this had been a really stupid idea. "I actually came here to ask a question—to get some spiritual guidance."

Again the priest didn't say anything right away. I heard another throat clearing, and then he spoke. "What is it, my child?"

If I told him the truth he'd think I was completely nuts. I was fairly certain that whatever a priest heard during confession was completely confidential—sort of a holy attorney/client privilege—but I didn't want to risk a visit to the rubber room, either. Just in case.

"I was just wondering whether—that is, I just wanted to know if you had any advice on dealing with the Devil."

"Excuse me, my child?" The accent sounded a little more pronounced. Latin American of some sort, but it didn't sound Mexican exactly. Maybe from somewhere in South America?

"Well, okay, I know there's exorcism, but since I'm not actually possessed—"

"The Devil represents temptation," the priest said, sounding as if he were trying to latch onto the only thing I'd said that might have made sense.

"Trust in God, and He will give you the strength to resist such temptation."

I hadn't paid much attention to God in my life. Somehow I'd always thought if He really did exist, He and I could work out any minor transgressions somewhere down the road. But I didn't think a statement like that would go over too well with a priest, so I just asked, "So...you're saying I should pray for help?"

"Prayer is your connection to the Holy Spirit," he said promptly. "By praying, you open yourself to God. If you are filled with God's love and his strength, then you can avoid the temptations of the Devil."

The priest obviously had no idea I was speaking literally of the Devil, not the temptations that people thought led from him, but I decided the point wasn't worth arguing.

Logic suggested that if there were a Devil, then there must be a God as well. And since Luke had actually spoken of some sort of rules, then it would follow that Someone must have set them. Did God know the Devil was here in Los Angeles, luring lonely females to their doom? Did He care? Or was there something else going on here that I simply hadn't figured out yet?

I had no idea whether my case merited divine intervention. Then again, asking for help couldn't hurt, either.

"Thank you, Father," I said at last. "I'll try that."

There was a soft sound from behind the latticed grille, as if the priest had uneasily shifted his weight. "If you're in some sort of trouble, child—"

"I'm all right," I said. "That helped a lot. Really."

And before he could say anything else, I slid out of the booth and headed for the nearest exit in a clumsy run/walk. I didn't want to risk him asking any other potentially awkward questions.

I'd never prayed before in my life, except for those rare moments when even agnostics send some sort of plea out into the universe. *Please, God, let me get into UCLA even though I blew chunks on the math portion of my SAT. Please, God, let me sneak into the house at 3 a.m. without getting caught by my parents. Please, God, let that not be the sound of my transmission failing.*

You know, that kind of thing.

Still, as I slid into the driver's seat of my car and turned the key in the ignition, I did as the priest had instructed. I clenched the steering wheel and thought, *Please, God, help me. Tell me what I should do.*

Of course I got no reply.

CHAPTER FOUR

EITHER GOD WAS OCCUPIED with more important things, or He had just decided my case didn't warrant any direct help. I went home, nuked a Lean Cuisine for dinner, and watched TV because I was too stressed out to try to read or do anything else constructive. I'd halfway been expecting some other sign of Luke's affections—a box of chocolates, more flowers, maybe my rent paid for the next year—but everything was as it should be, as far as I could tell. What I really should have done was put in a good hour at the gym, because I knew that too many more meals like the one I'd had on my birthday, and I could kiss my size-six jeans good-bye. However, when push came to shove (i.e., when I crossed the intersection where I should have turned right to go to 24-Hour Fitness), I just couldn't do it. As far as I could tell, being in shape was highly overrated. It certainly hadn't helped my love life any.

The next day passed without any flowers, or anything else out of the ordinary. Oh, there was some minor drama at work when the press passes for the fundraising gala at the Museum of Natural History went missing, but they eventually turned up—you guessed it—buried under the rubble on Roger's desk. And so it went. I did whatever work crossed my desk, surfed the Internet, and posted another entry on my private blog about my adventures in Catholicism.

So I went to a priest for help, which even at the time I thought was really reaching, but I didn't know what else to do. I should have known I wasn't going to get any helpful advice. Maybe there are still some priests out there who believe in the Devil as a real entity, or at least a real force in the universe, rather than the inner voice of our lesser selves, but I didn't get one of those today, that's for sure. And of course I couldn't be specific, couldn't tell him what's really going on.

Not that the priest would have believed me anyway. I have a hard time believing all this myself, and I've met Luke, heard him casually admit that he's the Devil. I guess I figured a priest would have some insight on this sort of thing, and really, who else can I even talk to about this? Nina would think I've gone completely batshit crazy if I tried to tell her, and she's the only person I would even try to confide in. Micaela's so busy, she doesn't need to hear about my problems, and Jennifer's wrapped up in her wedding plans, and...

Oh, well. Looks like I'm flying solo on this one.

That day I did force myself to go to the gym, even though I crapped out after about thirty-five minutes. Still, thirty-five minutes was better than nothing, and I felt a little bit better about myself by the time I was done. I let myself in my apartment, listened to my one and only phone message (from Nina, trying to schedule a belated birthday dinner now that her sinuses had finally unclamped), and then opened up my laptop so I could check my email.

Mostly it was the usual junk, the stuff that gets through no matter how much your ISP beefs up the spam filters. A few daily logs from a couple of Yahoo groups I belonged to, mostly for writing critique circles to which I had never actually contributed anything. At one point I'd harbored a few random literary ambitions, but as time wore on and I didn't write anything much beyond the entries in my blog, I realized those dreams were getting as stale as week-old bread.

Then, something from him. The email address was Luke.Nicolini@gmail.com. I didn't know anyone else named Luke, and although he hadn't given me a last name, this one seemed to fit.

So the Devil's Italian? I thought, grinning despite myself. I clicked on the email to open it.

One line: *Wear comfortable shoes. See you at seven tomorrow.*

And that was it.

Comfortable shoes? What the hell? Was he taking me mountain climbing?

The more I thought about it, the more ominous it sounded. I mean, if he were taking me out for another decadent meal, he wouldn't be worried about my footwear, would he?

Since most of the day had been spent in radio silence, I'd been harboring the vain hope that perhaps he'd decided I wasn't sport enough and had moved on to bigger and better things. The email, however, shot down that idea pretty effectively. As far as I could tell, the date was definitely still on.

Okay, God, I thought. *You can step in here whenever you like. Really.*

No answer, of course. Maybe all my years of blissful agnosticism really had ticked Him off.

Nothing from Danny, either, despite his posturing about not giving me up without a fight. Typical. Not that I really wanted to hear from him, but a snotty email or a wounded message on my answering machine would have at least proved that he'd meant what he said.

Fine. I could handle this. After all, no matter what sort of game Luke was playing at, so far he'd done nothing that would have roused my suspicions if he were anyone other than the Devil. Maybe I should stop holding that against him. Maybe he had turned over a new leaf.

Maybe you ought to get your head examined, I told myself. *Preferably by someone who's not Freudian. I can only imagine the field day some shrinks would have with this.*

Probably I would have had less contempt for the whole psychoanalysis industry if it weren't that my father was a very successful psychologist. He certainly hadn't been able to keep himself from making a mess of his own family. But that was a can of worms for another day.

In the meantime, I had to take stock of my closet and figure out what I had in the way of sensible shoes….

By the time Friday evening rolled around, I was pretty much a bundle of twitching nerves. I made some completely stupid mistakes at work, but luckily one of the editors caught them before I told the art department those articles were okay to go to press.

"Having a bad day?" the feature editor asked as he tossed the marked-up layouts onto my desk.

"Long week," I said. I really didn't feel like explaining to Brian Matthews (who was one of those people whose world always seemed perfectly ordered) that I was having some issues in my personal life. Besides, he had problems of his own to deal with. I knew he'd been hoping for the executive editor position and was mightily put out when Roger got it instead. It probably didn't help that Roger was such a disorganized mess.

Since Jacqui knew I had a second date with my mystery man, she let me flee a few minutes early so I would have enough time to get ready. I'd already pretty much lined up what I was going to wear, but an extra fifteen minutes never hurt anyone.

The phrase "comfortable shoes" led me to believe we probably weren't going anywhere too fancy. There seems to be a corollary that the more glam your footwear is, the more painful it has to be. So I'd picked out a pair of flat brown boots that still looked very smart because of the buckle detail at the ankles, my favorite pair of jeans, a white button-up shirt, and a tweedy fitted jacket in muted greens and browns. Put together, the ensemble looked very *Town and Country,* very English gentry rusticating for the weekend.

I slipped in a pair of plain gold hoops, and decided against a necklace. But a few Christmases ago my father had given me a heavy gold ring set with a square-cut green tourmaline, and I put that on as well. Then I fiddled with my hair, trying to decide whether I should pull it back or wear it down. In the end I went with leaving it down—with it pulled back in a barrette, I looked just a little too much as if I were about to go fox hunting or something.

After all that I started to wonder why I was wasting so much effort on my appearance. Did I really care what he thought? *Should* I care? I mean, here I'd been having minor freak attacks all day at the thought of seeing Luke again, worrying whether this night would be my last or something, and yet I was being a typical girl and futzing *ad nauseum* with my hair. Something was definitely wrong with that picture.

I made a sound of disgust and threw the hairbrush back in its drawer. At that inopportune moment I heard a knock at the front door.

Great. Despite my efforts to remain calm, I felt my heart begin to beat more quickly in my chest. I took a breath, tossed my hair over my shoulder, and went out into the living room. My fingers trembled as they worked the deadbolt.

Wonderful, I thought. *He's not even inside, and you're already a big ball of goo.*

I wrenched the door open. He stood outside, looking casually gorgeous in a black leather jacket over a white button-down shirt and dark jeans.

"Hi," I said. Wow, that was brilliant.

"Good evening," he replied. Then a corner of his mouth lifted as he looked at me. I'd continued to stand in the doorway, blocking the entrance. "May I come in?"

I hesitated. Maybe I shouldn't let him in. If I let him in, maybe that would give him some sort of strange power over me, just like—

"I'm not a vampire," he said, lip curling a bit. "I promise I have no dastardly intentions."

For someone who said he couldn't read my mind, he was doing an awfully good job of it. But I didn't want him to see that he'd gotten to me, so I stepped aside and let him enter my modest living room.

Compared to his newly acquired home in Hancock Park, it wasn't much. But I'd carefully selected each piece, from the chenille-upholstered couch to the rustic-looking tables from World Market, and I had to say I was proud of my apartment. It was warm and welcoming, in shades of soft tan and brown with accents of brick red. I hated cold-feeling houses, which was partly why I'd disdained his first choice of that modern '50s place in the Hollywood Hills. Likewise, I didn't much care for the way Traci—I refused to call her my stepmother—had decorated my father's house. She'd brought in sleek, uncomfortable furniture and expensive modern art, all of which made the place look more like a gallery than a place where people actually lived. Whatever. It wasn't the house I'd grown up in, after all, and they had to live in it, not me.

"It suits you," he said, after a brief glance around the living room.

"Um—thanks," I replied, feeling a little awkward. I wondered if he'd somehow discovered that I'd tried to enlist the big guns for a little divine assistance.

"You'd better get a coat," he advised. "It's chilly out."

Feeling even more mystified, I went to the hall closet and retrieved the brown leather ankle-length coat that was my end-of-season splurge at Loehmann's last spring. The coat always made me feel chic and tall, and I figured I needed all the help I could get at this point.

After I'd locked up and we'd descended the stairs to the ground level, I got another surprise. Instead of the big dark-green Bentley, a fire-engine-red Jaguar convertible sat at the curb.

I shot Luke a questioning glance.

"This is a little more maneuverable," he explained. "Better for tight spots."

That sounded…dubious…but, not knowing what else to do, I went ahead and climbed into the passenger seat after he'd opened the car door for me. He got in the car, started it up, and headed east toward La Brea, then turned left.

"So where are we going?" I asked.

"Hollywood first," he replied.

Hollywood? Not really my destination of choice, even though the city really had done quite a bit to improve its reputation the past few years. And at the end of January, it wouldn't be quite as overrun with tourists as it was the majority of the time.

It was still busy, though—Friday nights could be horrendous, with everyone trolling along both Hollywood and Sunset Boulevards. Even though the police really tried to crack down on random cruising, it was still pretty obvious that a lot of the people who shared the street with us didn't have a particular destination in mind. They were more interested in showing off their tricked-out cars. The Jag could more than hold its own, luckily.

We turned right on Hollywood and headed east, crawling along from light to light. It was the sort of traffic that would have made me chew the dashboard in frustration, but Luke threaded his way through the packed cars with ease. Finally he turned down a side street and parked in a pay lot.

As I followed him back out to Hollywood Boulevard, I realized what our destination was. I'd never eaten there before, but Musso & Frank's Grill was a landmark, a restaurant that had been in the same location for more than eighty years.

"You sure do know how to pick them," I commented, as he held the door open for me and I went on into the building, which was clubby and dark. I felt as if I'd stepped back in time to the '50s.

He smiled. "Let's just say that I do enjoy the finer things of this world."

That much was obvious. Not bothering to reply, I watched as he spoke in a brief undertone to the maitre d', then trailed along after them to a high-backed booth upholstered in red leather. After we were seated and handed heavy menus that looked as if they'd been around since Hollywood's heyday, I said, "I still don't see where the comfortable shoes come in. If I'd known we'd be coming here, I would have dressed up a bit more."

The amused look never left his face. "Don't worry—I saw several other people in here wearing jeans as well. You Southern Californians are remarkably relaxed about your dress codes."

Well, I couldn't argue with that. I'd seen people wearing T-shirts in expensive restaurants and sporting flip-flops at cocktail parties. Micaela told me she'd once spotted someone wearing tennis shoes at an Oscar party, but since I hadn't been there, I couldn't confirm that sighting.

"The chops are particularly good here," he said. "In case you wanted something besides steak."

Personally, I was the kind of girl who couldn't ever get tired of steak, but I thought I'd give the grilled pork chops a try. Luke requested a porterhouse from the red-jacketed waiter who took our order, asked for wine recommendations, and settled on an Australian cabernet.

"What is this all about, really?" I asked, after the waiter had returned with the wine, poured a measure into each of our glasses, and then departed with an air of having bestowed a great favor. "All this wining and dining? This captain of industry act you've got going? I just don't get it."

"Back to that, are we?" He let me stew in my own juices while he took a sip of wine.

"Yes, 'back to that.' Did you really think I would stop asking you why you wanted to see me so badly?"

"I'm curious, Christa. Do you question all the men you've dated as to why on earth they could possibly be interested in seeing you?"

"Of course not." I allowed myself a mouthful of wine. It was good—fruitier than the Bordeaux we'd shared a few evenings earlier. "But you can't tell me the situations are exactly equal. I mean, those guys aren't—they're not—"

"Not the Devil?" For the first time, his smile looked a little tight around the edges. "How many reassurances do I have to give you?"

"As many as it takes to convince me you're not up to something."

He was silent for a moment. Then he stared straight at me, the blue eyes catching my own. At that particular second I felt as if I couldn't do anything but look back at him. His gaze seemed to bore into the depths of my soul.

"I swear that my intentions aren't evil," he said. "No soul-snatching or *Rosemary's Baby.* I promise."

He'd said as much to me before, but for some reason this time I found myself beginning to believe him. Yes, there was obviously something going on here. I'd be an idiot if I didn't recognize that much. But whatever that something might be, I was starting to think it didn't involve any sort of sinister objective.

The waiter arrived with our food at that point, and I had to wait until he had safely departed before I could reply.

"I'll stop with the questions," I said, "but only because I'm hungry, and these chops look delicious."

Luke shook his head slightly and said, "I suppose I'll have to accept that for now." He raised his glass toward me, as if conceding the point, and the rest of the dinner passed peaceably enough. I didn't ask any more awkward questions, and tried to keep the tone of the conversation light. The booth seemed private enough, but the sorts of things I kept thinking I'd like to discuss weren't topics I really wanted overheard. I could only hope that we'd be someplace less public later on.

As it turned out, we ended up somewhere extremely not private: Griffith Observatory.

We parked the Jag in the parking structure at Hollywood and Highland and caught a specially designated tour bus to take us up the hill to the Observatory. The site did have parking, but at that hour on a Friday night? Forget about it. I wondered if Luke's "opening doors" somehow failed to extend to good parking karma.

It felt odd to sit next to Luke on the crowded bus; we'd never been in such close physical proximity before, and once or twice I felt his knee brush against mine as the bus took a particularly tight turn on the uphill grade. Strange, too, to sit next to this being who looked like a man as we were surrounded by faces of every color and every age: I saw what looked like church or school groups, couples out on dates, families making a night of it. All so human, all so ordinary.

Except one, of course.

The Observatory wasn't completely unfamiliar to me. My parents took Lisa and me back when we were around ten and eight, respectively—I knew we couldn't have been much older than that because Jeff hadn't even been born yet. We all piled into my mother's Volvo and trekked up the 5 Freeway into L.A., stopping at Philippe's downtown for beef-dip sandwiches before making the final leg of the journey to Griffith Park. We watched a laser show that accompanied the music from Pink Floyd's *Dark Side of the Moon,* gawked at the Tesla coil, and stared in awe at the Foucault pendulum. Although this evening we weren't exactly hiking up the hill, as I saw some people doing, the planetarium still had a lot of steps and ups and downs, so I was glad of Luke's advice that I wear comfortable shoes.

No laser show this time, but honestly, I found the presentation given in the planetarium to be even more engaging. We all sat there in the dark, watching as an amazingly intricate map of the heavens was projected on the smooth dome of the ceiling above us, and listened to the astronomer who was giving the talk discuss space exploration and the mythology surrounding the various constellations. The whole time, though, I couldn't help thinking about the man who sat next to me. Had he witnessed the birth of these stars? Could my mortal brain even begin to comprehend everything he must have seen and done throughout his long, long existence?

Feeling a bit chastened, I remained silent as we filed out of the Observatory proper and wandered through the halls. Luke paused by the Tesla coil to let a group of excited elementary school kids laugh and point at the coil before being swept on by a pair of harassed-looking teachers. I wondered if they were getting overtime pay to herd their students up here after hours.

"He was a true genius," Luke murmured, after the hubbub had died down a bit.

"Who?"

"Tesla." The static discharge from the coil cast odd shadows across Luke's face as he added, "So many people have no conception of how much he really contributed to this world. You can thank Edison for that."

"Thomas Edison?" I asked, feeling a little stupid. I had to admit that I didn't know a lot about Tesla, but school kids in the United States got Edison's genius drummed into their heads from an early age.

Luke began to walk toward the doors, and I followed him. We emerged into the open area outside the front entrance, where spotlights illuminated the beautiful Art Deco building and the astronomers' statues that stood in the center of the circular drive. Although the day had been clear and mild for late January, by now the air was quite cold, and I found myself glad of the leather coat Luke had suggested I wear.

"Edison," he said, after we took up an isolated position against a railing that overlooked steep hillsides and gave way to a staggering view of the Los Angeles cityscape, "was a jumped-up hack who stole ideas left and right and strong-armed those who would oppose him."

"Wow," I remarked, after pulling my coat a little more closely about me, "so much for that diorama I made in the fourth grade with Edison inventing the light bulb."

Something suspiciously like a snort reached my ears. "It's amazing, the impunity with which history gets rewritten."

For some reason, hearing him speak so nonchalantly of people I'd only read about in history books brought home more than anything the reality that he was much more than a mortal man. It was easy to forget when I sat across the table from him at a restaurant, or watched him drive a car, or even (or maybe especially) when I sat next to him on a crowded bus and felt his leg touch mine.

"There was even some debate as to whether Edison should end up in Hell for his various nefarious acts," Luke said, in tones so casual you'd think he was discussing whether to have soup or salad with dinner. "Unfortunately, God won that one."

"Uh, God?" I asked. Having someone mention God the way I'd off-handedly refer to a coworker in a conversation was a little disconcerting.

"Most cases are fairly clear-cut, but every once in a while we have a difference of opinion."

"I'm guessing God has the final say," I ventured, and Luke actually laughed.

"Yes," he said, his voice sounding ruefully amused. His face was in profile to me as he stared out over the drop-off and toward the shimmering lights of Los Angeles. The wind had picked up, and I saw it ruffling at his heavy dark hair. A few clouds began to blot out the stars; the forecasters had said a storm would be moving in over the weekend, and it looked as if they might be right.

Luke and I had this little section of the viewpoint to ourselves. I supposed the night air was now cold enough that most of our fellow tourists had decided to stay indoors. Angelenos aren't the most hardy lot when it comes to chilly temperatures. Maybe it was the isolation that gave me the courage to ask, "What's it like?"

He turned toward me then. "What?"

"Hell."

With a shrug he replied, "It's different things for different people."

"What's that supposed to mean?"

Even in the dim reflected lights from the Observatory, I could see him smile slightly. "If you're worried about ending up there, don't be."

I hadn't even realized I was worried about my eventual fate until he said that. Whatever else, if the Devil says you're not going to Hell, then you probably aren't.

"Hell is actually far less populated than some might think," he went on, the smile fading as he spoke. "Those who have killed, those who have willfully sought the destruction of others, or whose actions have brought about the pain and suffering of many—yes, those are the people who will end up in Hell. But taking the Lord's name in vain, or telling lies, or any of the other thousand and one transgressions people commit day in and day out—no, it takes much more than that."

His words were obscurely comforting. Oh, there were some things in my past I wasn't proud of, but at least it sounded as if the cosmic balance sheet was stacked in favor of the regular guy.

"What's the worst thing you've ever done?" he asked.

That one was easy. There were worse things than overstating the charitable contributions on your income tax or wishing that the person who just cut you off on the freeway would drop dead of a sudden thrombosis. "Standing up Anthony Whitman for the senior prom," I said.

"Tell me."

"Don't you know already?" I demanded.

"I know Anthony's side of it," Luke replied imperturbably. "I want to hear your side."

Was it just me, or had the temperature suddenly dropped about ten degrees? I pulled the coat more tightly against myself and wished I'd thrown on the cashmere muffler my sister bought me for my birthday a few years ago. I sighed, then said, "Anthony asked me to the senior prom—I assume you know what those are."

"Of course."

Right. He knew everything, didn't he? Except, apparently, what was in my head. Thank God for small favors. "Anthony was a nice guy, but he was sort of a geek, and I had a crush on someone else—"

"Greg Lopez."

I felt as if I'd just been pole-axed. "How did you know that?"

"Because *he* knew."

Well, that settled it. I definitely was not going to attend my high school reunion next summer. There was no way I could face Greg Lopez, even after ten years, if he actually knew I'd been mooning over him for most of our senior year. And here I thought no one had known about my infatuation with him, that it had been this big secret —

"Anyway," I said, deciding I was already in deep enough, "when Anthony asked me to go I said yes, because everyone kept telling me that if I didn't go to senior prom I'd regret it for the rest of my life. And then the night before, I realized I just couldn't do it. I didn't want to go with Anthony and have to sit there all night and watch Greg dance with Mandy Lewinson, and probably hang all over her, too. So I called Anthony and told him I'd come down with the flu and was puking all over the place."

"I see." Luke's tone was so neutral I couldn't tell what he was thinking.

"It was a horrible thing to do. I knew that even as I did it." The irony of it was that I did have prom regrets for the rest of my life…just not the sort of regrets people were probably thinking of when they talked me into going in the first place. "The really awful part was that Anthony had scrimped and saved to buy those prom tickets and rent a tux and whatever, and then he was out all that money. I found out afterward that he had the stereo stolen out of his car and couldn't even afford to replace it because of the money he'd blown on a prom he ended up not even attending."

"It didn't end there, though, did it?"

"No," I replied. "I felt so awful about what I'd done that I emptied out my savings account and bought him a car stereo, then left it for him on his front doorstep. He never knew where it came from."

"And that, my dear," Luke said softly, "is why you're not going to Hell."

For a long moment I was silent. I didn't know what to say. Even though I tried to make amends, I still hated what I had done. Anthony was a nice guy and didn't deserve the treatment he'd gotten from me. I was a coward over the whole thing. I should never have agreed to go in the first place.

Who knows? My putting up with Danny's neglect over the past six months could have stemmed from misplaced guilt over the way I'd acted to a similarly geeky but generally nice guy. Sometimes it's really hard to tell why we do what we do.

Luke said, "You're getting cold. Let's get down off this hill and someplace warm where we can get some hot coffee."

"Sounds good," I said. I'd have to order something decaffeinated, but a nice warm decaf latte suddenly sounded like a bit of Heaven on earth.

We made our way back over to the stop where the buses would return us to the parking garage. By then it was almost ten o'clock, and the place had begun to close down anyway. The interior of the bus was cozy and warm, since it was so packed with people. It felt good to sit down and let the chatter in various languages surround me. It was comforting in an odd way.

Once we were back down at the bottom of the hill, we found a Starbucks at the Hollywood and Highland center (not that difficult, really—you can't throw a rock in Los Angeles without hitting a Starbucks), ordered our poisons of choice, and talked about the planetarium. Of course we couldn't pick up the thread of our previous conversation, since the coffee shop was crowded and noisy, but I had actually enjoyed myself and wanted him to know it.

Afterward, we retrieved the Jag and headed west toward my apartment. I was beginning to wonder whether my choice of a decaf latte had been the best one; a few times I could feel my eyelids dropping and started awake. Well, it had been a long day.

Probably Luke noticed, but he didn't say anything. In silence he turned down my street, then pulled up at the curb. Although my block was usually fairly crowded, since most of the apartments there didn't have garages the way mine did, somehow he always managed to get a spot out front. So much for my wondering whether or not he could use his cosmic powers to finagle a decent parking space.

It's good to be the Devil, I thought, and felt a sudden urge to giggle.

By that point I was a little more used to his practice of coming around to help me out of the car; I waited in the passenger seat until he had opened the door and extended his hand. I knew now that his touch really wouldn't feel any different from anyone else's, but I still experienced a little shiver as I laid my hand in his.

He followed me as I headed up the stairs, rummaging in my purse for my keys the whole time. I wasn't too worried about making noise, since Al, my neighbor across the landing, worked graveyard for the phone company and would have already left for his shift.

I had just inserted my key in the lock when Luke said, "I would very much like to kiss you."

Somehow I managed to reply, "I'm not sure that's such a good idea."

"Why not?"

I'd been half-turned away from him to open the door, but I left the key dangling in the lock and made myself face him squarely. *Because I'm afraid I'll like it too much,* I thought, but of course I couldn't actually tell him that. Instead, I answered, "It's still too soon for me."

"Ah." Those blue eyes scanned my face; I wasn't sure what he saw there, but he apparently decided not to press the point. "Then I'll just have to hope that 'soon' becomes 'now' in the near future."

Part of me wanted him to pursue the matter. It had been a long time since I was with anyone who attracted me this much, and I wanted to know what his mouth would feel like against mine—but I was also frightened. No matter how pleasant the evening, or how many times he'd reassured me that his intentions were honorable, I couldn't yet forget who—more to the point, *what*—he was.

"We'll see," I said, in a voice that sounded shaky even to myself.

Maybe that was all he needed to hear. He'd been looking rather solemn up until that moment, but a sudden glint entered his eyes. "Until next time, then." He inclined his head slightly, then moved away from me and began to descend the steps.

I stood on the landing for a long moment and listened as his footsteps retreated across the path that cut through the lawn and connected with the sidewalk. There was a *thunk*, as of a car door closing, and then I heard the silky growl of the Jag stirring to life. Finally I let out a breath I hadn't even realized I'd been holding, and with trembling fingers turned the key in the lock.

Was this how the cowering mouse felt when the circling hawk finally turned and flew away?

Interlude

"I FEEL LIKE AN IDIOT," Asmodeus complained. He glared down at his ill-fitting jeans and baggy T-shirt, which advertised some long-defunct heavy metal group.

"This isn't a beauty contest," Beelzebub replied coolly. Possession always felt odd at first, like shoving your feet into a pair of shoes that were a size too small. But the potential benefits here far outweighed the momentary discomfort. He had taken over the body of Vincent Nguyen, since Beelzebub judged that particular young man to be the marginal leader of Danny's housemates, while Asmodeus now inhabited the form of Zach O'Connell, a spotty individual whose limbs all seemed about half a foot too long.

They stood in the kitchen of the home the possessees shared with young Master Koslowski. As was the case with most bachelor abodes, its general cleanliness left a good deal to be desired—dirty dishes were stacked in the sink, and a pile of empty pizza boxes rested on the counter-top. And was that a roach scuttling away behind the overflowing trash can in the corner?

Well, the filth could be ignored. Bad as it might be, the cluttered little house was still worlds better than Hell.

He went on, "Just play your part. The sooner our goal is accomplished, the sooner we can be out of here."

Asmodeus made a disgusted sound. "No wonder this Zach's only lay is his left hand."

Of all the—Beelzebub ground his teeth and pushed his glasses farther up his nose. "Is that all you can think about?"

"No, but I do look forward to at least getting some action when I go slumming. That girl in Rio—"

Asmodeus did have a decidedly skewed set of priorities, the attractions of mortal women being high among them. Beelzebub could never quite understand the fascination, since sex to him seemed the messiest of businesses, complete with some of the most ridiculous facial expressions seen in both this world and the next. Now, however, was certainly not the time to discuss such things. "What you do on your own time is your business," he said coolly. "However, we have more important things to attend to here. Danny—" He broke off as he heard the front door slam. In a quick undertone he added, "He's home. Stay sharp, and follow my lead."

Without bothering to look if Asmodeus was following, Beelzebub moved out into the cluttered living room. Game consoles and cartridges littered the ground in front of the large LED television. Danny stood in the middle of the room, arms crossed, a frown creasing his forehead.

"Something wrong?" Beelzebub asked.

Danny looked up, and his frown deepened for a second. "Well…"

"Something go wrong at work?" Beelzebub felt safe enough asking this question; even though Victor and Danny worked at the same company, they spent most of their shifts out on service calls and often didn't see each other at the actual office for days at a time.

"No…no, work was okay." With an impatient gesture, Danny loosened his necktie and then flung it over the arm of the couch. "It's Christa."

"Christa?" Beelzebub repeated, in carefully neutral tones. Mustn't give away his eagerness to discuss that problematic girl.

Danny hesitated. Like most young men, he and his roommates didn't spend much time discussing their personal lives—from what he could tell, Beelzebub wasn't sure Victor and Zach even *had* personal lives—so no doubt Danny was reluctant to go into any detail.

Still, it appeared the young mortal's desire to unburden himself outweighed his need to keep his personal life private. He gave a little hitch of his shoulders and said, "I think she's seeing someone else."

"Who?" Asmodeus/Zach blurted, and Beelzebub ground his teeth. Subtle.

But apparently Danny didn't appear to notice anything odd about the question. "I don't know," he replied. "She won't tell me anything."

"That's harsh," Beelzebub said, in what he hoped were appropriately sympathetic tones.

"Yeah," Danny agreed, and plopped himself down on the couch. Looking droopy as a hound dog, he picked up the remote for the television but didn't actually turn it on. The little black device dangled from his hand as if he'd forgotten what it was for.

"Maybe we could help," Beelzebub suggested.

Still frowning, Danny asked, "How?"

Beelzebub opened his mouth to reply, but Asmodeus forestalled him by saying, "I think we should follow him."

Wonderful. He should have known better than to trust Asmodeus to behave himself. "Impulsive" didn't begin to describe him. Time to do some damage control—

Too late. Danny said, "You'd do that for me?"

Asmodeus grinned. Zach did have amazing teeth, despite his overall unprepossessing appearance. "Sure. I've been reading up on it. Trust me—I'll get all the info you need on this guy."

Somehow I doubt that, Beelzebub thought. He couldn't really see Lucifer being too patient about a post-adolescent gamer nerd tailing him in a beat-up Chevy Nova. Unfortunately, he couldn't think of a way to dissuade Asmodeus without giving too much away in front of Danny.

Instead, he gritted his teeth, then said, "I don't think we should rely on just one method of gathering information."

Danny still looked as if he were impersonating a hound dog. "What else can we do?"

Mortals were so easily persuaded. "Do you think she's emailed this guy at all?"

"Probably." Some of the fuzzy look left the young man's eyes. "You're thinking of hacking her email?"

Beelzebub repressed a smile. "That would probably be the easiest thing to do."

"Unless you can think of something else," Asmodeus added, hitching up his oversized jeans. Somehow they managed to be both too big and too short at the same time.

"There's her blog," Danny said. He straightened, then set the remote down on the couch next to him. "I don't know much about it, though—she keeps it private."

"Not a problem," Beelzebub replied at once. "I'll just get her passwords."

For a second Danny looked puzzled, and then he brightened. "Keystroke capture?"

"You got it."

Asmodeus tried to nod sagely, although Beelzebub was fairly certain the other demon didn't know what keystroke capture even was. Technology had never been high on his list of interests, and he'd never been as good at gleaning necessary information from the minds of his possessees as Beelzebub.

"A keystroke logger would be easiest," he said. "Tomorrow's their weekly staff meeting—I'll install it then."

Danny looked dubious. "Won't she notice?"

"It just looks like part of the wiring. She'll never know it's there. Anyway," Beelzebub continued, "I can come back to retrieve it a couple days later. You'll just have to get her out of her office for a while so I can retrieve the device and any passwords it captures."

"I think I can manage that," Danny said. "I'll take her to lunch or something. An hour should be enough, shouldn't it?"

Beelzebub nodded. He didn't know for sure if an hour was sufficient, but he'd make it work. An hour was better than nothing.

"Okay, I'll call her. She should go along with the whole lunch thing—she's always said we don't go out enough." For a few seconds a look of indecision hovered over Danny's features. "But—it's kind of underhanded, isn't it? I mean, I know she started seeing this other guy, but we never said we couldn't date other people, and—"

Oh, for Lucifer's sake—"You want her to yourself, though, don't you?" Beelzebub broke in.

"Well, yeah—"

"All's fair in love and war," Asmodeus put in expectedly.

The cliché seemed to do the trick. Danny paused, and appeared to clench his jaw. "You're right," he said.

Perfect. Who would have guessed that Asmodeus' lack of intellectual depth might actually come in handy one day?

"All right," Beelzebub said. "Just let me know the time once you've got it set up. Then we'll find out some more about this mystery guy she's seeing." Once Danny discovered Christa's new love interest was the Devil, Beelzebub knew the young man would do everything in his power to split up the budding romance. Danny took his religion seriously; he'd be on a mission to save not just his own relationship with Christa, but her immortal soul as well.

Faced with such a two-pronged attack, the young woman would have no choice but to waver. She hadn't struck Beelzebub as the courageous type. He was certain her lack of backbone would be quite enough to keep Lucifer in Hell where he belonged….

Chapter Five

THE METEOROLOGISTS HAD BEEN RIGHT; I woke up Saturday morning to the sound of rain pattering on the driveway under my bedroom window. Great—there was nothing better than a forty-mile drive in the rain, especially when people in Southern California seemed to lose whatever limited driving skills they had every time water fell from the sky.

Still, if my mother's plans included dragging me down to Laguna Beach to whatever latest organic eatery she'd discovered, better to do it on a rainy day. At least that way the little seaside town wouldn't be quite so overrun with tourists.

I picked up my phone and saw that it wasn't so late that I could avoid going to the gym that morning. There was also an alert for a missed call. I hadn't given Luke my number, but that didn't count for much. My heart began to race as I pushed the button to call voicemail, then plummeted just as quickly when I recognized my father's voice coming out of my cell phone's tiny speaker.

Apparently he'd gotten back into town the day before and wanted to know if I could swing by his place after I'd seen my mom.

"I could take you to Tutto Mare for dinner," he said. "After lunch with your mother, you're probably going to need a decent meal. Give me a call and let me know what your plans are." And then he hung up.

Considering the meals Luke had been buying me this week, the last thing I needed was another big dinner, but I also knew my father had a point. Anyway, I'd already planned to put in a truly grueling session at the gym to burn off whatever guilt I might have had regarding those luscious pork chops from the night before or the garlic mashed potatoes that had gone along with them.

After changing into my gym clothes and allowing myself a small container of yogurt for breakfast, I took my place on a treadmill at 24-Hour Fitness with the rest of the Saturday-morning masochists. Recalling my father's promise of a big dinner out tonight, I grimly settled in for at least forty-five minutes of slogging. My personal best so far was an hour, but I was feeling more tired than I had any right to be, considering that I'd been in bed before midnight.

My thoughts kept pulling themselves toward Luke, even though I tried very hard to keep my mind on other things, such as alternate routes I could take if the 5 Freeway got completely bogged down, or what I could wear that would be appropriate for both whatever sprout-and-twig place my mother would take me to and Tutto Mare, which was a fairly upscale seafood restaurant located in Newport Center. Unfortunately, none of that was terribly stimulating. Instead I kept hearing the sound of Luke's voice, seeing his face as he stood on the landing and asked whether he could kiss me.

It seemed as if the more time I spent in his company, the harder it became for me to remember he was something more than a man. Maybe that was his intention—for me to become so familiar with him that his true identity was no longer a barrier.

And then what?

Well, that was a good question. I somehow got the feeling this wasn't just about sex...assuming he was capable. Probably; otherwise, why take on the form of a human man at all? Had he done this before? Was I just the latest in a long string of mortal conquests? Maybe he needed a lay once a century to keep on his game. I just didn't know.

Exactly. I didn't know anything, and although he'd let slip a few interesting tidbits, they'd all been calculated to put me at my ease, not to give me any more information about why he'd come to me, of all the women on the planet. The choice snippets he'd told me seemed, in retrospect, to have been carefully chosen to put me off the scent, to get me distracted by anything but the central question of our relationship.

If you could even call it that, considering we'd only seen each other twice. The sad thing was that even in our limited time together, Luke and I had had more meaningful conversations than I'd had in the entire six months I'd been dating Danny.

Danny, who seemed to have disappeared off the face of the planet. Not that that was particularly unusual, but his silence seemed almost ominous. What was he up to?

Probably nothing, as usual. Maybe he had a gaming convention or something to go to. Repressing a shudder, I recalled the time when he actually dragged me to one of those a few months ago. I'd gone along, because at the time I'd still thought we might actually work out as a couple, even though his parents acted like I was the Whore of Babylon or something because I wasn't Catholic. They were so hardcore they'd even had portraits of the Pope hanging on the walls of their living room.

At any rate, Danny had looked like a *GQ* model compared to the collection of misfits, nerds, and downright freaks I saw at that gaming convention. It didn't help that there weren't many other women there, especially ones in skinny jeans and high-heeled boots; the conglomeration of geeks in attendance kept staring at me the way a starving dog would stare at a steak, and I'd finally faked a headache and made Danny take me home.

But he hadn't mentioned any events of that sort coming up, and he usually did tell me about them, in a half-wistful, half-cajoling way: "If you'd just give it a chance, you could have a lot of fun!" Yeah, right. I'd cop to playing games on my phone while waiting at the doctor's office or something, but I certainly didn't devote large chunks of my life to gaming the way those guys did.

Well, Danny would just have to take care of himself, and Luke as well. Not that I had any doubt as to his capacity to keep himself occupied. God knows what the Devil did in the hours when he wasn't wining and dining me. But maybe He didn't, either. I still hadn't exactly figured out that particular relationship. There hadn't been any animosity in Luke's voice when he spoke of God—if anything, they sounded like a manager and a subordinate who usually got along fairly well but who every once in a while had a difference of opinion.

That didn't sound much like what I'd read about Lucifer, about the supposed war in Heaven and all that, but maybe the passage of time had mellowed things. Maybe one of these days we'd be someplace private enough that I could actually try to get straight answers to some of my questions.

Then again, that could be asking for trouble. I was beginning to wonder if I could trust myself to be alone with Luke for anything longer than five minutes.

It was a good thing I'd planned alternate routes down to Orange County, because, as I'd worried, someone had decided it was a really good day to wrap his car around a light pole. I had to make a detour that took me a good bit out of the way and actually put me on a freeway that ran closer to the coast. Ironically, the change in route meant that I was going to drive right by the exit I would have taken to get to my father's house. But of course I couldn't go there now—I still had lunch to get through somehow.

I did use some of the time I spent sitting in traffic to finally call Nina back and try to set something up with her for a belated birthday get-together. She still sounded a little cloggy, but she protested when I said we could just postpone things until she was all the way better.

"I'm fine," she said. "I'm going stir-crazy anyway. Let's get out and do something."

"All right," I said. "As long as it doesn't involve food. After this week I don't think I want to ever eat again."

"Another big date, huh?"

"He took me to Griffith Observatory."

A few seconds of silence as Nina digested that statement. "Wow, that sounds really...fun."

"It was," I replied. "It was lovely."

"'Lovely'? I don't think I've ever heard you use that word to describe a date before."

"I guess I never had a date before that deserved it."

Nina remarked, "I'm impressed. So when do I get to meet the wonder stud?"

I winced. "Um—"

"Yeah, I know. 'Our relationship is in a delicate beginning stage, and I don't think it's time yet to introduce him to my friends.'"

Despite myself, I laughed. "Something like that." With a grin, I added, "Tell you what—you introduce me to Gina, and I'll introduce you to Luke."

"That was underhanded."

"All's fair." The words hadn't left my mouth before I began to wonder, *So is this love...or war?*

"Fine." But I could tell Nina wasn't upset with me, because I heard a little undercurrent of laughter in her voice. "Have a good day with your mom, and tell her I said hi."

"Will do," I replied, and then we made our good-byes. I hit the "end" button on my phone and tossed it back into my purse.

Although I'd been down to Irvine just a scant month earlier for the holidays (no "Christmas" in my mother's house...she just refers to the winter celebration as her solstice observance), it seemed as if the place had gotten even more crowded in the intervening time. The developers appeared intent on covering every square inch of land with over-priced tract houses, and shopping centers sprang up in the sections that weren't occupied by over-extended homeowners and renters.

Following my parents' divorce, my mother had gotten possession of the house where I'd grown up. It was located in Woodbridge, a subdivision located pretty much in the center of the city, and the homes around it were well-maintained, many of them expanded as much as city ordinances would allow. My parents had never bothered with additions or any of that, since the place had four bedrooms to start with, but it was freshly painted a few years back and so blended in fairly well with the rest of the neighborhood. I doubted you could say the same for its interior.

True, most of the furniture had stayed the same country-ish oak that had been in place ever since I could remember. But after my father moved out, my mother began to indulge her passion for folk art and ethnic crafts until the house began to look like an overcrowded shop. No wonder my brother spent so much time roaming around the city with his friends, looking for places they could hang out on their bikes and skateboards before the Irvine P.D.

caught up with them and forced them to move on to the next hangout.

I just wished my mother would wake up and realize what a slacker Jeff was turning out to be. He wasn't a bad kid—despite spending the hours he wasn't free-floating around town holed up in a friend's room and smoking weed. My father had been pretty much hands-off ever since my parents split up, and my mother spent so much of her time taking classes on basket weaving or throwing pottery or whatever else had lately taken her fancy that she seemed to have no clue that her youngest child was on the fast track to nowhere. Now, I didn't pretend to be some huge over-achiever. I certainly wasn't my sister, with her million-plus in real estate sales and her mortgage broker husband. But even I had done the best I could to try to live life for myself, away from my parents. Jeff, from what I could tell, seemed content to spend the rest of his days living in the bedroom he'd occupied ever since he was five years old and sponging off my parents. From time to time he'd get a part-time job, but none of those seemed to last very long.

Even though I knew it was uncharitable of me, as I pulled up into the driveway I found myself hoping that he wouldn't be home. Probably not; he tried to avoid the family togetherness thing as much as possible, and going out to lunch would have required putting on a clean shirt. Besides, he hated the whole organic/vegan thing as much as the rest of us. My mother fed him top-of-the-line holistic stuff, and then he went out with his friends and spent his pocket money on McDonald's and Del Taco.

The rain had lightened up a bit as I headed south, but I still needed my umbrella to get from the car to the front entry relatively unscathed. I rang the doorbell and waited a few seconds until my mother answered the door.

Looking at her was always sort of strange for me. We were a lot alike—same straight dark hair and big brown eyes, same short little nose and rounded chin. For years she colored her hair to keep the gray at bay, but after the divorce she let it pretty much go, and now it had heavy silver streaks through it. She also put on weight immediately after my father took off, but once she went on her vegan diet she lost most of the extra pounds and got pretty trim. Actually, she looked damn good for someone her age, so it gave me hope that I'd be able to hold up fairly well as the years went on.

Still, coming face to face with her was always like meeting up with an older version of myself, and it could be kind of disconcerting. It didn't help that she invariably wore jeans and flowing, boho-style tops that made her look younger than her fifty-six years, despite the gray in her hair.

She hugged me and told me I was looking wonderful—her standard greeting—and then led me back into the house, chattering away about this fabulous new place she'd found in Laguna whose chef was a huge proponent of the whole raw food movement, and how much I was going to adore it. I sighed inwardly, steeling myself for a meal composed of hummus, pine nuts, and God knows what else, and managed to smile. At least I could look forward to getting some real food in me after I met up with my father later in the afternoon.

Some vaguely Celtic new age–sounding music played softly in the background, and the house smelled of patchouli. Sometimes I really did wonder if my mother thought it was still the '70s or something. I still couldn't quite figure out why my parents—who met at Berkeley—had ever decided to settle in staid Irvine all those years back.

"So what's new?" I asked, hovering in the living room as she went to retrieve her purse. "Any new projects?"

My mother worked as a freelance book designer, and she made a decent living at it. Of course, the continuing support from my father probably didn't hurt, but she did have a steady stream of jobs coming through, mainly from small presses that couldn't afford full-time designers.

She emerged from the kitchen, clutching an oversized faux-suede bag (no leather products for my mother) and smiling. "Oh, yes, a wonderful new book from Chanson Press about the baskets of the Chumash people. It's very exciting."

Well, at least she was able to combine two of her great loves. I could see two examples of her own handicraft perched on one edge of the fireplace surround. Good thing she never actually lit a fire in there—too wasteful of natural resources.

"Sounds great," I said. Then—because as much as I hated to drive in Laguna, getting in a car with my mother behind the wheel was a surefire recipe for disaster—I asked if she wanted me to drive to the restaurant.

"Oh, you don't have to do that—" Her protest sounded a little half-hearted, though. I think deep down my mother knew she was a lousy driver.

"No problem," I said hastily. "Um...is Jeff coming?"

"No," she replied. "I think he was going to the movies with a friend. I told him he should see you, since it was your birthday and everything, but he said you'd understand."

Which was Jeff code for *Hey, sis, hope you have a good day, but I don't really give a crap whether I see you or not*. I still hadn't decided whether the feeling was mutual or not.

My mother and I shared an umbrella as we went back out to the car. For a second I worried that she might to try to convince me that driving her Toyota hybrid would be better than the Mercedes, but since the rain was coming down harder now and the Mercedes handled beautifully in wet weather, she apparently decided safety won out over conservation.

I backed the car out of the driveway and headed back down to the 405. From there we'd pick up a highway that wound its way through the hills and on into Laguna. For a while we were both quiet; I needed to focus on the road, and I thought she could sense that. But after I pulled onto the 133 and slowed down to about fifty to accommodate the winding, slick pavement, my mother stirred in her seat and gave me a thoughtful look.

"Something seems different about you."

"I'm a whole year older," I replied, without lifting my gaze from the road.

"No, I think it's more than that."

Well, I've met the Devil, I thought. *And he sent me flowers for my birthday.*

I didn't say anything, though. That was a conversation I really didn't feel like getting into quite yet.

"How's Danny?" she asked, her voice altering subtly. Now, my mother is probably the world's most understanding person. She didn't even rant and rage and despair when my father left. *We've become different people,* she'd said, looking somewhat wistful, but that was about it. With Danny, though, I always got the definite vibe that she didn't quite think he was good enough for me, even though she would never say such a thing out loud.

"Fine," I said, lifting my foot off the accelerator as we hit the inevitable crawl that started at Pacific Coast Highway and backed up onto the 133 by a distance determined only by the quality of the weather. Since it was raining buckets, I only had to wait about three phases of the light before I could turn left onto PCH.

"It's on the right, about two streets down," my mother instructed. "There's parking in the back—"

I caught a glimpse of the restaurant in time, and turned right, then right again into a cramped parking lot. Still, that was better than a lot of places around here, which often had only street parking. For a few minutes we were occupied with getting out of the car and into the restaurant without being soaked in the process. It wasn't until we'd been seated at a small table toward the back and handed our menus that my mother was able to pick up the previous thread of the conversation.

"You don't sound very enthusiastic," she said. "Is everything all right?"

"Oh, sure," I muttered. What I wasn't enthusiastic about was the contents of the menu. No meat, of course, but not even anything with dairy in it. I was overcome by sudden visions of cheeseburgers and fries and bit my lip, forcing my mind away from such forbidden fruit. "We just had a little spat a few days ago, that's all," I added. I figured it couldn't hurt to cheer her up a little bit with the prospect of Danny and me having difficulties.

"A spat?"

The waiter showed up, and my mother ordered an herbal iced tea. I asked for the same, since nothing else was remotely appealing.

Then she requested some scary-sounding kind of wrap, and I ordered the pesto pizza, since I couldn't see anything else on the menu that didn't frighten me. We handed the menus back to the waiter, and my mother fastened me with a penetrating look, the sort I used to get in high school when I tried to lie about how late I'd been out the night before.

"He forgot my birthday," I said flatly.

"Oh, dear," she said.

"Yeah. As you can imagine, I wasn't too thrilled about it." The waiter placed the iced teas in front of us, and I figured I might as well go for it. "But that's all right, because I've actually met someone else."

"You have? Who?"

That was a good question. "Um, just this guy. His name is Luke."

"What's he like?" she asked.

If it had been my father or my sister, probably the first question they would have asked would be, "What does he do?" But this was my mother, and of course she cared more about this unknown suitor's personality than what he did for a living.

Unfortunately for me, neither question offered an easy answer.

"Charming," I said, after a long pause. "Intelligent. Good-looking."

"Sounds good so far," she replied, smiling. "Does he work in publishing as well?"

"No—he's—he's sort of independently wealthy." That was good enough for now. At least it explained the cars and the house in Hancock Park.

She lifted an eyebrow, as if she didn't completely believe me. But, being my mother, she didn't press the issue. "So you're not seeing Danny anymore?"

"Not exactly," I said. "I guess I thought I'd see what it was like to go out with a few different people at the same time. It's not as if Danny and I were serious, anyway."

"That's not like you, Christa."

That was for sure. Up until this point my entire romantic life had been an exercise in serial monogamy. Even when it wasn't really working out, as it hadn't been with Danny, I was always afraid to try seeing several people at the same time. Nina didn't have the same scruples; she made it sound as if she were seeing only the unknown Gina, but I didn't know for sure. During college she usually had at least three guys on the string at any one time.

"I guess not," I admitted. "But maybe it's time I tried something different."

She opened her mouth to reply, but then the waiter showed up with our meals, and I had to spend the next few minutes listening to her gush about the food and how wonderful it was and how healthful, yadda yadda. To me, it tasted as if I were eating the dining-room table run through a blender and covered with pesto, but somehow I managed to keep taking bites and nodding enthusiastically. If it made her happy, I could suffer for a few hours (or maybe more, depending on what this stuff ended up doing to my digestive tract, but I was just going to cross my fingers and hope for the best).

After that she went into a panegyric about the benefits of yoga and encouraged me to take it up. Now, I had to admit that my mother looked fabulous, and if yoga helped her to achieve her current tone, then kudos and all that. But yoga scared me a bit; I worried that I would get myself twisted up into some sort of human pretzel shape and wouldn't be able to get out of it.

I made some sound of demurral, and then she said, "And I just participated in a croning ceremony, and it was the most empowering—"

"A *what?*"

"A croning ceremony, to celebrate reaching the third stage of life and achieving a certain wisdom."

Abandoning all attempts to finish off my pesto and buckwheat monstrosity, I laid down my fork and stared at her. A crone? My vital, still-attractive mother? Oh, I knew she'd said she wasn't interested in pursuing any further relationships, that she was done with that part of her life, but I just figured it was because of the hurt resulting from the divorce and that eventually she'd get back into the dating scene. Women her age and older got remarried every day.

"Don't you think you're a little young to be calling yourself a crone?" I asked at last, trying not to sound overly incredulous.

"Some of the women in my group are as young as forty-nine," she replied. "It's just an acknowledgment that we've moved beyond the mothering stage and are ready to become active wise women."

"Moved beyond the mothering stage"? What, did that mean she was finally going to kick Jeff out of the house and tell him to shape up?

I opened my mouth to ask the question and then shut it with a mental sigh. That was between her and Jeff; I'd been out of the house pretty much since I was eighteen and left to attend UCLA. Maybe the "mothering" she'd referred to was simply being of an age to have children.

"I'm glad it's working out for you," I said finally. It seemed to me the path she'd chosen was one of personal exploration, and if that was what she wanted, then I'd just have to support her. Despite my current difficulties, I couldn't imagine not wanting to have a man in my life, but maybe during the past five years she'd come to an understanding of her own strengths and abilities, and had realized she would enjoy going it alone from here. Telling her that she was too young to call herself a crone or that she should just get some highlights and sign up with a dating service would only let her know I didn't understand or approve of her choices.

She smiled at me, and I returned the smile. I wanted to pat myself on the back for being so mature about the situation, but oddly enough, I just felt tired. And I still had to deal with my father and the dreaded Traci later that afternoon.

It was closer to six than five when I finally dropped my mother back home and then got on the road once more to head into Newport Beach. During our lunch the rain had tapered off, and she'd wanted to take me shopping amongst the various boutiques and trendy little stores that filled Laguna's downtown area. Since garnets were my birthstone, she bought me a beautiful silver necklace and a pair of earrings set with the wine-colored gems as a belated present. I also spied a truly awesome embroidered black suede jacket in one of the stores, but I decided to pass it by, since I knew any gushing over it would have earned me another lecture about the cruelty of wearing real leather or suede. Maybe that was true, but my feet hated shoes made out of synthetics, and so far comfort had won out over scruple every time.

My father lived in a pseudo-Mediterranean McMansion about half a mile from the ocean. The house had a gorgeous view from the back-yard, a black-bottom swimming pool, and about four thousand square feet of pretentious living space. I still shuddered to think what it must have cost.

When I pulled into the driveway, I saw Traci's white Escalade sitting there as well. Don't ask me why she felt the need to leave it outside when they had a perfectly good three-car garage. Actually, do ask me—I knew it was because she wanted every-one to see her new piece of automotive extrava-gance. The point of a Cadillac SUV eluded me any-way; it wasn't as if she was ever going to take the damned thing off-road.

I went up to the front door and rang the bell. My father answered it almost immediately, since I'd called as I was getting on the freeway to let him know I was about fifteen minutes away. He looked good, with a fresh Hawaiian tan. Or maybe he'd just gotten a spray tan so he could have the look with-out the sun damage.

"How's the birthday girl?" he asked.

"Fine," I replied. I didn't bother to remind him that my birthday was days ago. With everyone's crazy schedules, my birthday had somehow bloated into a birth-week.

"Starving?" His eyes twinkled. He'd had to suffer a few of my mother's macrobiotic experiments over the years as well. I wondered if that was part of the reason why he finally cleared out.

"Not quite, but probably I will be in a half-hour or so."

"Well, I made early reservations, since I figured you wouldn't want to wait."

"Sounds great," I said, following him into the family room.

Traci was in there, lounging on one of the leather sofas. She had the 60-inch flat-screen tuned to some reality show featuring a bunch of equally plastic-looking people, but she picked up the remote and clicked it off when she saw us enter.

"Hi, Christa!" she chirped.

"Hi," I said, sounding distinctly lackluster. Probably I should have tried to muster at least a modicum of false enthusiasm, but both the spirit and the flesh were weak at that moment.

"So are Lisa and Nathan meeting us at the restaurant?" Traci inquired, standing up and brushing at her close-fitting taupe suede trousers. No scruples over animal cruelty in this household, that was for sure.

"Oh, are they coming, too?" I wished I'd known that. I always had to mentally prepare myself for extended periods in my sister's presence.

For a second my father looked a little uncomfortable. "Well, she wanted to be part of your birthday dinner, too, so I thought it would be good for all of us to get together."

This was just getting better and better. But I knew any sort of protest would make me sound like I was a bad sport, so I mustered a smile and said, "It'll be good to see them. Lisa and I always talk about getting together, but our schedules, you know—" I waved a hand, hoping he'd bought the lie. Frankly, Lisa and I talked maybe four or five times a year, if that, and mainly to plan holidays or family birthdays.

Luckily, though, my father didn't seem to be paying me that much attention. He smiled and nodded, then went and fetched a coat for Traci, since going upstairs to get it herself seemed to be out of the question. She looked tanned as well, her mid-brown hair streaked liberally with blonde. Her French manicure was almost blinding.

"So how was Hawaii?" I asked, praying that my father wouldn't take too long.

"Great, really great. We found this fabulous new restaurant in Kona—"

I let her natter away, not really listening, until my father returned and we all piled into the Escalade to go to the restaurant. Of course I had to get in the back seat, which was all right; at least I could just stare out the window at the lights of Newport sliding by and try to ignore the inane chatter in the front seat as to whether they should listen to the jazz station or talk radio.

Some days I really wondered why my father ever bothered to marry that woman. Oh, she was decorative enough, if in a typical sort of way, and supposedly she was a fairly successful interior designer before the two of them got together and she took up her current life of hardcore shopping and travel, but I had yet to hear her string two intelligent words together.

Of course, I might have been a little biased.

Tutto Mare was located at the edge of Newport Center, yet another Southern California homage to commerce. The restaurant was modern yet somehow still warm, its airy spaces and clean lines offset by expanses of burnished copper and smooth travertine. My sister and her husband Nathan already waited for us there, and we exchanged the obligatory greetings and hugs before the hostess gathered us all up and seated us at a large table at the far end of the main dining room.

We settled ourselves with my father at the head of the table, Nathan at the foot, and my sister and I sharing one side while Traci had the other to herself. My stomach was beginning to tell me it was not happy with the nuts and twigs it had received earlier, so I decided a nice big swordfish steak was probably the way to go. The waiter came and took our drink orders; as much as I would have liked a glass of wine, I had a long drive home after this and decided to stick with mineral water.

Finally we all had our beverages, and the talk around the table quieted down a bit. My father cleared his throat and said, "We're here for Christa's birthday" —and he raised his glass toward me— "but I also have some very important news for you all."

I shot a mystified look at Lisa, and she raised her shoulders. At least she didn't know anything more than I did.

For some reason my father reached over and took Traci's hand in his. "I just wanted you here so I could tell all of you the happy news." Grinning, he announced, "Traci and I are going to have a baby."

CHAPTER SIX

AN AWFUL SILENCE FELL. My stomach, which had already been doing some interesting gyrations as it tried to digest the wood chips from my lunch earlier, flip-flopped. My father continued to grin, but Traci's smile began to look a little pasted on.

I blurted out the first thing that popped into my mind. "Aren't you too old for that?"

If I'd thought the silence that followed my father's pronouncement was bad, the one that resulted from my ill-considered question was positively hideous.

Finally Traci said, shooting me one of the most evil glares I've ever received, "I'm only thirty-nine."

"Oh," I said. "Right." Okay, she might only be thirty-nine, but my father was going to be fifty-seven in May, which meant he'd be the ripe old age of seventy-five when he got around to sending this kid off to college.

"So when are you due?" my sister Lisa asked, in what I thought of as her sparkly real-estate agent's voice. I could tell from a certain tautness in her jaw line that she wasn't exactly thrilled with this particular piece of information, either, but unlike me Lisa hadn't contracted a sudden case of foot-in-mouth disease.

"The end of June," Traci said promptly. "We wanted to wait until we were sure and that everything was progressing normally until we told everyone."

If it really had been that touch-and-go, I questioned the wisdom of their jetting off to Hawaii for the past ten days, but whatever. Maybe Traci had wanted to get in one last round of vacationing before she was stuck in Newport Beach with nothing to do but watch her waistline expand and drop large amounts of cash at trendy maternity boutiques.

I wanted to ask, *Does Mom know?* but realized that question would be even less welcome than the whole age gaffe. Probably I should have realized that this particular disaster might occur at any given time, since Traci was so much younger than my father. Honestly, as the years went on and they never discussed having kids, I'd just assumed Traci didn't want any.

But obviously she had wanted them, or at least had gotten it into her head that a baby was the latest accessory she needed to make her life complete. I'd rather think that than consider the possibility of my father really wanting more kids. Because if that were the case, then I'd begin to wonder if there was something deficient in all of us, something he'd wanted from a child but hadn't yet gotten. We were all bright and attractive (well, the jury was out on Jeff on the first part of that statement, even though he cleaned up pretty well), but none of us was exactly a genius or a prodigy. However, if my father had hoped that Traci's genetic contribution would bring him a Nobel laureate or the next Bill Gates, I had a feeling he was going to be sadly disappointed.

While all these thoughts were passing through my head, I found myself getting angrier and angrier. How dare they, anyway? Wasn't this world over-populated enough? Had my father even stopped to think that he was the age where he should be expecting his first grandchild, not his fourth child? And bringing it up like this, at a dinner that was supposed to be for my birthday. Very nice. Thanks so much.

"Do you know what you're having?" Nathan asked. He shot a considering glance in my direction, as if he'd started to guess the reason for my continuing silence. Despite the fact that he was a mortgage broker, he was actually a fairly nice guy who displayed flashes of intuition I wouldn't have thought possible in someone who'd been misguided enough to marry my sister.

Traci gave a simpering little laugh. "Well, I had an amnio because, well, I am past thirty-five. But Stephen and I decided we wanted it to be a surprise, so we asked them not to share that part of the results with us."

"I suppose it's more fun that way," Lisa put in. Her smile was starting to look a little tight around the edges. I wondered suddenly whether she and Nathan had been trying to get pregnant as well, with no luck. She'd always said she didn't want to start a family until she was at least thirty, but she'd hit the big three-oh this past October. If they really had been trying with no success, I could see why Lisa's expression reminded me more of someone who was grimacing in pain than actually grinning.

For the first time my father seemed to detect a notable lack of enthusiasm on my part. His gaze settled on me, his hazel eyes looking concerned. "You're very quiet, Christa."

"Sorry," I said, gulping at my mineral water. At that moment I really regretted not ordering a glass of wine. "I guess I was just thinking."

"About?" It was his psychologist's voice, neutral, gently probing.

I really hated it when my father pulled that stuff on us. We were his kids, after all, not his clients, or the groupies who paid big bucks for the seminars he gave one weekend a month on personal growth and family dynamics. "So are you going to cut Mom off when the baby comes?"

"I hardly think this is the time to discuss that, Christa. Your mother already knew the situation with Jeff couldn't continue indefinitely."

Okay, maybe they'd already hashed through that particular point. I'd often thought to myself that my mother needed to give Jeff more of a push, make him realize he couldn't live with her forever. However, now that it looked as if there might be a definite end point to the support my father was willing to pay for him, I found myself rushing to his defense. My brother, who lately had been a source of some impatience for me, suddenly seemed in definite need of a protector.

"Who's to say Jeff isn't just acting out because his father took off to marry someone almost half his age?" I snapped, then realized I had gone way too far.

"Christa!" my father and sister exclaimed almost at once.

Lisa looked really angry. Now, she wasn't a huge fan of Traci, although she was willing to make nice and play "happy family" just because that's what people are supposed to do. But I had broken the cardinal rule. I had brought up the divorce when we'd all agreed to tiptoe around that point. Worse, I had made it quite clear that I thought the breakup of my parents' marriage was mostly my father's fault.

Oddly, though, I didn't feel guilty. I guess I should have—here we were supposed to be having a celebratory family dinner, and instead I'd turned it into a scene. Well, all right, not quite a scene. Most of the conversation had been carried on in normal tones, so unless the people around us were actively eavesdropping, they probably couldn't hear what was being said. However, I flushed with righteous indignation. It felt good to have finally said what I thought instead of biting my lip and avoiding a confrontation.

The weird thing was that Traci shot me a strangely triumphant look, as if my outburst was exactly what she wanted. Why? So I could alienate my father? Maybe she thought having him on the outs with his first family would give her more power in the relationship, power that could only be increased by having a baby. I knew she merely tolerated us, just as we only tolerated her. We didn't have anything in common, and no reason to like one another except that my father had decided—in a fit of insanity—to marry her.

But as much as I would have liked to push the matter, the sad fact was that I really didn't want to upset my father any more than I probably already had. Despite my continuing irritation with Traci and the feeling that something had gone subtly wrong with the universe ever since my parents split up, I really did love him. He'd been a good father, there for our concerts and plays and awards ceremonies, taking us to the park on the weekend, gamely trying to build a playhouse for us in the backyard even though he had less mechanical ability than I did.

Sometimes things just don't work out between people, I thought. *That doesn't necessarily make them bad.*

"I'm sorry," I said at length, knowing they needed to hear the words even if I didn't really mean them. "I guess you caught me by surprise." And then, because my father still looked troubled, I added, "Probably just low blood sugar."

"Curse of the nuts and twigs," he said, the beginnings of a smile lifting at his mouth.

Lisa glanced from him to me, eyebrows pulled together in puzzlement, and then she gave a sudden relieved laugh. "Oh, lunch with Mom, right?"

"Unfortunately, yes," I replied, and a little of the tension went out of the air.

Nathan essayed a smile. Traci looked as if she could have cheerfully strangled the lot of us, but because we'd managed to avoid a meltdown, she had to shoehorn a cheerful expression onto her features. It was actually sort of funny to watch her twist her tight-skinned face—never capable of much movement at the best of times—into something approximating good humor.

By way of an olive branch, I asked Traci which room they were considering converting into a nursery, and she was off and running. The second guest bedroom had already been selected, she informed me, and the painters were coming next week. As she went into details that mattered probably only to her and my father (and his interest was debatable; I thought I saw his eyes start to glaze over as she launched into a discussion of layette tables), I patted myself on the back for skillfully maneuvering the conversation into safer territory. Then the food came, and the rest of the meal passed without incident.

A few times, though, I saw a hurt look come and go in my sister's eyes, and wondered if she'd ever tell me the truth about how she felt regarding this new addition to our family. Probably not. Some sisters shared that kind of closeness, but not the us. We tended to keep our secrets from one another.

I figured it was just as well. Even if Lisa were the kind of sister I could have confided in, I think I would have had a hard time explaining to her how I ended up dating the Devil.

The evening felt interminable, but in reality I was back on the freeway and heading north by nine o'clock. The rain had begun to fall again, unevenly and in fits and starts. For some stretches the road was almost dry, and in others water hit my windshield with such intensity that I had to ratchet up the wipers a notch or two. I almost welcomed the rain, since it made me concentrate on my driving and not the unwelcome news my father and Traci had dumped on us.

As we left the restaurant, there was another round of congratulations. I think my voice sounded almost normal as I said it would be fun to go shopping for those cute little baby booties and all the other paraphernalia an infant needs. But on the way back to my father's house from the restaurant, I couldn't think of anything else to say, and I just stared out at the rain and wished I could transport myself back home instantly. If Luke had been with me, I probably could have.

He wasn't there, though, and, weird as it seemed, I almost missed him. I supposed it was just because when I was around him he made me feel as if his entire attention was focused entirely on me. This dinner, even though it supposedly was in honor of my birthday, had been pretty much hijacked by talk of the baby and Traci's plans for him/her. As the middle child, I was sort of used to being overlooked, but something about the whole evening just rankled. I tried to tell myself I was being selfish, and probably I was tired and PMS-y to boot, but I knew it was more than that.

Maybe I'd just fix myself a nice hot bath when I got home. I'd never been much of a bath-type girl, more from lack of time than anything else, but I tried to treat myself once a month or so if the spirit moved me. My apartment's single bathroom had both a tiled shower stall and an actual tub, and I dutifully scrubbed out the tub every other week even though I hardly ever used it. I had some bath salts and candles, and I could turn up the stereo in the living room so I'd still be able to hear it down the hall.

The more I thought about it, the more the bath sounded like a good plan. Time to pamper myself, time to relax, time to try to forget all the craziness that had dominated my life for the past week. Then I could get a good night's sleep and wake up the next day with a fresh outlook on life.

I parked my car in the garage, and hurried around to the front of the building and up the stairs. The rain had let off a bit, but I still felt a few drops hit my face and hands. I wanted to be safely under cover before it let loose again.

After scrabbling for my keys, since once again they'd migrated to the bottom of my purse, I unlocked the deadbolt and let myself in.

Luke looked up from his place on the couch and smiled at me. "Good evening."

I let out a little scream and dropped my key-chain. Blushing furiously, I bent down to retrieve it and hoped the dim light of the one lamp he'd switched on hid my flushed cheeks. *Cool reaction,*

Christa, I scolded myself. Then again, it's a little startling to think you're coming home to an empty house and instead to open the door and find the Devil sitting on your couch.

"How the hell did you get in there?" I asked.

"Don't you remember that comment I made about doors opening for me?"

Crossing my arms, I retorted, "Yeah, well, in this part of the world we call that breaking and entering."

As usual, his only response was a smile. "I wanted to see you."

"Okay, so you're seeing me." To cover my confusion, I hurried through the living room and set my purse down on the floor next to the side table in the dining room.

"You sound upset." His voice was very close; obviously he'd followed me.

"Of course I'm upset," I replied, turning to face him, my arms crossed protectively across my chest. "I just got home and found the Devil sitting in my living room."

"It's more than that."

Eyes narrowing, I glared at him. "Oh, I suppose you already know all about what happened at dinner with my father, Mr. Omniscient."

"I know some of it." The look he gave me seemed almost pitying. "But I don't know how you feel about the situation."

"Oh, I should think that's pretty obvious!" I snapped.

Without comment, Luke extended his hand. A glass of pale wine suddenly appeared in his palm, and he placed it in my own hand and wrapped my fingers around the stem. "It sounds as if you could use this."

I hated to admit it, but he was right. I didn't bother to sip at the wine; I lifted the glass to my lips and took a healthy swallow. It figured that he'd given me the pinot grigio I'd almost ordered at dinner and then decided to pass up.

"Better?" he asked.

"A little," I admitted.

"Then come and sit down."

Not bothering to protest, I followed him back into the living room. Luke didn't attempt to sit next to me on the couch. Instead, he took a seat in the wing chair that was located to the right of the sofa and which formed an L-shape around the coffee table.

"By way of correction," he said in an off-hand tone, "I'm not omniscient. There is only One who can claim that particular ability."

"Well, that's a relief," I remarked. A few more swallows of the wine, and I began to feel a little less wild. "But you obviously know enough."

"True." He leaned back in the chair; a glass identical to the one I held appeared in his left hand.

"This news about your father and his wife upsets you. Why?"

"Why?" I echoed. "Because—because—" And I broke off, wondering what it was that really *had* set me off so badly. Well, besides the fact that it's mildly freaky to acknowledge your father is doing the horizontal mambo with his second wife. I mean, I knew that in an intellectual way, but it was a lot more difficult to ignore that sort of thing when the fruits of their nocturnal activities were about to become very obvious in the next few months. So, all right, icky and all that, but I was a big girl; I could handle the idea that my father was still a sexual creature.

No, if I took a real hard look at the situation, what upset me so much was the realization that now there was no way my parents would ever get back together. If you'd ever asked me that point-blank, I probably would have laughed out loud, but somewhere in the back of my mind there was this little niggling hope that the whole thing with Traci had been a horrible mistake and that one day he'd dump her and go back to my mother. With a baby on the way, however, that tiny little hope had melted away like ice hitting a hot skillet.

"Because I was stupid and thought that maybe my parents would decide the divorce was a bad idea and that they really should be with one another," I said at last, my tone hard, brittle, full of scorn for my self-delusion.

"That's not stupid," Luke replied. "That's just being human."

Frowning, I helped myself to another gulp of pinot grigio and then shot him a suspicious look. "Are you sure you're the Devil?" I asked. "You're starting to sound more like Jesus to me."

He laughed. "I assure you, I'm not He."

No, I supposed not. There was something dark and complicated in Luke's face, even during relaxed moments such as these, that I somehow doubted would have shown itself in the visage of the son of God.

"You assume," he went on, "as most people do, that because I'm the Devil I'm somehow the source of all evil."

"So you're telling me you're not?"

"Hardly."

I straightened and set my wine glass down on a coaster on the coffee table. "So where does evil come from?"

Tilting his head to one side, he regarded me intently. "From you."

With a nervous laugh, I replied, "So I'm the source of all evil?"

"I meant that as the general 'you.'" Luke sat up as well, then leaned forward and rested the wine glass on one knee. Tonight he wore all black—trousers, V-neck sweater, black T-shirt underneath. He managed to look casual and elegant at the same time, and

I found myself wondering what my family's reaction would have been if I'd appeared this evening with him in tow. I guessed they all probably would agree that I had traded up. He added, "After all, God is a big believer in something called free will."

"So all the horrible things that happen in the world are our fault," I said slowly.

"Not all. Some are simply natural disasters. People may throw up their hands and cry, 'Why would God let such a thing happen?' But no one stops to wonder what would happen if God put His finger on the fault to keep the quake from happening, or lifted His hand to push the hurricane aside. The consequences of intervention sometimes can be much worse than what would have happened if the original event had been allowed to occur unimpeded."

I had to admit that I'd never really thought about it that way. Then again, I didn't quite have Luke's perspective.

"But so much of the rest of it—the murders, the rapes, the abuse, the wholesale slaughter of innocents—all that comes from the demons within." A sardonic light entered his eyes. "Not from the Devil without."

"So what *is* your role, then?" I asked. "Was there really no war in Heaven? What about 'it's better to reign in Hell' and all that?"

Luke's lip curled slightly. "Actually, of all my portrayals, I have to say I am rather partial to Milton's. I'm almost sympathetic there."

Since my knowledge of *Paradise Lost* was pretty much limited to that one quote, I really couldn't comment. Instead I reached down, picked up my wine glass, and took another sip, waiting.

The wry set of his mouth never changed. "'Prison warden' is the closest approximation, I think."

That almost sounded plausible, but I still got the feeling he wasn't telling me the whole story. Was it possible that humankind had gotten the tale completely twisted around?

"So you're saying you never challenged God," I said.

"No, I'm not saying that at all," Luke replied coolly. "I did mention that we'd had differences of opinion on occasion."

"And you ended up running Hell."

"Precisely." He lifted his shoulders and then added, "Someone had to do it."

Feeling more than a little overwhelmed, I drained the last of my wine and set the glass back on its coaster. Not for the first time, I wished I weren't so completely ignorant of Christian mythology and belief. Some random stolen minutes with Wikipedia weren't exactly adequate to get me up to speed enough that I would be able to know if he were telling me anything close to the truth...and whether I was even asking the right questions.

"I guess running Hell isn't a full-time job," I commented.

"What makes you say that?"

"Well, if it were, I doubt you'd be spending quite so much time hanging around me."

"Like any other manager, I have subordinates who can look after things in my absence."

And who's that? I thought. *Beelzebub? Asmodeus?* I couldn't recall any of the other demons' names from my Internet studies, but I supposed it didn't really matter.

I suddenly realized we had wandered far off the topic of my miserable evening and the fallout from my father's and Traci's announcement, but maybe that had been Luke's intention all along. It was sort of hard to feel sorry for yourself when you were getting distracted by big concepts like good and evil and the origins of Hell. Still, I figured it was worth trying to steer the conversation back toward its original focus.

"So I suppose you're going to tell me that I should exercise my free will and not let Traci and her impending special delivery get to me?"

Luke had a sort of faraway look in his eyes, but after I asked him that question, he immediately seemed to snap back into the present. "I think you should do whatever helps you to cope with the situation," he replied. "Just know that your feelings on the matter won't change the course of events that have been set in motion."

Geez, he was starting to sound just like my father. It was always, "Well, how does that make you feel?" or "Feelings aren't good or bad—they just are." I suppose those were valid comments, but when you're feeling as if your life is slowly circling the drain, sometimes it's nice to have someone say, "I agree—they're wrong, and you're right, and it basically all sucks."

I launched a hostile glare in Luke's direction and replied, "You know, your psycho-babble doesn't change the fact that I'm seriously irritated by the whole thing. It's just not fair—"

At that statement he gave a short laugh and shook his head. "Please don't get started on the whole 'fair' argument. Nothing is fair, Christa. It just is."

"How very Zen of you," I snapped, then stopped before I said anything more. If someone else had handed me that line, I probably would have told them to shove it. But I realized that Luke had a perspective on the situation I couldn't possibly begin to comprehend.

For a moment he remained silent, watching me carefully. It had been a long day, and I hadn't bothered to reapply any lip color after leaving the restaurant, but I didn't think he was paying attention to any of that. He was looking at *me*, not my exterior. Somehow I got the feeling that even with all his long years of observing human beings, he hadn't spent much time thinking about our individual problems or concerns.

At the moment, however, I didn't want any more metaphysical discussions or lectures about how this latest spike strip in the highway of my life wasn't of any real import compared to the grand sweep of human history. Okay, I couldn't really argue that point. I knew that eventually I'd get over it, and I'd probably even think the little bugger was cute if it ended up taking more after my dad than Traci. Right now, though, I just wanted someone to tell me that yeah, this pretty much stank—and not just for me, but for Lisa and Jeff particularly. How my mother would take the news, I wasn't sure. Very likely she'd just light another incense stick, go into a lotus position, and meditate on the cycle of life and birth. Or she could fly into a rage and get one of her buddies from her croning circle to put a hex on my father's private parts, although I somehow doubted that.

"You aren't particularly close to your sister." Luke's voice sounded calm, barely questioning.

"No," I said.

"She's very upset," he went on. "She and her husband have been trying to conceive for almost two years now. She kept telling everyone she wasn't interested in starting a family yet because she didn't want people to know they had been unsuccessful so far."

I stared at him. His face held almost no expression, but those dark blue eyes were narrowed, intent upon my face.

It hurt. It hurt more than I thought it would, since I'd spent a lot of time over the years discounting my sister. Our temperaments were worlds apart, and I'd mocked the things that were important to her—money and the big house and the successful husband—partly because I didn't seem to have any expectation of attaining them myself. Of course, I wouldn't have minded a husband somewhere down the line. But I hoped when the right guy came along, I'd know he was the one for me because our personalities suited, not because I was impressed by the size of his bank account. Apart from that, though, Lisa was still my sister, and to have her infertility thrown in her face by Traci and my father, of all people, must have been both humiliating and painful.

"I didn't know," I said slowly, feeling like an idiot. Shouldn't a sister have known these things?

"Lisa is not one to confide in others," Luke replied. "Her world is composed of surfaces, and when something moves beneath that surface, she has a difficult time understanding or dealing with it."

"Still—"

"She hasn't even spoken to your mother of these things. Why, then, would you think she'd discuss them with you?"

He was right, I knew, but I still felt even more like a failure as a human being. Oh, families spent years not speaking to one another, but we weren't that bad. We could be civil and friendly and even loving. But we all had fences around ourselves, lines in the sand we never crossed.

"I don't know," I said, after an uncomfortable pause. "I guess because it's what I think sisters should do."

Luke set his own empty glass down on the coffee table. I wondered briefly whether those wine glasses, which he had conjured into existence just a while earlier, would continue to sit there after he had gone, or whether they would simply evaporate.

An uncomfortable tightness began to build in my chest. Part of me wanted to just break down and start crying then, but I didn't want to do that in front of him. I had no idea how many private moments of pain he might have observed over the years. Mine, however, I wanted to keep to myself.

I rose. "I think maybe you should go now. Thanks for the insight and everything, but—"

He stood as well, a graceful unbending of his tall frame from the wing chair's confines. "If that's what you want."

Was it? Crazy as it sounded, all of a sudden what I really wanted was for him to hold me, to take me in his arms and reassure me that everything was going to be fine. Even I knew that wasn't necessarily true, but sometimes it's the human contact we need, not the words we say.

"Could you do me a favor?" I asked abruptly, a little amazed at my own audacity.

"What?" His expression never changed.

Maybe it was the wine hitting my bloodstream that gave me the courage to ask, "Could you just—just hold me for a minute?"

He didn't say anything. Instead, he took a few steps toward me, then reached out and wrapped his arms around me, pulling me close to his chest. I'd known he was some inches taller than I, but it wasn't until I stood there with the top of my head barely reaching his chin that I really noticed the difference in our heights.

I could hear his heart beating as I laid my head against his chest, slow and strong and steady. His sweater felt almost indescribably soft against my cheek.

Cashmere, I thought irrelevantly, then let myself relax into his embrace. It felt good. Maybe it was anti-feminist or reactionary or just plain old unevolved, but right then I thought there was nothing better than letting a man hold you, having him make you feel safe and protected. For a second I thought I felt something brush against the top of my head. Maybe he had touched his lips to my hair. I couldn't be sure.

All I did know was that I could have stood there forever, listening to the healthy, human heartbeat and feeling the warmth of his embrace. Did it even matter that he was the Devil?

That was dangerous territory, though, and as much as I had needed the physical contact at that moment, I knew I should pull away, stop things before they could progress any further.

I lifted my head from his chest and stepped back. My face felt flushed, but maybe he wouldn't notice. "Thank you," I said, hoping my voice sounded steady. His heart rate might have been slow and undisturbed, but mine was racing like a Ferrari let loose on an open highway.

"Did that help?"

His tone was so neutral I couldn't tell whether he was genuinely concerned or being sarcastic. I decided to go with the former and replied, "I think so."

"I—enjoyed it."

I couldn't help smiling then. "So did I." Knowing part of me wanted much more than that embrace, but certain that doing anything else would be a huge mistake, I moved toward the door. "I didn't see your car outside," I began, and he smiled back.

"Oh, I took the easy route." The blue eyes laughed into mine, and he added, "Sleep well, Christa."

And then he was gone. No loud bang, no puff of smoke. Now you see him, now you don't.

"God," I said weakly. Not that God had been of much help in any of this.

The glasses still sat on the coffee table. Shaking a little, I gathered them up and took them into the kitchen, where I placed them on the counter next to the sink. I'd deal with them in the morning. For now I just wanted to go to sleep and put the day's events behind me, if only for a little while.

Maybe then I could ignore the dawning realization that Luke might be the Devil, but he was also the nicest guy I'd met in a long time.

CHAPTER SEVEN

WHEN I CHECKED MY PHONE the next morning, I saw that I'd missed a text from Nina the night before. She suggested drinks around seven, and said I should call her when I had a chance.

Drinks sounded good. Hell, if I'd had any champagne lying around, I would have been whipping up a mimosa for myself on the spot. Lacking bubbly, I settled for straight orange juice.

The apartment felt empty in a way it never had before. Stupid, I knew, because I'd always lived there by myself. I wished Luke could have been there with me, squabbling over who got the Calendar section of the *L.A. Times* (reading the paper was a ritual I'd acquired from my parents and still hadn't given up), and sharing the pot of extra-strong French roast I made up.

God, I was being a moron. One hug, and suddenly I wanted him to move in with me and share the joys of domestic tranquility. Yeah, right. Besides, in the unlikely event that we actually did end up cohabiting, logic would suggest I'd be moving in with him, not vice versa.

Not that logic had anything to do with any of this.

The night before I'd finally resorted to my mother's old standby of chamomile tea to get myself to sleep. I'd kept feeling his arms around me, remembering the warmth and strength of his body. I liked the slightly husky, rough edge to his voice, and his heavy dark hair, the kind of hair that made you want to run your fingers through it. I'd felt a pleasant tingle as I recalled that delicate touch on the top of my head. It had to have been his lips pressing ever so lightly against my hair. What else?

All in all, I exhibited all the classic symptoms of someone falling heavily in lust, and I told myself to stop being such an idiot. It had taken two cups of chamomile tea and an extended session of dumping my frenzied thoughts into my private blog before I felt capable of anything approaching sleep.

Oh, God, I let him hold me tonight. I don't know what I was thinking. Maybe I just didn't want to think. I wanted to feel safe, wanted to feel…I don't know, cherished or something. And I did; that's the crazy thing. All that crap with Dad and Traci and the baby just sort of… melted away, if only for a few minutes. I don't pretend to understand what Luke's thinking or what his motives are in pursuing me, but in those moments when he held me, I thought he did care.

The Devil, caring about someone? Maybe that doesn't make sense. I don't know. I'm sure no expert on what even regular guys are thinking, and Luke is an order of magnitude beyond anyone else I've ever been with.

But if all this is just some sort of act, just his way of maneuvering me for his own purposes, then someone should nominate him for an Oscar.

Even after I'd gotten my feelings off my chest, I tossed and turned, waking up more than once during the night. I wished I could say that I dreamed of him, but I didn't—I just remembered disjointed scenes that included my mother, my biology teacher from high school, and a large pink hedgehog discussing sexual versus asexual reproduction. When I woke up, I could sort of see where the inspiration for that one came from, but it still didn't explain the hedgehog.

The coffee should have helped me focus, but I couldn't concentrate on the paper and its coverage of the latest shenanigans in Washington, and finally I laid the front-page section aside. I didn't even really know why I kept getting the Sunday paper, except that it was a family tradition I'd sort of kept up long after I was out of the house. Half the time I didn't even read it, but that particular morning I was looking for anything to keep me occupied. My seven o'clock drinks date with Nina seemed very far off.

However, I still had my "chores" to do—laundry, housework, all the wonderful, exciting stuff that inevitably gets pushed back to the weekend so it feels as if you never really get a day off. I'd just finished washing the breakfast dishes (and the wine glasses Luke had left behind the night before), when my phone rang.

"Shut up," I told my pounding heart. Really, I was starting to wonder whether I should get my blood pressure checked.

But it was Nina's voice I heard, not Luke's. "Are we still on for tonight?"

"Of course," I said. "I thought that's what your voicemail was about."

"Well, if you'd bothered to actually listen to it, you'd have known I told you to call me to let me know if seven was all right."

"Oh." Was that really what she had said? Probably, but my brain seemed to be anywhere but here these days.

"Are you all right? You sound a little weird."

"I'm fine," I said. I wondered whether I should tell her about my impending little brother or sister and then realized she was going to find out sooner or later. Voice flat, I added, "Traci is pregnant."

A long pause on the other end of the line. Then Nina said, "Well, that's it. I'm calling in the troops. I think Jennifer said she was getting back into town late last night, and those Nazis Micaela works for have to give her a day off every once in a while, or she can sue. I'm sure I read that somewhere."

"You don't have to—" I began weakly, but I should have known Nina would bulldoze right over my protests.

"When was the last time the four of us all got together, anyway?" she asked. "You need your friends with you." She hesitated, then said, "Are you okay? Do you want me to come over now? Maybe we could go catch a movie or something."

I really did think about it for a minute. Maybe it would be better to get out for a few hours. But I had laundry in midstream and grocery shopping to do, and I didn't want to sound like such a wimp that I couldn't manage a few hours without my friends to prop me up.

"That's all right," I said, forcing myself to sound upbeat but determined. "I've got a million things to do today. Just make sure one of you guys is ready to be the designated driver, because I'm planning on getting plowed tonight."

"That's the spirit," Nina replied. "*Illegitimi non…* whatever it is. But seriously? A baby? At their age?"

"Traci was happy to point out to me that she's only thirty-nine."

"Really?" Nina sounded surprised. "She looks older than that."

I couldn't help laughing. So much for all the Botox and highlights. "See?" I asked. "I feel better already."

"Hang in there, kid. Reinforcements are coming."

"Thanks," I said, and we made our good-byes and hung up.

I just wished I didn't feel so guilty that the chief source of my unease wasn't the upcoming addition to my family, but the man who had stood in my living room and held me only twelve hours before.

As promised, Nina managed to gather up both Jennifer and Micaela and bring them along. I'd put on my new embroidered wine tweed jacket with the velvet panels, my favorite pair of dark jeans, and some dark brown kitten-heeled boots and thought I was looking pretty good—at least until I opened the door and took a look at Nina. She had on a slinky jersey top in a dark green that somehow caused her eyes to glow like a cat's, and the jeans she wore made her legs look as if they went on forever.

Oh, who am I kidding? I thought. *Her legs* do *go on forever.*

Jennifer was put together as usual, in a pale blue cashmere twin set and gray slacks. She looked like the proper offspring of a lady who lunched, which was exactly what she was. Jennifer came from Pasadena and was a former Rose Court princess. Not queen, but still, princess isn't too shabby. Besides, she'd achieved what the rest of us (well, with the exception of Nina) were still just dreaming about; she'd gotten engaged this past fall, and her wedding was slated for the end of May. Her fiancé was a surgical resident at Huntington Memorial hospital, she had gotten a great job with a local P.R. firm, and she had her life pretty much together.

In direct contrast, Micaela appeared to have just slouched off the set of the latest film she'd been working on—and considering her schedule, that might have been the simple truth. Her dark hair was put up messily in a clip, and she wore a weather-beaten suede jacket over what looked like a man's white T-shirt. Not exactly the greatest attire for martini sipping at Lola's, but on a Sunday night we had a better chance of slipping in under the radar.

"Happy birthday!" Jennifer said, handing me a floral gift bag with some opalescent ribbons hanging from it.

"Oh, you didn't have to—" I began, and Micaela broke in,

"I'm glad you said that, because I've had no time to go shopping lately. But—at great personal sacrifice—I've offered to be the designated driver."

I laughed. "Sounds good to me!"

Jennifer's present turned out to be a beautiful spice-scented candle and a carved marble pedestal for it to rest on. Both in warm, earthy colors that would go perfectly in my living room. Trust Jennifer to pick out exactly the right thing.

"It's gorgeous," I said, and went to give the candle and its holder a place of honor on the mantel.

"My present," Nina announced, "is that all your drinks are on me. But not you freeloaders," she added, shooting a mock-severe glare in Jennifer's and Micaela's direction.

"I would've been a cheap date anyway," Micaela said, "considering I'm going to have to lay off after one drink. But whatever. Shall we?"

I gathered up my purse and then locked the apartment, and we all went downstairs and piled into Micaela's Honda CR-V. We headed over to Fairfax and then turned left, making our way up into West Hollywood. The streets around us were still fairly crowded, but nothing like they would have been if we'd attempted this outing on a Friday or Saturday night.

Since Nina was the tallest, she got to ride shotgun, and from her perch in the front seat she kept pestering Micaela for details on her current movie shoot. "Oh, come *on*," she said. "You can tell us something. It's not like we're going to leak information to the *National Enquirer* or something."

"Nope," said Micaela, lifting one hand to casually flip off a Porsche who had darted in front of us and then slammed on its brakes.

"Oh, please," Nina retorted. "I know it can't be another Harry Potter movie, and we're in L.A. and not New Zealand or something, so it's not the next *Avatar*. What else could be so top secret?"

"If I told you, it wouldn't be a secret anymore."

Jennifer and I both laughed, and Nina looked over her shoulder and gave us a quick green-eyed glare.

"No comments from the peanut gallery," she snapped.

"All right," Micaela said, just as she slowed to a stop so she could make a left into the parking lot. Someone behind us honked, and she muttered "asshole" before adding, "Channing Tatum's in it."

Even Jennifer made an excited little squeak at that.

Nina demanded, "Really? You're not messing with me?"

"Nope." There was a minuscule break in traffic, and Micaela took advantage of the opening to shoot her mini SUV across Fairfax and into the parking lot, nearly knocking down a startled-looking valet in the process.

"And is he that gorgeous in person?" Nina asked.

Micaela put the vehicle in park and then gave all of us a wicked grin. "Better."

Nina and Jennifer both sighed, and I wondered how long Nina's "bi" phase was going to last. I hoped she didn't do this sort of hetero mooning around Gina. For myself, well, I had to agree that Mr. Tatum was pretty hot, but since I'd been on the receiving end of attention from someone equally hot over the past few days, I didn't feel quite so transported. I wondered what Nina *et al.* would think of Luke. I was sure Jennifer would pretend that she'd made a much better catch, but although Phil, her resident, was a nice guy and really brilliant, he wasn't going to win any beauty contests. Nina would probably give me an encouraging "You go, girl," and no doubt Micaela would hand Luke her card and tell him he had an interesting look and that he should think about getting some head shots to casting agents. I loved Micaela, but sometimes she could be awfully single-minded.

I was glad that we'd waited until Sunday night to come here, though; Lola's certainly wasn't empty, but at least it wasn't a total mob scene. We snagged a cozy table in one of the side rooms where they had live music on Friday and Saturday evenings. I could see the empty place where a band might set up, but no one was playing tonight. The only music was some low-key jazz coming out of discreet speakers placed around the room.

I decided to start with an apple martini, since Lola's claimed to have originated the drink. After that I could branch out to something a little more exotic. The waiter took our order—a Cosmo for Jennifer, another appletini for Micaela, and a dirty martini with two onions for Nina—and we all settled back into our seats. We also got a couple of appetizers because, as Nina pointed out, even if I didn't want to eat a full meal, I shouldn't be drinking on a completely empty stomach.

"So really?" Micaela asked, after our drinks arrived and we'd all taken our first sips. "A baby?"

"Yep," I said, savoring the sweet-sour taste of my drink and thinking that what it reminded me of the most was a highly alcoholic green apple Jolly Rancher. "Due at the end of June, I guess."

Jennifer shook her head. "It seems a little irresponsible to me. I mean, how old is your dad going to be when this kid graduates from high school?"

"Seventy-five."

"That's just wrong," Micaela remarked. She twirled the plastic stir stick in her martini, probably to occupy herself so she wouldn't drink it too quickly.

Wrong. That was a good word for it. The whole situation had begun to take on an air of unreality, as if it were happening to someone else. Maybe it would start to seem a little more real once I had an actual infant to deal with. I was just thankful that I lived far enough away that they couldn't really call on me for babysitting duties. Not that Traci would probably even trust me with her precious little bundle of joy. No, I was certain they'd get a nanny or *au pair* or something. *I hope she's really pretty,* I thought viciously. *Then Dad can run off with her next.*

While that revenge fantasy might have been appealing, I doubted it would ever happen. For one thing, I was fairly certain Traci would do everything in her power to make sure that whoever they did hire to help with the baby was unattractive. Newport Beach probably abounded with horror stories of that type, and while I didn't think much of Traci's mental abilities on an intellectual level, I had to admit she could be cunning enough when the situation required it.

"Does your mom know?" Nina asked.

I lifted my shoulders before swallowing the rest of my appletini. "By now? Probably. I mean, Lisa probably called her." Of course, I didn't know that for sure, but Lisa tended to take her position as the oldest child seriously. Any time something needed handling, she was the one to do it.

Nina skewered one of her cocktail onions with the plastic stick and stuck it in her mouth while I tried not to shudder. I still couldn't see how she stood those things. "But you haven't heard anything?" she said.

"No." Which, on the face of it, was a little odd. Usually my mother would have called me to see how I was handling news of such magnitude. Her silence seemed to signal one of two things: either she was so upset that she didn't want to talk to anyone, or for some reason Lisa hadn't yet worked up the nerve to tell her. Neither explanation was at all reassuring.

"Well," Micaela said, then hesitated. She'd just finished the last of her appletini and looked slightly wistful. Sounding a little too hearty, she continued, "I'm sure she'll work through it."

Jennifer had a dubious expression on her face, as if she wasn't sure at all, but I guessed tact prevented her from coming out and saying so. Instead, she remarked, "I think we need another round," and lifted a hand to flag down the waiter.

He reappeared, carrying the crab cakes and quesadillas we'd ordered, then took our request for the next round. Looking sour, Micaela asked for a Diet Coke, while I branched out into a caramel apple martini, and Jennifer and Nina both stuck with their original choices.

"Anyway," Jennifer said, with the air of someone who wanted to get on to the good stuff, "Nina was telling me that you'd met someone new?"

"Well, um—sort of," I replied, feeling a little cornered. I flashed Nina a sideways glare, and she gave an almost imperceptible lift of her shoulders by way of apology.

"'Sort of'?" she echoed. "I mean, he *did* take you out on your birthday, didn't he?"

"Does this mean you broke up with Danny?" Micaela demanded suddenly.

"No, I did not break up with Danny," I said. "I'm just trying this whole dating more than one guy at once thing. I mean, it worked well enough for Nina in college."

"Oh, yeah, that was great," Micaela remarked, her tone caustic. "Who was that guy—Eric?—you know, the baseball player—"

Nina and I both answered at once. "Aaron."

Micaela waved a hand. "Whatever. Anyway, Nina, it was *so* much fun having to stall him in the hallway that one time you got your dates mixed up, and he showed up while you still had David Lippman in your room. You barely got David's pants back on and him out the window before Aaron came charging in."

I'd actually forgotten about that. Sometimes Nina's man-juggling had gotten a little complicated. "I'm not being quite that extreme," I said with a laugh.

The waiter reappeared with the next round of drinks, and I plowed on into the caramel apple martini. This one really did taste a lot like the Halloween treat of my childhood—with an added kick.

"Well, if you do dump Danny for good, let me know," Micaela remarked. "I'll take him off your hands."

I choked on a mouthful of martini. "What?"

Nina and Jennifer both gave her disbelieving stares.

She looked back at the three of us and shrugged. "Hey, I think he's kind of cute. Besides, your biggest beef with him is neglect, right? Well, with my schedule, I need a guy who isn't clingy. Sounds like a match made in Heaven to me."

"Don't be so sure about that," I said.

"Why not? At the very least we could just be fuck-buddies or something."

Boy, was she off-base. "Sounds like a great plan, except for the part where he's a rabid Catholic who doesn't believe in premarital sex."

My comment made all three of my friends snap their heads around to give me a shocked look.

"You're kidding, right?" Nina asked.

"Nope," I said, then took a large sip of my martini. Yummy.

Her tone accusing, she said, "You never told me that."

"Well, it's sort of embarrassing, isn't it?" I said. "I mean, who likes to go around advertising that they're a forced celibate?"

Jennifer shook her head once again, and Micaela said, "Hey, I can still work with that. I'm Catholic, too, you know."

Nina made a skeptical noise. "Yeah, right."

"Uh, yeah," Micaela retorted. "All right, so I haven't exactly been observing lately. But my family is—there aren't a hell of a lot of Methodists in Boyle Heights, in case you hadn't noticed."

"Sounds great to me," I commented. The rapid-fire martinis were starting to make me a little swimmy. "I'll put a bow around his neck and send him on over to your place next chance I get."

"You are too much," Jennifer said. "He's a person, not a DVD you can swap back and forth."

I shrugged. I knew that Micaela was half-joking, and so was I, but it really wasn't that bad an idea. I didn't want to leave the boy completely off on his lonesome, and Micaela was right—between her screwy schedule and his tendency to disappear for long stretches, she and Danny would probably make a much better couple than he and I ever had. Of course, there was the minor complication that he'd never expressed even the slightest interest in Micaela, but that could be corrected without too much trouble.

"Not even oral?" Nina asked suddenly. Talk about one-track minds.

"Okay, TMI!" said Jennifer, sounding more than a little exasperated. "I'm trying to eat a crab cake here."

Oh, right, there was food. I leaned over and snagged a section of quesadilla. After biting off the point and savoring the spicy cheese and black bean salsa, I replied, "Not even that."

"Honey, no wonder you've sounded tense lately," Nina said.

You don't know the half of it, I thought. After all, sexual deprivation is no fun, but it's even worse when you've got more than a year of tension bottled up, and then you meet a guy who swings your gauges over into the red. I guessed I probably should have just counted myself lucky that I hadn't torn Luke's clothes off the night before.

Then, unbelievably, *his* voice.

"Christa?"

I paused, martini glass halfway to my mouth, then turned to look back up and over my shoulder. Luke stood there, a martini of his own in his right hand. He wore a dark suit of such casual elegance it had to be Armani or something similar, with a deep wine-colored shirt underneath.

Speak of the Devil, I thought. Then, *Is he following me?*

"Oh, um, hi," I said lamely.

Nina made an ostentatious throat-clearing noise.

"Right," I added. "Luke, this is my friend Nina—and Jennifer—and Micaela."

He extended his hand to each of them in turn, wearing that gorgeous half-smile of his. "Ladies."

Jennifer's gray-blue eyes were about the widest I'd ever seen. Micaela gave Luke a frankly appraising glance. And Nina—well, Nina was looking from Luke to me and then back again, with about the same expression you might expect from someone who had just spotted a UFO. Or a unicorn.

"I didn't know you were coming here," I said, my tone about two shades away from outright accusation.

"I'm meeting a business associate for some drinks. He happens to be partial to the melon martinis here."

Business associate? What kind of business associate would the Devil have? I tried to look past him to see if some other well-dressed denizen of the underworld was loitering near the bar, but none of the men there stood out in particular. Lola's attracts its share of L.A. hipsters, but no one else in the bar radiated that air of indefinable chic which Luke seemed to possess in spades.

"Is he, now?" I asked, eyes narrowing a bit.

Luke's gaze caught mine, and I thought I saw the corner of his mouth quirk ever so slightly. Then again, it wasn't very well lit in there. I could have been imagining things. "I'll let you ladies get back to your evening. It was very nice meeting all of you."

With that he gave us all a nod and another smile, then sauntered off in the direction of the entry to the main restaurant.

Naturally, Nina was the first one to break the stunned silence that followed his departure. "Oh. My. God," she said at last.

Close, but no cigar, I thought.

Micaela set her Diet Coke down on the table and let out a low whistle. "Girlfriend, he is *fine*."

"Where on earth did you meet him?" Jennifer asked.

"At The Grove," I said. "We just sort of—bumped into each other."

"And you had the guts to pick him up?" Nina demanded.

"Well, actually—" I couldn't help smiling. "It was sort of the other way around."

There was an impressed silence.

"That's great," Jennifer said, after a short pause. "That means he must really be into you."

"I think so," I replied cautiously. "I don't want to rush anything, but—"

"Rush it," Micaela said. "Believe me—you don't want to miss out on a piece of that."

If it weren't for him being the Devil, I would have been inclined to agree with her. I certainly wasn't the sort of girl who indiscriminately hopped into bed with men, but it had been a long time. There were exceptions to every rule. And, as Micaela had pointed out, the guy was fine.

"So how many times have you seen him?" Nina again, always wanting to know every little detail. I loved Nina to death, but she was used to being the center of attention, the one who attracted all the guys (and women, too, apparently), and the fact that I'd somehow managed to snag one at least several steps above my usual pay grade had, I think, aroused just the tiniest bit of jealousy.

"Well, my birthday, of course," I replied. "And then Friday night—we went to Musso & Frank's and then to the Observatory—"

"The Observatory?" Micaela asked, eyebrows lifted. "Since when are you into astronomy?"

Nina cut in, "Christa said it was 'lovely.'"

Micaela gave a little laugh, but Jennifer, bless her, came to my defense. "And it probably was. I think it was great that he came up with something besides just the same boring old dinner and a movie deal."

"Thank you," I said. "Then he came over for drinks last night—"

"You never told me that," Nina said.

I guessed I hadn't. Right then I wasn't sure whether that was simply because it had slipped my mind or because I really didn't want to discuss Luke with her. I think I'd been hoping to keep things low-key for a little while longer. Well, he had sort of put the kibosh on that by showing up here, of all places. He'd made it sound as if it were simply a coincidence, but I knew better than that.

Without trying to seem too obvious, I looked off in the direction he'd disappeared, but I didn't see him. Oh, well.

"So he came over for drinks—" Micaela prompted.

"That's all. We had a glass of wine and talked, and then he left. I'd had sort of a rough day, after all."

"That's it?" She looked disappointed. Maybe she was trying to live vicariously through my (so far) nonexistent sex life.

"He was very supportive about the whole thing with my father and Traci," I added.

"You told him that?" Nina sounded shocked.

"Sure. Why not?"

She gave a dismissive shrug, but she did appear to be genuinely surprised. "Honey, I make it a rule never to drag guys into my sordid family life until we've been going out at least a month."

"You don't have a sordid family life," I pointed out. It was true; her parents still had a very solid marriage, and Nina's equally gorgeous younger sister was a star student at Columbia University.

"Okay, whatever. I just figure, why dump the angst on them in the beginning and scare them off?"

I had to admit that was a valid point—in most cases. However, Luke already knew all about what was going on with my family, so there would have been absolutely no point in trying to hide things from him.

"It was fine," I said. "I don't think I scared him off. After all, he came over to say hi to all of us. And he held me for a long time last night before he left."

"Held you," Nina repeated.

"Yes," I said. *And it was wonderful*....

"Looks like we've got a keeper here," Micaela remarked.

Jennifer nodded. "He does sound awfully nice, Christa. What does he do?"

That question again. I didn't think a reply of "guarding the souls of the eternally damned" would fly here, so instead I just trotted out the old "independently wealthy" line again.

The slightest gleam entered Nina's green eyes. "You know guys will say that when they're actually just unemployed."

"Oh, really?" I retorted. "Then unemployment benefits must've gotten a big bump-up lately, considering he picked me up for our first date in a Bentley Arnage."

"Holy shit," Micaela said, in respectful tones. Out of all of us, she was probably the only one who might have previously seen one of those cars in person. You got a lot of exposure to that sort of thing when you worked in the film industry.

Another silence fell. I took advantage of the break in conversation to flag down the waiter and order another round. Remembering Luke's mention of the melon martini, I requested one of those and looked over at Nina and Jennifer. Micaela was still forlornly nursing her Diet Coke.

"I'm good," Jennifer said. "Some water, though, please."

"Another Downright Dirty for me," Nina said. "I'm not driving."

"Rub it in," Micaela sighed.

The waiter departed, and Nina chewed meditatively on her last cocktail onion. "So somehow you managed to find an unattached, gorgeous, rich man who likes to hear you talk about your messed-up family and who enjoys buying you expensive dinners."

"And who sends me roses," I added.

"Roses," Micaela said, her tone flat.

"Yes. He sent them the morning after our first date."

Nina and Micaela exchanged a significant glance. Jennifer just looked pleased that at least someone in this town knew how to treat a girl on her birthday.

"Well, that settles it," Nina said at last. "Either he's a serial killer, or he's the world's only perfect man."

"Oh, ha-ha," I replied, but my sarcastic tone sounded a little weak to me. Now, I knew Luke wasn't a serial killer, but I also knew he wasn't the world's only perfect man. Technically, I didn't think he could be called a man at all.

Bringing up that point, however, would only result in disbelieving stares and a few pointed questions asking whether I'd switched medications lately. So I simply went on, "He's not a serial killer. I already checked his refrigerator. No body parts."

"Thanks, Nancy Drew," Nina said, but I thought she'd gotten the point. Even if she might be a little jealous, she did care about my happiness, and I thought I'd made it clear that the remarks were getting a little annoying.

Micaela remarked, "In that case, you need to get him to elope right away—and make sure you get out of any pre-nups he might try to push on you."

Mercifully, the waiter came back with our drinks at that point, and I took my melon martini and sipped at it, ignoring that last comment. I knew the jokes were just part of the way we interacted. However, it was a little hurtful to think they didn't believe I could hold on to a guy (at least a guy as fabulous as Luke) for any length of time without tricking him into a precipitous marriage.

Jennifer, being the peacemaker of the group, apparently noticed my stony silence and pushed the conversation in another direction, asking what the three of us thought of seafoam green for her bridesmaid dresses. We were all in the wedding party, and already my involvement in Jennifer's upcoming nuptials had taken roughly three times as much effort as I'd thought it would. Still, I knew she was probably trying to keep me from getting more upset than I already was.

Micaela made a caustic remark to the effect that seafoam green would make both her and me look as if we were dying of seasickness. I had to agree;

some greens worked on me, but not anything that pale. Nina said she thought it would be great with her eyes, and Micaela sighed. Then Jennifer ventured that maybe she could go a *little* darker, but too dark and it wouldn't work for a late spring wedding, and—

I tuned them out, shifting slightly in my chair. Movement out of the corner of my eye caught my attention, and I focused on the next room, where I saw Luke stride away, probably heading to the front door. Beside him walked another man, older, also in a dark suit. He was not as tall as Luke, his gray hair was thinning, and his nose was definitely oversized, but in the glimpse I caught I liked his face. There was something very kind in it, I thought, something gentle and unassuming. The stranger looked a little out of place in a restaurant that usually was filled with a hip crowd of twenty- and thirty-somethings, but he didn't appear to notice that he stood out like a crow at a polar bear convention. He smiled, maybe at something Luke had said, and then the two of them passed out of my line of sight.

Puzzled, I turned back toward my friends, but I still wasn't paying much attention to their conversation. Instead, I wondered about the strange older man who must have been Luke's "business associate." He didn't look much like another demon in disguise. But who…?

My heart seemed to stop in my chest. No, it couldn't be. It had to be someone else.

"Are you all right, Christa?" Jennifer asked suddenly. "You look like you've seen a ghost."

"I'm fine," I said, but my hand shook a little as I set my glass down on the table.

It wasn't possible. Or was it?

Had I just seen God at Lola's Martini Bar?

CHAPTER EIGHT

DANNY CALLED ME MONDAY MORNING, sounding diffident even for him. "Um…I was wondering…."

"What?" I snapped. My head was pounding, even though I'd taken a couple of ibuprofen about an hour earlier. So much for the wisdom of not mixing alcohol in order to avoid a hangover. Or maybe I just hadn't eaten enough to cushion the vodka. In any case, Monday morning was turning out to be even less of a picnic than usual.

"I thought maybe we could have lunch on Wednesday," he said.

That sounded a little weird. We hardly ever went out to lunch, even on the days when he had appointments in my building. Then again, maybe he was just trying to do some damage control. I thought of Micaela's comments of the night before and grinned slightly. No doubt Danny would turn about fifteen shades of red if he knew she had been discussing his potential as a "fuck-buddy."

At any rate, I didn't see the harm in having lunch. Maybe we could have a rational, adult conversation in which I told him that I'd rethought the situation and decided I couldn't see him anymore because I wanted to pursue a relationship with the Devil.

On second thought….

"Okay," I said, after a pause I hoped he hadn't noticed. "Do you want to pick me up, or should I just meet you someplace?"

"I'll pick you up," he said immediately. "I thought we could go over to the Beverly Center or something—maybe California Pizza Kitchen?"

Danny loved CPK. I could think of several other places in the vicinity that I'd rather go, but after my past few days of grand dining, I was willing to be magnanimous.

"Sounds great," I replied. "Is twelve all right?"

"Sure," he said. "I'll see you then."

I made an affirmative sound and then hung up. I figured I had a fifty-fifty chance of him actually showing, let alone on time. Probably better to bring along a Lean Cuisine to throw in the freezer in the break room at work, just in case. Also, I'd make a point of meeting him out in front of the building. I didn't want him bumping into Jacqui and maybe earning me some more grief when I returned to the office. She kept hoping he was permanently out of the picture, and I didn't want to disabuse her of that notion.

Besides, by the time lunch was over with, it was entirely possible that Danny and I would be through.

I didn't hear from Luke at all on Monday, which worried me. Not that I was really expecting another vase full of roses, but I thought he'd at least call or email after I got home. Nothing though, and I felt a pang as I closed up my MacBook Air and went into the kitchen to make myself a salad for dinner.

Wow, you're some independent modern woman, I thought. I hoped that by mocking myself I might get my sense of perspective knocked back into place. *Can't you even go a day without some contact from Luke without feeling like you've lost your last friend?*

Apparently not; after all the goings-on of the week before, my cozy little apartment had begun to feel downright confining. Nothing satisfied—not checking out the usual online sites I visited, or the book I had been reading, or even the hundred-plus cable channels that still couldn't offer anything to distract me. My mother probably would have told me that I needed to take up some sort of handicraft, something to occupy my hands when my mind didn't want to cooperate with anything else. But I'd tried to learn how to crochet when I was in high school and hated it, and sewing had never appealed, either.

Instead (and this should have been a clear signal of how desperate I was feeling), I called my sister.

She seemed surprised to hear from me. "Is everything all right?" she asked.

"Um, sure," I responded. "I was just wondering if you'd told Mom."

Lisa didn't bother to ask about what. "Yes," she said. "I talked to her this afternoon, in fact."

"Oh," I said. "How did she take it?"

"About the way I expected. She said something about Traci becoming more evolved as a person once she became a mother, and then she said she was sure Dad must be thrilled."

Typical. I almost wished my mother had ranted and raved; it would have seemed a more normal reaction to me. "Well, that's healthy," I ventured.

"No," said Lisa, sounding very cool, very flat, definitely unlike her usually sparkly sales–super-power self. "I don't think it is. She has serious denial issues. But she'll never admit it—she'll just keep going on about how having a cleansed colon is somehow the key to enlightenment. Or whatever."

That bitterness was not Lisa at all. Although I'd had no reason to disbelieve what Luke told me about my sister and her husband trying to get preg-nant, it wasn't until I stood there and listened to her monotone delivery that it really came home to me he'd been telling me the truth.

"Um—" I hesitated; Lisa and I had never been ones for personal conversation. "Are you okay? Is there anything you want to talk about?"

"No," she said immediately. "I guess I'm just tired. I took two new listings today, and I've been running around like a chicken with its head cut off."

She was lying—getting new real estate listings usually charged Lisa up the way a jump would rejuvenate a tired battery. But I knew better than to challenge her on it. The lie was her way of telling me to back off.

So instead of saying anything else, I just told her, "Well, thanks for talking to Mom. I'm glad she handled it so well."

"Better than some people," Lisa said cryptically. "Listen—I've got to go. My work cell is ringing." And she hung up.

I sat there for a moment, staring down at my phone, then sighed and set it on the coffee table. With a feeling of futility, I picked up the remote control for the TV and began flipping through the stations, all the while telling myself I didn't miss him. Not really. Not that much.

When I came into work the next morning, though, I found a small brown-wrapped parcel sitting on my desk. Puzzled, I picked it up and turned it over. There were no UPS or FedEx labels on it, nothing to indicate where it had come from… which probably meant only one thing.

Trying to keep an idiotic grin off my face, I rummaged through the top drawer of my desk until I found a letter opener. Then I cut through the clear packing tape and carefully unwrapped the heavy brown paper. Once I pulled it away, I saw that it had concealed a book. An old one, too, judging by the scuffed leather binding. I turned it over in my hands to read the gold lettering on the spine. *Faust*, it said, then, in a slightly smaller font, *Goethe*.

Inside was a note, wrapped around a heavier piece of card stock. *I thought it might amuse you to get a little background,* the note read, written in Luke's heavy black hand. *Highly inaccurate, of course, but a worthy diversion for an evening.*

I pulled out the little card and realized it was a ticket —a ticket to the L.A. Opera performance of *Faust* for this upcoming Saturday night.

Opera? Was he serious? I'd always thought of opera as an acquired taste, one I'd never bothered to acquire. Compared to a lot of people in my age group, I actually had fairly eclectic taste in music, partly because my parents had played anything and everything as I was growing up. I couldn't stand rap, and modern country left me cold, but otherwise I listened to everything from Elizabethan chamber music to Arcade Fire. I'd discovered that Middle

Eastern music was a great background track for doing housework—you could really groove while pushing the vacuum cleaner around.

For some reason, though, I'd never really gotten into opera. Isolated pieces, sure, but I'd never been able to sit down and listen to a whole opera all the way through. Still, even I knew that going to the opera was a big deal, a very high-end night out.

This thought led me to the dismal realization that I had absolutely nothing to wear. Really, the world didn't offer a heck of a lot of opportunities for dressing up these days. I had one plain black sheath I'd bought a few years back, since Jennifer had convinced me every woman needed to own a Little Black Dress, but that was about it for evening attire. And my LBD, while a very nice Jones New York piece, just didn't seem quite festive enough for the occasion.

I checked my watch. Nine o'clock. Nina should be up and around by now, although she usually didn't have to start work until ten.

Her cell rang four times, and I worried that maybe she'd left it someplace or was in the shower or similarly unavailable. But she picked it up just before it rolled over into voicemail.

"He wants to take me to the opera," I said without preamble.

"What—Christa?"

"Yeah. Look, Luke is taking me to the opera Saturday night."

"Really? How *Pretty Woman* of him."

"Very funny. Any clothes advice?"

"Where are your seats?"

Fumbling a bit, I shoved the phone between my ear and shoulder and reached down to pick up the ticket. I squinted at the tiny print and said, "Um… Grand Circle?"

I heard Nina expel a breath. "Wow, this guy doesn't mess around, does he?"

"I assume those are good," I said.

"The best," she replied. "It's L.A., so you'll see everything from jeans to tuxes, but if you've got seats in the Grand Circle for a Saturday night per-formance, I say you go red carpet."

"Red carpet?"

"Gown. Important gown. No little black dress, no skimpy cocktail slip number. No way."

Great. Well, at least now I knew where the rest of the birthday money my father had given me was going to end up.

"Hey," she went on. "I've got to run a piece out to a client in West Hollywood today anyway. How about I meet you for lunch and we go shopping?"

I'd actually feel a lot better having Nina along. Although she wasn't exactly an opera devotee her-self, I knew her father was a big fan and had season tickets. For all I knew, Luke and I might bump into

Dr. Nomura and his wife in the Grand Circle. I sort of had a feeling that Nina's plastic surgeon daddy didn't exactly have season tickets in the cheap seats. At any rate, she knew how to dress for the opera, and I didn't.

"Sounds fabulous," I said, trying not to sound too relieved. "You can keep me from making any horrible gaffes."

"Not a prob. I'll be by a little before noon."

I said thanks and hung up, then picked up the book once more and really looked at it. The leather-bound volume had the faint musty smell I always associated with used-book stores; when I opened it, I saw the text was printed in both English and German on facing pages. I couldn't tell a lot from the imprint, as it was solely in German, but I did see a date: 1895.

Definitely not something Luke had picked up at the local Barnes & Noble. Feeling a little awed, I carefully wrapped the brown paper back around the book and then stowed it in one of the locking compartments that sat above my built-in desk. The opera ticket I slid into the bill compartment of my wallet so it wouldn't get bent.

The rest of the morning went by more slowly than I would have liked; I supposed I was just eager to get out and go shopping. After all, how many times in your life do you actually get to buy an "important" dress? Not many, unless you're a celebrity who spends a lot of time on the red carpet.

But the time passed, as it always did, and at about five minutes to noon I got a text from Nina that she was out waiting for me at the curb and to hurry so she wouldn't get busted for double parking. I scooped up my purse and was outside at lightning speed, then squeezed myself into the front seat of her little BMW Z4. It was a cute car, but I still couldn't comprehend why someone as tall as Nina would want something that low to the ground.

"I thought we'd go to Loehmann's," she said. "The last time I was in there it looked as if they'd gotten another shipment of post-holiday evening wear, so I'm hoping we can get a deal."

I thought that sounded like a good plan, and told her so. Then I hung on for dear life as she squealed away from the curb and headed west on Wilshire. From there she hung a right on San Vicente, bringing us up to the Loehmann's that backed up to the Beverly Center.

We'd gotten there ahead of the lunch rush, but the place was still fairly crowded. Luckily, though, the racks toward the back where the formal wear was kept didn't have quite as many women browsing through them. Deals are great, but if you don't have any place to wear it, grabbing a five-hundred-dollar gown for ninety-nine bucks isn't going to do you much good.

I took one rack and Nina another, and we got down to work. Technically, I was a size six, but different designers sized their clothes differently, so we couldn't judge just by what the tag said.

Pushing aside a few items that looked like refugees from prom circa 1985, I came across a beautiful beaded Sue Wong number. I pulled it out for Nina to inspect. "What do you think?"

She looked up from the rack she'd been digging through and frowned. "Nice, but everyone always wears black. Try to find some color."

Personally, I liked black. It was slimming, and since I was dark-eyed and dark-haired, it looked pretty good on me. But I knew she was right— every woman always went for black first, so it would be nice to find something in a different shade that would suit me.

After pushing my way through some more gowns, I found something in a gorgeous dark teal that would have been perfect. When I pulled it out, though, I saw that it was just cocktail length, and I knew Nina had been hoping for a true evening gown. Still, it wasn't bad for a second-string choice, so I draped it over my arm and kept working.

Then I heard Nina say, "Oh—oh—" And she lifted this amazing red number up for my inspection.

"Weren't you the one making *Pretty Woman* cracks?" I asked, although I couldn't take my eyes off the gown.

"This doesn't look like that dress at all. Besides, red has always been great on you. And it's a size six."

Well, that cinched it. I went over to Nina and took the dress from her, then headed over to the dressing rooms. I had to wait in line before I could even get in, but that was all right; somehow I knew this gown was The One.

It could have been made for me. The shirring on the bodice molded to my curves and made my waist look incredibly small, and I loved the little godets around the hem. I looked at the tag. The label said "Vera Wang," and it had originally retailed for almost eight hundred bucks. Now it was marked down to $199. I thanked my father mentally for the wad of birthday cash, since it would more than cover the dress and any shoes, etc. I needed to go along with it.

I looked at myself in the mirror and gathered up my hair at the back of my head, testing how the gown would look with an up-do. The red seemed to bring a glow to my cheeks and made my eyes look velvety and dark. I couldn't wait to see how the whole thing worked once I had a real hairstyle and a little more makeup than my customary mascara, blush, and lip gloss.

Red's my favorite color, Luke had told me that first evening. He'd probably believe I chose this gown specifically because of that. Well, let him. I knew it looked great, and that was why it was going home with me. Still, I couldn't help thinking it would also work really well with the red satin underwear I'd bought at Victoria's Secret…and I wondered whether Luke would get a chance to see that as well.

While I was in the dressing room, Nina located a pair of strappy silver sandals for me, as well as a gorgeous pair of chandelier earrings.

"No necklace?" I asked.

She shook her head. "Nope. Too much, with a pair of earrings like that. If you look at actresses on the red carpet, it's either a great necklace and little studs, or big earrings and no necklace. Maybe a bracelet, too, but I didn't see anything I liked. It's all right. Just let the dress speak for itself."

Since Nina could probably teach Learning Annex courses on style, I decided to take her word for it. We tried to find a wrap that would work with the dress, but nothing seemed right.

"I'll just have to freeze to death, I guess," I said after we gave up and I had gotten in line for the cash register.

"Nobody freezes to death in L.A.," Nina replied sensibly. "Besides, you won't have to be outside all that much. Better to be cold than to wear a wrap that doesn't work with the dress."

Of course, the standard mantra: style over comfort. But that was all right. I couldn't help feeling a little spasm of excitement as I handed over the dress, shoes, and earrings to the cashier.

By that point I was already running late, so there was no time to eat. Nina dropped me off back at work, and I went to my car first so I could hang the gown from the hook in the back seat. Then I scrounged my emergency container of yogurt from the refrigerator in the break room and went back to my office, tingling with anticipation and wondering if there were any way to speed up the week so Saturday would get here more quickly. Probably not—even for Luke—so instead I sent an email to the Gmail address he'd used before.

Thank you for the book, I wrote. *I'm really looking forward to the opera.* I paused, thinking that sounded awfully formal and stilted. On the other hand, writing *I'm dying to see you again* wasn't exactly a good idea if I were going to keep with the whole "playing it cool" strategy. Instead, I just wrote, *I hope to hear from you soon,* and sent the email before I could obsess over it anymore. After that, I picked up the layout that had come in while I was out with Nina and forced myself to concentrate on work, and not immediately pounce on my computer every time a new email message popped up. None of them were from Luke, however, and after a while I'd gotten myself back into a state almost resembling sanity.

Almost.

I went home in a mood dangerously close to a funk. It was wonderful to have received the book and the opera ticket, of course, but I would have liked a little more personal contact. Probably I was just being selfish—who knew what claims the Devil had on his time?—but I'd found myself craving even an email or a phone call the way a junkie craves his next fix. Not good, not good at all. I'd thought I was maintaining some sort of equilibrium—barely—but that seemed to have changed suddenly. Why?

Because you let him hold you, you idiot, I told myself. *Before that it was safely casual, despite his claims of wanting to kiss you, but after you realized what it felt like to have his arms around you, it wasn't so easy to push him away, was it?*

So had I irrevocably screwed up? Had I passed the point of no return? And did I even care?

I turned left onto my street and saw the red Jag sitting there…and Luke himself, lounging on the bottom step, holding a book and looking as if he hadn't a care in the world. My heart jumped straight up and seemed to lodge in my throat.

Somehow I managed to pull my car into the garage without smacking it into the side of the building. I debated as to whether I should leave the gown hanging in the back seat or not, but it was safely swathed in opaque plastic, so he wouldn't really be able to see what it was. Hands shaking, I gathered it up, along with my purse and book bag, and went out front to meet him.

He stood as I approached and greeted me with a smile. "Miss me?" he asked, and although his voice was teasing, his eyes were not.

All sorts of flip answers popped into my head, but for some reason I didn't feel like using any of them. Instead I met his gaze squarely and said, "Yes."

Someone else might have looked smug. Luke just smiled and said, "Then I'm glad I followed a hunch and stopped by." His gaze traveled to the gown I carried, safe in its covering of plastic. "Been shopping?"

"I was fresh out of opera wear," I responded. Since it was cold out, and I didn't want to keep standing in the dubious light provided by the fixture at the bottom of the stairwell, I started scrabbling in my purse for my keys. The bulky gown wasn't helping much.

"Ah. May I?" He reached out and plucked the dress and its hanger from my arms.

"Thanks," I said, then added, "Just don't peek."

The laugh lines around his eyes deepened a bit. "Of course not."

Finally I grabbed hold of the lanyard keychain I'd been using since high school and pulled the damn thing up out of the recesses of my bag. Maybe it was time to switch to a smaller purse.

Luke followed me up the stairs and into my apartment. I set down my purse and book bag, then reclaimed the gown from him so I could go hang it in my closet. He waited in the living room, book tucked under one arm.

"What are you reading?" I asked, after I'd come back out and given the place a quick look around to make sure there weren't any embarrassing dirty dishes or other clutter anywhere. Usually I tried to tidy up the place either right before I went to bed or before I left in the morning so I wouldn't come home to a mess, but I'd been a little distracted the past few days and honestly couldn't remember if I'd followed my usual routine. Luckily, though, the place seemed mostly in order.

"This?" He pulled the hardback out from underneath his arm. "Just amusing myself."

I shot a quick glance at the cover. "The *Da Vinci Code?* You're kidding, right?"

"I told you I was amusing myself."

Since I hadn't been expecting company, I didn't have a lot to offer by way of beverages. However, I did have a few bottles of wine stashed away in the countertop rack in the kitchen. "Glass of wine?" I asked.

"Absolutely." After setting his book down on the coffee table, he followed me into the kitchen and inspected my meager wine collection with some interest. "Let's have the pinot, shall we?"

It figured he would choose the best one out of the bunch. I hadn't even bought it myself; Nina had brought it over when we were having a "girls' night in" a while back, but we'd never gotten around to opening it.

My bottle-opening skills were shaky at best, so I handed the corkscrew to Luke and let him have at it. Of course he pulled the cork out so smoothly he might have been using one of those fancy gas-powered openers instead of the simple waiter-style corkscrew I owned.

"Glasses?" he inquired.

I fetched a pair from the cupboard and set them down on the counter. He poured an equal amount of wine into each, and then handed one to me.

"To unexpected meetings," he said.

Taking the glass, I replied, "I'll drink to that," and sipped at the wine. A dark rush went over my palate, tasting of warm fruit ripened on sandy hillsides. Damn, that was good.

He drank as well, and got an approving look on his face. I made a mental note to have Nina choose my wines whenever possible.

"So," I said, after we'd wandered back into the living room, "*The DaVinci Code,* huh?"

"Are you mocking my choice in reading material?"

"Um…yes."

"I suppose it does seem a bit odd." He lifted the glass to his lips and took another swallow of wine. "But the inaccuracies amuse me."

My stomach decided that particular moment was a great time to growl. Loudly. I felt the blood rush to my cheeks, and hoped he hadn't heard.

But of course he had. "Hungry?" Luke asked.

"Well, yes," I said. "I spent my lunch hour shopping, so all I had was some yogurt, and—"

"I suppose I should have offered to take you to dinner," he mused.

"Oh, that's all right," I said hastily. "I've been out so much lately anyway."

"Then I'll have it come here. What would you like?"

Was he serious? I shot a glance at him from beneath my lashes and decided he must be. Probably conjuring up a meal was no big deal for someone who possessed his powers.

"Don't laugh," I said.

The blue eyes crinkled at the corners. "I promise I won't."

"I really just want a cheeseburger."

"A cheeseburger?"

"You asked."

To his credit, he didn't laugh, but I could tell he was amused by my request. "Thy will be done," he said. "Cheeseburgers and pinot noir, God help me."

And with that the coffee table suddenly covered itself in a white cloth, and in front of me was a plate with a huge cheeseburger, exactly the way I liked it, with lettuce and tomato and Thousand

Island dressing. A similar plate appeared in front of Luke, although his burger looked as if it had bacon on it as well. Both plates were well-garnished with seasoned fries.

"Now, that's what I'm talking about," I remarked. "That smells heavenly."

At the word "heavenly" I thought I saw him start a bit, but then he shrugged and leaned forward to pick up his burger. I did the same, and took a huge bite. It tasted as good as it smelled. Who cared if the meal was going to earn me an extra half-hour on the treadmill tomorrow? That burger was definitely worth the sacrifice.

After a few more bites, my stomach felt sufficiently sated that I could slow down a little and actually engage in conversation once more. "So what inaccuracies were you talking about?" I asked. "Let me guess—Jesus and Mary Magdalene were just really good friends."

"No," he replied, setting down his burger and picking up his wine glass. With a shake of his head, he drank, then added, "Jesus might have been the Son of God, but that didn't mean he was dead below the waist."

I choked.

"Are you all right?" Luke inquired, sounding oh-so solicitous. But the glint was back in his eyes— the devilish glint, if I could be allowed to call it that.

"Fine," I said, after retrieving my own wine and gulping enough down that it dislodged the troublesome piece of ground beef in my throat. "So you're saying that, well—"

"Of course. But there were no offspring from that union, so there goes the central conceit of Mr. Brown's book. Really, I have no idea why anyone would ever think such a thing."

"I don't see what's so strange about it," I argued, "if you're willing to accept the idea that Jesus was enough of a mortal man to have a physical relationship with a woman."

"Because that would have negated his entire reason for being here," Luke replied calmly. "Jesus, being the spirit of God made manifest on this earth, and coming here to die for men's sins and grant them redemption, would certainly not leave any children behind. Otherwise, his eventual resurrection would have no point. So what if he died on the cross? His heirs would still live on, carrying the divine seed within them. No, he lived and died, and did the work God intended for him. End of story."

I sat there silently for a moment, trying to digest what he had just said. My coping mechanism for dealing with Luke's presence seemed to have been to shove the truth of his identity far back in my mind, and to concentrate on only the surface things—the sound of his voice, the way he looked at me, all the little things that made him seem just like a mortal man. But when he made statements like that, when he spoke as someone who knew these things as irrefutable truth—well, that brought the reality of the situation crashing down on me.

"You were there," I said at last.

"Of course. I had my role, just as He had His."

My world's foundation begin to feel shakier and shakier. I'd been raised to respect other people's beliefs, but my parents hadn't practiced Christianity, and they'd never taught my siblings and me that Jesus was truly the son of God. Of course they'd said he was an enlightened man, a prophet and seer, but so were Buddha and Krishna and Mohammed. Luke, though, seemed to be telling me Jesus really had been divine, and I didn't know what to make of that.

Unsure as to how I should respond, I retreated to the safety of sarcasm. "Oh, that's right," I remarked. "They showed you in *The Passion of the Christ,* wandering through the crowd. You were pretty freaky-looking, though."

"Filmmakers," Luke said, "rarely get the details correct. Are you going to eat those fries?"

With a start, I realized that I'd been neglecting my meal. As usual, I'd eaten the important part first—the burger—and left the fries as filler. I silently pushed the plate toward him and watched as he added some ketchup to the fries before plowing into them. I didn't recall seeing the bottle of Heinz before that, but with Luke around that didn't mean much.

"So you've always looked like this?" I asked.

He had to finish chewing before he could reply. "More or less. Of course, this is a much better haircut."

I couldn't help it. The giggle bubbled its way up into my throat, and the next thing I knew I was laughing so hard I could feel the tears starting to leak out the corners of my eyes. I heard him begin to laugh as well, and it took me a minute before I recovered myself enough to say, "Well, that puts some perspective on the whole thing."

"Most definitely." He raised his wine glass and gave me a sort of salute. The smile never left his mouth.

Wine sounded like a good idea. I had some more of mine, and then Luke asked, "Finished?"

I nodded, and the detritus of our impromptu meal disappeared off the table. "Whew," I said. "My mother sure could have used you around when I was a kid and she had to cook Thanksgiving dinner. Of course, even back then we had to get the lectures about free-range turkeys, but—"

"Christa."

I paused, and glanced over at him. He still looked amused, but there was no mistaking the deadly serious way those deep blue eyes met mine.

Something inside me seemed to turn over. Mouth dry, I watched as he rose from his seat and came to stand next to me. He reached down with one hand, and I took it, standing so I faced him.

Before I could really register what was happening, he cupped my face in his hands and brought his mouth against mine.

Every nerve ending in my body seemed to explode. I couldn't have stopped him even if I'd wanted to, and I didn't. All I wanted was to feel his lips touching me, to taste wine as his tongue met mine. Suddenly I was pressing my body against his, my hands reaching up to tangle in the heavy, rich hair.

I don't know how long the kiss lasted. Eventually we broke apart; he seemed calm enough, but I was gasping like someone who had just swum the English Channel. My knees were rubber. I barely retained enough hold of myself to keep from collapsing right then and there.

"Ah," he said at last. At least his voice sounded rough and husky, not quite as controlled as he probably wanted me to believe. "You continue to surprise me, Christa Simms."

Somehow I managed to recover the power of speech. "Well, I'd hate for you to get bored this early on."

"Far from it," he replied.

That was all the encouragement I needed. I pressed myself against him once more, and he gave me another of those depth-charge kisses—you know, the kind that make you feel as if you've been blown back into another dimension. Did I even want to know where he'd learned to kiss like that? You wouldn't think the Devil would have much experience, but maybe he was just naturally good at that sort of thing. Exposure to all that sin over the years must have had some sort of effect.

It took a little longer for us to break apart this time. Or maybe it was just that the cumulative effect of his mouth on mine had begun to rob me of some much-needed oxygen. I didn't know. All I did know was that I'd never had someone kiss me into something resembling semi-consciousness before.

"Okay, you have to stop," I said at last, trying to draw some air back into my lungs. "Or I'm going to end up in the hospital."

"I believe you initiated the last one," he replied, but he did take a step back, giving me some much-needed breathing space.

"True," I said.

Then he reached out to run a hand down my hair. He had a strange expression on his face, an odd mix of curiosity and tenderness. "Maybe we should leave it at that for now," he said, after the slightest of pauses.

The urge to tear off his clothes was almost overwhelming, but from somewhere I dug up a measure of self-control. I took a deep breath, and then another. "That might be a good idea," I replied. Otherwise, we were probably going to end up doing it on the living room floor, and I sort of wanted my first time with him to be a little less trashy than that.

"Until next time, then," he said. Leaning down, he brushed his lips against my cheek, and even that feather-light touch was enough to get my blood racing.

"Until then," I whispered, and then he slipped out, leaving me standing in the center of the room. For a long moment I stared at the door, as my heart finally managed to resume something resembling a normal rhythm.

Was I damned for wanting him?

Did I even care?

CHAPTER NINE

AFTER THE EVENTS OF THE NIGHT BEFORE, the prospect of meeting Danny for lunch seemed particularly anti-climactic. But I figured it would give me the chance to make a clean break; I knew after that kiss with Luke there wouldn't be any more nonsense on my part about trying to see both men at the same time. People date multiple partners (and sleep with them, for all I know) every day. I just wasn't that sort of person, though, and it would be cruel to give Danny any more false hope. If he even had any.

He picked me up in his little white Nissan truck. Shockingly, he was only about five minutes late, and I knew he must really be making an effort.

Too little, too late, I thought, but I couldn't help feeling a little sorry for him.

We didn't talk much on the way over to the Beverly Center. I had no idea what to say, and he seemed tense and nervous. Maybe he'd already picked up on the "you're about to get dumped" vibe. Even though I knew it would be better for both of us in the long run, it still didn't make the short term any easier to face.

Luckily, though, we didn't have to wait long for a table, and after about five minutes we were seated at a booth next to the window. Not that there was much to see today; another storm had come in, and the day outside was gray and gloomy.

Remembering the delicious but oh-so-caloric cheeseburger of the night before, I ordered a grilled chicken salad with dressing on the side. Also, I was feeling sort of bloated, since my period had started just that morning. I would have worried about it ruining my weekend, except that my doctor had put me on some great new pills about six months earlier, and now I only had to deal with the inconvenience for three days instead of six. You just gotta love modern science.

Still, I still knew I was a little off, and I made a mental note to think twice before I said anything so I wouldn't let my hormones do the talking. I waited until after Danny had placed his own order for a barbecue chicken pizza (his favorite) before asking, "So how was your weekend?"

"Great," he said, although his tone indicated that it had been anything but. "Victor and Zach and I had a LAN party Saturday night, and then on Sunday I upgraded my video card."

I wanted to say, "Whoo-hoo! Party!" but that would have been downright rude. Victor and Zach and Danny shared a little one-story house on the edge of Culver City and generally indulged one another's geekdom to almost pathological levels. Privately I referred to them as the "Lone Gunmen," from the similar trio of crazies on *The X-Files,* which I binge-watched the summer between my freshman and sophomore year in high school, mainly because I had a serious crush on '90s-vintage David Duchovny. Maybe Danny would have been a little easier to deal with if I'd been able to pry him away from his partners in crime, but I knew that was never going to happen.

At any rate, LAN parties and upgraded computer hardware were pretty much par for the course. I tried to look impressed and said, "I'll bet Warcraft runs a lot better now."

"Oh, yeah!" he said enthusiastically. "I kept having problems with jumpy movement, but now it's so smooth you'd swear you were watching a DVD. I just wish I'd done it months ago."

I assumed what I hoped was an expression of polite interest. Well, if nothing else, Danny was definitely reinforcing my resolve to call it quits. Right then I couldn't believe that I'd put up with more than six months of this stuff.

"Anyway," he said, his face sobering quickly, "how was your weekend? Big date, right?" Those last three words were uttered in a tone of snottiness so extreme it sounded as if he were channeling some backstabbing teen at cheer camp.

"Just on Friday," I replied. *Cool, keep it cool,* I told myself. "Saturday I went to Orange County to see my parents, and Sunday night the girls took me out for drinks."

"Oh." For a second he looked a little surprised, as if he'd thought for sure I would have spent all weekend in some wild sex-fest with his unknown rival.

I wish, I thought, and despite everything, a little chill ran down my spine. If just kissing Luke was that spectacular, what would it be like for him to make love to me? Any rational arguments I might have made against taking such a step seemed completely feeble at that point. If I weren't going to follow this thing to its logical conclusion, then I should never have let him kiss me in the first place. And keeping him from kissing me seemed on a par with stopping the Earth in its orbit—not only was it physically impossible, but it would have had catastrophic consequences to boot. At least, that was what I told myself. I didn't want to think what would have happened if I'd turned into the ice queen again and sent him packing.

The waitress came back with some water and disappeared immediately afterward. Danny took a sip and then said, "Look, Christa, I just want—I want to apologize."

I felt as if he'd taken that glass of water and splashed it in my face. "Uh—what?"

Not meeting my eyes, he continued, "I guess I—well, maybe I sort of took you for granted. And I shouldn't have. You're great—you're really, well… um…great."

It might not have been the sort of eloquence that could turn a girl's heart, but I felt awful all the same. Why did he have to be nice now, when all I wanted to do was end things so I could run off into the sunset with the Devil?

Swallowing hard, I said, "Look, Danny, I—"

"No, really," he interrupted. "I guess I didn't even realize how I felt about you until you told me that you wanted to go out with somebody else, too. It just—well, it freaked me out. I don't want to share you."

Three weeks ago those words would have been music to my ears. At this point, though, I was angry more than anything else. Boy, that was typical, wasn't it? I'd just been a superfluous adjunct all those months, and then the second Danny realized someone else might be interested in me, suddenly I was the love of his life.

I almost snapped, *Hey, it's your lucky day—you don't have to share me, because I'm dumping you!* But I managed to hold my tongue long enough to allow the impulse to pass. Hormones were so much fun.

Instead, I helped myself to some water, then said, "I wish you could have told me that a while ago."

"I know," he said. "I guess I just didn't think about it until now. I always thought you'd, you know, be there."

Of course, right at that moment the waitress showed up with our food. I busied myself with pouring out the precise amount of dressing required to give my salad some taste without totally upping the fat and calorie quotient. If nothing else, the activity gave me some time to think.

This wasn't going to be easy. Then again, whatever was?

Even though eating was the last thing I wanted to do at that moment, I lifted some grilled chicken to my mouth and forced myself to chew. Danny had already dug into his barbecue chicken pizza.

"Well," I said, "I'm glad that this has made you stop and think about things."

He glanced up from his food, his gray-blue eyes hopeful.

I suddenly felt as if I were about to kick a puppy, but I had to go on before I completely lost my nerve. "But I just don't think it's going to work out for us."

The blood seemed to rush from his cheeks. He put down his half-eaten slice of pizza and said, "What?"

Keep going, I told myself. *You can't back out now.* "I've been thinking, too, Danny, and although I really like you as a person, I just don't see us having much of a future together."

In stunned tones he asked, "I don't—why not?"

"Besides having nothing in common?" I retorted.

"What do you mean?" he demanded. "We both like the same music, we—we —" The words trailed off as apparently he stopped to think about what precisely we *did* have in common.

As for the claim about liking the same music, well, that wasn't too difficult, considering I'd listen to just about anything. Danny tended to favor esoteric heavy metal bands from Europe whose names I couldn't even pronounce; generally, I thought they were all right, but I felt the same way about pretty much everyone from Glenn Miller to Adele. Other than that, he and I really had no common interests. I was Mac; he was PC. I liked indie films and a good romantic comedy; he liked action movies or gore-fests. I liked Thai; he liked Chinese. And so forth. That didn't even take into account the enormous chasm separating our religious backgrounds.

As a wise man once said, "You say potato, I say po-tah-to." A rational person probably would have called it off months ago.

"You see?" I asked, in gentler tones than I thought I'd be able to summon. "People need more than that to build a relationship on. It just wasn't working, and I think deep down we both knew it."

Danny's mouth grew tight. "Funny how you didn't figure any of this out until *he* came along."

"'He' who?"

"This guy you met. Whoever he is. He must really be something to make you want to throw away someone you've been with for six months."

You have no idea, I thought, but I knew better than to say anything that would reinforce Danny's feelings of inadequacy. "I think we're better suited," I said carefully. "But that has just as much to do with me as it does him. This isn't about him, anyway. It's about you and me. And I'm telling you that I would have felt the same even if I hadn't met someone else."

"You really expect me to believe that?"

Suddenly tired, I replied, "Hey, you're going to believe what you're going to believe. I'm just telling you my side of things."

His face twisted. Again I experienced a rush of guilt; this couldn't be easy for him. Here he thought he'd had something good going, a girlfriend who was leagues beyond anyone else he'd dated (and I wasn't just saying that to puff myself up; I'd seen a couple of photos of his previous girlfriends), and now she was pulling the plug. That just had to suck, no matter what he might have done to deserve it.

Maybe I was fooling myself. Maybe I wouldn't have had the guts to break up with Danny if I didn't have somebody else already waiting in the wings. I didn't know for sure, and second-guessing myself wasn't going to help the situation anyway. All I knew was that right here, right now, I had to make an end to it.

"I'm really sorry, Danny," I said at last. "But we're done." I fumbled for my purse and pulled out my wallet. "I don't expect you to pay for my lunch, so—" And I dropped a twenty-dollar bill on the table.

"You don't have to do that," he replied mechanically. Then, as he seemed to grasp the fact that I was leaving, a spasm of panic crossed his features. "No, really. You don't have to leave. You *can't* leave."

God, he was making this awkward. "I think it's better if I go. I can just catch a cab or something back to work—"

"No!" he burst out, so loudly that a few heads at neighboring tables swiveled in our direction. "I mean, that's silly. We're civilized people—we can at least finish our lunch, right?"

His urgency seemed really out of line with my actions, but whatever. I settled back in my seat, wondering how on earth I was going to get through the next half-hour or so.

Calmly I said, "All right, Danny. If you feel so strongly about it."

A look of relief passed over his face. "Great, um—thanks, Christa. I'm sorry—I just—well, you know, this is tough."

You've got that right, I thought, then sighed and picked up my fork. This was definitely going to be one of the longest meals of my life.

Several centuries—all right, approximately half an hour—later, Danny dropped me back off at work. He cast a nervous glance around, and said, "Uh—good-bye, I guess."

"Good-bye," I said, then added, so the farewell wouldn't sound so harsh, "Take care of yourself, okay?"

He managed a smile. "You, too."

I shut the door to his truck, then turned and walked back into the building. It had to be done, but I still felt like crap.

My feelings of guilt evaporated, however, when I entered my office and saw Victor Nguyen, one of Danny's roommates, hastily backing away from the keyboard to my Mac.

"What the hell are you doing in here?" I demanded.

He blinked. "Upgrading your Norton Antivirus. Didn't you get the email?"

"No," I said, shooting him a wary look.

Victor also worked for IT Solutions—in fact, I was pretty sure Victor had gotten Danny his job in the first place—but I hadn't received any emails about an upgrade. Besides, Danny usually got the assignments at my magazine. Since we'd had lunch plans anyway, why hadn't he just asked to perform the upgrades?

"I'll have to check on what happened to your notification email," Victor said, dark eyes expressionless behind his wire-rimmed glasses. "Anyway, you're good to go. Just let us know if it stalls or causes any problems."

"Oh, I'll definitely let you know if there are any…problems." I didn't bother to keep the suspicion out of my voice. How convenient that Victor should be snooping around my computer while I was out to lunch with Danny. No wonder he'd panicked at the thought of me leaving early—he'd probably known I'd walk in and catch Victor in the middle of…what?

I couldn't tell for sure, and Victor had the poker face I so woefully lacked, so there was no point in questioning him further. Instead, I just crossed my arms and waited as he gathered up his briefcase and brushed past me.

I caught the faintest gleam of triumph in his eyes. Or maybe it was just a reflection off his glasses.

At any rate, I waited until he was safely gone and then plunked myself down at the keyboard. Heart racing, I went through my emails to see if I could find anything incriminating there, but the only contact with Luke on this computer was that one innocuous email in my "Sent Items" folder. There wasn't much they could glean from that—except of course Luke's email address. And what could they do with his email account, really? Bombard him with pleas for financial help from nonexistent Nigerian bankers and send him penis-enlargement advertising?

The only other personal things on the computer were a few abandoned to-do lists and my various Internet bookmarks, none of which could possibly be of much use. So why bother at all? Or had Danny been driven so distracted he was just reaching out blindly for anything that might explain my sudden defection?

I went a little cold then at the thought of my private blog, but it was locked down with a very long, very random password, one that wouldn't be easy to hack. Even my online banking password wasn't as complicated. I should be safe enough.

Still, it had been a complete invasion of my privacy, and one that might possibly get both Danny and Victor fired if I could prove they'd really been snooping. I picked up the phone and started to dial Jacqui's extension—I figured I could at least verify whether the antivirus install was completely bogus or not—then slowly placed the handset back in the cradle. As irritated as I was, I really didn't want to get

Danny fired. He had enough to deal with already. Besides, as far as I could tell, they'd just found a dead end. Okay, ten points for original thinking, but five for actual execution.

All the same, from now on I was locking my office door when I left for lunch.

The rest of the afternoon passed in a blur. We were approaching the final deadline for getting this issue out the door, so naturally that was when all our freelancers roused themselves and started to send in their material. I ended up working almost an hour over. Of course, I probably could have gotten out on time if I hadn't told Jacqui the happy news about my breakup with Danny. I lost more than an hour of my life listening to her alternately congratulate me, talk about the uselessness of men in general, and try to worm more information out of me about Luke. Somehow I finally managed to extricate myself, but the delay put me behind the curve, especially considering that I still had to go to the gym and try to work off that cheeseburger.

It was past seven o'clock by the time I made it back to my apartment. I had a slight feeling of anticipation as I turned the corner onto my street, but tonight there was no Luke waiting for me on the bottom step. Not that I could blame him; a spattery half-hearted rain was falling, and it wouldn't have been very comfortable.

When I opened my laptop, though, at least I had an email from him. *Business takes me away tonight,* it said. *I've left you something to pamper yourself with, though. Check the refrigerator.*

Eyebrows lifting, I pushed myself away from the dining room table where my laptop sat and went on into the kitchen. Upon opening the refrigerator door, I found a takeout container filled with my favorite corn chowder, as well as an elegantly packaged salad. A little split of sauvignon blanc sat there as well.

Something warm and wonderful filled my chest. The only other time I'd really experienced anything similar was back in my sophomore year of college, when I fell hard for Brad McAllister, who'd been in my abnormal psych class. We had what felt like a perfect romance for most of that year—right up until the point when he decided to transfer to Stanford. Despite that, though, he'd really been a great boyfriend, always coming up with thoughtful little things to do for me, coping with my hormonal mood swings, even remembering to get me flowers for my birthday and Valentine's Day. I'd been a wreck at the end of that year after we broke up, but he'd still become the unconscious yardstick against which I measured all my other love interests. So far, no one else had really come even close…until now.

It seemed petty to even wonder what "business" could have called Luke away. After all, it wasn't as if he gave me the third degree over how I spent every single second of my day. Besides, it probably wasn't healthy for me to expect to see him every night. I didn't want him to think I was a complete clinging vine, after all.

So I emptied the container of soup into a bowl and put it in the microwave, then pulled out one of the glasses he'd left behind several nights ago and poured myself the wine. I was feeling a little crampy, but between the wine and the warm soup I thought I could manage without the help of any painkillers. From the top of the refrigerator I retrieved an old serving tray and then put my meal on it. I figured if I were really going to be decadent I'd put my feet up on the couch and eat while watching TV. That position would help the slight ache in my lower back as well.

Only about five minutes had gone by, though, before my phone rang. At least I'd left my cell out on the coffee table, but I still gave it an exasperated glance before deciding I'd better answer it.

The caller ID said it was Nina. Good thing, because otherwise I wasn't sure I would have recognized the frantic voice on the other end of the line.

"Ch-christa?"

I asked, "Nina?"

"Thank God you're home—I tried earlier, and you weren't answering your cell—"

"Sorry—I was really bogged down at work today, and I had to stay late." Maneuvering myself into an upright position, I wedged the phone under my ear while I transferred the dinner tray to the coffee table. "What's the matter?"

"She—she *dumped* me!"

"Who—what?"

"G-Gina! She said she could tell I wasn't serious about 'the lifestyle' or I would have told my parents about her. She said she refused to be with someone who couldn't get out of the closet!" The last word came out mostly as a strangled sob.

Damn. It must be something in the air. I said, "Oh, wow, Nina—I'm really sorry."

"I mean, you'd think she'd be a little more understanding. This was the first time I'd ever, well, you know—"

"Yes," I said, hoping she wouldn't go into graphic detail. Of course I'd support Nina in whatever choices she made, but that didn't mean I wanted to hear all the inside info, so to speak.

"But no! That wasn't good enough for Miss Lesbianation! She said I was a coward and a hypocrite and—"

I broke in. "Well, you know that's not true. I mean, you never told her you were a lesbian, right? You told me you were bi."

A long silence on the other end of the line.

"Nina," I began, in warning tones.

"Oh, don't give me any crap, Christa! Like I knew what I was doing!"

Actually, I thought she did. Rather, she probably *thought* she knew what she was doing. Nina had always been a player. In that she had always seemed a lot more like a guy to me. Lots of different relationships, no deep emotional attachments. She'd always been in it for the thrill. And at that stage in our lives, her behavior hadn't exactly been off-putting to men. I didn't know a lot of guys who would say no to a gorgeous woman who just wanted to have some fun and who wasn't looking for anything lasting.

So when Gina came along, and Nina thought it was time to try something new, she didn't stop to think that of course Gina would react very differently from the men Nina had been with previously. Why not another fling? What was the harm?

Obviously Gina hadn't seen it that way.

I'd known Nina for ten years. I loved her—she was fun and bright and outrageous. But I also knew she had a really difficult time whenever someone wanted to get serious. That was always the signal for her to move on. Whether she'd been hurt at some point before I met her and therefore kept things light so she couldn't be wounded again, or whether she simply didn't have it in her emotional makeup to form deep attachments, I still wasn't sure. However, if Gina had been expecting Nina to confront her parents, proclaim herself to be gay, and go off to live in lesbian bliss forever, Gina had definitely picked the wrong gal. I guess she'd just discovered that for herself and broke it off before things could go any further.

Nina didn't get dumped. Nina was always the dumper, not the dumpee. I had the uncharitable thought that a good deal of her current outrage was probably due to that fact, not because she'd been all that attached to Gina.

I also knew, however, that I didn't dare point out what seemed pretty clear to me. Part of being friends with someone is knowing when to speak your mind and when to shut the hell up.

So instead of uttering some of the home truths that had bubbled up to the front of my brain, I made sympathetic noises and told her that was terrible and did she want me to come over so I could take her out for a drink or something?

I really didn't want to. I'd just gotten comfortable, and all I wanted to do was keep my feet up, finish my wine, watch some mindless TV, and then go to bed, where I would (I hoped) dream of Luke. Being a friend means putting yourself out there when necessary, though, so I just waited to hear what Nina wanted.

"No," she said at last. "I don't need you to come tearing out here. I've made a date with a nice bottle of Jose Cuervo Reserve, and I think I'll call in sick tomorrow."

"Good plan," I replied, trying to keep the relief out of my voice. "Go shopping and buy yourself something completely frivolous."

"I plan on it," she said. "I saw this amazing pair of Christian Laboutin shoes over at a shop on Montana. They're fierce, and they will be mine."

"Nothing like a little retail therapy," I agreed. "I'd call in and go shopping with you, but we're shipping the magazine starting tomorrow, and the only excuse for not coming in is death. Or maybe Ebola."

Nina laughed. "That's all right. I'm just glad I was able to get hold of you." She paused, then said, "Thanks, Christa."

"I'm here if you need to talk more," I replied. "I'll probably be up until eleven if you need me."

"Thanks," she said again. "But I plan to get so drunk that I won't be able to find my phone, let alone navigate my contacts list. 'Night."

I heard the click of the phone hanging up. After a second, I pushed the button to send my cell back to its home screen and then set it back down on the coffee table.

My soup had gone cold, but I didn't feel like getting up to reheat it. Instead I finished the last few spoonfuls, thinking of Luke, thinking about Nina and all the crazy things people did so they wouldn't have to be alone.

Was falling for the Devil all that much different?

I overslept the next morning, and hurried into work in a foul mood. My disposition didn't improve any when I realized that the last article I'd been waiting on still hadn't been sent to me. Goddamn freelancers. You'd think they'd be a little more professional when their livelihood depended on turning in quality work on time. Most of them were, really, but we had a couple of bad apples we nevertheless kept hiring because they were good enough that we had to overlook their chronic lateness.

After I'd cleared off my desk, I started roaming around the Internet, visiting the Fug Girls site, checking to see if a couple of items I'd spotted on the Victoria's Secret website had been put on sale yet. It had been a few days since I'd logged into my blog, so I figured adding another private entry might be a good way to kill some time until the next piece of work came along. That was the problem with getting a magazine out—it was definitely a case of hurry up and wait. The second the freelancer's article came in, I'd have to massage it and then rush it over to the art department so it could get laid out, but until then I didn't have much to do.

But after I'd logged in, I found myself staring at the blank field where I'd planned to write about the breakup with Danny, and maybe Gina's breakup, and realized I didn't feel like writing about that at all. I didn't want to write about relationships ending, not with things just beginning with Luke, all shiny and fresh and new.

Because I was restless, and because I couldn't think of anything better to do, I started noodling with the layout of my blog. I chose another theme, then changed the background color and the font. That didn't take me very long, though, so I started roaming through the other menus to look at all the options I hadn't really investigated previously. Usually I'm a cut-to-the-chase sort of person when it comes to that sort of thing—I just want to get the account set up as quickly as possible so I can get things moving. But since I was trying to waste time anyway, I went into the account settings and clicked on the "manage logins" option. I didn't even know what it really was for.

Basically, it showed a list of my previous logins, along with the IP address and the time stamp. It took me a minute to figure things out, because it was set up for Greenwich Mean Time, not local time. However, I hadn't accessed my blog since Monday night, and the list of logins showed that, according to the account manager at the site, I'd logged in just the day before. What the hell?

I was very careful with my passwords. I didn't give them out to anybody, and I had a group of about six I rotated amongst my various online accounts. And because I used the blog as an online diary, I'd come up with something even more complex to guard that particular site. I hadn't logged in to my account, though—I'd been out to lunch the last time the blog site thought I had entered my password.

Out to lunch—

The realization hit me, and I swore. Goddamn Victor sneaking around while Danny kept me busy at the restaurant. No wonder Danny had a minor freak attack when I tried to leave early. It hadn't been the realization that I was really dumping him—it was the thought that I might come back and catch Victor doing…well, I didn't know exactly *what* he'd been doing, but it sure as hell wasn't installing an antivirus program.

Fuming, I got up from my chair and stalked down the hall to the art department. Jesus was actually pretty savvy on the technical stuff. If the magazine had had only Macs to maintain, we probably could have dispensed with IT Solutions' services altogether. I wanted to see if he had any ideas about how Victor could have gotten my password when I knew I sure as hell hadn't written it down anywhere.

Jesus was doing his own 'net surfing when I peered inside his office. He started a bit when I stuck my head in the door, and then minimized the window for his browser so I couldn't see what he'd been doing.

"Really, I don't care," I said. "I'm waiting on Goldsmith just like everyone else."

He relaxed a little, then raised an eyebrow. "So what's up?"

"I have a technical question to ask you about computers."

Fingering his goatee, he said, "Okay—but it'd better be about a Mac, or I can't help you."

"It is," I replied. I stepped all the way into his office and then asked, "If you needed to get someone's password for logging into an online account, how would you do it?"

"Ask them for it?"

"Very funny."

He swiveled his office chair back and forth in a thoughtful way. "If you're not a hacker, probably the easiest thing to do is put a key logger on your computer."

I crossed my arms and frowned. "I'm not sure I follow you."

He stopped the annoying movement of his chair long enough to answer, "A key logger is a little device about yay big." He held up his thumb and forefinger about an inch and a half apart. "Install one of those suckers on the connection between your keyboard and the computer, and it keeps a log of everything. Then all you have to do is run a program that accesses the keystroke log and it'll pull up everything—passwords, commands, all the text you've typed, that sort of thing." Still with that raised eyebrow, he asked, "What's the matter? You think someone's been messing with your computer?"

"No," I said hastily. "It's just something a friend and I were talking about last night."

"Uh-huh?" Jesus sounded skeptical, but luckily for me he didn't press the point. He just swiveled the office chair back around to face his monitor and brought the browser window back up. "Sounds like you girls need to get out more."

"Very funny," I said, but I'd heard enough. Frowning, I walked back into my office and started going back to every online site I'd ever used where I needed a password and began changing all of them. Maybe that was locking the barn door after the horse had been stolen, but it made me feel the tiniest bit better. And I didn't care if my Mac blew up—I was damned if I was going to let anyone from IT Solutions touch my computer again.

Of course, that didn't solve the teensy little problem of Danny and Victor reading my entire private blog…or the fact that now they knew all about me and Luke.

What they'd do with that information, I shuddered to think.

Interlude

"He's the *Devil*?" Danny repeated, looking rather like someone who had just swallowed a large dose of battery acid.

Beelzebub affected a negligent shrug. "That's what her blog said."

"But—" The young man hunched over and twined his fingers in his overlong hair. "How is that possible?"

"Maybe she's just nuts," Asmodeus put in.

Danny lifted his fingers from his hair, which remained standing up in a pair of tufts closely resembling horns. Ironic, Beelzebub thought.

"No," Danny said at once. "She's not crazy. I mean, she can be moody and all, just like most girls, but I don't think she'd say something like that unless she really meant it."

"So you think she's telling the truth?" The disbelief in Asmodeus' voice was clear. Nicely done.

Beelzebub tried not to look his compatriot in the face, because otherwise he'd run the risk of letting his own expression of disinterested concern turn into one of pure amusement. Danny wasn't watching either one of them, but rather a blotchy stain in the center of the carpet. Still, one wrong step here, and the whole scheme could fall apart.

"Yeah, I think she is."

"Do you believe in the Devil?" Beelzebub inquired. Good thing Victor's delivery was fairly deadpan most of the time; it was a lot easier to ask that question when he could keep his tone flat and just barely accusatory.

Danny's response was immediate. "Yeah. Of course I do."

"For real?" Asmodeus put in, still playing the role of skeptic.

"Yeah, for real." Scowling, Danny got up from the couch and stalked into the kitchen, where he pulled the last bottle of beer out of the fridge.

Interesting. None of the trio were big drinkers, although Zach tended to consume more than the other two. And of course Asmodeus had taken advantage of the fact. Danny was actually lucky even that one bottle of Anchor Steam had escaped unscathed.

"So what are you going to do about it?" Beelzebub asked, after Danny had taken a few bracing swallows of beer. Excellent. If he got himself somewhat tipsy, he would be in a far more suggestible state.

"Do?" Several hearty mouthfuls of Anchor Steam followed the first ones. "Um, this guy is the Devil, Vince. What exactly am I supposed to do about it? And I already didn't have a chance, based on what you told me about his house and his cars. So on top of all that, he's the Devil? I'm thinking the odds aren't exactly in my favor."

Beelzebub exchanged a quick glance with Asmodeus. Mortals were horribly weak, of course, but he'd expected this Danny to put up a bit more of a fight over his Lady Fair. If they couldn't get the young human to stir things up, they'd have to resort to far riskier methods, ones that would increase their chances of getting caught.

To his surprise, he heard Asmodeus say, "Well, uh, what about her immortal soul and stuff?"

That got him, Beelzebub could tell. Danny's head went up, and he paused in the middle of lifting the beer bottle to his lips. "Her what?"

"Her soul. You obviously believe in that, too—I mean, you still go to church every Sunday with your parents. What do you think your priest will say if you go to confession and tell him you let your girlfriend get stolen by the Devil?"

Nice, very nice. Beelzebub reflected that perhaps he had been too hard on Asmodeus previously—his fellow demon was showing a nice streak of low cunning that certainly hadn't been in evidence for the last few centuries.

A tortured crease appeared in Danny's brow. "I—well, probably he wouldn't be too happy with me."

"So do something about it," Beelzebub put in. "Go talk to her."

"What, now?"

By Tartarus, this young mortal was dense. "You have to wait for the right time. She saw me leaving her office today and wasn't too happy about it. I think a cooling-off period is in order. In fact, I think you should just let things lie for a few days. Let her think you didn't find anything. Then go get her when her defenses are down. You'll have a better chance of success that way."

Danny was still frowning, but he did manage a nod. "Yeah, that could work—"

"Sounds like a great plan," Asmodeus added.

Without replying at first, Danny upended his beer and drained the last of it. Then he looked down at the empty bottle with sorrowful eyes. "That was the last one."

"Maybe you should go get some more," Beelzebub suggested. It would be helpful to have the young man out of the house for a bit so he and Asmodeus could talk in private.

"Are you sure I should drive?"

"After just one beer?" Asmodeus mocked. "Give me a break."

Danny squared his shoulders. "You're right. It's only a couple of blocks anyway."

A sane person would have just walked, but Beelzebub had long ago come to the conclusion that the inhabitants of this so-called "City of Angels" were all crazy—they'd jump into a car to go a distance that should only have taken them a few minutes by foot. But he also knew that suggesting such a thing to Danny would look suspiciously out of character, since Victor Nguyen was the type who'd drive his car to the bathroom if he could get it to fit down the hallway.

"You want anything?" Danny asked as he fished his car keys out of his pocket.

"I'm good," Beelzebub said at once. *Now, there's a lie.*

"Me, too," Asmodeus added.

Danny nodded and headed out the front door after depositing his empty beer bottle on the coffee table. Both demons waited until they heard the sound of a car starting up in the driveway. After a few more seconds, Beelzebub let out a breath.

"That could have gone badly," he said.

"But it didn't."

"I can't believe *he's* willing to throw in *his* lot with these pathetic mortals. I'd kill myself within a day."

"Yes. Although—" And Asmodeus hesitated.

Beelzebub was in no mood for his partner's whimsical shifts in subject. "Although what?"

"There *are* certain distractions."

Not that again. "Nothing is enough to distract me from the foolishness of these people."

Asmodeus glanced away. "I agree that *he* seems to be wasting his time with this girl. She's certainly nothing to write home about. If *he* had any taste, *he'd* be going after her friend Nina."

"*He* shouldn't be 'going after' anyone at all," Beelzebub gritted. "*His* job is to run Hell, not to chase tail. Especially if that piece of tail is *his* means of getting back to Heaven."

"Agreed. Only—"

A low growl escaped from between Beelzebub's teeth. Good thing Danny wasn't around to hear it; nothing of this earth was capable of emitting such a sound.

But Asmodeus, having heard that sort of thing countless times before, appeared unfazed. In fact, he looked downright wistful. "I wouldn't mind a chance at Nina's tail."

Focus, Beelzebub told himself. *Focus. If you rip Asmodeus' head off right now, someone will be bound to notice.*

For of course doing such a thing would only damage the mortal body Asmodeus now inhabited. Danny's grasp of the situation was shaky enough. The last thing he needed to deal with was a beheaded roommate awaiting him at the end of his beer run. That would most certainly distract him from his crusade to save Christa Simms from the Devil.

No, satisfying as it would be to show Asmodeus exactly what he, Beelzebub, thought of the other demon's preoccupation with human women, he would have to control himself. He clenched his puny mortal fists and reminded himself of what was at stake here. It would all be worth it in the end. The possession of this paltry body, Asmodeus' puerile obsessions—all of it could be brushed aside, as long as the status quo was preserved and Lucifer remained where he was meant to be.

In Hell.

chapter ten

ALL MY WORRY SEEMED TO BE FOR NOTHING, since I didn't hear anything else from Danny, and no screaming headlines appeared in any of the tabloids proclaiming that the Devil walked the earth (at least, no more so than usual). Maybe Danny had decided I was just kidding, although why anyone would make that sort of joke, especially in a private blog no one else was supposed to see, I had no idea. Or maybe (and this seemed more likely) he was huddled with the rest of the Gunmen, trying to figure out the best way to take down the Prince of Darkness.

Since Luke hadn't said anything about getting together before we saw each other on Saturday night, I pried Nina out of the house, and the two of us went out to the movies on Friday. I didn't want to eat a big meal, as I still felt a bit puffy, and I had to fit into the red dress the following night. So I used the excuse of having to stay at the office just late enough that we wouldn't have time for dinner before the movie. I wasn't sure whether Nina bought it or not, but she didn't argue. At least I was able to feel virtuous about eating a Weight Watchers frozen meal instead of whatever calorie-fest we might otherwise have indulged in.

We met in Westwood, since it was a halfway point between my office and her place in Brentwood. It was also completely mobbed, but going to school there for four years had taught me the goat paths and less popular parking garages, and I was able to meet Nina in front of the theater with some time to spare.

She stood there, arms crossed as she scowled up at the marquee. Obviously, her mood hadn't improved much. "Going to the movies this time of year sucks," she said. "There's nothing good out."

"Hi, Nina, nice to see you, too," I replied.

That made her stop and look at me. Then she shook her head and gave a short, humorless laugh. "Yeah, I'm a real party. Sorry—I'm still cranky."

"Well, you have every right to be."

She shrugged. "Maybe. In a weird way, it's sort of a relief. She was getting awfully demanding there at the end. I think I'm going to switch back to guys. They're not so high-maintenance."

For which the entire straight male population of Los Angeles thanks you, I thought. But I only said, "Well, whatever works."

"Right now nothing is working for me," Nina replied, tossing her heavy curls back over one shoulder. A few feet away, a couple of guys in UCLA jerseys stopped and stared. "I'll get over it. Anyway, everything all set for the big date?"

"I think so," I said. "Mani/pedi at eleven, and Bethany was able to squeeze me in at four for hair and makeup."

I still felt sort of strange about all the preparations I'd made for attending the opera, but Nina had assured me they were necessary. It had taken me a moment to recall the last time I'd even had a manicure—I think it was right before my cousin's ill-fated wedding a couple of years ago. Pedicures in the summer, sure, just because painting your own toes is a pain in the butt. Besides that, though, my hairstylist was taking care of my up-do, and another girl in the salon was going to do my makeup, since Nina had told me she didn't really trust me to do an adequate job. I wasn't one of those girls who never wore any cosmetics, but I liked keeping it simple. Simple, however, was not what you paired with an evening gown.

Turning away from Nina, I looked up at the movie listings. Unless we wanted to wait almost an hour, we were stuck between choosing a romantic comedy, which I would have liked but wasn't sure Nina could handle at the moment, or a psychological thriller which, according to the reviews, wasn't all that thrilling.

"So which is it going to be?" I asked.

Nina shrugged. "Whatever. Actually, shocking as it may sound, I'd rather watch the comedy. It's got Gerard Butler in it. Even if it's stupid, at least I can stare at him for the next two hours."

So much for Nina's journey to the "dark side." It sounded to me as if she were pretty firmly back in hetero territory. Then again, I had to admit that Mr. Butler was definitely worth looking at.

We went up to get the tickets, and I couldn't help feeling a little smug. Movie stars were fun to dream about, but I had someone equally stare-able taking me to the opera the next night. The thought sent a little tingle down my spine.

If nothing else, I couldn't wait to see what Luke looked like in evening wear.

Well, fabulous, naturally.

He'd told me he would pick me up at six, but I'd been ready for about twenty minutes by that point and was hovering nervously in the living room, occasionally stopping to peer through the blinds to see if he'd shown up yet. Thank God the weather had decided to cooperate. It was clear and cold, but the rain had taken itself off for a few days.

Then I saw the Bentley glide to a stop at the curb, and after a few seconds Luke got out. Looking at him in his tuxedo, I thought, *James Bond's got nothing on you, baby*. It seemed a little childish to be watching him through the blinds like that nosy neighbor from *Bewitched*, so I stepped away from the window and waited, listening for his knock.

Even though I'd been expecting it, my heart beat a little faster when I heard the light rapping on my front door. Taking a breath, I stepped forward and opened it.

He looked even better closer up. I don't know what it is about a guy in a tuxedo, but Luke just oozed gorgeousness.

His gaze fell on me, and I could see his eyes widen slightly. For a few seconds we both stood there in silence, partaking in mutual admiration, until he cleared his throat and said, "You're beautiful."

"So are you," I blurted, and then he laughed.

"For you," he said, handing me a bouquet of red roses from seemingly out of nowhere.

"Uh—thanks," I said, taking them a little awkwardly. Maybe someday I'd get used to the way he made things materialize out of thin air. "They're beautiful."

The flowers matched my gown perfectly. I wondered what he would have come up with if I'd been wearing black.

"Let me just go put these in some water—"
I began. But the words had hardly left my mouth
before a crystal vase appeared on the coffee table,
ready to go with water already inside. I shot Luke
an amused glance. "Now you're just showing off."

"I am?" Without waiting for a reply, he neatly
plucked the roses out of my grasp and put them in
the vase. "We should be going—the reservations are
for six-thirty."

"Reservations?" I echoed. "Really? How…
mortal of you! What happened to doors opening
and all that?"

"On special occasions I do try to observe the
correct protocols."

"And this is a special occasion?"

His gaze lingered on my mouth, and then flickered for the barest second to the low neckline of
my gown. I could feel the blood rush to my cheeks.
"I hope so," he replied, a world of meaning in those
three small words.

I didn't think I could manage a reply. Instead, I
leaned down and picked up the little silver beaded
evening bag I'd bought to go with my ensemble.
After double-checking to make sure that my lip-
stick, ticket, and house key were inside (the purse
wouldn't accommodate much more than that), I
turned to him. "All right—I think I'm ready."

He glanced at my bare shoulders. "It's quite
chilly out."

That particular point had been worrying me as well, but I said casually, "Oh, it's all right. I couldn't find a wrap I liked, so I figured I'd just go without."

Something soft and indescribably warm draped itself around my shoulders. I looked down and saw that a coat of silvery-gray fur had, like the roses, appeared out of nowhere.

As beautiful as it was, I knew I couldn't wear it. "Luke, it's gorgeous, but I can't wear fur. I don't believe in it, and besides, if my mother found out, she'd skin me alive!"

His blue eyes laughed at me, at what he no doubt thought were foolish mortal scruples. "Don't worry, my socially conscious little friend. It's not real."

"It isn't?" I asked in dubious tones, and reached down to stroke the amazingly soft material.

There was an undercurrent of amusement in his voice, but he sounded neutral enough as he said, "They do wonders with synthetics these days, don't they?"

Fine—if I had to be a source of constant mirth for him, so be it. At least now I didn't have to worry about freezing my ass off. I just hoped, as he ushered me out of the apartment and down to the car, that no over-zealous animal rights activists would do as I had and mistake my faux fur for the real thing. Dodging balloons filled with red paint wasn't exactly my idea of a fun Saturday night activity.

Luke didn't bother to head back to the freeway. Instead, he pointed the huge car east on Wilshire toward downtown Los Angeles. Street lights seemed to stay magically green for us much longer than they should have, and I reflected that, among other things, the Devil was obviously a handy person to have around when dealing with L.A. traffic. On a Saturday night, though, there weren't a lot of cars heading into the downtown area. That section of town had a high concentration of financial buildings, law offices, and other commercial facilities, most of which didn't have much business on the weekends. A little farther south than we were going lay the Fashion District, which was very busy seven days a week, but even those shops would have closed up by this hour.

I watched the buildings and other cars move outside the car windows as we made our majestic way through the streets. More than once I saw people on the sidewalk stop to stare at the Bentley as it glided past. Maybe I wasn't quite Cinderella at the ball, but I definitely had the feeling that I'd stepped into another world as I sat there in my evening gown with the luxurious coat nestled against my bare neck.

We didn't speak. I think Luke could tell I was enjoying the ride itself as I drank in the sights and even the smells. I love the scent of leather, and the car was redolent of very fine hides, as well as the slightest spiciness that I thought might have been Luke's cologne. Soft classical music emanated from the speakers. I didn't know what it was, but it sounded vaguely familiar. Mozart, probably.

A little while later we reached downtown, and we came to a stop outside an elegant older building. A valet hurried over and opened the door for me, extending a hand to help me out of the car, even as Luke came around to the sidewalk and gave him the keys. The kid's eyes widened slightly—I had the feeling he didn't get to park a Bentley every day— but he nodded and hurried over to the driver's-side door.

Luke extended an arm. "Shall we?"

I took it, reflecting that a girl could definitely get used to this sort of lifestyle. He opened the door for me, and we stepped inside.

The building was lovely, old but meticulously restored. What surprised me, though, was that the maitre d' led us through the main dining room and on into a separate chamber, an incredible room with a fountain in the center and gorgeously coffered ceilings. Only one table occupied the cavernous space, which had been decorated with some of the most amazing floral arrangements I'd ever seen.

Feeling a little apprehensive, I shot a questioning glance up at Luke. "All this, just for us?"

"Just for you," he corrected, and pulled out a chair for me.

The maitre d' handed me a menu as Luke took his own seat. Not even bothering to look at the elegant leather-backed bill of fare, Luke said, "We'll start with the *capesante in padella*, and a bottle of the Schiopetto sauvignon blanc."

"Very good, sir." He gave the two of us a slight nod and then disappeared back the way we had come in.

I had no idea what he'd just ordered, but I figured I'd better just trust him and go with the flow. My surroundings almost overwhelmed me. What kind of strings had Luke pulled, and what kind of expense had he gone to, in order to procure this room for just the two of us? Under normal circumstances it looked like the sort of space that would have been used for banquets or possibly small wedding receptions.

"You don't do things by halves, do you?" I asked.

"Not usually, no," he replied. "Besides, I wanted to take you out to dinner, but I also wanted some privacy."

"Heck of a way to do it," I said, waving at the slightly echoing chamber around us. From somewhere I heard soft background music which sounded like a string quartet, but it couldn't completely mask the slightly hollow sound of a large space that didn't have enough people to fill it.

Luke smiled. "Perhaps."

At that moment our waiter appeared with a bottle of white wine, which he deftly opened, and then poured out a precise quantity into each of our glasses. Task accomplished, he deposited the bottle in a silver wine bucket that had been placed off to the left of Luke's chair and asked, "Anything else, sir?"

"Not for the moment."

The waiter nodded and left. Luke raised his wine glass toward me, and said, "To trying new things."

I wondered precisely which "new things" he was referring to, but decided it probably would be better not to ask. Instead, I lifted my own wine glass and smiled at him. "To new things," I repeated, then drank. The taste was clean and cool, with the slightest hint of a mineral flavor at the finish.

"I think you'll enjoy *Faust*," Luke went on, as if the only thing in the world he possibly could have been referring to was the opera itself. "The music is really quite exquisite, and the story involving…even though it's a pure fabrication."

"So no one ever sold you their soul?" I asked, only half-joking.

For a second he was quiet, holding the glass of straw-colored wine in his hand. The reflection of the votive candle at the center of the table glimmered against its surface, gold on gold. "People have tried," he said. "But you can't sell that which is not yours to give."

"Are you saying our souls aren't our own?" That idea didn't sound very appealing to me.

"You misunderstand me." Finally he lifted the glass to his lips and drank, then replaced it on the cloth-covered tabletop. "Of course your soul is yours, and yours alone. That's why you can never sell it or give it away."

Frowning, I thought that sounded like circular logic. I sipped my own wine, then said, "I'm afraid I'm not following you."

Once again he smiled. "God gave men souls, and free will. But a soul is not a commodity—it is a part of you, like the color of your eyes or the sound of your voice. It can't be separated from you, any more than you can bottle your eye color and sell that."

"So why all these stories about people selling their souls to the Devil?"

The smiled faded. "If a person comes to the psychological point where he feels his soul is of no worth to him, that it can be traded for wealth or power or any of the other temporal things he might crave, then he has lost touch with the bit of grace God has granted him by giving him a soul in the first place. Once a person is in such a state of mind, he allows himself to commit whatever acts he feels are necessary, because he has 'lost his soul,' so to speak. It's a way of giving up responsibility for one's actions. You know—'the Devil made me do it,'" Luke added, with the familiar glint in his eye.

Well, that actually made some sense, although I had to sit and think about it for a minute. After sipping at my wine as a cover for some serious cogitation, I finally asked, "I'm not—I'm not imperiling my immortal soul by having dinner with you, am I?" Even though I tried to keep my tone light, I had the feeling my inner anxiety seeped through a bit.

At that he laughed outright. "Hardly. I asked, and you accepted. You haven't made any bargains with me, or with yourself—except possibly to have a good time."

"Some people might say that 'having a good time' is the quickest route to Hell," I remarked. "But they're never any fun at cocktail parties."

"Exactly. Besides, why would God have given humans a capacity for enjoyment and the ability to experience pleasure if he didn't actually want them to do so? This is what I find difficult to understand about so many of the tenets of people's faith—that self-denial and self-abnegation somehow leads to enlightenment."

"And it doesn't?" If that were really the truth, then I guessed all those monks I'd read about in my history books, the ones who wore hair shirts and fasted and scourged themselves, must have felt pretty stupid after they died and realized it had all been for nothing, that God actually would have preferred for them to go out and eat meat and drink wine and get laid.

"Sometimes. But only because the person in question has cleared his or her mind of enough extraneous things to do so. It's certainly not guaranteed." His gaze moved past me, and I turned slightly to see the waiter arriving with our appetizer.

He laid down the plate between the Luke and me, and then set smaller plates in front of each of us. I didn't know what it was, but it smelled delicious.

"And for the entrée?" the waiter asked, and I cast a guilty glance at my menu. I'd been so busy talking to Luke I hadn't even thought about what I wanted to eat.

Seeming to notice my discomfort, Luke asked, "If you'll allow me?" and gathered up both our menus.

Normally I would have gotten on my feminist high horse about a man presuming to place an order in a restaurant for me, but somehow I knew I could trust him to get me something I liked. I nodded.

"For the lady, the *filetto alla rossini,* and for me the *entrecote di manzo peppe rosa.* And a bottle of the '99 Ornellaia."

"Excellent, sir." The waiter took our menus, smiling. I could only imagine that whatever Luke had ordered, it was very expensive.

"So what am I eating?" I asked, turning to my neglected appetizer.

"Bacon-wrapped scallops. They go beautifully with this wine, I think."

Scallops had never been on my top ten list of favorite foods, but I did love bacon, so I figured I'd give it a try. The blend of flavors turned out to be amazing, though, subtle and smoky, and the clean, light taste of the wine seemed to both cut through it and harmonize with the dish.

The Devil was apparently both an epicure and a hedonist. However, since at the moment I was reaping the benefits of his predilections, I wasn't about to argue. No wonder the stories painted him as the one who led people into temptation—it was hard not to be tempted by the sorts of pleasures he'd given me so far.

I could only imagine what others might soon follow.

Dinner was a decadent dream, and the opera sublime. The experience of actually sitting there, watching the entire spectacle and hearing those perfectly trained voices bring the tragedy to life, was so different from just listening to a CD that it hardly seemed to be the same art form. *Faust* is sung in French, and I'd worried that I wouldn't be able to understand anything that was going on, but those nifty supertitles they projected above the stage took care of that problem. By the end I was so caught up in the story and the haunting beauty of the music that I had to breathe deeply and concentrate on not crying. Maybe Luke would have understood, but

I've never found it a good idea to dissolve into a weepy mess while on a date, especially when your eye makeup has been meticulously applied by some Southern European eyebrow expert and probably wouldn't survive the ordeal.

To say I'd never experienced anything like the opera would be an understatement—my parents had taken the family to a few musicals when I was younger, but that's not the same thing. For one thing, this crowd was better dressed and better behaved. In fact, the audience was so somber and respectful that the standing ovation at the end actually caught me by surprise. I laid aside the opera glasses Luke had given me and stood, clapping until my palms tingled.

After that we had to deal with all the confusion of navigating the crowded halls of the Dorothy Chandler Pavilion amid the mass exodus to the parking structure. Luke took my hand and steered me through the throngs without incident. It wasn't until we were in the warm, leather-scented confines of the Bentley that he spoke.

"So you enjoyed it."

"Very much." I leaned back against the headrest, not caring what I might be doing to my hairstyle. It had served its purpose. "I didn't know it could be so—so—"

"So what?"

I turned a few words over in my head, then answered, "Thrilling. Exhausting. Uplifting."

"I'm glad." The car moved forward in little fits and starts; it was probably going to take awhile for us to climb our way out of the garage. "I've followed opera for quite some time now."

Of course you have, I thought. *You've been there since the beginning, haven't you?*

That made me think of all the different voices he must have heard over the years, all the different venues where he'd seen these works performed. The Pavilion was lovely, elegant and spare in a late-'60s sort of way, with its blond wood and modern chandeliers, but I wondered what it would be like to see an opera performed in an old theater in Paris, or Milan, or even New York.

Finally we inched our way out of the parking structure. To my surprise, though, Luke didn't turn the car south back toward Wilshire. Instead, he headed north on the Hollywood Freeway.

I turned in my seat to look at him. "Is there some after-party going on that you forgot to mention?"

He kept his gaze straight ahead. "I thought we could go back to my place for a drink."

Normally that comment would have sent up all sorts of warning flags. You know, the "he's going to take you back to his house and have his wicked way with you" warning flags. But I thought about it for a minute and realized I didn't care. At this point I had the thought that it might be a race to see which one of us could rip the other person's clothing off more quickly. He'd probably win—I was wearing a lot less than he was.

"That sounds good," I said, hoping he couldn't hear the edge of nervous anticipation in my voice.

Without comment, he got off the freeway at Vermont, then headed south to Beverly Boulevard. Fairly soon we were back in the high-rent district near the country club where his home was located. He turned down a side street, then another. Within another minute or so, the wrought-iron gates that shielded his driveway swung inward, and we came to a stop under the porte-cochere.

I waited while Luke came around to open the door for me and tried to ignore the butterflies in my stomach. Just because he had invited me back here didn't necessarily mean he intended for the two of us to go to bed together.

Yeah, right, I thought. *And the NSA isn't reading all my emails.*

However, I thought I maintained my cool pretty well, except for the part where the stiletto heel of my sandal caught in the mat at the side door. I would have pitched over on my face if Luke hadn't caught me by the elbow.

"Maybe a drink isn't such a good idea," he said with a laugh.

"Very funny," I retorted. "You try walking in three-inch spikes and see how well you do."

"I think I'll pass on that one," he replied, relinquishing my elbow and pushing the door inward.

The side entrance opened into a short hallway that branched out to the kitchen on one side and then continued into the main part of the house directly in front of us.

"Go ahead to the living room," Luke said. "I'll be there in a minute."

I nodded and kept moving forward, hoping that I was recalling the layout of the place correctly. Soft light from a series of wall sconces illuminated my way, and without too much trouble I found the center hall and the living room beyond it. A low fire burned in the enormous hearth. The real thing, too, not one of those bogus contraptions of ceramic-composite logs and gas flames. No doubt he'd willed the fire into existence as we entered the house, along with the series of pillar candles that flickered from both the mantel and the low, heavy table that fronted the sofa. The air was warm and smelled faintly of sandalwood and spice.

Great setting for a seduction, I thought, and kicked off my uncomfortable shoes. Again I felt that uneasy thrill in the pit of my stomach. Even putting aside the fact that he was the Devil, Luke and I had known each other for less than two weeks. All right, if we were counting time elapsed in actual evenings together rather than calendar days, then I'd probably spent more time with him than I had with some of my previous lovers before I ended up in bed with them. But still....

I shook my head at myself. "Previous lovers," my ass. There was Alex Akullian, whom I'd lost my virginity to during the summer between high school and college, mostly because I refused to start college still a virgin. A big gap between Alex and Brad, the love of my sophomore year. Another exciting dry spell that lasted until well after I had graduated and which was finally broken by a five-month relationship with Scott Tanaka. That one had actually been going fairly well—until his company transferred him to London. End of story. Then finally the wonderful Danny, although I wasn't sure I could really count him since we'd never actually made love.

All in all, it was a pretty pathetic roster for a single girl living in a city as supposedly happening as Los Angeles, but unlike Nina, I couldn't jump into bed with someone just because I thought he had a nice ass. With the others, I'd truly believed I loved them...with the possible exception of Alex Akullian. No excuses for that one—you do some stupid stuff when you're just eighteen.

So did this mean I loved Luke? Oh, I was completely infatuated by him, and pretty seriously in lust if my physical reactions to his mere presence were any indication, but it's still a big leap from that to love. Especially when I had to consider that he wasn't even truly a man. I'd always needed to believe there was some sort of future in every relationship I pursued, but what possible future could I have with someone like Luke?

At that inopportune moment he returned, carrying a bottle in one hand and a pair of small crystal cordial glasses in the other. My face must have given something away, since he gave me a piercing look before setting the bottle and glasses down on the cocktail table.

"Everything all right?" he asked.

"Fine," I said automatically. Although I found him very easy to talk to most of the time, the subject of where we were headed seemed fraught with problems. I just didn't want to go there yet.

One eyebrow lifted as he gave me the lie, but he remained silent as he pulled the cork from the squat bottle and poured some dark garnet-colored liquid into each of the glasses. "Here," he said.

I took the fragile little glass from him and asked, "What is it?"

"Port. I think you'll like it."

Up until that point, I'd only come across references to port in the historical romances I indulged in every once in a while when I wanted to entertain myself without fully engaging my brain. Port had always sounded like a fussy Victorian drink to me, out of place in a world of martinis and mojitos. But what the hell.

Lifting the glass to my lips, I took a very small sip. The liquor was sweet and rich, tasting of deep, dark grapes with a raisin-y undertone. I could feel the warmth pulse its way down my throat, gentler than the kick you got from brandy or cognac. Damn—if only I'd known what I'd been missing all these years.

Ignoring the knowing smile on Luke's mouth, I drank again. "You are *the* corrupter of the innocent, aren't you?" I asked at length.

"I prefer to think of it as 'broadening horizons,'" he answered.

"Rationalization," I shot back, but I had to admit that he had a point. At any rate, just looking at the curve of his mouth and the strength of those shoulders under the proper evening jacket made me hope that my horizons were going to get broadened very soon.

Almost as if my thoughts were a trigger, Luke drained the rest of the port in his glass and then set it down on the table. I did the same, recklessly tossing back the contents of the little glass even though I knew the stuff had to be much higher-octane than regular wine.

He pulled me into his arms then, his mouth finding mine. I tasted port, smelled again the faint spicy scent that seemed to permeate his hair and skin. His hands moved over my bare shoulders, and the flare of desire I felt as his skin touched mine exploded through me like a match setting off gasoline.

We kissed until I was gasping for air, and even then his lips moved against my throat, finding just the right sensitive spot behind my ear. My fingers reached up, fumbling with the unfamiliar knots of the bow tie at his neck. Then it was loose, and I flung it down on the couch, shakily moving on to pull at the studs down the front of his shirt. A series of metallic little pings sounded as they hit the wooden floor.

Probably we would have ended up right on that floor, or at least the sofa, if it weren't for Luke's ability to whisk us from one place to another in the blink of an eye. The next thing I knew, we were standing in a chamber slightly smaller than the living room, but with an enormous canopied bed. Another hearth occupied the far wall, and a fire burned there as well, providing the only illumination. A huge Persian rug covered the floor, soft against my bare feet.

Could I have stopped him at that point? I didn't know. For an eternity we stood there, staring at one another as our breaths sounded, ragged in the half-lit room. Then our mouths met again, and this time his hands were moving down my body, pushing the straps of my gown off my shoulders, sliding it down until I stood there only in the red satin underwear I'd bought at Victoria's Secret, on a night that now felt as if it had taken place a century ago. Likewise, I pulled off his tuxedo jacket, and then went to work on the rest of his shirt buttons.

His body was as beautiful as I had thought it would be—strong and toned, not particularly defined, but solid. The faintest dusting of dark hair trailed down his chest and disappeared into the waistband of his pants.

A flash of his teeth as he grinned in the semi-gloom. "I told you red was my favorite color." His fingers worked the front closure of my bra, and I gasped as he pulled it away and cupped my breasts in his hands. I moaned as he touched me, even as I worked the button on his pants and then pulled down the zipper. Although he didn't stop touching me, somehow he managed to step out of his trousers, kicking them to one side.

And then we were on the bed, his body pressed against mine as his hand slid down beneath my underwear, his index finger unerringly locating just the place to touch me…there. I moaned even more loudly, lying back and letting him stroke me. His breath came warm against my breast, and I felt his tongue touch me, swirling against my skin. The climax came with shocking suddenness—I'd never come that quickly in the past, but then, no one had ever been able to make me feel like this before.

I lay there gasping for a few seconds, then turned over and feverishly reached for his underwear, pulling it off, my hands wrapping around him, feeling the strength of his arousal. His breathing quickened, and I bent and took him into my mouth, tasting him, the heat in my body increasing as I heard him give out a low, strained moan.

Then he said, "Enough," and pulled away, pushing me under him.

"Yes," I whispered, and he was inside me, our bodies moving as one, the warmth of his flesh against mine. It was as if we'd been made to fit together—no false moves, no awkward miscalculations. I felt the surge in my veins again, and knew that I was about to come once more.

I climaxed just a few seconds before he did. With a groan that sounded as if it had been ripped out of him, he exploded inside me, the heat of his orgasm like a small supernova at the very core of my body. We clung together, both gasping, as the waves of passion slowly receded.

How long we stayed like that, I wasn't sure. Eventually, though, reality set in, and I eased myself away from him to find the bathroom and get myself cleaned up. When I returned, he still lay there in the bed, his dark hair mussed and sticking to his brow, the blankets pulled halfway up his chest.

Did the Devil even sleep? I didn't know for sure, but he was giving a pretty good imitation of it. Lifting the covers, I carefully slid into bed next to him. For a long moment I stared at his profile as it was silhouetted against the glow from the dying fire. I knew better than to say the words aloud, but I couldn't help thinking them.

I love you…I love you…I love you.

CHAPTER ELEVEN

Dim light slanted across my eyelids. I blinked, then looked up at the heavy drape of blood-colored velvet above my head. Last night I'd barely registered the fact that this bed had a canopy, but now I could see a little more clearly. The sheets were dark red as well, along with the heavy brocade comforter that now lay in a crumpled wad toward the foot of the bed. The overall effect was womblike, to say the least.

Luke's voice came from somewhere over to my right. "Rested?"

I started, then clutched the sheet against my naked torso. Not that he hadn't seen my body already, but somehow what happens between two people in the dark gets overridden by the light of a morning after. My hair was a disaster, half still pulled up and held in place by some very determined bobby pins, the rest tangling over my shoulders.

"Um, yes," I said. Rolling over, I saw him standing next to the bed in a white T-shirt and a pair of black sweatpants. He held a dark glazed mug in each hand. The thick smell of fresh coffee drifted slowly toward me.

"I thought you could use this," he said, and extended one of the mugs.

Still clutching the sheet against my bare breasts with one arm, I sat up and took the coffee from him with the other hand. "Thank you."

"I suppose this could be awkward," he went on, his tone casual. "Would it put your mind at ease if I told you that I had a wonderful time last night?"

"Uh…so did I," I replied, then bent my head to sip at the coffee. The heat in my face told me I was blushing furiously once again, but at least this time I had a good excuse.

"And that I certainly don't mean for last night to be our only time?" His voice sounded teasing, but when I glanced up at him, he looked serious enough. His hair was mussed as well, but in an adorable bed-head sort of way. A trace of dark stubble showed on his cheeks.

"Okay," I said. "If you insist." I kept my tone light, but the pressure in my midsection eased a bit. At least it didn't sound as if he meant for this to be a one-night stand.

"Some breakfast after the coffee?"

That sounded wonderful, but I felt a little used up. What I really wanted was a long, hot shower. A change of clothes would be nice, too. I hated the thought of sneaking into my apartment still wearing the previous night's evening gown. I wouldn't exactly call it the walk of shame—I certainly wasn't ashamed of what I'd done—but it would still be a dead giveaway for letting my neighbors know that I'd gotten got lucky the night before.

"Sure," I replied, then hesitated.

"Over on that chair you'll find some of your clothing. And I have toiletries for you as well in the bathroom." His eyes gleamed at me, impossibly blue. "Meet me down in the kitchen when you're ready." Then he leaned down and kissed me, just a swift touch of his lips against mine, but it was enough to get my blood racing all over again. After that he turned and went out through the door that led to the hall.

I should have known he'd have all the contingencies figured out. Glancing over at the chair he'd mentioned, I saw a pair of my jeans, a sweater, and a bra and panties folded neatly there, just waiting for me. On the floor beneath the chair were my flat brown boots, with a trouser sock tucked into each one. Shaking my head slightly, I pushed my way out of the oversized bed—I had to be careful getting out, as it was a good deal higher than what I was used to—and went over to the chair. After picking up the stack of clothing, I wandered down the hall, found the bathroom in the same place I'd left it last night, and set my clothes down on a marble-topped chest at the far end, under the window. Sure enough, sitting on the counter was my little striped cosmetics bag. All the necessities were tucked away inside: toothbrush, deodorant, moisturizer, even my purple container of birth control pills. So much for Luke using me to conceive the Antichrist.

I poured some water into the heavy glass tumbler I found next to the sink, popped a pill, then went over to the shower to turn on the hot water. Like my own bathroom, this one had a separate tub and shower stall, but there the similarity pretty much ended. In keeping with the rustic, Tuscan-villa feel of the house, this bathroom was completely tiled in shades of cream and rust and dark blue. Every so often one of the tiles had a little hand-painted vine-like design on it. Although the place had probably been built in the early '20s, the fixtures were up-to-the-minute Moen pieces that looked as if they should be in a museum. The water was hot, and felt wonderful. Inside the shower I found my regular Biolage shampoo and conditioner, along with the vanilla sugar soap I loved so much.

All in all, everything had been provided to make the experience as enjoyable as possible, and I felt myself relaxing as the glorious massaging shower head pounded hot water against my neck and shoulders. No matter how great the sex, the aftermath can be messy, and it felt awfully good to get clean again.

Then I thought I sensed movement out beyond the frosted glass of the shower door. I froze, soap still in my hand. The door opened, and Luke stood there, naked as I was, and obviously ready for another go-round.

"I decided I couldn't wait," he said, and entered the shower. Reaching out, he pulled me against him, then smothered my mouth with his as his hands moved to cup my breasts.

After the first second of shock, I responded with equal passion. How many times do you get to make love in a shower, after all? Reaching down, I took him into my own hands, using the soap as lubricant. His breathing grew harsher and more rapid. He leaned back against the tiled wall, his eyelashes dark crescents against his water-flecked cheeks.

The orgasm came quickly. I had a quick thought that it helped to do this sort of thing in the shower—no muss, no fuss. But after a few seconds of slumping against the wall, Luke straightened, then slowly knelt, his lips moving down my torso until his mouth reached the damp triangle between my legs. And then it was just his tongue, and the waves of pleasure that pulsed through me until I almost collapsed. My shaking fingers found the metal bar of the washcloth hanger, and I gripped it so I wouldn't fall down in a heap on the floor of the shower stall.

He stood, his hair looking almost black as it lay wetly against his head. His breathing still sounded a little hurried, although nowhere close to the post-marathon gasps I was taking. That heart-stopping smile touched his lips. "Mind if I borrow some of that soap?" he asked.

Eventually, of course, we made it out of the bathroom and down to the enormous kitchen, which faced out on an equally expansive backyard that featured a black-bottom pool and an artfully landscaped herb garden off to one side. Land was at a premium in this part of town (well, to be honest, it was at premium almost everywhere in Southern California), and I wondered how much this little piece of Tuscany in L.A. had cost. Five million? Six? But I guessed housing prices were just a number when you happened to be the Devil.

"How do you like your eggs?" Luke asked. "Oh, wait—scrambled well. Right?"

Again, there was no point in asking how he knew that. Instead, I inquired, "So do you actually cook?"

"Of course not. Eating, as with so many other mortal...activities, is an enjoyable occupation, but I'm afraid I don't feel the same about cooking."

He pointed to a smaller chamber that opened off the kitchen, sort of a sun room, but one which obviously had been intended as an adjunct eating area. Windows framed it on three sides, offering an excellent view of the herb garden, which probably would have looked more welcoming if the skies hadn't turned gray and brooding again. People seem to think it's always sunny in Los Angeles, and maybe we have more sun than a lot of other parts of the country, but January through March was our rainy season. This year in particular had been fairly wet, although the walkways outside looked dry for the moment.

Right after Luke gestured in that direction, breakfast just sort of…appeared. Plates of eggs and bacon steamed gently into the air, a rack of toast materialized in the center of the table, and a pot of coffee and a mug sprouted into existence next to each plate.

"Nice trick," I said. "I should have you come over to help with my laundry."

He didn't bother to reply, but instead shook his head, then went to the table and sat down. I followed him and took a seat as well, unfolding my napkin and putting it in my lap before I helped myself to a bracing swallow of strong coffee.

Was it possible that I could still trade casual remarks with him as if last night's intimacies had never happened? But I supposed that was the way things usually worked out; after all, we couldn't spend the entire day mooning into each other's eyes and having sex. Then again....

I could feel the familiar warm sensation grow in the pit of my stomach. Whether it was the afterglow from our shower escapades or a tactile memory of the way he had felt inside me the night before, I knew I was ready for him again, wanted him once more. Did he sense it? Did he feel the same way?

At that moment I didn't think I could trust myself to look directly at him. I lifted a forkful of eggs to my mouth, tasted, and gave a nod of approval. "Just the way I like them," I said. Of course.

Even though my eyes were cast down toward my plate, somehow I felt the weight of his gaze on me. "Good. You know I want only to please you."

That comment finally made me look upward. How many women would kill to hear a man say those same words to them? Was I a horrible person for still wondering, even after the night we had spent together, what exactly his plans for me were?

The other thing that made me more than a little uneasy was the fact that I could sit here and try to second-guess him, yet still know I loved him. Oh, I couldn't have said why, exactly. It was more than his good looks, the solicitous way he treated me, or even his sly sense of humor. Add to those the way the hair waved back from his brow, the sound of his voice, the million and one other things that made him uniquely Luke, and you might have a start. Maybe.

I guessed he was expecting a response, so I said, "Oh, you've definitely pleased me—no doubt about that."

"And you've pleased me as well." He smiled. "More than pleased me. Mankind's obsession with the physical act of love makes much more sense to me now."

Shocked, I said, "So you'd never—"

Eyebrows lifted, he replied, "There's not much opportunity for that sort of thing in Hell, I'm afraid."

Well, damn. I set down my fork and stared at him. His face wore its usual half-amused expression, but something about the set of his mouth told me he didn't want me asking a lot of questions. If I'd even known which questions to ask.

I figured it was better to leave it alone. If Luke wanted to confide in me at some later point, then he could. If there was one thing I'd learned in this life, it was to keep my mouth shut when it became obvious that my questions were unwelcome.

I said lightly, "You're an awfully fast learner, then."

Some of the tension seemed to go out of his jaw. "Thank you, Christa," he replied.

We ate in silence for a few minutes, and then he said, "So what would you like to do today? I'd thought of perhaps going to the beach, or over to the Huntington Library in San Marino, but the weather doesn't look as if it's going to cooperate with outdoor activities, I'm afraid."

I followed his gaze out the window and saw that it had in fact begun to rain again. It was the sort of day that made you just want to cocoon, to stay indoors and explore the offerings on Netflix, listen to music, or even randomly surf the cable TV stations to see if anything caught your fancy.

"No weather control?" I teased.

"That power lies with a greater authority even than mine," he said gravely, although I guessed he was teasing me back…just a little.

"Well," I said, after I had drained the last of my coffee and set down the mug, "I think I know of a few indoor activities that should keep us busy…."

I couldn't see myself, of course, but I think for the first time the gleam in my own eyes matched the one in his.

As it turned out, I didn't make it home until almost eight o'clock that night. Even then I had to plead exhaustion as well as a certain soreness—there are limits to how many times a woman can have sex in a twenty-four-hour period, no matter what the porn industry might want people to believe. Luke finally relented and drove me home, my evening gown packed carefully in a little case he gave me that also contained my shoes and my cosmetics bag.

I would have come home earlier, using my undone laundry as an excuse, but he'd only laughed and said it was taken care of.

And so it was—after he left, I went into my bedroom to stow the gown in my closet and saw that everything had already been washed and hung up, or folded and put away in my dresser. Talk about your modern conveniences; the Devil was obviously the ultimate labor-saving device.

At last I remembered to dig my cell phone out of my purse. The little alert icon for a missed call was showing on the home screen. It never failed. Holding back a sigh, I pushed the button to call voicemail.

"You have five new messages," the machine voice intoned once I connected, and I winced. Why was it that no one ever called when I was actually sitting around and *waiting* for a call?

The first one was from my sister and time-stamped around seven-thirty the previous evening. "Christa, call me as soon as you can. I'll try your email, too."

The second call was from Jennifer. She said she knew I was probably out with *him* (her emphasis, not mine), but that we really needed to get moving on the whole bridesmaid dress thing, and when would I be available to come into Pasadena for a fitting?

Not any time soon, I thought, but I made a mental note to call her back.

The third call was once again Lisa, this time at around nine o'clock this morning. "I don't know where you've gotten to," she said, sounding increasingly waspish. "Did you forget to charge your cell phone again? Call me as soon as you can."

Calls four and five also came from my sister, the last one clocking in only about twenty minutes before I got home. By the end she sounded as if she could have cheerfully twisted my head off at the neck. "I don't know what's the matter with you," she snapped. "People have cell phones for a reason. Did you go out of town or something?"

True, I probably should have remembered to check my phone, but honestly, I'd gotten tired of the attitude people have where they think you should be reachable twenty-four/seven. I mean, how the hell did they think we all managed back when we only had—God forbid—land lines?

Deep cleansing breaths, I told myself. After all, she wouldn't have called that many times if it weren't important.

Still, I wasn't looking forward to the scolding I knew I was going to get when I finally did call Lisa back.

I sighed, willed myself to remember what a fabulous evening (and morning, and afternoon) I'd spent with Luke, then picked up the handset and dialed my sister's home number. It was a Sunday evening, so she should be in.

The words "hi, Lisa, it's Christa" were barely out of my mouth before she went into full-blown attack.

"Where the hell have you been? I've been calling and calling—"

"Yeah, I know that," I said. "I had a date."

"All weekend?" she demanded.

"Well, actually, yes."

A few seconds of silence as she digested that statement. Then she said, "Fine, but why didn't you take your cell phone with you?"

"I did have it. I was just…busy."

"Okay, whatever, but while you've been off playing footsie with Danny, I've been holding down the fort over here."

"I wasn't with Danny," I said.

Another silence. "Fine, whatever, I don't need to know the sordid details of your personal life. All I do know is that Traci's in the hospital, and Dad's a wreck, and you've been MIA the whole frigging weekend—"

I cut in. "Traci's in the hospital? What happened? Did she—" And I paused, unsure as to the best way to phrase the question. Had she lost the baby? Was that why my father was a "wreck"?

"She slipped and fell on the patio Saturday afternoon, and then she started spotting. Dad took her over to Hoag, and they think they have everything stabilized, but there's a very good chance she's going to be spending the next five months off her feet."

Ouch. Being a bum every once in a while and spending the day in bed or on the couch while you read or watched movies was one thing. Having to stay flat on your back for months at a stretch, especially for someone as active as Traci, would be a complete nightmare. "That's awful," I said at last.

"Yeah, it is, and I've been staying with Dad as much as possible, but I have about fifty gazillion phone calls I need to return. You sure picked a hell of a weekend to go AWOL."

Nothing like a good old-fashioned scolding from your big sister, especially one served up with a side helping of extra guilt. "Look, I said I was sorry. What do you need me to do?"

"Visiting hours are over at nine. Dad's still at the hospital, but he needs someone there with him, and I've already been there most of the weekend." Lisa paused and said, "If you left right away you'd probably still make it in time. Earlier today the doctor said they might let Traci go home as soon as tomorrow afternoon, but that's still iffy. I've got a home tour tomorrow morning that I just can't miss, so I need you to stay down there."

Which meant calling in sick to work. Not a huge deal—I hardly ever got sick, so I had a bunch of leave on the books. And luckily this issue of the magazine was mostly wrapped up. Still, the thought

of having to babysit my father all day and act concerned about Traci to boot didn't appeal very much.
Maybe there was something just wrong with my
moral makeup, but I hadn't been thrilled about this
baby in the first place. Frankly, I was more worried
about my father's reaction than anything else.

But Lisa had already done her duty, and it was
time for me to take a shift. "All right," I said. Luckily,
I was already mostly packed, since I hadn't yet put
away any of my toiletries. I could just throw some
clean underwear and a change of clothes in the little
case Luke had given me and get out the door in
less than five minutes. On a Sunday night the traffic
should be fairly light, and if I didn't hit any snags on
the freeway, it was conceivable that I could make it
to the hospital before nine. "I'll be out of here in a
couple of minutes."

Lisa didn't bother to say thank you. "I'll let Dad
know you're on your way," she replied, and hung up.

I'd just started to head down the hallway to
my bedroom when the phone rang again. Great. I
hoped it wasn't Lisa with a fresh round of guilt. That
sort of thing could really slow a person down.

I looked at my cell phone's screen; it was my
father on his cell. I snatched up the handset. "Dad?"

"I'm glad I caught you." He sounded a little har-
ried, but not too bad, considering.

"I'll be on my way in just a minute—"

"It's really not necessary. I tried to tell Lisa that, but you know how she is when she gets the bit between her teeth."

Did I ever. Once she had a notion lodged in her brain, it took dynamite to blast it out. Part of me thought uncharitably that she was probably just angry with me for being out of touch all weekend and wanted to send me running off down to Orange County even though there might not be a good reason for me to do so.

"Are you sure?" I asked. I tried very hard not to let any relief show in my tone. "I really don't mind coming down to help out."

"Traci's tired and already asleep. I wouldn't want to wake her up. And the hospital gave me a list of at-home care professionals. I've got someone meeting me at the house in an hour to get things prepared. I appreciate the offer, but there's really no need for you to come down here. Maybe in a day or so, after Traci's settled back at the house and ready for visitors."

He sounded calm and plausible, just as he probably did when speaking to one of his patients. But he was there and of course had a much better idea of what Traci did and didn't want. Frankly, I didn't think I'd really appreciate a vaguely hostile stepdaughter seeing me if I were in her condition.

"All right," I replied. "If that's what you both want."

"It is." He paused, then said, "I know you were less than thrilled when you heard about the baby."

I opened my mouth to utter some sort of denial but realized that was useless. My father wasn't stupid, after all. "Well, it just seemed a little…strange," I said, after stopping to wonder whether I should be honest or diplomatic. At that point, though, I was too tired to be diplomatic. "I mean, you're going to be retirement age when the kid is just in elementary school."

"Men my age become fathers every day."

Somehow I doubted it, but I didn't want to get into a raging argument on the subject. "Okay, maybe in Hollywood," I admitted. "But we're not exactly celebrities. Whatever. I know you can certainly afford to have a baby, and if Traci wanted one, then fine, I guess. It's just…" I trailed off. Maybe this wasn't the best time to be having this conversation. On the other hand, I didn't know when I'd have the opportunity again to talk to him one on one. I decided the hell with it. "It's just that it seems to me as if the family you had wasn't enough. Like you wanted to try again so you could get something better."

"You know that's not true."

No, I don't, I thought. *I mean, you dumped Mom so you could trade up for a better model, so why not do the same with your kids?*

He went on, "I will always love you and Lisa and Jeff. Having another child isn't going to change any of that. I've always done my best to be there for you, even with the divorce."

I wanted to argue, but that much was true. Even though my graduation from college had come post-divorce, while he was courting Traci, my father had made it a point to attend the ceremony, and had handed me the keys to my car that very same day. At the time his generosity had floored me, although he'd laughingly dismissed my stammered protests that it was too much. "Just think of how much money you saved me by graduating in four years and not being on the six-year plan," he'd said, and wouldn't hear any more on the subject.

"I also want you to know that I appreciate your offer to come help," he added. "I know you're not particularly fond of Traci."

I would have done it for him, not her, but I didn't bother to tell him that. "I'm really sorry about being out of contact," I murmured.

He chuckled. "Ah, that. Lisa was definitely beside herself. That must have been some date."

Blood flooded my cheeks. Thank God my father couldn't see my face. I managed to say, "Uh—yeah, it was."

"I take it this is someone new?"

No hesitation with that reply, anyway. "Yes."

"He must be pretty special."

"What makes you say that?"

"I don't know—you sound different More cheerful." Still with that little bit of a laugh in his voice he asked, "You're not pregnant, too, are you?"

"God, no!" A baby was definitely the last thing I needed, but I had pretty irrefutable biological proof that I wasn't pregnant. "No—it's just—he's—well, yeah, he is amazing, actually."

"Good," my father said. "It's about time someone showed up who was good enough for my daughter."

And that, Alanis, I thought, *is irony.* I had a sudden urge to burst out laughing, but I only said, "He's a great guy."

The phone beeped in my ear, and he said, "I'm getting another call. Give me a call tomorrow afternoon, after I've gotten Traci settled. Plan?"

"Plan," I replied, then took the phone into the dining room and set it on the side table so I could charge it.

As I headed back to my bedroom for the second time, a disquieting thought surfaced in my mind. Had Luke known that my sister had been desperately trying to get in touch with me for most of the weekend? I wasn't sure how this whole omniscient thing worked. Obviously he possessed knowledge about everyone around me, even though for some reason he couldn't get inside my head (thank God… literally). Did being the Devil mean that you were tuned into everyone's lives at once? Or maybe his powers functioned more like satellite TV—the stations might be broadcasting all the time, but when they were accessed and for how long was in the control of the person with the remote.

I had no idea. Even if I had asked him to explain his powers to me, I wasn't sure I could have understood. After all, the human mind, intricate as it is, has its limits.

So all right, maybe I should assume he had known. And if I assumed that, then he had deliberately kept me occupied all day even though my family needed me. I chewed on that thought for a moment and decided I didn't like the taste very much. Up until now Luke had been the soul of consideration, the very antithesis of his supposed persona, but maybe there really was a darker side lurking in there. After all, he *was* the Devil.

A full moon broke out of the clouds just as I reached up to close my bedroom curtains. A silvery wash of light shimmered against the puddles in the courtyard below, and I paused to stare down at it.

Maybe Luke really hadn't known anything. After all, he'd admitted to me a few days ago that he wasn't completely omniscient. Still, he'd been awfully familiar with my family and their activities…too much so, actually.

Brooding about it wasn't going to help the current situation, though. I pushed those nagging thoughts away as best I could while I got ready for bed. By that point I was so bone-weary I thought I'd fall asleep the second my head hit the pillow, but for some reason sleep had decided to run off to the Bahamas.

I couldn't stop thinking of Luke, the way his arms had felt around me, the scent of his skin and how my body responded to his. An aching wave of desire passed over me, and I curled my hands into fists, willing it away. My doubts suddenly seemed silly and foolish in the face of my need.

I don't pray, but that night I prayed I would dream of him.

CHAPTER TWELVE

I DIDN'T DREAM AT ALL. It figures. I should have known from my futile pleading with God in the parking lot of St. Gregory's that he wasn't listening to me. Or maybe he was, but wanted to see how I would handle all this on my own. Maybe this was some sort of test. If so, I got the impression I was flunking pretty badly. Somehow I found it hard to believe that God actually wanted me to be having hot monkey sex with the Devil, but it was a little late to be worrying about that now...especially when the aforementioned sex was the best I'd ever had.

The next morning felt like ten Mondays instead of just one. My in-basket looked depressingly full, considering we'd just finished shipping off the last issue of the magazine. The one guarantee about my job was that the cycle never ended. No sooner were you done with one month than the next was poised to get started, all shiny and eager like a new puppy.

No email from Luke, either, which both puzzled and worried me. I hoped he wasn't going to turn into another Danny—I'd had enough of the whole on-again/off-again thing to last me a lifetime.

And guess who showed up around ten-thirty? None other than Mr. Industrial Espionage himself.

He walked straight into my office, removed the stop that had been holding the door open, and let it close behind him. Then he said, "We need to talk."

"Hi, Danny," I replied, still glaring at the half-ed-ited article on my computer screen. Did no one in the world know what a comma splice was anymore? I added, in conversational tones, "You know, I could get you and Victor fired for that crap you pulled last week."

At least he didn't bother to deny it. "I was des-perate," he said.

Giving up, I swiveled my chair away from the computer screen so I could face him and then took off my glasses. "Give me a break."

"Well, I had to do *something*. Here you'd taken off with this rich, good-looking guy, and—"

"Wait a minute," I said, frowning. "How do you know he's a rich, good-looking guy?"

Danny flushed, then apparently found some-thing really fascinating to stare at in the weave of the carpet at his feet. Finally he mumbled, "Zach followed him."

I screeched, "*What?*" even as Danny winced. Good thing he'd shut the door.

Looking as if he'd be perfectly happy for the earth to open up and swallow him at that point, Danny said, "It was Zach's idea. He'd found this whole article on the Internet about how to follow people so they don't know you're following them… some CIA guy wrote it or something."

I found it more likely that it had been written by some high school kid with an overactive imagination, but whatever. Geeks could be so gullible sometimes. "So when did this James Bond maneuver take place?"

"Uh…a week ago Saturday night."

"I was in Orange County that Saturday," I pointed out.

Danny's face twisted, and for a second his pleasant features looked downright ugly. "So you said… but Zach saw this guy's Jag parked in front of your house."

I hadn't, but that meant absolutely nothing. After all, Luke was a master of letting people see only what he wanted them to see. "That doesn't explain why Zach was there to see it."

"Because even though you'd said you were going down to Irvine to see your mom, I had a feeling you'd be seeing him again. And I was right."

"So you sent Zach out to spy on me because you were too chickenshit to do it yourself?"

He flinched, but answered, "No, Zach volunteered to do it. That's what friends do for each other."

I wasn't sure if engaging in morally—if not legally—suspect behavior was exactly the best way to prove your friendship with someone, but the Lone Gunmen had always followed their own weird code of what was right and what was wrong. "So Zach followed Luke from my house back to his place."

"Right. And he told me the guy had this huge mansion, and at least two other expensive cars besides the Jag, and—"

Interesting. I'd only seen the Bentley. I wondered what else Luke was hiding in his garage. Fixing a look of what I hoped was bored contempt on my face, I asked, "So is being rich and owning nice cars a crime?"

"No," Danny said. "But Christa—this guy's the Devil!"

"And what evidence do you have to support that, except for a few comments I made in a private blog that you guys hacked? Maybe I was making a joke. Maybe," I added, thinking of my father and his love for Carl Jung, "I was just using that as a metaphor, a way to express the shadow that people repress."

As usual when I'd said something that he didn't entirely understand, Danny ignored that last comment. "Whatever," he sneered. "That doesn't explain how this guy can leave his house driving one car and then come back driving the other one."

"Maybe he was picking one up from the mechanic's or dealer's and leaving the other one behind," I suggested.

"Nice try, but Zach thought of that. He went and peeked in the garage window and saw that big green thing—"

"The Bentley."

"Yeah, that, and then like half an hour later the guy comes driving up in the same car! Explain that." Danny crossed his arms and shot me a triumphant look.

Well, I couldn't explain it, because I knew it was entirely possible that Luke could have left the house with one car, become disenchanted with it for some reason, and swapped it out when everyone in the vicinity's head was conveniently turned. I also knew I couldn't admit that to Danny, so instead I went on the defensive. "Great, so Zach looked in the garage. Now we can add trespassing to the list of misdemeanors involved here."

"Like anyone's going to care when we tell everyone that the Devil is living here in L.A.!"

Despite the fact that I knew no one would probably believe him, I still felt a little trickle of unease thread its way down my spine. The last thing I needed was for Danny to go public with this whole mess. If nothing else, I really didn't feel like explaining the situation to my family if I could possibly avoid it.

"Go ahead," I said, knowing the only way to handle this was to call his bluff. "All it will get you is a hot date with a straitjacket and some serious anti-psychotics."

For the first time Danny appeared a little unsure of himself. Maybe the comment about the straitjacket really had gotten to him. It also looked as if he'd decided he had committed himself to this course of action and so was determined to see it through to the end. "You'd like to think that," he retorted. "I talked to my priest, and he said it's entirely possible the Devil is walking amongst us."

I quelled the urge to jump over the desk and throttle Danny with his badly knotted necktie. "All that proves is that your priest is as crazy as you are," I said, not caring how rude I sounded. "From what I've read, the Catholic Church really isn't that keen to get involved in discussions about the Devil. Your priest may be old school, but I doubt he's going to get much support from his higher-ups."

That appeared to stymie him for a moment, but then Danny said, "Yeah, but you know what's really interesting about this whole discussion? Not once have you said, 'No, Danny, he's not the Devil.'"

"'No, Danny, he's not the Devil,'" I said immediately, with a curl of the lip. "Feel better?"

"No." He crossed his arms and glared at me. "Because I know you're lying."

"Really? Have you developed psychic powers all of a sudden?" Maybe the scorn I injected into my voice would help cover up my growing sense of unease.

"No," he replied, his eyes boring into mine. "But I know you." And with that parting shot he threw open the door and marched out. He probably would have liked to slam it behind him, but it was on one of those overhead gas spring thingies and would never have cooperated.

I stared at the shut door for a moment, thinking of all the things I should have said and didn't. Then, because I couldn't come up with anything better, I said, "Well, shit."

My mood didn't improve any when I finally got a chance to log into my personal email account, only to find a terse email from Luke. *Business takes me away,* it read. *See you on Thursday evening.*

Great. Just great. Not for the first time I wondered exactly what this "business" of his was and why he, as the Devil, couldn't bend his schedule to fit his own needs. Of course, there had to be Someone above him calling the shots, but what did that mean, precisely?

I didn't know, and it seemed as if I wasn't going to find out any time soon. Scowling, I hit the "respond" button and typed, *Call before you come over, please,* then sighed and backspaced over what I had just written. That sounded too curt, even if I did happen to be more than a little ticked off. Instead I wrote, *I hope everything is all right. Could you please call before you come over?* and sent it off into cyberspace before I could second-guess whether I was being a doormat or not. After all, the beginning stages of a relationship were difficult enough without factoring the whole supernatural-being element into the equation.

Was Luke playing games? Pursuit, followed by evasion? Did he think that was the sort of thing I enjoyed? Well, I didn't, and if he thought he could get away with it just because he'd gotten me into the sack, he was about to discover he was sadly mistaken.

The phone rang. I picked it up and barked, "What?" before I stopped to think that probably wasn't the most professional way to answer the phone at work.

Jennifer's voice. "Geez, Christa, who woke up on the wrong side of the bed this morning?"

"Oh…sorry," I said. "I thought you were someone else."

"I'd hate to think who." She paused, then asked, "Are you having problems with Luke already?"

Already. Now there was a nice, confidence-inspiring thing to hear from a friend. I said, with some asperity, "I wouldn't call it problems. He's just busier than I would like. I won't get to see him again until Thursday."

"Well, there is such a thing as taking a relationship too quickly. You don't want him to think you're totally needy, do you?"

"No," I replied slowly. So what if I found myself craving his touch, the sound of his voice, that smile of his the way an addict craves a crack pipe? I needed to be an adult about this. "I, well—I miss him. But at least he did say he'd see me later this week."

"There you go," Jennifer said, with a false heartiness in her voice I didn't buy one bit. Her tone lowered conspiratorially as she went on, "I have a foolproof plan for you."

"What?" I couldn't say I completely trusted Jennifer's advice about men. She hadn't dated much in college, but I had to say that once she found her target—Phil, the guy who was going to be the big-shot surgeon—she zeroed in like an ICBM. Maybe she knew something I didn't.

"Pot roast," she said.

"Excuse me?"

"So it sounds like he's been wining and dining you, taking you out and showing you the town. But you should really make him dinner."

"Gee, what a great idea…except for the fact that I can't cook." This was her big plan to keep Luke firmly at my side?

"You can follow directions, can't you?"

"Well, yeah."

My unenthusiastic tone must have been getting to her, because Jennifer said, a little waspishly, "Cooking is just following directions. I have a great recipe for roast that you do in the crock pot—set it up before you leave for work in the morning, and you'll gave a great dinner when you get home. I'll email the recipe to you when I get home tonight and can pull it up from my desktop there."

"Pot roast, huh?" Not that I had anything against roast; my mother used to make a great one back in the days before she decided meat was murder.

"Yes," Jennifer said. "I made it for Phil, and three days later he proposed. Coincidence? I doubt it."

I protested, "Look, Jen, I'm not really trying to get Luke to propose to me—"

"Go to the kosher butcher up on Third," she continued inexorably. "He's got great roasts."

"Kosher?" I asked. My mind was spinning. "But we're not Jewish." At least, I wasn't, and I sort of doubted that Luke followed any religion, for obvious reasons.

"That's got nothing to do with it. Kosher butchers have great cuts of meat because they've got to follow stricter rules. My friend Sarah told me that in high school."

Sarah and Jennifer had been best friends since third grade or something, and Sarah was going to be Jennifer's maid of honor (thank God, since that was more work than I thought I could deal with at present). I started to ask what Jennifer was doing discussing roasts with Sarah back before they had even graduated from high school, then thought better of it. Jennifer's goal had always been wedded bliss. If she'd lived a hundred years ago, she would have been one of those girls who had her hope chest stocked before she even turned sixteen.

Okay, fine, I'd bow to a higher authority. What I didn't know about roasts could probably fit into a cookbook of its own, but if this recipe was as foolproof as Jennifer said....

"He does eat red meat, doesn't he?" Jennifer asked, sounding suddenly suspicious. Old school in every way, she'd had a nasty bout following some tofu my mother had sprung on her unexpectedly back when we were in college and she'd come down to Irvine with me for a long weekend.

Now that I stopped to think about it, I'd never seen Luke eat anything except red meat. I would have said he was just an über-crazed paleo-diet follower, except that pretty much all those servings of red meat had been matched with equal helpings of potatoes or some other equally heinous carbs.

"Oh, definitely," I replied.

I couldn't see her face, but the feeling of relief that rippled down the phone line was practically palpable. "Thank God," she said. "Anyway, I was actually calling to see if you could make it up to

Pasadena for a fitting this Saturday afternoon. Nina said she's available, and Micaela has some time off for once because they just went into an emergency rewrite and halted production for a week."

That couldn't be good. Still, I knew it happened every once in a while, and if the shutdown gave Micaela a few treasured days off, more power to her. I hated to commit time when I had no idea what (if any) plans Luke had for the weekend, but to be fair, Jennifer had the first claim on my time.

"Sure," I said. "Just tell me when."

"Two o'clock at Abbey Rose. It's on Green Street."

"Got it," I replied, jotting furiously on the little pad I kept next to the phone. "I'll see you then."

"I can't wait to hear how the roast worked out for you," Jennifer burbled, and then hung up.

Neither can I, I thought, and wondered exactly what I'd just gotten myself into. Then again, I'd always heard that the way to a man's heart was through his stomach. I'd just have to see whether that particular piece of folk wisdom could be applied to the Devil as well.

I did email Luke again to tell him that I wanted to cook dinner for him on Thursday, and at least he replied to tell me that sounded wonderful. Now all I had to do was put the whole thing together without it turning into an unmitigated disaster.

The kosher butcher, a sweet man by the name of Saul Eisenstein, fixed me up with what did look like a lovely sirloin-tip roast. All I had to do was tell him that I was making dinner for my boyfriend, and he was all smiles, telling me it was so good to see a girl actually cooking for her man. He hoped I would eat plenty, since I looked awfully thin. I smiled and thanked him, blushing a little that he would consider me too slender (since in L.A., as everywhere else, popular thought had it that one could never be too rich or too thin. As a size six in the land that created the double-zero, I felt like a heifer sometimes). I made my escape clutching a paper-wrapped parcel before he could start pushing anything else on me. I figured it was better to get through this one roast before I went on to anything more ambitious.

Thursday morning I got up a half-hour early to prep everything. I felt a little nervous, since cooking was definitely not my area of expertise. But I followed Jennifer's instructions step by step and found it really wasn't as hard as I'd thought. She'd even told me how to nuke the potatoes for a couple of minutes in the microwave before putting them in the crock pot, since they didn't cook at the same rate as the meat. I actually did own a crock pot, unbelievable as that might sound. Traci had given it to me for Christmas a few years back, and at the time I'd thought it was about the most useless present I'd received in a long while. It had been sitting, forlorn and neglected, in the back of one of my cupboards, but I promised it that if everything turned out okay tonight, I'd give it lots more use in the future. Anyway, I layered in the ingredients as instructed, then threw in a cup and a half of port, the "secret weapon," as Jennifer referred to it in the recipe she'd emailed me.

Somehow I resisted the urge to run home at lunch to check and make sure everything was all right. Maybe it was Jennifer's dire warnings about what would happen if I lifted the lid to the crock pot prematurely, or maybe it was just my habit of not really wanting to know the worst until absolutely necessary. Whatever the case, I kept myself busy all day, then skipped the gym and made a beeline for my apartment exactly at five o'clock.

The smell that greeted me when I opened the door was beyond heavenly. I hurried into the kitchen and peered as best I could into the crock pot. Since the lid was coated with heavy condensation, I really couldn't see much. But it smelled fine, so I had to assume everything was all right and go ahead with the rest of my dinner preparations. They weren't terribly involved, since the bulk of the meal was of course residing in the crock pot, but I still had to set the table, run to the bathroom and wipe down the countertops, and generally make sure everything was as ready as I could make it. I'd told

Luke to come over around six-thirty, since it was a weeknight, and I didn't want to eat dinner too late.

I'd just pulled out the Caesar salad kit I'd bought the day before and stuck some rolls into the oven to heat up when I heard the knock at the door. The whole day I'd been feeling mildly irritated with Luke for abandoning me for most of the week, but right on cue my heart began to beat a little faster once I knew he was outside on the landing. God, I was such a pushover.

"For you," he said, when I opened the door, and handed me a smallish pink box, the sort you get from a bakery.

"Uh, thanks," I replied, then pushed the lid open with one finger so I could see what forbidden fruits lay inside. I wasn't sure exactly what it was, except that it looked luscious and dark-chocolate-y.

"Chocolate truffle tort," Luke said.

"It looks fabulous," I managed, although I couldn't help wondering how many extra laps I was going to have to do on the treadmill to work off that particular bit of decadence.

Luke stepped past me into the living room, then stopped and gave an appreciative sniff. "That smells wonderful."

"I hope so," I said, moving on to the kitchen so I could put the cake in the refrigerator. "I'm kind of new to this."

"If it tastes even half as good as it smells, then I'm sure it will be fine."

Surprisingly, it actually did turn out to be very good. The meat was so tender that even with my less than optimal cutlery Luke was able to slice it easily, and the gravy and vegetables were equally delicious. From somewhere—I didn't see him bring it in, not that it mattered—he produced a bottle of lovely Bordeaux, and it really brought out the seasonings in the roast. All along I'd been thinking that the meal had to be a dismal failure, since pretty much every movie I'd ever watched or book I'd ever read had the heroine flubbing royally whenever she attempted to do something similar, but I'd actually acquitted myself pretty well. Whether that was due to some heretofore untapped culinary talent or whether it was simply because Jennifer's recipe actually was, as she claimed, foolproof, I wasn't sure. I supposed it really didn't matter one way or another.

The whole time I wanted to ask Luke what he'd been up to the past few days but didn't quite dare. After all, he did have Hell to run, even if he managed occasionally to leave things in the hands of a subordinate. I also wanted to inquire as to whether he'd known about Traci's incident of the previous weekend, but again my cowardly side took over. I decided it was probably better not to ask.

At least I scraped up the courage to inquire, "Did you know that Danny had one of his loser friends follow you back to your house?"

Luke smiled, his glass of Bordeaux poised a few inches away from his lips. "Of course."

"And you're not going to do anything about it?"

"What would you suggest?"

Good question. I lifted my shoulders, then said, "I don't know. But it seems as if you shouldn't just let them get away with it."

He gave a shrug to match my own. "They're harmless. If it amuses them and makes them feel as if they're in control of the situation by following me around, then let them."

Sometimes Luke seemed awfully *laissez-faire* for the Devil. "Fine," I replied. "But Danny keeps threatening to expose you for what—who—you really are."

"He can try."

I sipped at my own Bordeaux and raised an eyebrow.

Luke went on, "Even if by some miracle he convinced someone in authority to investigate me further, they would find nothing. I have everything an upstanding citizen of this country should have— Social Security number, clean credit record, no history of trouble with the law. They could even perform a complete physical on me and still find no anomalies…although I would prefer to avoid a full body-cavity search if possible."

"Very funny," I said, although I was far from amused.

"Don't you think I would have done everything in my power to make absolutely sure I blended seamlessly into this world of yours? What would be the point otherwise?"

That was the real question, wasn't it? What, precisely, was the point? His revelation the morning after we'd slept together that he'd never been with a woman before sort of shot down my "lay of the century" notion. After all these millennia, why would he choose to be physically intimate with a mortal woman? I was no Helen of Troy; mine certainly wasn't a face that could have launched a thousand ships or caused a man to start a war. Up until Luke, Danny was about the best I thought I could do.

I set down my fork and gave him a direct look. "Why don't you tell me what the point is, Luke?"

He didn't pretend to misunderstand me. "That again."

"Yeah—it'll be 'that again' until you actually give me a straight answer."

"Do you have so little confidence in yourself?" he inquired. The blue eyes met mine; unfortunately, I was the first to look away. "You're bright, beautiful—"

I made a disbelieving noise.

He continued without pausing, "I think you're beautiful. And if I feel that way, what should it matter what the rest of the world thinks?"

"So you're saying the rest of the world doesn't think I'm beautiful?"

For the first time Luke began to appear a little impatient. "No, that's not what I'm saying. For whatever reason, you have these preconceived notions about yourself, that you're merely adequate, the girl others overlook—"

"Well, watch me show up at a party with Nina and see how many guys pay attention to me instead of her," I snapped.

Unperturbed, Luke replied, "A wise man once said, 'Comparisons are odious.' Why do you persist in comparing yourself to someone who is so obviously different from you?"

"Well, because—because—" I flailed about for a moment, then muttered, "because it's just what people do."

"People often do stupid things," he said. "Don't be one of them."

I couldn't really argue with that. Comparing myself to others and invariably coming up short was something I'd been doing since I could remember, starting with my over-achieving sister and ending with Nina, whose outstanding gorgeousness was enough to put almost anyone in the shade. Was it so hard to accept that Luke might have seen something in me no one else had? Normally I would have said yes, except for the fact that he was here, sitting in my apartment, and telling me how wonderful he thought I was.

"All right," I said at last, then smiled. "Ready for some dessert?"

"I thought you'd never ask," he replied. He stood and took me by the hand, pulling me against him and giving me a warm, Bordeaux-flavored kiss.

Oh, yeah. That was exactly what I wanted. I kissed him back, pressing up against his body, and then we proceeded to the much-anticipated finale to the meal.

And the chocolate torte wasn't bad, either.

Interlude

BEELZEBUB HAD HALFWAY EXPECTED to be called in for this interview. After all, *he* had been spending a great deal of time away from Hell; it was only natural that *he* should expect some sort of report of the goings-on during *his* absence.

Good thing *he* had been so distracted, or he might have noticed that *his* trusted lieutenant had been AWOL a good deal of the time as well. Beelzebub had tried to limit his times in Vincent Nguyen's head to the occasions when the young man was actually in Danny's presence. Extended possessions could be exhausting, and there was no point hanging around in that unfortunate specimen's cramped cranium when he was going about his daily duties or hunched for hours over a computer desk, playing some infernal online game.

So Beelzebub felt fairly confident that he'd put in enough face time here in Hell that no one should have noticed anything too out of the ordinary. Still, he knew he had to be on his guard. Despite *his* current unfocused state, the Lord of Hell was no fool.

He waited now in an audience chamber at the palace. Why it was called the palace, Beelzebub wasn't sure. "Palace" conjured for him images of fluffy human excess, and this building—this fortress—was anything but fluffy. Constructed of slabs of black basalt, with slit-like windows through which an unceasing chill wind blew, it had never been intended for comfort. Not even Lucifer was allowed that distraction, here in the heart of *his* kingdom.

A door on the far side of the room opened, and he entered. At least *he* had discarded the ridiculous human garments *he'd* been wearing topside; dark robes flowed around *his* tall form as *he* approached Beelzebub.

Still, *he* looked different, and for a few seconds Beelzebub couldn't say exactly why. Then it struck him.

Lucifer, the Prince of Darkness, looked happy.

Well, that wouldn't do at all. Happiness had no place in Hell. Hell was supposed to be the very antithesis of happiness. And yet here was its overlord looking as if *he* were about to burst out whistling at any moment. *He* practically glowed as *he* halted a few paces away from *his* servant.

There could be only one explanation.

He must have gotten laid.

Beelzebub clenched his jaw. It was one thing for Asmodeus to commit a series of libidinous indiscretions every time he set foot on Earth. Minor philandering could be overlooked if necessary, and Beelzebub had long since given up on changing his fellow demon's lusty ways. But it was quite something else for proud Lucifer, the lord of the underworld, to have surrendered *his* honor to some whey-faced little mortal who wasn't worth even a second's consideration.

Although he fought to keep his face expressionless, some flicker must have caught his master's attention. *He* frowned, then asked, "Is there something you'd like to say to me, Beelzebub?"

At once Beelzebub inclined his head. "Not at all, my lord. I merely wait to give my report."

He waved a hand. "Report, then."

"An attempted breakout in the Fourth Quadrant has been suppressed," Beelzebub said.

Really, when would these lost souls learn? There was no place to run. Even if the guards let them leave the heavily secured zones where the damned were kept—for their own protection more than anything else—all they could do was wander the trackless wastes of the underworld until they met up with something far more frightening than the demons who'd been set to guard them. There was no death here, of course, but dismemberment hurt now just as much as it had when the prisoners were alive. The only difference was that they'd receive no relief in death. They'd only continue to hurt until one of the guards came along and sent them back to one of the safe zones.

His mouth compressed slightly, but all *he* did was nod.

"And the guards in the Second Quadrant are requesting that the next batch be sent to either Three or Four. They say it's getting too crowded."

Usually *he* would have asked a few questions at this point, but again all Beelzebub received for his trouble was another abstracted nod.

He said, "That's all. It's been quiet."

Then he paused for a second, gathering his thoughts. While he had no idea exactly what sort of deal his master had worked out with the man upstairs (Beelzebub refused to even think His name), he guessed that time was of the essence. After hearing Danny's report on how Christa had reacted to his attempts to get her away from Lucifer, Beelzebub knew she was made of tougher stuff than he had originally thought. At the very least, it seemed clear that she had a stubborn, independent streak, something he wouldn't have expected of someone who seemed so outwardly insipid. And so he'd come up with a plot that he thought might just work.

Assuming an expression of mock concern, he added, "If I may, my lord—"

His eyes, which had seemed focused on something very far away, snapped back into focus. "What, Beelzebub?"

"You seem…preoccupied. Is it the girl?"

If the Lord of Hell's eyes had seemed focused before, now they seemed to narrow into a pair of dark-blue laser beams. "So you know about that?"

"Nothing much, my lord. Your business is your own. But since some were inquiring as to your frequent absences of late, I did a bit of checking. Pardon my presumption."

Then he waited, hoping he had managed to impart the correct mixture of arrogance and apology to his tone. A too-meek Beelzebub would arouse his suspicions immediately.

"I suppose you think I've lost my mind."

"As I said, my lord, your business is your own."

He crossed *his* arms and said, "You would be correct in that."

This remark's delivery was so mild it could hardly be called a rebuke, but Beelzebub heard the touch of steel within.

Careful, he thought.

Then he replied, "Still, anyone who has known you as long as I have, my lord, would have noticed a change in you. A lightness, if I may be so bold."

He said nothing, but merely lifted an eyebrow.

Since it hadn't been an outright denial, Beelzebub felt he should press on. "But now you seem…troubled."

"Is it that obvious?"

"Only to one who knows you well, my lord."

His eyes went unfocused again, shuttered. Beelzebub guessed *he* was thinking of that silly chit. Then *he* murmured, "This is proving to be more difficult than I had thought."

"My lord?"

"Things seem to be going well, but I keep thinking I should do more."

Beelzebub held his tongue. He feared any comment now might prevent his master from continuing to say what was in *his* thoughts.

The Lord of Hell turned away from him and toward one of the narrow windows. *His* hair ruffled slightly in the wind that blew through the chamber. Still in that quiet, contemplative tone, *he* went on, "I've done everything I could think of—wined and dined her, listened to her concerns about her family, been there for her in every way. And yet she still hasn't said it."

Said what? Beelzebub wondered, but he knew better than to ask. Still, *his* words had given him the perfect opening.

"If I may, my lord—"

His master turned. "You have a suggestion?"

"My lord, it seems that young women enjoy it when men give them gifts. I would suggest that you give her something she's truly wanted, whether it's some bauble, or something a bit more…substantial."

"Substantial?"

Now or never. "Is there something she feels she lacks in her life? A better home…perhaps a more fulfilling career?"

That seemed to sink in. *He* nodded, eyes narrowing. "She has expressed some dissatisfaction with her current position."

"Well, then. It would seem your way is clear, my lord."

Again his master was silent. Another nod, and then *he* turned and swept from the room without so much as a farewell.

Not that Beelzebub minded the curtness. Courtesy was not a currency much in use in Hell. Besides, it seemed he had planted a seed in *his* mind, one he hoped would bear dark fruit.

He somehow guessed that his master's paramour would have a slightly different reaction from the one *he* expected.

CHAPTER THIRTEEN

ROGER MCKINLEY, THE MAGAZINE'S EDITOR, called me into his office the following morning. Now, Roger and I didn't normally have much contact besides the usual handing-off of layouts to proof, or the occasional phone call where he needed me as backup on some fine point of grammar or syntax because a freelancer was giving us grief over something we'd changed in an article. I liked Roger, but my job just didn't require a lot of one-on-one contact with him.

As usual, he looked vaguely rumpled and a little unfocused. Roger was a native of Southern California, just as I was, but he had always looked sort of English to me, too pasty for Los Angeles. Someone could have cast him as Tim Roth's younger brother with no problem.

Feeling somewhat uneasy, I took the seat he indicated and folded my hands in my lap. I hoped I hadn't committed some heinous copy-editing *faux pas*, but even if I had, Jacqui was technically my supervisor, and it would have been her place to give me a dressing-down.

"Well, Christa," Roger said. His pale brown eyes, which always reminded me of weak tea, were focused somewhere above my right shoulder. I resisted the urge to twist around in my seat to see what he was actually looking at. "It appears Brian has decided to leave us."

"Really?" I asked, wishing I didn't sound quite so much like a complete idiot. The news surprised me, though; I knew Brian had been less than thrilled to be passed over for the position Roger now held, but I hadn't thought he was upset enough to actually leave the magazine.

"Really," Roger repeated. "Apparently he was just offered a position at TMZ, and he's decided to take it. Can't blame him—it's a good career move."

I nodded, and wondered why Roger had bothered to call me into his office to tell me this. Maybe he wanted me to organize a farewell party or something, although that was usually the sort of thing Jacqui would do.

"At any rate, that leaves the feature editor position open. I'd like to give it to you, Christa."

For about five seconds I just sat there, staring at him, wondering if something had gone catastrophically wrong with my hearing. Had Roger just offered me an *editorial* job?

Oh, it was something I'd secretly dreamed about. My degree was in journalism, after all, and even though I liked copyediting, I had to admit there wasn't anything very glamorous about it. From time to time I'd written little snippets for our News section or done anonymous restaurant and movie reviews—you know, the little pieces that are only a paragraph or two long and are always just attributed to "Staff." But it was kind of a leap to go from that sort of thing to the actual feature editor position, which was basically second-in-command to Roger.

My vocal chords decided to function again. "I—I'm honored, Roger," I began, and he waved a hand.

"Don't tell me that you're honored," he said. "Tell me if you'll take it."

"I'll take it," I said immediately. I might have been shocked, but I wasn't stupid.

"Wonderful," he replied. "I'll let Jacqui know. Of course she'll have to start advertising for your replacement, so I'll have to see how soon you can actually start writing. But I have a few assignments I know Brian probably won't get to, so I'm going to email those to you so you can start planning."

I stammered a thank-you, and he smiled. "Glad to have you on board," he said. "I always thought you were wasting yourself in the copyediting position."

The ringing of his phone saved me from having to make a reply; I just nodded and walked out of the office, wondering when I was going to wake up.

It took me about an hour of bliss before I began to smell a rat.

The euphoria lasted through my informing Jacqui of the promotion and sending off some excited emails to family and friends. She was happy for me, of course, but her happiness was tempered by the fact that she was losing her copyeditor. Looking for new people is never fun, and although a lot of the time the editorial assistant would have naturally been moved into that position, this time around it wasn't really an option. Stephanie, the current E.A., had only been on the job for about three months. Although she was fine for certain elements of her position, she wouldn't know a misplaced modifier if it came up and slapped her across the face. Also, I had the feeling Jacqui had hoped that one day I'd take her job, even though being the managing editor wasn't really my cup of tea. Frankly, I hadn't really looked forward to dealing with bickering advertisers and babysitting the production staff.

Whereas feature editors got to go to film premieres and gallery openings, interview local movers and shakers, and generally lead a fairly exciting life. And that didn't even take into account the sizable bump-up in salary which accompanied such a promotion. It was also the only editorial position I would ever have had a true shot at, since I wasn't really qualified to be the fashion editor, and as for being the food editor—well, that wasn't going to happen in this lifetime. Still, I was younger than any of the other editors by at least a decade, and I'd always thought I'd have to do some serious time at the magazine before I would ever be considered for such a lofty position.

All in all, it sounded too good to be true… which meant that it probably was.

Luke?

Of course. He could probably snap his fingers and make me President of the United States. Thank God my ambitions never reached that high. But my current situation was just as problematic, if on a slightly lesser scale. I'd accepted the job, which meant I'd have to do my damnedest to be as good at it as I possibly could. I just didn't know if my best would be good enough. It wasn't quite like working at *Time* or *Newsweek* or even *Vogue* or *Harper's Bazaar*, but the position of feature editor, besides the obvious perks, carried a lot of responsibility with it. Any screw-ups would be highly visible.

And what should I do next? Confront Luke with my suspicions? That would be the right thing to do—get it out on the table, let him know I didn't appreciate him meddling with my life in such a high-handed way.

Whether or not I'd actually have the guts to do that was an entirely different proposition.

The phone rang. I started, then peered at the display. My mother. I supposed that made sense; she was on her home computer pretty much all day, so naturally she'd be the first to get the email.

I took a deep breath, then reached over and lifted the handset.

"Christa, that's wonderful news! I'm so proud of you!"

Right then having my office chair swallow me whole sounded like a pretty good proposition. Unfortunately, it showed no inclination to do that, so I was forced to reply, "Um…thanks, Mom."

Her voice sharpened a little. "You don't sound very excited."

"Oh, I am, I really am," I said hurriedly. Whatever doubts I might be having, I knew I certainly couldn't pass them along to my mother. One of us should be enjoying this, if nothing else, and I wasn't about to open the whole "my boyfriend is the Devil" can of worms. I couldn't do much about Danny and his adolescent predilection toward spying on me, but I sure as hell wasn't going to start spreading that information voluntarily. "It's just a big step. I guess I haven't really processed the fact that I'm going to be an editor yet."

"Well, you'll do great, I'm sure. Those awards you won for journalism, your grades—I knew you'd get there one day."

I wanted to say that I really didn't think a couple of second-place finishes for articles I wrote for the high school newspaper qualified me to be in line for a Pulitzer, but whatever. For all her airy-fairy clothing, rampant veganism, and general save-the-planet mentality, my mother wanted her children to do well. In an enlightened and responsible way, of course, but having a daughter who was feature editor at the biggest regional glossy rag definitely was going to earn her some points.

"It's exciting," I said, after a pause that I could only hope she didn't notice. "I'll get to go to a lot of fun events and meet interesting people. I won't be stuck in the office all day."

I should have known what was coming next.

"It would be great if you could cover more social issues, and include more vegan restaurants in your reviews."

People's agendas constantly amazed me. I never really had any, besides making it through another day and maybe at some point finding someone that I thought I could share the rest of my life with. Maybe my mother's constant crusading had turned me off the whole socially conscious thing. She'd just never gotten over the Berkeley mentality. At least she hadn't taken to growing pot hydroponically in the garage. I hoped.

The fact that she thought I could somehow turn the magazine into a force for good made me want to burst out laughing, though. Although we did the occasional "in-depth" piece on some hot-button local issue, the truth was that we existed to cover a certain type of lifestyle, a lifestyle that only a small fraction of the population actually enjoyed but one which a whole lot more people aspired to. It was sort of like me buying *Vogue* and poring over all the gorgeous couture clothing inside; I certainly wasn't going to run out and purchase a thirty-thousand-dollar Versace gown, but that didn't mean I didn't like to look at it. There's always the vague hope that maybe someday your circumstances would change, and suddenly you'd be eating at the Ivy and driving around in a Bentley.

Hmm. Well, I supposed I'd gotten the Bentley part of it already (sort of), although I didn't see too many Versace gowns on my horizon.

At any rate, the only way we'd be covering the sort of stuff my mother was interested in was if one of her pet causes became the latest in thing in Hollywood. Maybe that was more likely now than it had been a decade earlier, but I still wasn't going to hold my breath on any crusades for raw food any time in the near future.

I had an out on that one, though. "Uh, actually, the food editor covers restaurant reviews and interviews with chefs and that sort of thing," I told my mother. "I'd be covering people in the community, local events, that stuff."

"Well, it's still very exciting," she said. "So when do you start?"

"I don't know for sure. It kind of depends on how quickly they can get a replacement for me in here. I may be having to juggle both jobs for a little while." That was going to be a party, but Roger had made it sound as if he wanted to start transferring some articles to me right away. Oh, well, a little overtime never hurt anyone.

We chatted for a little while after that, not about much in particular, and then I said I needed to get off the phone and back to work. My office is fairly relaxed on the whole personal calls thing, but I still didn't want to abuse it. Besides, what I really wanted to do was ask my mother how she felt about the whole Dad/Traci baby mess, even though I knew work wasn't the place to do it. So I just shoved that particular question to the back of my mind and hoped I'd have a better opportunity to discuss the situation in more depth at a later date.

After that I got congratulatory emails from Jennifer and Nina (who said we needed to have another martini night to celebrate) and a quick note from my sister that sounded pleased but had a certain undercurrent of snottiness I couldn't quite put my finger on. Maybe she couldn't bear to think that she might not be the Golden Child of the family for a whole five minutes.

Roger stopped by to give me a press kit and a pair of passes to an upcoming "Women in Film" festival that was going to take place the following week. "Your first big assignment," he said, smiling a little. "I've assigned Lee to do the photography, so mainly what I'm looking for is an overview of the event, some good quotes, mini-reviews of the spot-lighted films—that sort of thing."

I nodded, hoping I didn't look as terrified as I felt.

"H.R. is getting together a press photo badge for you," he went on. "It should be ready by the end of the day. You've got two passes to the festival, so feel free to take a plus-one."

"Thanks, Roger," I said. Well, at least for once I'd be the one taking Luke somewhere interesting instead of always the other way around.

To my surprise, Roger gave me a conspiratorial wink, leaned forward slightly, and said, "The first one is always the hardest." Then he straightened up and sauntered out, leaving me to stare at the materials scattered across my desk and pray that I really could pull this off.

In one of those weird "Coincidence? I don't think so" moments, Luke called a while later to offer his own congratulations. I'd blind-copied him in the list of people I'd sent the email to, but normally he wasn't that quick to respond.

He wanted to take me out to dinner to cele-brate, and where did he propose to take me?

The Ivy. Of course. Now, Luke had told me he couldn't read my thoughts, but maybe he'd been lying about that as well. Or maybe he'd just figured it was about the hippest place he could think of to take me. I didn't know, and challenging him then and there didn't seem like a very good idea. So I said that sounded like a lot of fun, agreed that sev-en-thirty would be fine, and then hung up, already stressing about what I should wear.

Under normal circumstances, a mere mortal like me wouldn't have had a chance of getting a good table at the Ivy on a Friday night, especially at such short notice. However, although I was a mere mortal, Luke certainly was not, and I guessed he'd be able to wrangle the best seat in the house. Even A-list celebrities didn't stand a chance in a smack-down with the Devil.

So while I wasn't worried about getting snubbed by the maitre d', I didn't want to embarrass Luke or look out of place. As always in matters of sartorial confusion, I picked up the phone and called Nina.

I had to catch her on her cell; it turned out she was driving up to Malibu to supervise the installa-tion of a pricey piece of modern art in some pro-ducer's oceanfront mansion.

"The Ivy, huh?" she asked. I could hear a weird background whistling noise and guessed it was the wind blowing across her sunroof. Nina tended to drive with it open as long as rain wasn't actually falling. The day outside was actually quite pretty, from what I could see through my office window—big puffy white clouds, dark blue sky. It wasn't really warm enough to be driving around with an open sunroof, though.

"Yep," I said. "I tried looking up some references online, but the most I could get was 'dressy casual.' Isn't that an oxymoron?"

"Not in L.A.," she replied. "Probably not a dress—it'll look as if you're trying too hard. I'd say your most expensive pair of jeans, a jacket, and a nice camisole underneath. And a really good pair of strappy shoes."

The priciest jeans I owned were a pair of dark-wash True Religion pants that I'd found at Loehmann's for the bargain basement price of ninety-nine bucks. That was a huge savings off retail, but if it weren't for the fact that they made my butt look great, I would never have spent even that much. I still worried that somehow my mother would find out how much I'd paid for them and give me grief over my extravagance. Actually, Loehmann's was my best supplier of designer duds at copyeditor prices— pretty much the rest of the ensemble I started mentally assembling had come from there as well. The shoes (a pair of sling-back Jimmy Choos), however,

I'd snagged at the Barney's warehouse sale at the Santa Monica airport.

"I think I can manage that," I said.

"I want a full report. Food, celebrity sightings, everything."

"Deal. Thanks for the help."

"No prob," Nina said, and then I heard her sigh. "Whoever thought I'd be living vicariously through *your* social life?"

Not me, that was for sure, but I was also pretty certain Nina wouldn't really want to hear that. I just said, "Oh, it's not that big a deal. I'm sure regular people eat at the Ivy, too."

"Name one. Besides yourself, that is."

"Uh—" I actually didn't know anyone who had gone there. It was a little out of my price range and that of most of my friends, even Nina.

"Exactly. Listen, gotta go—I'm pulling up at the house now."

I said good-bye and hung up. At least with Luke picking me up a little after seven I would have plenty of time to get myself pulled together. No time for a hair appointment or anything like that, but my hair was actually pretty easy to deal with. Naturally straight and thick, it just required a few passes with a ceramic iron to get it to premium gloss. Besides, anything else, and it would look as if I'd fussed with it too much, which according to Nina was a no-no. I wasn't about to comment on the irony of spending a lot of time getting ready so that it would look as if you hadn't spent a lot of time getting ready.

I also didn't want to stop and think that maybe I was obsessing over preparing for dinner because that way I wouldn't have to think about how I could possibly confront Luke over my precipitous promotion.

Considering our destination, I figured Luke would show up in the Bentley. The Jag was beautiful, but compared to Bentleys, they're a dime a dozen in Southern California. But after I followed him down the steps and over to his customary premium parking spot, I stopped dead, wobbling a little on my Jimmy Choos.

Sitting at the curb was a gleaming piece of silvery blue metal so elegant and muscular that it could only be one thing. I looked over at Luke, raising an eyebrow.

He actually grinned. Oh, I'd seen him smile quite a bit, but there was a world of difference between the sort of subtly amused smiles he'd given me in the past and the look of unadulterated glee he flashed me now. "I've always had a sneaking desire to be James Bond," he said, and opened the door for me.

I couldn't help laughing. Was it possible for me to still be angry with him on one level and yet still so thrilled by his presence, by the odd flashes of the person I thought I could see sometimes beneath the outer sophistication?

Apparently it was, since just sitting that close to him in the lush yet high-tech interior of the Aston Martin succeeded in getting my heart rate and respiration up to seriously elevated levels. I'd recognized the car right away; I'd seen all the latest Bond films (up until I'd met Luke, I hadn't thought anyone could wear a suit better than Daniel Craig). Besides, I probably knew more about cars than I had any right to, thanks to my father's automotive obsessions. Well, Danny had mentioned seeing a third expensive car in Luke's garage, even though he hadn't identified it. Maybe Zach, the spy, hadn't recognized the Aston Martin for what it was. Zach had his own geeky fixations, but I didn't think he'd was much of a James Bond fan.

"Hiding any more exotic automobiles?" I asked, after we'd pulled away from the curb and were heading west on Wilshire. The thrumming power of the V12 hidden under the hood seemed overkill for the Friday night stop-and-go traffic that choked the streets.

"No," Luke said, turning right on Robertson. "The house only has a three-car garage, unfortunately. Maybe I should expand it."

"What, you want one for every day of the week?"

Another flash of that boyish grin. "Maybe."

Whatever else he might be doing on earth, obviously the Devil was having fun playing with the big-boy toys. Not that I could blame him. Cars can be very sensual things, and I suddenly wondered what it would feel like to be blazing at wide-open throttle on a deserted highway somewhere, to hear that massive engine really perform in the way it had been intended, to sense the speed of the asphalt rushing beneath me at velocities that were definitely not legal anywhere west of the Autobahn.

"It's very sexy," I said, wondering a little at my own daring.

He didn't look over at me, but I could see one of his eyebrows lift slightly. "You like it better than the Bentley?"

I said, with a curl of the lip, "Didn't you tell me yesterday that comparisons were odious?"

That got a laugh. "So I did. I must confess to wanting to make something of a splash. Even Bentleys can be seen around town, but the dealer assured me there were only three of this model currently in Southern California. I figured those were fairly good odds."

"Unless Jay Leno is eating at the Ivy tonight, too."

He shook his head, grinning. "We'll find out soon enough."

The restaurant was coming up on our left; somehow Luke managed to maneuver the car around to make a U-turn that brought us up directly in front of the valet station. Even in a place as used to money, celebrities, and upscale automobiles as the Ivy, I could see heads turn as Luke made his way over to the sidewalk. A valet hastened to open the passenger door for me. Maybe the restaurant's patrons were trying to see if Luke and I were famous. After all, who else would be riding around in a car like that?

Praying I wouldn't wobble too much on my spike heels, I took Luke's hand as he helped me out of the Aston and on to the maitre d's station. The Ivy is known for its outdoor dining, even in the winter, but Luke had secured us a premium table near the fireplace in the front room, for which I was glad. I didn't have a problem with *al fresco* dining when the season allowed it, but I never understood the logic in huddling under those outdoor gas heaters and trying to pretend it was still eighty degrees out when everyone was bundled up in coats.

I couldn't be sure whether it was because they really did think Luke was the local version of James Bond or simply that "doors opened" for the Devil. Whatever the reason, we were shown to our table immediately by a staff that was all smiles. Once we were seated, I kept shooting surreptitious glances around the room, trying to see if I recognized any celebrities, but although most people there were glossy and perfect, they didn't look famous.

"I promise I'll tell you if any movie stars show up," Luke said from behind his menu.

"I wasn't looking," I said hastily, opening up my own menu.

The familiar sly smile was back. "Of course you weren't."

Our waitress appeared, as flawless as the restaurant's patrons, and Luke said, "I think a bottle of champagne is in order, considering why we're here." He glanced up at the waitress and requested some Cristal, then said, "I think you'll find that lobster goes very well with champagne."

"I can imagine," I replied, giving him a smile that felt weak even to me. Champagne. Great. Now how was I supposed to tell him I didn't think I should be celebrating at all?

To cover up my growing unease, I pretended to peruse the menu, scrutinizing it the way an IRS agent would dissect a questionable tax return. Luke was right—the lobster salad would probably go best with the champagne, and that way I'd still have enough room for dessert. I'd heard the desserts here were fabulous.

Then the waitress came back with the champagne and a silver bucket, and proceeded to push out the cork without the precious liquid inside fizzing up or spilling. That was a talent I lacked, but I supposed it was one you'd have to develop quickly if you were opening bottles that cost hundreds of dollars.

We placed our orders. Luke waited until the waitress had gone before he lifted his glass of champagne and said, "To your recent promotion."

I managed to mumble a thank-you and sipped my champagne. This was my first Cristal, and I had to admit it was awfully good. I actually could taste a difference between it and the lesser champagnes I'd drunk in the past, and I'm the first person to admit that my palate is far from developed. The bubbles seemed to evaporate in my mouth, and it had a wonderfully light taste that somehow reminded me of clover honey and almonds.

"That's amazing," I said, after I had helped myself to a second and third sip.

"Just another of this world's distracting pleasures," he replied, and his gaze seemed to rest on my mouth for a few seconds.

I had an acid flashback to how his lips felt pressed against mine, and a slight shiver worked its way down my spine. It just wasn't fair that he should be so damned attractive, so completely charming in his way. How was I supposed to fight against that? I wasn't sure I even wanted to. Okay, so he'd pulled a few cosmic strings and gotten me the job of my dreams. So what? It wasn't as if he'd offed Brian in order to get me the feature editor position. In fact, Brian had come out ahead in this particular diabolical machination, since he'd gotten *his* dream job at TMZ. No harm, no foul.

That was just self-serving rationalization, though, and I knew it. Luke couldn't go around disturbing the order of the universe just because he was trying to impress me or get on my better side. The truth of it was that I already cared for him; I didn't need favors or presents or other disguised bribes to get me to open my heart. Too late for that.

"Um…about the job, actually," I began, after I'd braced myself with a few more swallows of Cristal.

"Yes?" The blue eyes were unreadable.

"You didn't…I mean, did you…did you have anything to do with that?"

A long silence. The voices of the people around us rose and fell in their various conversations, but I couldn't distinguish any individual words. The sound was as impersonal and meaningless as surf breaking on a shore.

Finally Luke said, "Yes, I did."

I hadn't expected him to admit it so casually. What I also hadn't expected was the wave of anger that rushed over me. He'd replied as if the whole thing didn't really matter very much. When I spoke again, it was in a tone of choked fury that I still hoped wouldn't carry to the next table. "How *could* you?"

"How could I?" he repeated, looking a little confused. "How couldn't I, when it was something you wanted so much?"

"Because—because—" I found myself spluttering, and then had to regain my composure when the waitress appeared with my lobster salad and Luke's crab cakes. I managed to wait until she had departed before I snapped, "Because it's wrong! This is my career we're talking about, not a pair of shoes I saw in a store window!"

"Calm down," Luke said. His mouth still had its usual wry twist, but I thought I saw a hint of puzzled anger come and go in his eyes.

There were very few things that irritated me more than someone telling me to calm down. It was so condescending. "I am perfectly calm," I replied, striving to make my tone very cool, very cutting. "I am merely pointing out that what you did was wrong."

He took a sip of his champagne. "How so?"

"Because a job like this was something I wanted to earn for myself! I didn't want it just handed to me on a silver platter!"

"Oh, I see," Luke said. He gave me a sardonic look, complete with lifted right eyebrow. "Like the way you earned that car you drive?"

Well, of all the—I gritted my teeth and told myself that flinging a butter knife at his head probably wasn't the best response. "That was a *present*," I shot back.

"So was this," he returned, imperturbable as always.

Of course I knew the situations were completely different, but at the moment I was so angry I couldn't think of any way to articulate the finer points of the disparity. Cristal is meant to be sipped, but I just seized my champagne flute and downed the rest of the glass, then poured myself some more. Maybe if I got drunk enough I wouldn't remember how much I wanted to throttle him at that moment. "If you want to give me a present, then buy me a necklace or something," I said. "You don't just gift-wrap a career and give it to someone. How am I supposed to know if I'm any good if I didn't earn that job for myself?"

"How much of anything have you 'earned for yourself'?" Luke asked, and for the first time I could see a little of my own anger reflected in his eyes. "Your education? Bought and paid for by your parents. The deposit on that quaint dwelling you call home? Your father, I believe."

"I got my current job on my own," I retorted. I didn't want to let him see how much his words had stung. It was true that my parents had paid for my college. I hadn't even worked much while I was in school; I put in about fifteen hours a week as an English tutor while Micaela held down two jobs in an effort to supplement her scholarships and student loans. Of course, Nina hadn't worked at all, but that didn't make me feel much better.

"True," he said. "Although I believe you first got the editorial assistant job because the publisher's wife was an old college friend of your father's."

"What?" I gasped. I hadn't known that. No one had ever said anything to me about a connection between my father and Mrs. Donnelly.

"Well, your father avoided mentioning it because he knew it would have upset you."

Arguing with someone who was in possession of far more knowledge of the situation than you could ever hope to have was definitely frustrating at best and demoralizing to boot. To my horror, I could feel angry tears begin to prickle at the back of my eyes. Was I so incompetent, so unqualified, that the only way I could get a decent job was to have someone give it to me as a favor?

"You shouldn't have told me that," I muttered, looking down toward my neglected lobster salad and forcing myself to eat some, even though my roiling stomach told me food was the last thing it needed at that moment.

"Typical," Luke remarked, and this time he made no attempt to hide the mocking edge to his voice. "You mortals never want to hear the truth, do you? You want to live in a make-believe world where everything goes as planned, where everything is orderly and neat. Let me tell you something." He leaned forward, and for the first time since I'd met him I actually felt a ripple of true fear pass through me. What looked out as me through his eyes definitely was not human. "The world isn't an orderly place. It's full of death and pain and despair."

"Then what are you doing here?" I demanded. "If it's so awful, why all the running around in designer clothes and the fancy cars and the house? Why the wining and dining and seduction? Why?"

"Because it's still better than Hell, you foolish girl!" Following that statement I thought I saw a few widened eyes at the next table, and Luke obviously did as well, because he lowered his voice before he continued, "There are forces at work here you couldn't possibly comprehend."

"Try me," I said, forcing a bravado I certainly didn't feel into my voice.

His gaze shifted away from me. Suddenly he looked very weary. "I can't tell you that."

"Can't, or won't?"

"I can't."

From his tone I knew that I would get no further on that line of inquiry. I also knew if I dropped it, then I still might have a chance of salvaging the evening. But my pride had suffered a stinging blow because of that revelation regarding how I'd actually gotten my first job at the magazine. Part of me wanted to hurt him for telling me something that wouldn't make any difference at this stage of the game. Angry as I was, I could also feel the hurt start to claw its way up into my consciousness, like the first flare of agony when the pain medication begins to wear off.

"You've told me I didn't have enough confidence," I said, forcing the words past the choking sensation in my throat. "Well, how is securing this job for me when I've done nothing to earn it going to make me feel better about myself? Don't you understand what you've done?"

He stared over at me, almost expressionless, except for the tension along his jaw line.

"You tried to buy my heart," I said, and finally the tears welled up past all my efforts to keep them at bay. I could feel them begin to trickle down my cheeks as I added, "And you didn't even realize it was already yours." Then I pushed my chair back and stood, turning and rushing blindly through the crowded restaurant and into the cold night air. I had staggered almost halfway down the block before I realized he hadn't come after me. I stood alone on the street corner, tears stinging on my face, while a couple walked past arm in arm and gave me a curious look.

Angrily, I reached up to wipe the offending moisture from my cheeks. At least I'd had the presence of mind to gather up my purse as I fled the restaurant. Feeling chilled to the bone, I pulled out my cell phone. I always kept the numbers of several cab companies programmed in there just in case of date disasters, and I called one of them now.

I didn't dare allow myself to feel or think. I just waited alone there in the darkness, until the cab finally pulled up and took me away.

Chapter Fourteen

SOMEWHERE A PHONE WAS RINGING. With a groan, I pushed the covers off my head and then blinked at the light filtering its way through the curtains. As soon as I recognized the sunlight for what it was, my brain started to throb. It took a few more minutes for my battered gray matter to process the fact that someone must be calling me. I groped for my cell phone where it lay on the nightstand.

"Christa, where the hell are you?" Jennifer's voice, sounding more than a little pissed off.

"Uh—" I blinked again, trying to focus on the clock that hung across the room on the wall above my dresser. It couldn't really be that late....

Apparently it was. "You said you were going to meet me at Abbey Rose at two. It's now almost two-thirty. Did you forget?"

Probably the brain cells that were supposed to retain that particular piece of information had been obliterated somewhere between the first and second bottle of wine. I sat up, and a swirl of stomach acid splashed up against my esophagus. Not good. "Sorry," I mumbled, praying I wouldn't vomit there and then. "I guess I did."

A long pause. "You sound terrible. Is everything all right?"

No, it most assuredly wasn't, but I didn't feel like getting into it right then. "I can be out the door in fifteen minutes."

"You're sure?"

I nodded, then realized that was a stupid thing to do, first of all because Jennifer couldn't see me, and secondly because it made my brain feel as if it were sliding around inside my skull. "Sure," I replied, after the room stopped spinning.

"All right," Jennifer said, but I could tell she was definitely less than thrilled with me. "I'll just have all the other girls get their fittings done first. It takes about fifteen to twenty minutes with each person, so that gives you an hour."

"No problem," I said, then hung up.

Not a moment too soon, because at that point I had to push myself out of bed and run down the hall to the bathroom, where I threw up the remnants of last night's pity party. After I was done, though, I actually felt a little bit better. I staggered to an upright position, brushed my teeth not once, but twice, and then finally got in the shower and turned the water on as hot as I could stand it.

All right, so coming home and getting completely smashed after my fight with Luke probably wasn't the most mature thing to have done. At the time, though, it had seemed like a pretty good idea. Anything was better than the horrible empty feeling that had taken over once I realized he wasn't coming after me. For the record, I don't have a habit of drinking away my problems. Once in college, right after Brad left for Stanford, I did have a bit of a lost weekend. The problem with using alcohol to erase painful memories is that, once the buzz wears off, you're left with a really nasty headache in addition to those painful memories.

But last night I had completely lost it. I'd wanted to forget the inhuman look in Luke's eyes as he stared at me, the cold contempt in his voice. For the first time since I'd met him, Luke had actually acted the way I expected the Devil to behave. And, to put it mildly, I hadn't liked it very much.

Was it all over, then? Certainly by leaving me to make my own way home, Luke had sent a very clear signal. He wasn't about to come crawling after me, and at the moment, as much as it hurt to think about never seeing him again, I wasn't going to ask forgiveness when I hadn't done anything wrong. Okay, causing a scene at the Ivy probably wasn't the best way to have handled the situation. But in this case I actually felt I had the moral high ground. He was the one who had trespassed, not I. Maybe I'd shown a lack of judgment by confronting him in such a public place, but if making a foolish decision were actually a punishable offense, pretty much everyone I knew would have had to put in some jail time at some point.

Still, I felt absolutely wretched, and it wasn't just because I had a raging hangover. Once I got out of the shower, I opened the medicine cabinet and popped a couple of ibuprofen, then threw on some moisturizer, a little lip gloss, and some mascara. I looked like crap—dark circles under my eyes, skin pasty and blotched, but I didn't have time to apply any spackle to cover up the worst of it. *Don't cry,* I told my decidedly wan reflection. *Your eyes will get red, and you'll look even worse than you already do.*

Then I ran a comb through my wet hair, pulled it back with an elastic band, and hurried into my bedroom to throw on a pair of jeans and a sweater. What I really wanted to wear was my rattiest, most comfortable sweats, but I had a feeling that wouldn't go over very well with Jennifer. At least this way I appeared halfway presentable as long as you didn't look too close. By then I'd already used up fifteen precious minutes, so I grabbed my purse and hustled out of the apartment, telling myself my head didn't hurt as much as I thought it did and that the pain-killers would kick in at any moment.

All I could do then was pray to whatever capri-cious gods ruled L.A. traffic that there wouldn't be any accidents or freeway construction to slow me down on the trip into Pasadena. On a good day, when cruising at the speed limit was actually a pos-sibility and not just a foolish dream, the drive only took about twenty minutes. But I'd had times when those fifteen miles or so stretched into an hour of agonizing stop-and-go traffic.

Today, though, luck seemed to be on my side. True, Sundays usually were the lightest days of the week in terms of sheer volume, but all it took was one person to make an error in judgment for the whole fragile construct to fall apart like a house of cards. But I got onto the 10 Freeway and cruised east at a little more than seventy miles an hour. At that rate I thought I might be able to buy myself enough time to pull into a Starbucks I knew on Arroyo Parkway and get myself some desperately needed caffeine. After all, Jennifer did have five bridesmaids, so they probably wouldn't get to me until almost three-thirty anyway....

Even in the middle of the afternoon there was still a line at Starbucks. It moved quickly, though, and I only wasted about five minutes getting my grande French roast and a bagel. Normally I'm not much of a bagel person, since I have a real sweet tooth, but I didn't want anything sugary for fear it might upset my already abused stomach. The coffee was divine, though, and just what I needed. At that point I was ready to inject it directly into my veins.

Abbey Rose was a little designer wedding boutique on Green Street, not far from the historic Castle Green apartment building. Street parking could be a nightmare, but I seemed to have inherited some of Luke's parking karma and found a spot only a few doors down from the actual shop. Clutching my caffeine fix and praying that I'd regained some color during the time that had elapsed since I last looked in a mirror, I opened the door and let myself into the boutique.

Any hopes that my appearance wasn't as bad as I feared got dashed when Micaela looked over at me above a drape of deep sea–green silk dupioni and said, "Girlfriend, you look like crap."

"Hi, Micaela, nice to see you, too," I retorted.

Jennifer paused to glance up from the two tiaras she held, one in each hand. "Seriously, Christa—are you coming down with something?"

"Getting over it, more like," I replied, and crossed the shop floor to take a seat next to Nina on the overstuffed pink couch that faced the display area. On Nina's other side sat Sarah, Jennifer's long-time friend. The last of the bridesmaids, a girl named Nicole whom I didn't know very well, stood off to one side, flipping through what looked like a shoe catalog.

"What happened?" Nina asked.

I lifted my Starbucks cup and tipped some French roast down my throat. "Luke and I had a fight last night."

A chorus of "ohhhhhs" swirled through the room. Nicole glanced up from the catalog she was holding. The girl hardly knew me, but obviously she was more than ready to hear some dirt.

Of course Nina went where others feared to tread. "What happened?"

That was a tough one. I couldn't tell them the real reason for our argument, of course. Lifting my shoulders, I replied, "Let's just say we had a difference of opinion," then realized I had parroted Luke's own statement about his quarrel with God. Not that I could exactly equate a lover's spat with the fall of angels from Heaven.

"About…?" Nina inquired.

I fell back on an old standby. "Well, it's private."

Micaela made a huffy noise, but that could have been because the gal who was adjusting the fit of her gown had stuck a pin into her. "So is this a 'kiss and make up' kind of argument, or a 'get the hell out of my life' argument?"

Good question, although the fact that I hadn't heard from Luke since I'd stormed out of the Ivy was definitely a bad sign. "Um…somewhere in between, but probably more the 'get the hell out of my life' type."

She hesitated, then said, "I'm sorry."

Nina leaned over and gave me a quick little hug. "If he can't see how great you are, then he's a total jerk—even if he is completely hot."

"Nina!" Jennifer said, sounding completely exasperated.

"It's all right," I said hastily. The last thing I needed was for the two of them to start bickering. "If it's meant to work itself out, then it will. If not...." I trailed off and lifted my shoulders. "Anyway, I had a bad night, but I'm doing better now."

"Of course you are," Nina said, in tones of false cheer. "'Cause you've got all your peeps with you."

"Damn straight," Micaela added. Finally the seamstress was done with her, and she was able to step down off the little dais where the fittings were performed. "Um—does this mean I don't get a crack at Danny?"

I saw Jennifer roll her eyes.

"He's yours," I said wearily. "Even if Luke and I aren't together, at least this whole thing has made me realize that Danny is definitely out."

"How long were you going out with this guy?" Nicole asked out of nowhere. Maybe she wanted to feel as if she were a part of the conversation.

"Just a couple of weeks," I replied, and Nicole looked a little puzzled.

"He drives a Bentley," said Jennifer in tones of heavy significance.

I figured I'd better not mention the Aston Martin. Jennifer liked to pretend she was above the whole material-wealth thing, but I knew better. There was no way she would have gotten engaged to Phil if she hadn't been assured of having a husband who was guaranteed to make in the mid-six figures. No doubt if she'd been dating someone with Luke's kind of money, she would have chained herself to the steering wheel of the Aston Martin before letting him get away.

"Oh," breathed Nicole, who looked even more confused. Obviously she and Jennifer were cut from the same cloth.

Part of me managed to be amused, but I also felt myself growing a little angry, too. To someone looking in from the outside, I supposed that losing a guy who'd only been around a few weeks certainly wasn't the end of the world. A little disheartening, maybe, but the sort of thing you were supposed to recover from without sustaining any permanent damage. The problem was that I'd let myself fall for Luke, and hard. I guessed I only had myself to blame; I should have been more careful, not allowed him to somehow worm his way past my defenses.

He's the Devil. What did you expect? I thought. *That he was going to sweep you off into the sunset on a white horse and that you were going to live happily ever after?*

"Earth to Christa," Micaela said, and I snapped my head around to look at her.

"What?"

"Boy, that guy really does have your brain twisted inside-out, doesn't he? I asked you if you wanted to go over to Crown City Brewery after this for some drinks and a nosh. You look like you could use it."

My first instinct was to say no. After all, I'd had enough to drink last night to last me for weeks. On the other hand, some solid food wasn't a bad idea. Maybe I'd just skip the beer and go straight to the munchies.

I guess I hesitated too long, because Nina chimed in, "Come on, Christa. It's Saturday...well, okay, it's not Saturday night yet, but there's no reason we can't go have some fun. How about you guys?" she added, looking over at Jennifer, Nicole, and Sarah.

Nicole and Sarah both appeared a little startled to have been included in the invitation. Jennifer said immediately, "I can't—I'm meeting Phil for dinner, so late afternoon snacking is out. Besides, I need to watch what I eat for the next few months. The last thing I need is to be too fat to get into my gown."

I doubted that would happen; Jennifer was the sort of person who weighed her food portions.

As if taking their cue from Jennifer, both Sarah and Nicole shook their heads. "I need to watch it, too," Sarah said, and since she tended to be a little plump, I could see why she'd beg off. Nicole probably just didn't want to come because she didn't know us very well. She was another high school friend of Jennifer's who also went to the same church.

"Sounds good to me," I said firmly, since both Micaela and Nina had faintly disgusted expressions on their faces. I just hoped Nina wouldn't trot out some remark about uptight white girls, or this could get ugly.

But apparently my olive branch worked, because Micaela grinned and said, "Food therapy. Maybe some shopping, too, on the way over. I haven't had a chance to get out and do anything for weeks, and my debit card's burning a hole in my wallet."

"Uh-oh," I said, and for some reason Nina and Micaela and I all burst out laughing.

I loved them all in that moment, for their energy, their concern over me, and their attempts, however clumsy, to turn the conversation away from Luke. Hey, it even worked—for a whole fifteen seconds there I didn't even think about him.

It was almost eight o'clock by the time I got home. By then I felt unbelievably tired, but also oddly relaxed, as if spending those few hours in the company of my friends had started me down the first steps to healing. I hadn't written off Luke, but I knew if things really were over between us, I still had other people in the world who cared about me. As I came around to the front of the building from the garage, I saw someone waiting on the bottom step. My heart gave a single wild throb before I realized it wasn't Luke but probably the last person in the world I wanted to see—Danny.

"I need to talk to you," he said, before I could even open my mouth to demand why the hell he was loitering there.

"Now really isn't a good time," I replied curtly.

"Please," he said, and there was such a look of puppy-dog pleading in his eyes that I felt forced to relent.

"All right," I said, dragging out the words with some reluctance. "But I'm really tired, so I hope this isn't going to take too long."

His face sort of lit up then, and I felt like even more of a heel. If he thought that by talking to me he could change things between us, he was sorely mistaken, but maybe it would be better to let him have his say and be done with it. At least I could try to get a little closure with this relationship, since Luke's and my split still felt like a raw, gaping wound that wouldn't stop bleeding.

Trying to repress a sigh, I mounted the stairs, with Danny following close behind. After I had let us both in, I asked, since I wanted to sound halfway civil, "Do you want something to drink? I think I just have some bottled water, but there might be a beer hiding somewhere in the back of the fridge."

"Water's fine," he said. Danny never had been much of a drinker.

I went into the kitchen to get the water and figured I could use some as well. The food at Crown City was good, but I was still dehydrated, even though I had waved off any and all offers of beer. Frankly, right then the idea of drinking anything alcoholic made me feel a little sick.

When I went back out to the living room I saw that Danny had sat down in the armchair. It had been his usual seat when he used to come over and we'd hang out in the living room, but it still felt strange to look at him sitting there when the last man to occupy that seat was Luke.

That thought made me want to cry. Instead, I swallowed hard and thrust one of the glasses at Danny. "Here," I said, trying to keep any betraying huskiness out of my voice.

He shot me sort of an odd look, but accepted the glass and took a drink. I sat down on the couch and stared back at him with what I hoped was a slightly quizzical but also impatient expression.

"Look, Christa," he began, "I know you're still pissed off at me, but don't you understand that I'm trying to help you? Do you have any idea what you've gotten yourself into?"

A whole lot of lonely nights, was my first thought, and again that awful ache welled up inside me. God, I wanted it to be Luke sitting here in my apartment with me, not Danny, who kept giving me that anxious schoolboy look. I had the random thought that maybe I should just tell Danny that Luke and I had broken up. Maybe then he'd finally drop the whole thing. On the other hand, he might get the wrong idea and believe I was having second thoughts about ending our relationship, and that I absolutely did not want.

"What have I gotten myself into?" I asked after a brief pause.

"You're acting as if this only involves your social life or something, but you're endangering your immortal soul by trafficking with this person!"

At first I wanted to burst out laughing. Then I wondered if Danny had quoted that line directly from his priest or whether he'd at least paraphrased a bit. "Don't worry about that," I remarked, after I felt I could keep a straight face. "Luke already told me I wasn't going to Hell."

"Of course he'd tell you that," Danny retorted. "He has sort of a reputation for making things seem all great at first and then *boom!* Eternal damnation."

"Spare me the fire and brimstone," I said wearily. "If I even believed in any of that, I would never have taken up with Luke in the first place."

Eyes blazing, Danny leaned forward, the water glass clenched in his right hand. He looked like one of those people who get up and testify on what my father used to derisively refer to as "Jesus shows."

"How can you not believe it, when the existence of this person you call Luke proves that Hell is real?"

"Okay, let me rephrase that," I replied. "Maybe Hell exists, but even Luke told me that it's different things for different people. It's not some one-size-fits-all torture park."

"He told you that?" Danny asked, and the light in his eyes altered suddenly. He went from looking like someone possessed by missionary fervor to a geek who had just gotten to test-drive the latest game console. "What else?"

"Not all that much," I said, and immediately Danny's face fell. Maybe he'd been hoping that I'd gotten a topographical map of Hell or some other nifty artifact. "He also compared himself to a prison warden rather than the most senior inmate. Makes sense, I guess, since God doesn't seem to have too much trouble with him running around up here and driving expensive cars."

A scowl etched itself into Danny's forehead. I guessed he was chewing over what I had just told him and deciding which element to attack first. Finally he said, "Well, of course he'd tell you something that would make him sound better."

"And how does that make Luke different from any other man on the planet?" I asked nastily, then wished I hadn't. Danny looked as if I had struck him. I couldn't take it back, so instead I added, "All I'm saying is that he hasn't done anything to cause me—or anyone else, as far as I know—any harm. Does that sound like the source of all evil to you?"

No harm except misjudging me so badly he thought I'd happily take a job I hadn't earned. No harm except breaking my heart.

A little melodrama, Christa? I thought, and gave myself the mental equivalent of a slap across the face. *One pity party per week per customer.*

"No," Danny said at last, sounding reluctant in the extreme. "But that still doesn't mean anything. Of course he'd be on his best behavior with you."

And he was, I thought, remembering the sound of his laugh, the look on his face when I opened the door and he saw me in all my opera finery. And the feel of his arms around me, and the warm, spicy scent of his skin. I clenched my hands into fists and felt my nails dig into my palms. At least the immediate pain helped to drive away thoughts of Luke.

"Look, Danny," I said, facing him squarely and praying that he'd actually listen to me for once, "you and I are never going to agree on this, so let me just tell you a couple of things so you can get them through your head once and for all. First off, Luke knows all about your amateur-hour Hardy Boys impersonations. He knows Zach was watching the house and spying on him. Luckily, Luke thought it was more amusing than anything else, so I expect Zach doesn't have to worry about retaliation."

I let that hang in the air for a minute. I'd purposely left off mentioning that Danny didn't need to worry about retaliation, either.

My ploy seemed to work; Danny stared at me for a minute, obviously trying to work it out, and then he paled visibly. Good.

"Second of all," I went on, not giving him a chance to say anything, "even if by some amazing stroke of luck you got someone with any real authority to believe that Luke is the Devil, there's no way to prove it. None. He's got bank accounts, a credit file, and any other sort of identification a legal adult would have in this country."

"But he's not even human!" Danny burst out.

"Physically, he is," I replied. "He assured me of that. Do a blood test—you won't find anything strange. Put him through an MRI, CAT scan, whatever—that body is as human as yours and mine."

"Oh, really?" Danny sneered. "How would you know?"

I crossed my arms and stared back at him for a long moment. If possible, he went even paler.

"You—you didn't," he stammered at last.

Maybe I was being cruel. I certainly hadn't planned to rub in the fact that Luke had made love to me and it was fabulous, but I also didn't intend to lie, either. I could have made a crack about not being the one who had taken a vow of celibacy. I didn't, though. I said simply, "You might not want to ask any more questions if you don't want to hear the answers."

Danny looked away. I could see the muscles working in his jaw and felt a sudden rush of pity for him. He wasn't a bad guy—he just wasn't the right guy for me. That didn't mean I should rub his face in the fact that I'd jumped into bed with Luke less than two weeks after meeting him.

"Third," I said, and I made my tone as gentle as I could, "we both know that it really wasn't working out between us. We just kept limping along because we couldn't think of anything else to do. So even if Luke and I stopped seeing each other, it wouldn't mean that you and I had any sort of future together. Isn't it time we stopped kidding ourselves?"

For a long moment he said nothing but just sat there, looking down at the glass of water he still held as if he'd suddenly forgotten what it was. Finally he replied, "I guess so."

A sense of cautious relief filled me after those words. I supposed that sometimes you just had to beat people over the head with things before they finally got the point. And Danny, for all his cleverness with computers and numbers, could be remarkably obtuse when it came to human interactions.

"Besides," I added, "my friend Micaela thinks you're cute and wants your phone number."

"She does?" he asked, and he lifted his gaze from the glass at last. The hopeful puppy-dog look was back. "Uh—which one is Micaela?"

"Micaela Torres? You know—she works as a P.A. at Warner Brothers."

He obviously had to think about who she was for a minute. After all, Danny had probably only met Micaela at one or two parties during the six months he and I had been together. Her schedule was so crazy she didn't have time for much of anything else. After a bit he said, "Oh, right. I remember her. She's kind of hot."

A few weeks ago, that comment would have irritated me to no end. Now I was just glad to hear it—at least he sounded as if he were ready to move on. "So I can give her your number?" I asked.

A brief hesitation. Then Danny said, "Actually, I think I'd like it better if you gave me her number."

So the warrior picks himself up and steels himself to try again, bloodied but unbowed, I thought, repressing the urge to grin. "All right," I said, and he immediately pulled out his iPhone. I gave the number to him, and he entered it in his contacts, looking so adorably focused in a nerdy sort of way that I felt a stab of self-doubt. Was I really doing the right thing?

Yes, the sane half of my brain said. *Let him go. Don't hold on to something just because you're afraid to be alone.*

"Don't worry about Luke and me," I said then. "I'm a big girl. I can handle it."

Danny's expression grew troubled again, but after a few seconds it miraculously cleared once more. It was apparent to me he'd decided he had something new and shiny to focus on. If I wanted to throw away my immortal soul, that was my business.

I got up, signaling that I thought our conversation was at an end, and he followed me to the door. We paused there for a second, both of us staring awkwardly at each other. Then he leaned down and gave me a quick kiss on the cheek.

"If you need anything, just let me know," he said. "I want to be friends if we can."

"I'd like that," I replied, feeling a little overwhelmed. Maybe I'd underestimated him. Certainly I'd never thought that Danny would be handing me the "I hope we can still be friends line"—I'd always thought that would be my job.

"Okay," he said, then took in a breath, squaring his shoulders like a man about to head into battle. "Guess I'd better go."

And with that he was off, his sneakers squeaking a little as he moved down the stairs. They sounded very different from the soft slap of Luke's expensive leather-soled shoes.

I waited in the doorway for a minute. Then I shut the door, knowing that very soon I was going to have a long, drawn-out cry.

If only Danny had understood it wasn't my immortal soul that was in danger here…just my heart.

Interlude

THE LORD OF HELL REAPPEARED, face like a thundercloud.

Beelzebub fought to keep a grin from his lips as he thought, *I love it when a plan comes together.*

That dark seed he had sown had apparently grown into a wondrous plant, choking all life from Lucifer's nascent romance. Everyone who saw the Prince of Darkness stalking through the halls of *his* palace immediately discovered they had pressing business to attend to elsewhere.

Even Beelzebub decided to lie low, mainly because he wasn't quite sure he could contain his glee around his master. Not that it really mattered—*he* had immediately retired to the North Tower (Hell didn't have actual directions, but topside nomenclature could be pervasive), which was where *he* always tended to go when *he* wanted to brood.

Perfect. It seemed the little chit's independent streak had won out. Beelzebub felt a momentary flicker of respect for her bravery, then quickly quashed it. Most likely she had confronted Lucifer because she didn't have any real idea of what *he* could do to her if properly provoked. Ignorance and stupidity, while typically human, were nothing to admire. But he would acknowledge that she had played her part well. Actually, his master had done so as well. For all *his* power and intelligence, the Lord of Hell had fallen into Beelzebub's trap as neatly as a rabbit running into a snare.

A few centuries of black moods and hermit-like behavior were a small price to pay for knowing that Lucifer was back here where *he* belonged. Sooner or later *he* would snap out of it, would realize that *his* personal freedom was far more important than some promise of a return to paradise.

Beelzebub snorted. Paradise. That was one word for the place. Endless tedium, more like it. At least down here in Hell things could get interesting from time to time. He had no desire for eternal perfection. From time to time he lamented the fact that his master seemed to do little but rest on *his* laurels and make far more trips topside than *he* had any real need to, but those little foibles could be overlooked. After all, *he* was the one who had had the plutonium *cojones* to challenge the One Upstairs—it was only right that the Kingdom of Hell should be *his* reward. Even the most dedicated ruler might begin to find the bloom off the rose after so many millennia. But now *he* had probably realized that *he* had nowhere else to go and would reconcile *himself* to *his* situation as soon as *he* realized that there were far worse things than being the Prince of Darkness.

Like being mortal, for example.

Asmodeus flicked an imaginary piece of lint off the lapel of his new suit and cast a critical eye at the line and fall of the garments. Was the break at the hem of his trousers hitting in the right place? Or should he have the tailor let it out another quarter of an inch?

A subtle throat-clearing caught his attention, and he turned, expecting to see the familiar shape of Nanthan, a transplant from Singapore who was the only person in Los Angeles he trusted to create the custom suits taste required. Instead, an elderly man in a shabby tweed jacket beamed up at him.

That is, He looked like an elderly man. Asmodeus knew better, however.

"Sir," he said, and stood up a little straighter. Maybe Beelzebub would have thrown a little attitude in the newcomer's direction, but Asmodeus wasn't brave enough for that. Or perhaps he simply had a stronger instinct for self-preservation. Still, his mind reeled. What was God doing here, in a cramped tailor's shop on the outskirts of L.A.'s Fashion District?

God's eyes glinted. "Allan. That is what you've been going by lately, is it not?"

"Well, yes. Sir." Asmodeus couldn't quite figure out what to do with his hands and ended up jamming them in the pockets of his pants, thus ruining the lines he had been admiring just a moment earlier. He added, "I thought 'Asmodeus' might be a little difficult to explain."

"True." God moved farther into the shop and appeared to inspect the bolts of wool stacked next to the counter. "I've also noticed you've been doing a bit of possession."

Oh, hell. God tended to frown on such things, which was why doing it for extended periods of time was such a risk. *Get in, do your work, get out,* had always been Asmodeus' motto. But of course Beelzebub had to push things to the limit.

"Well, sir—I, that is, we didn't—"

God waved a hand. "No point in excuses, my boy. A bit of advice—I really don't think Beelzebub has your best interests in mind."

Asmodeus blinked. "No, I would suppose not. He has his best interests in mind. They just happen to coincide with mine."

"Do they?"

Frowning, Asmodeus stared down at the face of God. He wore an expression of mild curiosity and showed no other emotion. That meant absolutely nothing, of course.

"I mean to say," God went on, "that interfering with My plans is often a recipe for disaster."

"Disaster?" Asmodeus repeated, then attempted to swallow past the lump in his throat. This wasn't going well at all.

"Your master and I made a deal. Said deal did not include interference from meddlesome demons. Perhaps Beelzebub should have stopped to think. Perhaps then he would have realized that our friend Lucifer is not the only one who has a stake in this thing."

"Well, erm…I suppose You could be right—"

"I am always right," God replied imperturbably. "And it's not too late to fix things, regardless of what your compatriot might think. But I need your word that there will be no further meddling."

"You have it, sir," Asmodeus said at once. What else could he do, after all? Defying God to His face was never a good idea.

"I thank you for your cooperation." A twinkle entered God's dark eyes. "Perhaps a reward for good behavior?"

Reward? That sounded promising. What Beelzebub didn't know couldn't hurt him. "You are too kind, sir."

"I suppose I am." God crossed His arms and regarded Asmodeus thoughtfully. "You do spend quite a bit of time topside, don't you?"

"Well, yes, but—"

"No excuses necessary. Would you like to stay here?"

At first Asmodeus wasn't quite sure he'd heard the question correctly. Surely God couldn't be handing him the whole world on a platter. To be able to stay here, to never have to return to Hell—all in exchange for some simple cooperation?

He cleared his throat and said, "Very much so, sir."

The twinkle returned. "I thought you might say that. I don't believe you're quite ready for the same deal I gave your master, but let's see how things go. Say a trial basis of a year?"

Asmodeus wanted to inquire more as to the nature of the "deal" God had entered into with Lucifer but decided it would probably be wiser to just keep his mouth shut. A year he could handle. A year up here was a year not spent in Hell.

"Very good, sir." His mind raced, already moving on to what he should do first. A house, probably. And a car. Or several cars. He thought of the gorgeous automobiles his master had parked in the garage of *his* mansion and felt his heart race a little. Something exotic and expensive, something to catch Nina's attention—

"I'll leave you to work out the details," God said, breaking into Asmodeus' frenzied daydreams. "Enjoy yourself, and for My sake, stay out of *his* way."

Asmodeus nodded. Why would he want to interfere with Lucifer's life when his own had taken such a miraculous turn for the better? He had far more interesting things to do with his time.

God smiled and was gone, leaving Asmodeus alone in the tailor shop, his mind thrumming with possibilities.

CHAPTER FIFTEEN

MICAELA CALLED ME LATE SUNDAY AFTERNOON to ask if I'd given Danny her number. When I told her I had, I got a long pause as a reply. Then she said, "I wasn't sure you were really going to go through with it."

I replied, "I told you I would."

She hesitated again, then said, "Yeah, but after you and Luke…anyway, I wasn't sure whether you'd be having second thoughts about breaking up with Danny."

"That's the only thing I'm not having second thoughts about," I told her, with a bitter little laugh. "So he called you?"

"Yeah, earlier today. We're going to meet tomorrow evening for coffee. I figured I'd better start out easy. Anyway, I'll be back on set after that, and I probably won't have time even for coffee for a while."

I said, "I hope it goes well," and discovered I was actually telling Micaela the truth. Just because my love life had been torpedoed into shrapnel didn't mean she shouldn't give it a try. At first glance the two of them seemed like sort of an odd couple, but they were both really into film, which helped, and at least Micaela wouldn't care if Danny pulled a disappearing act from time to time. Then there was the whole Catholic thing. Danny's parents were very old-school Polish (his father had actually been born in Poland), and I thought they would have fewer issues with Micaela being Mexican than they had with me being a complete heathen. The relationship might not make it past coffee, but if it did they wouldn't have that particular complication to deal with.

Micaela, being the practical sort, just said, "We'll see," and we left it at that. It felt a little weird, setting up a friend with my ex-boyfriend, but we all knew there was a shortage of decent guys in L.A., and sometimes you just had to be open-minded about those things.

Not too long after that my father called as well, offering belated congratulations on the promotion and an offer to take me out to dinner some time during the next week or so.

"Sorry it took me so long to get back to you," he said, "but I haven't gotten much of a chance to check my email lately. Traci has been running me ragged."

"Oh," I said. "Sorry."

"It's all right," he replied with a laugh. "I just hired an LVN to come in and help, and now I'm trying to schedule as many appointments as I can. It'll keep me out of the house at least. And Traci can't complain, because more clients means more goodies for her and the baby."

He sounded so casual about Traci's materialistic behavior. Maybe, though, he sort of enjoyed it. After all, my mother had never really cared all that much about my father's earning power as long as there was enough to make the mortgage and keep food on the table. He'd always been much more interested in the finer things in life, starting with the cars and going on from there. I still remembered the argument they had when I was in high school and he'd gone out and bought a Porsche. The cost had nothing to do with it—by that time my father's practice was flourishing, and he could definitely afford the car. It was more that my mother thought it was completely impractical, and worse, extravagant. What was the point in having a two-seat roadster when you had three children?

At any rate, it had been just more proof of the widening gap between my parents. I'd often wondered exactly what my father saw in Traci (except the obvious), but maybe part of it was simply being appreciated as the superlative breadwinner that he really was.

"I'm glad everything seems to be working out," I said. "And Traci is doing okay?"

"So far so good. Of course it's a long time to the end of June, but the doctors say she's holding her own."

"Good," I replied.

"And how are you doing?" he asked. "How's this new man of yours?"

My throat seemed to close up. "Um…fine," I replied, in a tight little voice that didn't sound very much like mine.

A significant silence followed that statement. It's sort of hard to lie to a psychologist, especially when that psychologist happens to be your father. Then he said, "Do you want to talk about it?"

If there was anything more excruciating than having your father ask if you wanted to discuss your love life, I had yet to find out what it was. I cleared my throat and replied, "Um…not really. We just hit a rough patch. Either it will work out or it won't."

Another hesitation. "Okay," my father said. "but if he keeps giving you trouble, just let me know. I'll send someone over to break his kneecaps."

I managed to laugh at that, albeit a little weakly, and we went on to talk some more about Traci and the remodeling for the baby's suite. Just before I hung up, I said, "I love you, Dad." I rarely told him that, but right then it seemed important that I did.

"I love you, too, Christa," he said. "I'm proud of you. And if this guy can't figure out how great you are, then he doesn't deserve you."

"That's what Nina said," I replied.

"Wise girl, Nina. You can keep her around."

I laughed again, and then we said our good-byes and hung up. The conversation left me feeling a little bit better about life. Not much, but at that point I was ready for any improvement, however infinitesimal.

Before the Lone Gunmen indulged in their industrial espionage, I probably would have tried to work through my problems by writing in my blog—my online "dear diary." However, the bloom was off that rose. Of course I'd changed all the passwords, but the blog still felt…defiled. Dramatic word, maybe, although I couldn't think of any other way to think of it. At any rate, it didn't feel secure to me anymore, and so, after logging in one time and then spending five minutes staring at the blank field where I was supposed to be spilling my guts, I logged out and never went back to the site.

An even longer week followed that very long weekend. Work kept me busy, between juggling my copyeditor duties and starting to take over some of Brian's backlogged assignments. I planned to attend the Women in Film festival on Thursday, and Nina had agreed to be my "date" for the evening. Back before the shit had hit the fan I'd thought about asking Luke, but of course that wasn't going to happen. But Nina was more than happy to go along; it would give her a chance to get out and have fun, which she considered the paramount reason for existing in the first place, and it would also provide some fun celebrity-watching as well. Roger warned me that it was a small festival and probably not many A-list stars would be there. I didn't mind; even a D-lister would be worthy of a mention.

I tried to ignore the fact that Valentine's Day hit smack-dab in the middle of the week. It was hard, just because I knew that if Luke and I had still been together he probably would have planned something extravagant—that was just his way. Or at least the way he wanted to appear to me. Sometimes it was hard to know how much of what I loved about him was the true being underneath or just the public veneer he had presented to me.

The fact that I felt I was on the moral high ground in this particular conflict didn't help much, either. Sure, you can tell yourself that you did the right thing, but that's cold comfort when you're sitting home alone on Valentine's Day and eating Godiva truffles until you make yourself sick. At that point I didn't even care whether or not I'd be able to squeeze myself into my True Religion jeans for the film festival the following night. Who cares if the reporter is fat, after all?

But either my metabolism hadn't processed the chocolates in time, or the two days prior to that when I'd hardly eaten anything worked to my benefit. The jeans slid on with no protest, and I went through the process of glamming myself up for the night out half-heartedly at best. Who was I going to impress, after all? Of course there would be tons of better-looking women than I in attendance, starting with Nina and going on from there.

Sure enough, she showed up looking drop-dead in a pair of skinny jeans tucked into tight boots and an extravagant chocolate-colored suede jacket with a fur collar.

"Nice," I commented, when I opened the door and saw her ensemble. "Very JLo. I hope that's *faux*."

"Of course it's *faux*," she replied, sailing on past me. "I know better than to wear real fur in this town."

I didn't bother to reply, but just gathered up my bag, clipped the press photo ID to my lapel, and then gave her the extra pass. Her gaze fell on the half-empty box of Godiva chocolates that still sat on the coffee table. I'd forgotten to put it back in the kitchen after my binge of the night before.

"Self-medicating, I see," she remarked.

"Well, it's cheaper than crack," I said.

"I'm not so sure about that," Nina said. "But whatever. If that's the worst thing you've done since the two of you fought, I suppose you're doing okay." Her expression sobered. "I'm guessing you still haven't heard from him."

"No." *And I don't think I'm going to, either,* I thought. Surely he would have called me or come to see me by now if he were going to at all. That hurt now just as much as it did the first time I had thought it, but I knew I couldn't dissolve into a mess right then. I had a job to do.

Nina gave me a hard look, and nodded slightly. I knew then that she wouldn't bring the subject up again. If I wanted to talk about Luke, fine, she'd be there for me, but she'd known me long enough to understand that I tended to keep things inside. I'd never had much patience for the long angst-fests some of my friends indulged in every time they went through a breakup, even though some of those relationships had lasted only a few weeks. My one indulgence had been after Brad and I split up; in my defense, I had really thought I'd found the person I could spend a significant amount of time with, if not the rest of my life. Most of the time, though, the endless discussions and second-guessing that followed a breakup just seemed like an invasion of privacy to me, and my attitude hadn't changed much over the years. Did I really want someone else, even my closest friend, to know all the details of the thousand and one ways I'd died inside since last Friday night?

In silence I let the two of us out. Nina had offered to drive, and I'd accepted, since that would be one less thing for me to worry about. Twice during the preceding several days I'd almost rear-ended someone in the lurching traffic on Wilshire just because I'd been brooding over Luke and not paying attention. The last thing I needed tonight was to get in an accident while I was technically on the company clock. That would open up a whole legal can of worms I didn't think I had the energy to deal with at the moment.

The festival was being held in Hollywood at the Arclight complex, which was a large theater and restaurant built around what used to be a dome-style movie palace. The dome still existed, although completely refurbished and updated, but around it had been constructed a high-end multiplex that was sometimes put to use as a venue for premieres and festivals. The girls and I loved the Arclight because it had this great institution known as "21+ Screenings," which we referred to as "alcoholic cin-ema." Basically, if you were twenty-one or over, you could buy a drink in the bar and take it into the the-ater with you. More than one craptastic movie had been made bearable by this wonderful innovation. We kept wondering when it was going to catch on with other theater chains.

However, there wouldn't be any alcoholic cinema for me tonight. Roger wasn't expecting a huge piece on the festival—an opening spread, with a couple of partial pages to follow—but I still had to keep an eye out for any possible interview subjects, as well as generally observing the ebb and flow of the crowd and paying attention to which films had buzz and which didn't. I briefly hooked up with Lee Chiang, our photographer, and he informed me that Sofia Coppola was definitely there—he'd already gotten a few shots of her, and said that I should try to snag her for a few choice quotes whenever she reappeared. I nodded, then went back to circling the venue and hoping I didn't look as awkward as I felt.

Nina proved to be a great resource. She was a lot more sociable than I, and I watched her work the crowd and gather up some valuable intel while I was studiously taking notes on the films being shown and who had attended (and who hadn't).

The glaring lights of a TV crew off to one side caught my attention. I turned to see who they were interviewing, and it turned out to be Emma Stone. She looked amazing—and a lot smaller in person. I jotted some more notes in my little book, including several all-important details of her outfit, such as the impossibly skinny jeans, jeweled sandals, and beaded camisole, all of which wouldn't have been very appropriate for Los Angeles in mid-February if it weren't for the enormous turquoise shawl she had flung over one shoulder.

Then Nina came bounding up and said she had a possible Eva Longoria sighting down one hallway. "I'll come back with a full report," she added, then took off again, eyes glowing and hair bouncing. She reminded me of a kid on an Easter-egg hunt.

"You know that girl?" came a voice at my ear, and I turned to see an unfamiliar man, the sort of slick, attractive, well-dressed type that L.A. churns out in droves, staring thoughtfully after Nina.

"She's one of my best friends," I responded.

"Is she a model? Or an actress?"

"No," I replied. "She's the manager of a gallery in Santa Monica."

"Amazing," he said. "She has the sort of face that should be on camera."

True, but I knew that Nina couldn't care less about modeling or acting. She'd done some modeling back in high school, just local shows and a bit of print work, but she'd told me frankly that she hated it. "I never knew something could be so hard and so boring at the same time," she'd grumbled once to me, when the ten-thousandth person had asked why she wasn't a professional model.

"I don't think she's really interested in that sort of thing," I added. I figured it was nothing more than the truth.

"That's just because she's never had the proper representation," he replied. He fished in the pocket of his Italian dress shirt for a card case and pulled it out, then retrieved a business card and handed it to me.

The card identified him as one Allan D'Alessandro. He didn't look very Italian to me, but whatever. However, I did recognize the agency—it was one of the biggest in L.A. It appeared that Nina had pulled someone of importance into her slipstream.

"Aren't models supposed to be in their late teens or early twenties?" I asked. "Nina's almost twenty-eight."

He waved a hand. "These days age isn't so important," he said. "Besides, I could easily pass her off as twenty-two, twenty-three. Has she ever had acting lessons?"

"Um…I don't think so." I didn't know whether to be irritated or amused. Here I was at my first big reporting assignment, right in the middle of a happening Hollywood event, and instead of inter-viewing a celebrity or talking to one of the event organizers, I was playing pimp for Nina. It figured.

At that moment she came loping across the foyer area, curls bouncing. "False alert," she said. "But I did see Kathy Griffin."

"I'll make a note of it," I replied. "Oh, Nina, this is Allan D'Alessandro. He's an agent."

I could see a look of puzzled curiosity pass over her features, but she didn't have time to say anything before he cut in, "You have an amazing look, Nina. Have you ever thought about pursuing representation?"

"I'm not an actress," she said, her tone dubious.

He smiled, showing perfectly bleached teeth. Or maybe they were caps. "Acting can be taught. But it's a lot more difficult to fake looks like yours."

Nina lifted an eyebrow. "Really?"

"Really," he assured her. He barely glanced over at me as he said, "You don't mind if I borrow your friend for a while, do you?"

"Hey, she's a free agent," I replied. Then I shot her a look that said, *I can help you get rid of this guy if you want.*

Surprisingly, though, she said, "Why don't you buy me a drink, and we can discuss it?"

"Deal."

So they went off, and left me to stand there and stare after them with a look (I was sure) of baffled amazement on my features. Maybe Nina just hadn't pursued the whole acting thing because she hadn't gotten a good enough offer.

Still, I felt more than a little abandoned, a feeling that was mitigated slightly by the fact that right after they left, I turned around and almost knocked over Sofia Coppola, who's actually very tiny in person. She also turned out to be extremely gracious, answering my (to me, anyway) clumsy questions with care and thought. It turned out that we had a sort of mini-interview right then and there; about five minutes later she begged my pardon and said she had to move on, but that it was very nice to talk to me and she looked forward to reading my article.

That encounter helped to salvage the evening. I felt as if I hadn't made a complete idiot of myself, and I did get some good material. Then I met up with one of the organizers of the event, an intense redhead named Louise Steinberg, and we chatted for a while about emerging women directors and the importance of developing complex roles for women of all ages.

Between those two discussions and the notes I had taken earlier in the evening, I was pretty sure I had more than enough information to fill up the three and a half pages Roger had allotted for my article. Nina, however, was nowhere in sight, and I wasn't quite desperate (or mean) enough to pry her out of the bar yet.

Still, that left me rather at loose ends. I thought about ducking into one of the theaters and actually watching a segment of one of the films entered in the festival, but I worried that Nina wouldn't be able to find me if I disappeared like that.

I stood in the center of the lobby, irresolute, and then heard a half-familiar voice call out my name. "Christa?"

So I turned, and found myself looking at probably the last person I thought I would have ever seen at the Arclight. He'd filled out a little bit over the intervening years, but I still would have known him anywhere.

"Brad?" I responded, wondering what the hell he was doing here. Last I'd heard, he'd settled in the Bay Area permanently after getting his masters in anthropology at Stanford.

His gaze was frankly admiring. "You look incredible," he said, as if he hadn't dumped me all those years ago and left me to brave UCLA on my own.

"Thanks," I replied, and was suddenly glad I'd spent that extra ten minutes in front of the mirror before Nina arrived at my apartment.

"So what are you doing here?" he asked.

I lifted my press ID badge. "I work for *SoCal* magazine," I said. "But what are you doing here?"

"Good for you," he said, after looking at the badge and giving me an approving nod. "As for me—that's kind of a long story. You got a few minutes?"

"Probably more than that," I answered, since Nina still appeared to be MIA.

"Buy you a cup of coffee?"

I hesitated. After all, there had been a lot of weirdness in my life lately, and I wasn't quite sure what to make of the reappearance of the one true flame from my college years. Then again, I was dying to know what the hell he was doing here, of all places. "Sure," I said at last. "As long as it's decaf."

We wandered over to the restaurant/bar that occupied the far end of the lobby area and managed to snag the last unoccupied booth. As the hostess led us to our seats, we passed Nina and Allan D'Alessandro, who appeared to be in the middle of a hard sell. When Brad and I walked by their table, however, Nina's gaze flickered upward and then froze as she recognized who my companion was. Her mouth dropped, and I shot her a seraphic smile. For once it was fun to be the one flummoxing Nina instead of always the other way around.

Brad and I sat down, and then there was an awkward silence as we both tried to gaze at one another without appearing to outright stare. Finally I shook my head. "You know, it's sort of freaking me out to see you here."

"Believe me, I know." Brad gave me a rueful smile. "It's probably not the sort of place you'd expect me to turn up."

I nodded.

"I guess it started after my father died—I don't know if you heard about that or not."

"No," I said. I'd met Brad's father a few times, and he'd seemed like a genuinely nice person, and someone who was far too young and vital to have passed away so soon. "I'm sorry to hear about that."

A shadow seemed to move across Brad's hazel eyes, that dusky mixture of green and brown and gold I remembered so well. "It was pretty rough. Pancreatic cancer. He only had about three months from diagnosis to—well, you know."

I winced. That had to be one of the worst ways to go. And for it to happen to as good a man as Brad's father had appeared to be—well, it was the sort of thing that made you start to question what the hell God really was up to with the world.

"Anyway," Brad went on. Someone who didn't know him well would have thought he seemed somewhat detached from the situation, but I could see the tension in his hands as they wrapped around the menu, the downward droop at the right corner of his mouth. "He told me something right before he died. He told me to make a difference in the world, to follow my dreams and help other people follow theirs as well. That's why I'm here."

A little puzzled, I stared back at him. The Brad I remembered certainly wasn't into film, except in a casual "going to the movies on the weekend" sort of way. I hadn't expected him to be dabbling in film-making. "So you're directing or producing?" I asked.

"Producing, sort of," he replied. "When he got ill, my father sold his company. Made a huge profit. I decided to take my share and use it to help finance independent productions, give a leg up to talented people who couldn't get the time of day from the studios because their stuff wasn't mainstream enough."

Well, that sounded more like Brad. Although he certainly wasn't as rabid as my mother about such things, he'd had a strong crusading streak and was always donating his spare cash to various causes. What got him started in independent film I had no idea—after all, we hadn't seen each other for almost seven years—but I had to admit there were worse ways for him to be spending his money. In fact, awful as it might sound, I thought he would work really well as an interviewee for a sidebar to my article, one that gave some insight into the financial side of the small filmmaker.

"So one of your films is entered in the festival?" I asked, wishing there were a polite way for me to pick up my pen and start taking notes.

He nodded. "Yeah, I've been working with this amazing documentary filmmaker, Madeleine Czerny. She's really passionate, really dedicated."

Ludicrous as it might sound, I started to feel a little jealous. Somehow I sort of doubted that Brad had ever used those words to describe me. But I just made an approving sound so he would go on.

"Anyway, I don't know if you noticed her film on the program or not. It's called *Yesterday's Heroes,* and it's about the walking wounded coming back from Iraq and Afghanistan, about the psychological and physical difficulties they face, their problems dealing with the bureaucracy and the VA. I mean, these people risked their lives going over there for a bogus war, and then they got cheated by the same government that lied to them in the first place. When you hear some of these stories—" He broke off suddenly, and then gave a self-deprecating shake of the head. "Sorry—I tend to get the bit between my teeth and then keep going when I start talking about this stuff."

"No, it's fine," I said. "I think it's great that you get to do something you really care about. In fact—" I hesitated, then figured the hell with it. After all, I was here to gather material for an article. "Would you mind if I took a few notes for my article? Do I have your permission to quote you?"

"Um—sure," Brad replied, looking a little taken aback. Then his expression cleared, and he added, "The extra exposure would be great."

At that moment the waitress showed up to take our orders. I ordered a decaf café au lait, and Brad asked for a cappuccino.

While he was ordering, I pulled my pad and pen out of my bag and jotted down a few notes. It felt more than a little weird to be interviewing my former boyfriend for the piece, but this was my job now; I needed to be a little more thick-skinned. The waitress left, and I asked, "So how does this financing work? Do you sort of let it be known that you're willing to support these projects, or do you actually seek out aspiring filmmakers to lend them a hand?"

"A little of both," he said. "In Maddy's case, I actually knew her fiancé—he and I went to Stanford together."

A wave of inexplicable relief washed over me. So Brad's relationship with this Madeleine person had to be strictly professional. Then I wanted to smack myself. Why the hell should I care what was going on in Brad's personal life? Wasn't I still trying to work through the sudden derailment of my relationship with Luke?

Trying to hide my confusion, I stared down at the notepad and kept scribbling. I heard Brad say,

"I didn't really ask you to have a cup of coffee with me so we could talk business, though."

"Oh?" I said, and finally looked up, only to see him watching me with the earnest, level stare I remembered so well.

"No," he replied. "I've missed you, Christa."

Despite myself, I could feel a little flicker of hope stir somewhere deep inside. Maybe I could still salvage something from the wreckage of my love life. A long time ago, when I had been in one of my long dry spells between relationships, Nina told me my real problem was that I wouldn't let myself get over Brad. "You keep building him up as this dream boyfriend, but he left," she'd said. "I don't care if he was Prince Charming and JFK Jr. rolled into one—he's gone." At the time I'd almost hated Nina for that bit of brutal honesty, but I'd had to admit to myself she was right, even though I'd never say it to her face. I'd forced myself to move on after that, telling myself over and over that it was done, he was four hundred miles away, east was east and west was west and never the twain shall meet, and all that. It had almost worked.

But not well enough, apparently. Even with the specter of Luke hanging over me, even though Brad had deserted me all those years ago, part of me wanted him back. Badly.

I forced a sort of brittle lightness into my voice and said, "Really? I guess that explains all the cards and letters I've gotten over the past six years."

His mouth tightened. "Look, I did what I thought was best for my personal growth at the time. And Stanford worked out really well for me—I made a lot of good contacts, got involved with the community. I probably would never have linked up with Madeleine if I hadn't known Pete. Maybe I should have written you. At the time I thought it just wouldn't be fair. My life was up there, and yours was down here. And we all know how well those sorts of things work out."

That was true; I knew a few people who had tried the long-distance thing after they graduated from high school and then went on to separate college careers. The one thing all those relationships seemed to have in common was that they inevitably crashed and burned.

"Okay," I said. "I won't argue with that. So what's different now?"

"For one thing, I've moved back down to Santa Monica. There was so much to deal with after my father passed away, and then once I decided to get into financing independent film, L.A. just seemed the logical place to be."

I had to know. "So how long have you been down here?"

"About eight months."

Plenty of time to have looked me up, but I had to give Brad a break—his father had just died, and his whole world had been upended, from what I could tell. Pursuing an old girlfriend had probably been the last thing on his mind.

"I wanted to call you," he said, apparently interpreting my silence correctly. "But I didn't know if you were involved with someone, or whether you'd even give me the time of day—I know I left things badly." He took a sip of his cappuccino and asked, "So…are you?"

"Am I what?"

"Seeing anyone? Engaged? Married with two kids?"

My laugh almost sounded normal. Almost. "No. I was seeing someone for a while, but we split up." Even as the words left my lips, I wasn't sure to whom I was referring…Danny or Luke. Not that it mattered, since they were both effectively out of the picture.

Brad smiled. "Then maybe I've finally gotten my timing right. I really would like to take you out—for more than a cup of coffee. Are you busy tomorrow?"

Considering that my hot date for Friday night was a pint of Ben & Jerry's Chunky Monkey, the answer was definitely no. "Not really," I said.

"Then let me take you out for some real food—if that's all right."

I looked at Brad then—really looked at him, at the eyes with their warm, shifting hazel tones; the oversized nose that he'd always hated but which I sort of liked; the wide, friendly mouth. He'd never been what you'd call conventionally handsome, but I'd always liked his looks. Of course he didn't compare to Luke, but even Luke had told me to stop making comparisons. So I wouldn't.

"Ahem."

We both looked up to see Nina standing over us, her arms crossed and a patently false smile painted on her glossy lips. "Well, hi…Brad," she said. "Long time no see."

"Hi, Nina," Brad said, looking a little puzzled by her apparent hostility. Then again, he didn't know how many hours of Nina's life I'd wasted in agonizing over our breakup. "Christa and I were just catching up."

"Fab," she said. "Hey, Christa, I hate to be a party-pooper, but it's getting kind of late and I still have to drive you home—"

This from the girl who told the rest of us we were getting old when we wanted to head home at one…on a weeknight. But I knew what she was doing, and even though I didn't like it very much, I wasn't about to start arguing with her in front of Brad. Besides, he and I had already set up a date for the following night, so if Nina thought she could prevent further contact, she was sadly mistaken. And she was right—it was close to eleven, and I still needed to get my hand-written notes into my computer if possible. Then I could email them to myself at work.

"No problem," I said. "Thanks for the coffee, Brad. It was really great seeing you—and I'm looking forward to tomorrow night."

"Pick you up at seven?"

"Sounds great." I smiled, a little more broadly than I would have under normal circumstances, but the evil side of me was enjoying Nina's obvious ire. I gathered up my purse and then followed her out of the theater complex.

To her credit, she waited until we were safely ensconced in her Z4 before exploding. "Okay, what the hell?!" she snapped.

Innocently, I asked, "What do you mean?"

"Do not—I repeat, do not give me that shit! What the hell are you thinking? Brad 'he stomped on my heart and left me for dead' McAllister! Haven't you learned anything?" With a vicious gesture she threw the car into reverse and punched the gas. The little BMW jumped backward as if it had been kneed in the nuts.

"I know what I'm doing," I said, after my heart decided to dislodge itself from my throat.

"Oh, no, you don't." The car screeched to a stop at the parking attendant's booth. I began to pull out my wallet, but Nina just shook her head impatiently and practically flung a ten-dollar bill at the attendant. "Can you say 'rebound'?"

"That's stupid. I wasn't even dating Luke long enough to have earned an official rebound."

"Like the length of time you were together matters," Nina retorted.

"What's that supposed to mean?"

"It means," she said, turning left onto Sunset right in front of an oncoming SUV, "that you fell for that guy big-time. Don't lie and say you didn't—I know you too well."

An uncomfortable silence followed that remark. I should have known Nina would figure out exactly how crazy I'd really been for Luke. We'd been friends too long. "Maybe I did," I said in a small voice. "But I can't let that stop me from moving on, can I?"

"Of course not," she replied. "But you guys broke up barely a week ago. And if it were someone else, maybe I wouldn't mind. I saw what happened after Brad dumped you, though, and it wasn't pretty. Are you really saying you want to go through that all over again?"

"Circumstances are different now," I said. "He's moved back down here to L.A. And he as much as said he was sorry about how he handled things."

"And that's supposed to make it all better?"

Of course not, and I knew that as well as Nina. Still, a lot of guys wouldn't have even admitted as much as Brad had in our short conversation. I had to give him points for that. "It's a step," I replied finally. "Maybe this is just the universe's way of sorting things out."

Nina lifted an eyebrow, and again made one of those heart attack–inducing left turns onto La Brea. "'Whenever the good Lord closes a door, somewhere he opens a window,'" she said, in such treacly-sweet tones I knew she had to be quoting from something.

"What the hell is that from?"

"*The Sound of Music.*"

"Oh, rot, Maria," I snapped, and then we both began to laugh.

By the time we reached my apartment, her mood had been restored somewhat, and she was able to wish me good night with only the slightest trace of accusation in her tone. By that I knew, while she didn't really support my decision to see Brad again, she wouldn't try to stop me. Implicit in that understanding was the promise to be there for me if Round Two turned out to be as disastrous as Round One.

For myself, I didn't know exactly what to think. Had God finally stepped in? Was Brad His personal *deus ex machina*, the man who could save my heart and soul from the Devil?

I just wished I knew if I even wanted to be saved.

CHAPTER SIXTEEN

ALL DAY FRIDAY LITTLE PRICKS OF GUILT tormented me. Maybe Nina was right. Maybe I'd just said yes to Brad because I didn't want to deal with the emotional aftermath of my split from Luke. Maybe I was just trying to relive a part of my past instead of seeing what the future might have to offer. Then again, was there some predetermined amount of time that had to elapse before I could start seeing someone else? It wasn't as if I'd gone out looking for a new relationship; this one had pretty much been dumped in my lap. And if Luke really wanted to talk, he knew where to find me. Too many times in my life I'd apologized for things that weren't even my fault, and as much as I missed him—ached for him, if I really wanted to admit it to myself—I was damned if I was going to crawl back to him and beg for forgiveness when he was the one who had screwed up. If he was too proud to admit any wrongdoing, then so be it.

At least the article seemed to be coming together pretty well. I cleared out most of my copyediting duties in the morning and spent the afternoon organizing my notes into something resembling a coherent whole. Lee, the photographer, had already uploaded the images he shot onto the server we used for handling photos, and I actually had a lot of fun looking through them and deciding which ones to use. Then I had to write captions for the ones I selected. I didn't have the rough draft ready for Roger to look at until almost five, but at least I felt I had done a decent day's work and hoped he would approve of what I had written.

He'd already left by the time I dropped the story envelope on his desk; people tended to evaporate early on Friday afternoons, especially the staff members who had long commutes. Roger lived down in north Long Beach, so I couldn't blame him for pulling the disappearing act, but I still felt vaguely disappointed. It would have been nice to have a chance to discuss this, my first article, with him, but I supposed it could wait until Monday morning.

By the time I got home, I had about an hour before Brad was scheduled to pick me up. Since the date was supposed to involve dinner but nothing overly special, I didn't do much more than touch up my makeup, give my hair a quick once-over with the brush, and then change the flats I'd worn at the office for a slightly more stylish pair of kitten-heeled ankle boots. The last thing I wanted was to come off as desperate or trying too hard; casual but nice seemed to be the best angle to take here. I didn't want to acknowledge how nervous I actually felt. That was just silly, wasn't it? After all, I'd known Brad for years; it wasn't like going on a first date with the Devil or something. But maybe in a way that made things more difficult. We'd have the weight of a shared history affecting everything we did and said. I could try to convince myself that we were just starting over fresh, but that's never really the case—you can't ever entirely discount the past.

My minor preparations for the date left with me with a good amount of time to kill before I could logically expect Brad, so I took my laptop over to the sofa and opened it up, thinking I could roam around on the Internet, check my mail, and do whatever else it took to fill up that last useless half-hour.

Nothing much interesting in my email, of course—my mother sent me a recipe for some zucchini casserole that sounded vaguely nauseating, but I just replied that it sounded great and then, because I was too guilty to trash it altogether, moved the email into my "misc. Mom stuff" folder and promptly forgot about it. I really didn't get a huge volume of mail, since my spam filter was pretty aggressive, so there wasn't much new. In fact, one of Luke's emails was still visible in the inbox.

I know I shouldn't have, but I clicked on it and then sat there, feeling a painful tightness in my chest as I read the simple message. A roast sounds wonderful—thank you for cooking. *Yours, Luke.*

Yours, Luke. But he really hadn't ever been mine, had he? We'd just played at a relationship, after all. Luke had the whole moonlight and roses thing down pretty well, but the minute the situation got a little more complex, he'd pulled a disappearing act. I supposed I should have been grateful that I got out of the entanglement with only a few extra emotional scars.

Still, it hurt. It hurt a lot. I stared at the email for a long moment. Then I closed the window for my mail program and opened up the Firefox browser, forcing myself not to think about him, about what had gone wrong. Dwelling on it wasn't going to change anything, and I knew I'd better get myself together before Brad showed up and started asking questions. That's another problem with going on a "first date" with someone who already knows you well. There's no mystery.

But after spending some time canoodling on sites that I knew were guaranteed to give me a laugh, including The Onion and GoFugYourself. com, I felt my spirits improve somewhat. It's hard to take yourself too seriously when someone's doing an excellent job of mocking Lady Gaga's latest sartorial disaster.

Precisely at seven, Brad knocked on the door. He always had been the punctual type. I didn't have time to do much more besides close my laptop and set it down on the coffee table. Then I got up and let him in.

He looked good, wearing lived-in jeans, a dark shirt, and a brown leather jacket. Not quite as effortlessly chic as Luke, but still more than presentable.

"I like your apartment," he commented, after a quick glance around. "It looks like you."

"Thanks," I said, and then we both stared at each other until he began to grin, and I found myself grinning back.

"Awkward much?" he asked, and I replied,

"You have no idea."

"Well, I suppose we'll get over it eventually. Let's get something to eat—I'm starving."

"Sounds like a plan," I replied, then went to get my purse.

Brad's ride turned out to be an older-model Pathfinder, which felt awfully lumpy and bumpy compared to any of Luke's plush vehicles or even my own Mercedes. Then again, Brad had never been much of a car guy. With him it had always been what was practical, and I supposed the SUV was good for hauling things around.

"So what are you in the mood for?" he asked. "Mexican? Thai?"

"Oh, pretty much anything," I said, even though I knew he'd always hated it when I responded that way. He wasn't one of those guys who asked a question just for form's sake when he had already made his mind up as to what he wanted to do. He asked because he genuinely wanted the input. So I added hastily, "Mexican would be good." If nothing else, a margarita sounded like a great idea.

"I was hoping you'd say that," he responded with a grin.

We headed south to Olympic and then east. I didn't really recognize where we were going, and some of the neighborhoods we drove through were marginal at best. But Brad was a native, and I figured he knew where he was going, even if he'd spent most of the last seven years up in the Bay Area.

Sure enough, the restaurant we pulled up in front of looked perfectly respectable, and I thought I'd even heard of it, even though I'd never eaten there.

"El Cholo's got the best tamales in L.A," Brad said, just before handing the car over to the valet. It seemed that no matter where I went out to eat, it was impossible to park your own car. "And also the best margaritas."

"I'm all over that," I said. *The bigger, the better,* I added mentally.

It turned out Brad had reservations, and I lifted a skeptical eyebrow at him after we'd been seated. "So why bother to ask me what I wanted to eat if you already knew where we were going?" I asked.

His tone was apologetic. "Well, let's just say I hoped you'd want to come here. I got reservations at three different places, just in case…which means I'd better call the other restaurants and cancel."

I couldn't help shaking my head as he pulled out his cell phone and made a couple of quick calls. Just as he had hung up on the last one, the waitress came along and took our drink orders. Pretty much all of the margaritas sounded great, but I decided to go with the blue agave margarita, just because having a blue drink sounded like a lot of fun. Brad ordered a traditional version on the rocks, and then we lapsed into yet another awkward silence before she returned and rescued us by leaving behind some chips and salsa.

After a bit of companionable munching, I asked, "So do you think the festival helped with your film?"

"Oh, absolutely," Brad replied, looking relieved that I'd found an innocuous topic of conversation. "In fact, I spoke to a representative from HBO there who was really interested in picking it up for cable. So maybe it'll get a little more life than just making the indie festival circuit and a few art houses that are willing to take more of a risk than usual."

"That's great," I said. "I imagine a good part of working as an independent is learning how to network."

"You have no idea." He leaned forward a bit, clasping his hands on the tabletop. "You've got to be both a filmmaker and a marketer. Maddy's great at it, and I'm learning—I mean, I saw some of the marketing work my father's company did and even pitched in to help write press releases and that sort of thing every once in a while, but it's a far cry from that to convincing people the film you're backing is worthy of screen time. It's rough out there."

"I'll bet," I said. It didn't sound like much fun to me, but I'd always been the type who preferred to work behind the scenes. Last night at the festival had been both terrifying and exhilarating—I'd had to force myself to approach people and ask questions. Roger had said the first article was the most difficult, and I sincerely hoped he was right. Otherwise, I'd have to swallow my pride and tell both him and Jacqui that maybe I wasn't cut out for this sort of thing after all. "Do you have any other projects you're working on?"

He shook his head. "Not right now."

The drinks arrived, and I couldn't wait to pick up my margarita and take a long, cool pull at it. Nothing like the judicious application of some tequila to break the tension.

Because I could feel it. I didn't know for sure whether it was the result of natural awkwardness at sitting face to face with the man who had dumped me so egregiously all those years before, or whether the chemistry I'd always thought had been so good had altered subtly. Maybe it was just that we still had a whole lot of emotional baggage to deal with and weren't sure how.

Or maybe it was simply that I found myself wishing really, really hard it was Luke sitting across from me and not Brad.

Typical, I thought. *How many years did it take before you stopped wishing that Brad would miraculously come back into your life? And now that he's here, the only person you can think of is Luke? Get a grip, Christa!*

"So what else are you up to?" I asked. I made a vow then and there that I would keep the conversation going if it killed me…and if I looked into Brad's hazel eyes one more time and imagined Luke's vivid blue instead I'd pinch myself. Hard.

"Oh, I'm teaching a couple of anthro classes over at the local community college," he replied. "Might as well put that master's degree to some use. It brings in some extra cash, and I like it. A lot of the other adjunct professors have problems with the current climate, which keeps their hours below a certain level so the college doesn't have to pay them benefits, but I don't really need a full-time income right now, so in my case it doesn't matter so much."

He frowned. "Although I do agree that the policy is potentially damaging."

"And how's your family? Your mom?" I inquired hastily. Compelling as it might have been for the actual parties involved, I wasn't in the mood to hear him launch into an in-depth analysis of why the tight-fistedness of the California higher-education system was hurting the rank and file.

"Oh, fine," Brad said, apparently oblivious to the obvious red herring. "She went through a rough time, of course…we all did…but she's managing much better now. I think it was a relief for her to finally get the company sold, even though she really didn't want to let go of it at first."

Brad's father had been the sole owner of a company that sold high-end barbecues, outdoor fire pits, log sets, that sort of thing. I'd never really thought about how much money was actually in that business until I'd seen for myself how well his family had lived, but it had been very profitable. Probably it had been a wrench to sell the company, but it had thrived because of Mr. McAllister's passion for his products and his hands-on approach. I doubted that Mrs. McAllister or even Brad could have kept the place operating at the same level it had while Mr. McAllister was alive, so selling it seemed to me the most logical thing to do. "Well, I can see how that would be hard," I said. "I mean, it was your father's baby, right? But I'm glad it all worked out in the end."

"Yes, and the investments we made from the sale should keep all of us going for quite a while," Brad replied. "I'm trying to be a little picky about the projects I take on, though, because it's not the kind of wealth that's inexhaustible, naturally."

Unlike Luke's, I thought automatically, and I really did reach down under the table and pinch my left forearm between my right thumb and forefinger. Ouch. You'd think I'd learn. "And your sister?"

He sipped at his own margarita before replying. "Oh, she's fine, too. She's in her second year at San Diego State, although with the way they run that place it'll probably be another four years before she graduates. She wants to go into sports physiology and medicine, of all things."

Actually, that made a lot of sense to me, since Brad's little sister Melissa had been the sort of gung-ho athlete I found it almost impossible to relate to. I mean, more power to her and all that, but I just couldn't get my brain behind someone who obsessed over her backhand and who entered marathons as if they were just a walk in the park. Then again, she probably couldn't relate to me and my shopping pathologies, either.

"That sounds impressive," I managed to say, even though I found myself not much caring what Melissa's future plans were. In the year that Brad and I had dated, I think she and I had probably exchanged a maximum of twenty words.

"It makes her happy," Brad said. He tilted his head slightly and watched me for a few seconds, then added, "It's just killing you, isn't it?"

"What?" I asked, caught off-guard.

He grinned. "You're smiling and making all the correct responses, but somewhere in there you really wish you had the guts to rip me a new asshole for what I put you through. Am I right?"

Well, I supposed he was, but I didn't think I really wanted to give Brad the satisfaction of letting him know that. I suddenly recalled how I used to get annoyed by his know-it-all attitude. Had I really forgotten the way he used to say, "I know exactly how you're feeling, Christa," when I had known for a fact that he couldn't possibly know for sure? A couple of times I'd just wanted to hurl something hard at his head.

To throw him off a little, I smiled sweetly and said, "I don't know what you're talking about, Brad."

He gave me a skeptical look and drank some more of his margarita.

"Okay, fine," I said. What was the point in lying, after all? But the fiasco with Luke had taught me one thing: Never make a scene in a restaurant. "I've thought about it. But what's the point? It's over and done with. I thought we were trying a fresh start."

"We are," he replied. "I just wanted to let you know that if you wanted to bring any of that up, it's all right. I deserve it."

There was nothing like actual contrition to take all the energy out of righteous indignation. I shook my head and said, "If you really want a new asshole ripped, I'll call in Nina. I'm sure she's got a few choice words on the subject, since she was the one I dumped all my angst on back in the day. But I've gotten over it. Seven years is a long time."

"True."

Our entrées arrived at that point, and we both busied ourselves with our meals. Food is a great distraction. After a minute or so, though, Brad remarked, "You've grown up a lot, Christa."

I wasn't sure whether I should be flattered or offended. After all, everyone wants to achieve some emotional maturity in this life, but I thought I still had a long way to go. And if that were the case, it meant I had been even more immature back then than I had realized.

Not wanting to really go into that, I just replied, "Thanks," and helped myself to another mouthful of blue corn chicken enchilada. I figured I'd just stick with the whole "blue" theme throughout my meal. As I recalled, blue was Brad's favorite color.

"No, really," he said seriously. "I mean, I always thought you were a great person, even if you did tend to undervalue yourself, but there's something different about you…a sort of confidence I didn't see before."

Well, I guess that's what happens when you have raging-hot sex with the Devil, I thought. Of course I couldn't tell Brad that—God only knows what his reaction would be if I tried to convince him that the last guy I dated was actually the ruler of Hell—so again I was forced to merely say, "Thank you. Maybe it's the new job."

"Maybe," he said, but he shot me a speculative little glance, as if he thought there were something else going on but couldn't exactly put his finger on what.

The rest of dinner went by without incident, and afterward we decided the evening was young enough that we should go see a movie. We eventually settled on the not-so-suspenseful thriller Nina and I had passed on a couple of weeks earlier. Brad had never been the romantic-comedy type, and I delicately suggested that although I thought it was great he backed documentary filmmakers, I wasn't quite in the mood for something that heavy on a Friday night.

As expected, the film was a little lackluster, but at least it passed the time. I always liked going to the movies on dates because it gave me a breather from having to come up with fascinating conversation for a few hours. Afterward, Brad suggested coffee or dessert. I still felt full from dinner, though, and wasn't really in the mood for coffee, either. It had been a busy day for me, and right then all I really wanted to do was go home.

Of course, that proposition was fraught with problems as well. I had told Luke I didn't kiss on the first date, and that really was my general rule, old-fashioned though it might be. But how did you handle a "first date" with someone you'd had a long-term relationship with in the past? After all, even though technically Brad and I had maintained separate residences the whole time we were dating, the truth of it was that for a good portion of that period I'd practically lived with him. He had his own apartment, while I shared campus housing with Nina, Micaela, and Jennifer. As much as I loved them, I certainly wasn't going to have Brad stay over at my place. Anyway, Brad and I had a past together, and telling him I didn't think that we should kiss at the end of the evening seemed somehow juvenile and prudish.

On the other hand, I wasn't sure how I felt about kissing Brad. Even though I hadn't had any contact with Luke for more than a week, it still felt like cheating.

Maybe you should stop second-guessing yourself and just see what happens, I told myself as Brad retrieved his SUV from the valet. *Maybe he doesn't even want to kiss you.*

That seemed like a remote possibility, though, judging from the glance Brad gave me after he climbed into the Pathfinder and pointed it west on Olympic. Far from not wanting to kiss me, that look told me he probably wanted a lot more. That wasn't going to happen, though, even if I somehow managed to flush Luke from the memory banks long enough to concentrate on Brad. From what I remembered, he was no slouch in the kissing department, either.

A light, misty rain had begun to fall by the time we got back to my apartment. We hurried over to the stairs and then climbed up to the second floor, where we both hesitated on the landing. It felt public but really wasn't; my next-door neighbor worked nights, so I could have a hot-and-heavy make-out session there with no one really noticing. And better to kiss on the landing than to invite Brad inside. I was afraid what sort of message a suggestion like that might send.

"Well," I said, after I had fished my keys out of my purse. "I had a really wonderful time—"

And the next thing I knew Brad had taken me by the shoulders and given me a really thorough kiss. My memory hadn't been faulty; his technique was still wonderful.

So why didn't I feel anything?

Oh, I kissed him back. I knew I had to give this the old college try. My purse slipped from my fingers and fell to the ground, and I let Brad pull me against him as he continued to press his mouth on mine. He was a shade shorter than Luke, so I didn't have to go up on my tiptoes to reach him comfortably. His lips, which should have felt familiar, could have been a stranger's. I shut my eyes and tried to relax into it, tried to make myself respond. But all I could think of was how different he somehow felt from Luke, and how much I wanted it to be Luke kissing me instead.

After a few seconds, we broke apart. Brad looked a little puzzled, as if he'd sensed something was wrong but couldn't say exactly what.

Eloquent as always, I managed to say, "Um… wow…I wasn't expecting that."

His expression cleared. I could almost see him telling himself that he'd just taken me by surprise. "Well, I know about your 'first date' rule, but I figured we could make an exception."

"Oh, sure," I replied, feeling like an idiot and a fraud at the same time. I knew I couldn't possibly explain to Brad what was really going on, but I also couldn't decide how best to handle the situation. However, I figured it was best to keep things where they were and leave any really important decisions for later, when I might actually have my head screwed on straight. "But I think we should leave it there for now."

Brad frowned slightly, but said without hesitation, "Of course. I'm willing to take it slow."

Well, at least that would give me some breathing space. I smiled and said, "Thanks for understanding."

In answer Brad leaned down and kissed me again, a little more softly this time. It was a good kiss and I knew it, but that realization only underscored the fact that the wrong man was kissing me.

"Are you busy tomorrow?" he asked.

Despite myself, I laughed. "That's taking it slow?"

He smiled. "Well, maybe not exactly, but I was hoping…."

"Sure," I said without thinking. Maybe it was a bad idea, but at least I could give him a second chance and see how I felt. If I had the same reaction to him the following day, then at least I'd know it was because I really had gone certifiably insane and not just that I hadn't had time to adjust to seeing Brad again after all these years.

"Great. Is seven still all right?"

"Sure," I repeated, feeling a little dazed. All I really wanted at that moment was to go inside, crawl into bed, and sleep for about a hundred years.

"I'll see you then." Brad kissed me for a third time, again on the lips, but quickly—just his way of saying good-bye.

I nodded, not sure exactly what I had done. The keys to my apartment were still in my hand, so I turned and opened the door, then said, "Good night," before slipping quickly inside. I didn't want him to even try to follow me, so I closed the door just as hastily and hoped it didn't seem too rude.

Apparently not; I heard him whistling as he descended the stairwell. That was another thing I'd forgotten—Brad was a very good whistler. Obviously he was pleased enough with how the evening had gone, even if he hadn't been allowed back inside the sanctum.

For myself, I just wished I didn't feel so relieved. That was a bad sign, wasn't it?

Shaking my head, I dropped my purse on the floor and headed toward the kitchen. I was thirsty and thought a glass of water sounded like a good idea, even though I'd had a small diet Coke during the movie. Probably all those chips and salsa catching up with me.

I stopped short in the living room, though, and stared at my MacBook in consternation. I could have sworn that I had shut it before I went to answer the door. But it sat on the coffee table, open, the forest screensaver showing a serene progression of woodland images. Had I really been so out of it that I'd just thought I'd closed the damn thing?

Frowning, I touched the pad to deactivate the screensaver. My mail program stared back at me, even though I clearly remembered closing that window and opening Firefox. I should have been looking at the browser, not Mail. But there was my inbox—no new messages, but for some reason the email from Luke now had the little gray arrow next to its subject line, indicating that I had replied to it.

But I hadn't. I had opened it and read it, then closed the window. I hadn't responded.

Fingers shaking a little, I clicked on the "Sent Items" folder. Had some poltergeist decided to take up residence in my apartment and start playing mind games with me?

Sure enough, a reply to Luke's email was at the top of the list, with a time stamp of eight-fifteen. Of course I couldn't have replied to it then—I'd been five miles away at El Cholo. And although Danny and his friends were up to a little industrial espionage and outright spying, I thought even they would draw the line at breaking and entering. Anyway, my laptop always stayed at home—it had never even been anyplace where Victor Nguyen could get his prying fingers on it. And Danny and I had worked everything out…hadn't we?

The mystery message turned out to be short and sweet, just three words.

I miss you.

I cringed when I read the email. Oh, it was the truth, absolutely, but that still didn't mean I wanted my computer to be spontaneously sending off pathetic messages on my behalf. How the hell was I supposed to stick to my guns about not apologizing to Luke when my laptop had betrayed me and made me sound like some needy clinging vine?

Getting angry helped, because it kept me from being severely freaked out. Still, I wandered the apartment, checking to make sure I hadn't left the back door unlocked (no dice), and that all the windows were securely shut. Normally I'd leave one or two open, but because of the uncertain weather I'd closed them all and fastened the latches, since one or two had been known to blow open in the past if the wind kicked up enough. My apartment was locked down tight as a drum, and if someone had forced entry they had to be a career criminal or with the NSA, because I couldn't find any signs that anyone except me had been in the place. So how the hell had my computer sent off a reply to an email when I was miles away?

I shivered, even though I'd left the heater on while I was gone, and the apartment was warm enough. At that same second, I heard the little chime that signaled an incoming email message. Again my heart began to beat a little faster. I rushed over to the computer to see who it was from.

Not Luke. I saw that right away—there was no reassuring "Luke Nicolini" in the address line. It was completely blank, which was strange, since even spam has to come from somewhere. The subject line was also empty. Curiosity overcame my judgment. I clicked on the email and prayed that my Mac's superior virus resistance would cover my ass in case there was anything particularly nasty attached to the message.

There were no attachments. There was only one word:

Believe.

"Believe," I said aloud. Now, what the hell was *that* supposed to mean? Believe in what? God? The Devil? The power of love? That Nordstrom would finally put that pair of Marc Jacobs boots I lusted after on sale? What?

Of course I got no answers. That one little word just sat there, staring at me, surrounded by white space, until finally I swore and shut the MacBook so I wouldn't have to look at it anymore.

It would have been a lot easier for me to believe if I had known exactly what I was supposed to believe in.

CHAPTER SEVENTEEN

THE PHONE RANG PROMPTLY AT TEN O'CLOCK the next morning. I follow the ten/ten rule ("don't call before ten in the morning or after ten at night unless you have explicit permission or someone's dead"), so I figured it was probably Nina checking in to see how the date with Brad had gone. Sure enough, it was her cell number on the display. With a sigh I picked up my phone and headed for the couch; I had a feeling this might take awhile.

She didn't even bother to say hello. "So?" she asked.

"So what?" I said.

"So how did it go? Did you pledge your undying love to one another?"

"Very funny," I commented, then lifted the remote and turned down the sound on my stereo. I'd actually been up for hours; even with my roaming around the house and the general edginess that resulted from trying to figure out who had sent the mystery email the night before, I was still in bed by midnight. When Nina called, I had been trying to catch up with my housework, so my obligatory belly-dance music was blaring from the speakers. It was great for getting my energy levels up, but not so great as background music.

"You don't seem all that thrilled," Nina said. "Does this mean that the magic is gone?"

I hesitated.

"There's a whole book about this same thing. It's called *You Can't Go Home Again*."

"Boy, you're just full of zingers this morning," I said, my tone sour. "Is Allan D'Al-whatever going to get you a booking at the Laugh Factory?"

"You didn't answer my question."

"Maybe because I don't want to."

Nina was silent for a few seconds. Then she said, "I'm getting an 'I don't want to talk about it' vibe."

"How perceptive of you." I sighed. "Look, Nina, it was fine, but yeah, you're right, I wasn't getting a lot of sparks."

"Because of him."

I didn't bother to ask which "him" she meant. It sure as hell wasn't Danny. "Maybe," I admitted.

"I told you it was too soon."

"So pat yourself on the back for being right," I snapped, then said immediately, "Sorry, Nina—I just hate feeling like Luke's ruined me for all other men or something. I mean, I used to be absolutely nuts for Brad. Well…you know."

"Believe me, I do," she said, in tones of heavy significance. "Look, don't beat yourself up about it. People change. Just because you guys really clicked when you were back in college doesn't necessarily mean that you're right for each other now. I'm sure you thought of a gentle way to let Brad know that."

"Well…."

Nina's voice sharpened. "Oh, no, you didn't."

"Well…."

"Tell me you didn't sleep with him."

"Of course not!" I retorted, stung. "I'm not *that* stupid."

"So then?"

"So we kissed. And it's like I could tell he was a good kisser, but I just didn't care. It was awful. But—" I hesitated.

"But what?"

"But I still said I'd go out with him again tonight."

Nina made a disgusted sound.

"Well, I figured it would be better to give it one more try, just to see if I was having an off night or if I needed to work through some more stuff about

Luke before I wrote Brad off completely." That sounded lame even to me.

Obviously Nina was of the same opinion. "So you're going to magically get your Luke issues worked out before Brad picks you up tonight? That doesn't make a whole hell of a lot of sense."

"I don't know," I said. And the horrible thing was that I really didn't. My email had been empty of new messages this morning. No reply from Luke. No more mysterious notes from the ether, instructing me next to think or to dream or whatever else would be of absolutely no help in this situation.

"Geez, girl, and I thought I was the one who didn't know what she wanted."

"Maybe I should just become a nun," I remarked.

"Danny would love that."

For some reason, her comment made me burst out laughing, and after a second or two Nina joined in. Maybe it was the whole "if I don't laugh, I'll cry" mentality. I didn't know for sure. All I did know was that it felt awfully good to laugh.

"I guess I figured one more night couldn't hurt," I said at length. "He really did want to see me again, and maybe some more time together will help me decide if the chemistry's really gone, or whether I just need to stop obsessing over Luke."

"Well, you need to do that, regardless of what you end up deciding about Brad," Nina replied. "I mean, he was amazingly dreamy, but he's just one man. There are plenty more out there."

No, there aren't, I thought. Everyone wanted to be thought of as unique, but in his case that desire was the simple truth. Luke existed unto himself. It wasn't as if I could go back to Lola's with the girls and find another being just like him.

Of course I couldn't tell Nina that. I couldn't tell her the truth about Luke, and it wasn't my place to do so even if I thought she'd believe me. Even though it was fairly obvious he'd discarded me with as little concern as someone throwing away an empty soda can, I wouldn't let my hurt and anger allow me to expose him for who and what he was. I still loved him too much for that.

So I just said, "I know I need to get over him. It's just going to take me a while."

"And I'm not sure going out with Brad is the best way to do it," she replied. "I mean, I know you're going to do what you want. I can't stop you. But really, maybe you should slow down and think about what you're doing."

"You're right," I said, without really thinking.

"Excuse me? Could you repeat that? Speak into the microphone."

"Ha," I said. "I'm not so petty that I can't admit you might be right about Brad. I'll handle it."

"Good girl. Well, if you end up ditching him, give me a call. Allan told me about this really hot party that's going on in the Hills tonight."

"Oh, it's 'Allan' now, is it?" I asked caustically. I hoped the whole acting/modeling thing hadn't been just a ploy to get into Nina's pants. Then again, if Allan thought he was going to get away with that sort of thing around Nina and live to tell the tale, he wasn't as savvy as he looked.

"Shut up," Nina said. "We weren't talking about my personal life, we were talking about yours."

"Oh, so now Mr. D'Ala-whatsis is part of your personal life?"

"*D'Alessandro*. And shut up."

That made me laugh, as she had probably intended it to, and I promised that if I really did give Brad the brush-off I'd give her a call. I didn't think I would, though. If I didn't want to see him again, I figured I should at least tell him to his face and let him know that it had nothing to do with him and everything to do with me.

I hung up the phone and wondered what I used to do with my spare time before my life got so complicated.

Complicated life or not, I needed to go to the grocery store that afternoon, since I was out of just about everything. Grocery shopping in my neighborhood was sort of like planning a combat mission—everything depended on timing and preparation. For some reason, Saturdays around two o'clock tended to be dead, unless there was a big football game later in the day. But of course by mid-February football season was safely behind me, and I figured I could run in and get what I needed without losing more than, say, an hour of my life.

Both of the stores closest to me were owned by Ralphs, so it really just depended on which particular traffic nightmare I wanted to deal with. The Ralphs on La Brea was a little closer, but its lot was completely inadequate. The store at the Beverly Connection had more parking, but since it shared its parking structure with a bunch of other shops, sometimes you ended up having to park on a different level from the store itself and then bring your purchases up in the elevator. For some reason I found something fundamentally wrong with having to put a grocery cart in an elevator, so I decided to head to the La Brea store and take my chances.

Luck or God or chance or whatever force ruled the universe seemed to be smiling on me, since I pulled into the parking lot just as a minivan backed out of one of the choice spots in the row that faced the storefront. I aimed my Mercedes into the space before any of the predatory-looking cars that were trolling the lot could try to lay claim to it. As I got out of the car, I felt rather than saw several people giving me the evil eye, but I ignored them. It wasn't as if I had cut anyone off—they just weren't fast enough.

I selected a cart, made sure it didn't have any wobbly wheels or trash left inside (I hated that), and moved off to collect my purchases in an orderly manner so I could get out of there as quickly as possible. I hated grocery shopping anyway—spending money on consumables isn't my idea of a fun time. But even I needed more than the one ancient container of yogurt that currently resided in my fridge, so I resigned myself to stocking up and told myself that at least I only had to worry about feeding one person. Small comfort. I got the feeling that I could even get used to cooking on a regular basis if I were doing it for Luke.

The store really wasn't that crowded; the small-ish parking lot always made it seem as if there should be more people inside than there ever actually were. I trundled my cart along, moving in my usual pattern from dairy to frozen to regular dry goods, until I finally ended up in the produce department. Of course I wasn't a dedicated vegan like my mother, but I did tend to eat a lot of fruit; it was tasty and good for me, and I could feel somewhat virtuous when eating it.

I had paused by the apples, ruminating on the merits of Gala over Granny Smith (I hated Delicious, which as far as I was concerned were anything but), when I noticed a man who stood across the aisle from me, a shopping basket over one tweed-clad arm. He appeared to be in his late sixties and looked a little familiar, even though I couldn't really place where I'd seen him before. Then he smiled, and it suddenly hit me. The elderly gentleman from Lola's. The one who had been with Luke.

His gaze met mine, and for some reason I felt a little shiver run through me. Oh, he looked completely harmless—sweet and kind, actually, but there was something about the dark eyes under their heavy gray-frosted brows that made me want to stand up a little straighter.

"Difficult decision?" he asked. His voice was calm and a little deep, with just the slightest hint of an indefinable accent that sounded vaguely Eastern European. In fact, in appearance he reminded me of the elderly Jewish men who frequented the shops along Fairfax and Third Street, gray and tweedy and with an odd sort of shabby elegance.

I had the sudden idea that he wasn't referring to the apples, but I still picked one up and weighed it in my hand. "I'm partial to Galas, but I think they're getting a little out of season."

"Perhaps, but I think you'd still enjoy them the most," he replied.

"Then I'll take your advice," I said, and began selecting the most likely subjects out of the pile next to me.

"I'm glad to hear it," he said, then stepped a little closer. "Would you humor an old man and take another piece of advice?"

"Um, sure," I replied, as a ripple of nervous anticipation ran through me. But I just had to ask. "I—I have seen you before, haven't I?"

"Yes," he said, and gave me another one of those peculiarly sweet smiles. "I believe we have a mutual friend."

"Oh," I faltered, not sure of what I should say next. If this man was really who I thought He was, then no doubt He already knew all about Luke's and my difficulties. What He thought of the entire situation, I shuddered to think. "Is he—is he really a friend?"

The calm, dark gaze didn't flicker. "Oh, of course. We have known one another for quite some time."

Just an eternity or so, I thought. Well, at least Luke had apparently been telling me the truth about that. "So have you spoken lately?" I inquired, in a voice that shook only a little.

"Oh, yes." His mouth twitched, and I got the impression He was laughing at me, just a little, and completely without malice. "I've been treated to quite the diatribe on the nature of men's souls and the complete incomprehensibility of the feminine psyche. As if that were my fault."

I just had to ask. "Er…isn't it?"

He looked surprised. "No. At least, not completely. Poor Luke, he's always had issues understanding the whole concept of free will. To be expected, of course, considering his background. Still, it does lead to some confusion."

My head was reeling. Then again, it's not every day that you stand in the produce department of your local grocery store discussing free will and the Devil with God. If that was who this kindly old man actually turned out to be.

"Oh, your instincts are correct," He said, still smiling.

My mouth dropped a little.

"I suppose I should stop doing that," He mused, picking up an apple from the display and inspecting it minutely. "It does tend to put people off. Old habits are difficult to shake."

Feeling more than a little out of my depth, I just stared back at Him. I wasn't sure of the protocol in such situations, although dropping to my knees and prostrating myself didn't seem like a very good idea. For one thing, I'd be sure to attract attention, and for another, all I could hear in my head was the voice of God from that Monty Python movie about the Holy Grail where He snapped, "And stop groveling! I hate groveling!"

So I stood where I was, fingers clenched around the handle of my shopping cart.

"Wise choice," He said approvingly. "You wouldn't want to attract that sort of attention."

"So what should I do?" I asked at last. After all, if I'd actually been blessed with a private audience with God, I figured I should make the most of it.

"'Do'?" He repeated, looking a little surprised. "I should think that would be obvious."

"Well, it's not obvious to me," I replied.

"Oh, it is, even if you have chosen to blind yourself to the path you should take."

Was it possible to get disgruntled with God? I cocked my eyebrow and crossed my arms, waiting.

"I probably shouldn't tell you this," He commented. "Rules and all that." His dark eyes took on a certain twinkle. "However, since I created them, I suppose I can bend them as well. Have you heard of a certain saying, 'Pride goeth before a fall'?"

"Um…I think so." If pressed I could probably recognize about five sentences from the Bible, max, but that one sounded vaguely familiar.

"Proverbs, actually. The full quote is 'Pride goeth before destruction, and an haughty spirit before a fall.' Applicable to all sorts of situations, of course, but our friend Luke is particularly susceptible to the sin of pride, as I think you know."

I forced myself to nod. Wasn't it Lucifer's pride and arrogance that started the whole war in Heaven? I couldn't be absolutely certain, and at this point I supposed it didn't matter. After all, it seemed as if God had gotten over it.

Looking thoughtful, He replaced the apple He held on the display and then said, "But Luke isn't the only one who's guilty of pride, of course. Wasn't it hurt pride that caused you to become angry with him in the first place? Weren't your sensibilities wounded that he had simply handed you something which you thought you should have earned?"

"Well, he was completely out of line," I protested, then stopped. Maybe arguing with God wasn't such a great idea. I didn't want to get turned into a pillar of salt or something.

"True, but did you ever stop to think *why* he did it?"

That comment gave me pause. Had I? Or had I been in such a hurry to climb on my high horse that I'd never stopped to really think about why Luke would do such a thing in the first place?

"Um, no," I said at last, in a small voice.

"I can't agree with what he did," said God, "but in this one case his motivations were actually quite pure. He wanted to make you happy."

"He did?" I asked, feeling more like a worm than ever.

"Yes. So let Me ask you another question, and I trust you'll answer Me truthfully. Not that it matters; I'll know either way. But I think you should say it."

I swallowed, then said, "All right." It was more than a little disconcerting to be having a discussion with someone who knew what you were going to say before you even said it. Even Luke, with all his powers, hadn't quite achieved that level of omniscience.

"Do you love him?"

There was no point in trying to dance around the issue. I knew the answer…and I was pretty sure God did, too.

"Yes," I said.

A smile of beatific sweetness spread across His features. "Then the rest is simple, isn't it?"

"It is?"

"Of course. You must tell him."

That would be breaking the cardinal rule of modern womanhood; i.e., never tell a man you love him until you're about ninety-nine percent certain he's going to say it in return. Oh, well, rules were made to be broken.

"And that will just fix everything?" I asked, trying to keep the sarcasm out of my tone and only partly succeeding.

In answer, He reached out and touched the tip of His finger to my forehead. I felt a wave of tingling warmth spread out over my whole body, followed by a sensation of utter peace. For that one second I caught a glimpse of the inner calm my mother talked about whenever she tried to get me to do yoga. Still smiling, He said, "*Believe.*"

And then He was gone. Just like Luke—no puff of smoke, no clap of thunder. Whether by design or chance the produce section was deserted, so no one was around to witness the sudden disappearance of the kindly-looking old gentleman in the worn tweed jacket.

For a long moment I stood there, staring at the space He had occupied. With one shaking hand I reached out to pick up the apple He had replaced on the top of the display. It felt cool to my touch, completely ordinary, but I gazed down at it the way a pilgrim would stare at a holy relic. Maybe it was. I wrapped my fingers around it, then placed it reverently in my cart.

I took a deep breath. "*Believe,*" I told myself.

I hoped it would be that easy.

To say going back to my apartment after that encounter was a bit anti-climactic was like saying that *Titanic* was a big boat—woefully inaccurate and lacking any sense of scale. But I supposed even Moses had to go off and eat dinner or take a leak or whatever after he'd spoken to the burning bush. Mere mortals can't dispense with the common-places of life; we have them shoved in our faces on a daily basis. Besides, the act of hauling my groceries up the stairs and then putting them away helped me regain some semblance of normality. At least my hands finally stopped shaking.

So God wanted me to tell Luke that I loved him. Fine and dandy. Exactly how I was supposed to accomplish that, I wasn't sure. An email seemed tacky, and I didn't have his phone number—he'd never given me one. Pretty much all contact had been initiated by him. I did, however, know where he lived…or thought I did. I had a harder time remembering how to get to places when I hadn't driven there myself, but I did know his house was located off Beverly Drive on one of those exclusive streets near the country club. It might take a little work, but I thought I could narrow it down if necessary. Of course, I could always call Danny for the exact address, but the embarrassment that would involve seemed excruciatingly worse than simply driving around Hancock Park until I found the Italianate mansion that belonged to Luke.

Worrying about logistics helped to keep me from stewing over what I would say to Luke when—*if*—I saw him. Did God expect me to just blurt out, "I love you," and hope for the best? Was I supposed to apologize for flying off the handle and not giving Luke a chance to explain? Was *he* supposed to apologize for not thinking of the consequences of his actions? And what about the complete radio silence that had followed our blowout at the Ivy? What exactly had he been doing all that time? Sulking?

Waiting for me to come after him? In the final analysis, did it really matter?

That God had caused my little laptop to send off that pathetic "I miss you" message seemed obvious. Maybe it was His way of softening up Luke so that I'd have a fighting chance when I finally confronted him. I couldn't know for sure. Maybe God was trying to tell me that I didn't need to know. I just needed to believe.

The phone rang then, and I jumped. Since I had been standing in the kitchen after placing the last of the groceries in the refrigerator, I had to step into the dining room to dig my cell out of my purse where I'd left it on the table. A quick glance at the display.

Not Luke, of course. My sister.

I prayed there wasn't another Traci crisis to deal with. The last thing I needed was to go tearing down to Orange County when I'd finally steeled myself up to talk to Luke.

After pushing the "accept" button, I said, "Hi, Lisa."

"Oh, great—you're home!"

That was the Lisa I remembered—bubbling, her tone upbeat and happy. I'd never been able to figure out how much of it was an act she put on to convince everyone around her that everything was perfect in her world, and how much was really the result of being in a state of perpetual optimism. At times it had gotten a little tedious, especially when I wasn't in a particularly good mood, but it was a definite improvement from the brittle edginess I'd seen ever since my father had told all of us about Traci's impending bundle of joy.

"Oh, yeah," I said. "Just puttering around the house before I go out tonight. So what's up?"

"Nathan and I are pregnant!"

I'd always thought that was an odd expression, like the happy couple was going to be sharing all the fun of gaining weight, retaining water, and yakking in the toilet for the first few months, but I supposed it was just a way of making the father seem more included in the process. After a second or so of flabbergasted silence, I finally said, "Really? I didn't know you two were trying." God, I was such a liar.

But of course she didn't seem to notice anything odd about my tone. "Well, we really didn't want to say anything because it just gets everyone's expectations up. But we've been trying for almost eighteen months."

"Wow," I said, lacking anything better to offer. Not that Lisa needed any encouragement to keep babbling away.

"Of course, it's very early—I'm just about six weeks along—but my ob/gyn says everything looks fine and that I should be due around the middle of September. That means I'm going to be big as a house during the hottest part of the summer, naturally, but Nathan says I shouldn't worry about it, that's what air conditioning is for." She paused, presumably to draw breath; I hoped the baby wasn't suffering an oxygen deficit from the unimpeded flow of words.

"That's great," I said. "Have you told Mom?"

"Oh, yes, I called her first. She's very excited about being a grandmother."

I could imagine. My mother was probably already researching organic formula and cruelty-free yarn to knit politically correct baby booties. After a brief hesitation, I asked, "And Dad?"

"He's really excited, too. He says our babies can have play dates together."

My brain tried to ponder the weirdness involved in having an uncle/aunt who was young enough to have been a play date, then decided it really didn't want to think about it too hard. I knew that sort of thing did happen occasionally; I just never thought it would happen in my family.

"Nathan said we really just had to believe that it would happen, and it did."

I froze. "What?"

"I said that Nathan just told me to believe, and everything would work itself out." Lisa hesitated, then asked, "Are you okay? You sound a little strange."

"I'm fine," I said distantly. Was this one more cosmic smoke signal from God, just another way of convincing me that I had to follow His advice and believe, and the rest would fall in line? Or was it just random chance, a simple coincidence?

After talking with God, I'd gotten the distinct impression that nothing was coincidence.

"You're sure," Lisa said.

I knew I had to get my act together, because I certainly didn't want Lisa to think that I wasn't happy for her. I *was* happy, and relieved that they'd finally gotten what they'd been trying for all these months. As preoccupied as I might be with other matters, I had to give her the attention she needed right now. "Absolutely," I said, relieved that I sounded completely sincere. "You two deserve it. I'm really happy for you."

She gave a bubbly little laugh. "It hasn't really sunk in yet, I think, even though we've already started looking at baby furniture and all that fun stuff. Probably when my pants start to get tight I'll know it's really happening."

"Oh, that should be a ways off," I said. My sister was very dedicated about her exercise regimen, and I figured it would probably be some time before she really started to show.

"I don't know," she replied. "I'm already fantasizing about those chocolate milkshakes from In 'N' Out. It'll be so good to eat like a pig for once."

"Do I need to warn Nathan?" I asked with a laugh.

"I already did," Lisa said. "He just said, hey, whatever makes you happy."

Not for the first time I reflected on Nathan's innate superiority as a human being. I thought he would make a great father. From there my mind inevitably went off on a tangent as to what Luke would be like as a father. If he could even father children. If he ever spoke to me again. First things first.

"That's great," I told her. "We need to plan a celebratory dinner or something."

"Already ahead of you. We haven't nailed it down yet, but maybe tomorrow night—I'll get back to you as soon as I know more. I just wanted to tell you the news and not spring it on you at dinner like certain other people." Her tone was sly. Not that I could blame her.

"Good idea," I agreed, and then we exchanged some more chit-chat before I finally hung up and sat there for a moment, staring down at the cell phone I held and musing on the inexplicable nature of the universe.

I needed to go see Luke, and without much further delay. But there was something else I had to do first. I sighed, then dug Brad's phone number out of the desk drawer where I had put it. Even if Luke wasn't home…even if he threw me bodily off his property…I knew that Brad and I had no future together. Nina was right. You can't go home again. All you can do is keep moving forward and hoping for the best.

Believing.

CHAPTER EIGHTEEN

THE INTERVIEW WITH BRAD didn't go as well as I'd hoped. In the back of my mind I thought he'd just sigh and say, "Oh, I completely understand, we can't relive the past, have a nice life." The reality was that he ended up asking a few pointed questions about why I'd changed my mind, to which I replied it was none of his business. Then he said it actually was his business, since I'd agreed to go out with him a second time. I was forced to tell him that I couldn't see him ever again because I was in love with someone else, and that wasn't going to change any time soon. Then I made a nasty remark to the effect that he'd had his chance with me and blown it. This lovely conversation received its end punctuation via me hanging up and wishing I'd never agreed to go out with him in the first place.

All in all, not the sort of thing to put me in the best frame of mind to confront Luke, although Nina probably would have told me that any closure was better than none at all. Still, I was already feeling edgy and nervous, and the confrontation with Brad didn't help much. I made myself change out of my faded jeans and sweatshirt, take a quick shower, and put on something presentable before venturing out. Maybe my appearance didn't really matter all that much, but I didn't think that going out to have what could be the most important conversation of my life in a grubby UCLA sweatshirt and torn jeans was a very good idea.

So I put on my favorite True Religion jeans and a jacket, nice boots, and applied some makeup and brushed my hair. Thank God at least my hair was low maintenance enough—it just needed a few quick strokes of the brush to calm it down a little, and I was good to go.

But go where, exactly? I pulled up Google maps on my computer and zeroed in on the area where I was fairly sure Luke's house was located, but I honestly couldn't recall the name of the street. Still, I thought I had it narrowed down to a few blocks. From there I'd just have to hope that God was still watching over me and could give me a gentle nudge in the right direction. Otherwise, with my luck, someone would think I was casing the neighborhood for a robbery and call the police.

It had turned out to be a beautiful day. Southern California was enjoying a breathing space between storms, and so the area was dotted with large gray-white clouds, the sky in between them a deep, almost lapis blue. On days like this the smog lifted, and you could see the Hollywood sign clearly on the hills to the northeast. Far off to the west the ocean glinted like a narrow band of gold. A brisk breeze caught me as I descended the stairs to the garage, and I was glad I'd worn my tweedy wool jacket. At least I'd keep somewhat warm.

I headed east on Wilshire, and then cut up to Beverly from Highland and slowed down until I saw a street that looked sort of familiar. Since I did remember the house was north of Beverly, I turned left and hoped I'd chosen correctly.

Well, I hadn't. At first I couldn't really tell, because the neighborhood looked right; it was a mixture of Spanish-style and Tudor mansions (not McMansions like my father's, but the real thing, on very large plots of land), but none of them seemed to be Luke's. I supposed I shouldn't have been disappointed that I didn't get it on the first try, but I wondered if this were the universe trying to tell me something or whether it was just plain old bad luck. When I hit Oakwood, I turned right and thought I could use it to cut through, but no dice; it dead-ended at the country club. I wondered briefly whether I should just park the car there in the shadow of an enormous Norman-style chateau and have a good cry, but all that would get me was red eyes and a puffy nose. Instead, I turned the car around, maneuvered down another street whose name I didn't catch, and then went back out to Beverly and headed a few more blocks east before trying my luck with another side street.

That did the trick; I hadn't gotten more than a third of the way up the street before I recognized the pretty half-timbered mock-Tudor house that stood next door to Luke's Mediterranean-style villa. But even as I slowed down to approach the property and pull over and park the car, I knew something had gone horribly wrong.

A shiny Jag—not Luke's convertible, but a black XJ model—was parked out in front. Besides that, a tall, slender woman in a Chanel-style tweed suit was busily tamping a "For Sale" sign into the impossibly smooth lawn.

I didn't know what else to do, so I went ahead and pulled into the empty spot behind the Jag, then grabbed my purse and got out.

The real estate agent paused in her hammering and gave me a bright, professional smile. I knew the type, of course, since my sister was one of them. Always on, always polished, although I noticed the strong breeze had ruffled her stylish razor-cut bob into a disarray of perfectly streaked strands. Judging by the car, the suit might really be Chanel and not just a high-end knockoff.

"You must be haunting the MLS listings," she said. "I just got this one late yesterday. Janice Wilkerson." And she extended a well-manicured hand in my direction.

At first I didn't know what she was talking about, then realized she must have thought I'd come to look at the house. Of course a place like that was so out of my price range it wasn't even funny, but I supposed that since I had driven up in a nice car and was reasonably well-dressed, she'd decided to give me the benefit of the doubt. These days it was awfully hard to tell who really had money and who didn't, since people who were rolling in cash often dressed like slobs. Anyone who sold the kind of high-end homes that populated this neighborhood couldn't pass up even the possibility of a quick sale, especially since the housing market was still fairly lackluster.

"Um…right," I said. "I hope you don't mind."

"No, that's fine," she replied, still with that professional pasted-on smile. I wondered absently if she had to put Vaseline on her front teeth the way beauty contestants did to keep that unnatural smile going. "I don't have a lockbox on the front door yet, but the back door off the kitchen is open if you don't mind going in through the yard."

"No, I don't mind," I said hastily, then added, "Is it all right if I go in alone? I sort of like to get a feeling for the space by myself first." If he'd already hired someone to sell the house, then very likely Luke was long gone, but I wanted to be alone, just in case.

She looked dubious for a moment, then glanced over at my Mercedes and back at me. My appearance must have reassured her—after all, I didn't really look like someone who had shown up to rob the place—because after the briefest of hesitations she replied, "No, that's fine. I'll just be out here in my car, going over some paperwork. I've already put some information sheets about the house on the kitchen table, so you can pick one up to get the particulars of the square footage and so on."

"Great," I said, then shouldered my purse and headed down the driveway and under the porte-cochere. Past that the driveway extended to the detached three-car garage, but if I were recalling the layout correctly, there should be a side gate that led into the backyard off the drive. Sure enough, it turned out to be more or less exactly where I had thought it was located. I lifted the latch and let myself in.

It was very quiet. I knew that the city stretched around me in all directions, but here, in a place that was buffered on all sides by high walls and even taller trees, most of the incessant street noise that hung like smog over L.A. at all times had been effectively blocked.

Dead leaves floated on the surface of the pool, and the house had the indefinable forlorn air of a place that had been abandoned. Of course the lawn was still perfectly mown down to an inch of level green, and the herb garden off to one side and the flower beds around the borders were likewise weeded and neat, but it still felt empty and somehow sad. A cloud passed over the sun, and I shivered.

Not knowing what else to do, I turned and entered the house through the French doors that opened off the kitchen. As Janice Wilkerson had informed me, a pile of color flyers pointing out the particulars of the listing sat on top of the table where Luke and I had once shared breakfast. Had it only been a few weeks ago? It felt like years.

I picked up the flyer and learned that the house, built in 1922, had six bedrooms and seven baths in approximately six thousand square feet, and that she was asking five and a half million for it. Ouch. If I saved for the next twenty years I might be able to get together a quarter of the down payment.

Since I knew I had no real use for it, I set the flyer down on top of the pile and then squared it so it would still look orderly and perfect. After that I wandered down the main hall and into the living room, then paused there to look at the fireplace, now cold and dead as the rest of the house. Luke had kissed me here once, while a low fire burned in the hearth and the glorious final trio from *Faust* still echoed through my mind. But I could see no sign of him here; the place was devoid of any personal touches…no photographs, no half-read books lying on the coffee table, not even a remote for the stereo that had been cleverly concealed in the massive wall unit on the opposite side of the room. It looked as soulless and precise as a model home.

I knew there was no point in my going upstairs. Why, so I could look at the bed where he'd made love to me and torture myself some more? Apparently he was selling the house furnished, or at least had left everything in place so that it would show better. I wondered what he planned to do with the proceeds of the sale. It wasn't as if he needed the money.

What now, God? I thought. *I came chasing over here, and for what? To discover the home's current market value? To see how beautiful the hardwood floors really are? What?*

Of course I heard nothing, not even a soft sighing of the breeze that I could pretend was Him saying, *Believe….*

Luke's absence from the house felt like a hole in the world. Unshed tears formed a hard, burning knot in my chest, just above my solar plexus. I fought them back, though; the last thing I needed was for the glossy Ms. Wilkerson to come through the door and find me crying my eyes out in the middle of the living room.

I'd already thought up the excuses for leaving without taking a flyer. *It's a little too much space…it's too far for me to drive to work…I don't care for the paint color in the dining room.* Whatever it took to get me out of there with my dignity relatively unscathed.

I knew it was far too late for my sanity.

Jaw clenched, I made my way back to the kitchen. I figured it was safest to let myself out the way I had come in. For all I knew, the real estate agent had installed the lockbox on the front door while I was still roaming disconsolately through the downstairs rooms. I opened the French doors and stepped outside.

A shadow at the far edge of the garden caught my attention. I turned, and saw Luke standing there, watching me. For the longest moment I couldn't do anything but remain frozen on the top step, as his eyes met mine and an odd little wind blew a flurry of leaves past my feet.

He spoke first. "I knew you'd be here."

I found my voice. "I hoped you'd be here."

Another one of those uncomfortable pauses. After not seeing him for so many days, I found myself wanting to stare at him, at the heavy dark hair and long nose, the piercing blue eyes and thin but somehow sensual mouth. Actually, what I really wanted to do was run down the steps and throw myself into his arms, but my fragile self-control just barely managed to keep me from doing something so foolish.

"Someone told me that I was being a bull-headed fool," Luke said. "And that I should talk to you again before giving up entirely."

Sometimes divine intervention can come in really handy. "I think I know who you're talking about," I replied. "Elderly gentleman, favors tweed?"

Luke raised an eyebrow. "You, too?"

I shrugged. "Who knew that God liked to hang around in the produce section of the supermarket?"

To my surprise, he actually smiled. "He does have a way of turning up in strange places."

Feeling a little more brave, I made my way down the stairs and took a few hesitant steps in his direction. He watched me carefully, but he had his poker face on; I found it impossible to guess what he might be thinking. Was he just here because God had told him to come? Or had he gotten the benefit of a little divine advice as well?

Whatever Luke might or might not have going through his mind, I knew I had to say what was on mine. If God thought I'd let pride get the better of me, then I'd be humble. Apologies didn't come easily to me, but I had an idea they were even more difficult for Luke. Maybe if I showed him the way, we could get past what had been, in the final analysis, really a rather silly quarrel.

"I'm sorry," I said simply.

"You're sorry?" he asked. "For what?"

"For misunderstanding you," I replied. "For not stopping to think about what you'd tried to do." I hesitated, then added, "For running off like that and not even giving you a chance to explain."

"Accepted," Luke said, and a wry smile twisted his mouth. "Even though I'm probably the one who should have apologized first." He shot me one of those sideways glances I remembered so well. "You're not the only one who got a lecture on the sin of pride, although I have a feeling mine was considerably lengthier than yours."

A feeling of cautious joy began to spread through me. If Luke really had meant to send me packing, I doubted he'd be admitting that God had apparently given him what amounted to a good scolding. Maybe I'd have the strength to tell him how I really felt.

"So," he went on, and paused. The breeze caught his wavy hair and blew it back from his forehead, and I had to cross my arms and clench my hands at my sides to stave off the impulse to run my fingers through the heavy, rumpled locks. He shook his head. "I should have stopped to think about how you might receive such a gift. You'll forgive me if I tell you that in the past I've usually had to deal with people who possessed rather less…integrity."

"Oh, I don't know about that—" I began, feeling a flush spread across my cheeks. I didn't think I'd ever had anyone tell me I had integrity before. Then again, it wasn't the sort of thing that usually came up in day-to-day conversation.

"Well, I do," Luke said firmly, in a tone that allowed no argument. "You are an—unexpected person, Christa Simms. I went into this thinking I knew all the answers, and I have discovered that I know nothing at all."

Into what? I wanted to ask, but somehow I knew I shouldn't interrupt him, that I should just let him continue in this rare confessional mood.

"You've spoken to God," he remarked, and I thought I saw that little glint come and go in his eyes. "A rare gift, and not one that should be taken lightly, as you may well imagine. I hope, however, that you understand this is not something to be spoken of to anyone else."

"Who would believe me?" I asked logically, and he smiled.

"True. These days those who have actually had communication with God tend to be treated as madmen instead of visionaries." Luke's expression darkened, and he looked away from me, up into the dappled sky. At that moment another cloud passed across the sun, and he frowned. "And since I have spoken with Him as well, I know He has given me permission to speak frankly with you. In fact, He insisted on it. Pulled up the usual quotes…'the truth shall set you free,' and so on."

"Did it?" I asked, so softly I wasn't sure he could hear me.

But apparently he did, because he said, "That remains to be seen. You see, I haven't been completely honest with you."

My heart seemed to miss a beat. "What do you mean?"

"During our first meal, you accused me of having an ulterior motive for seeking you out, and I believe I brushed off that comment. In fact, you were speaking the truth."

Here it comes, I thought. *So what is it, really? My immortal soul? Playing Mary for his unholy son… although this one certainly wouldn't be a virgin birth.* I swallowed, and somewhere in the back of my mind I finally heard God's voice.

Believe.…

"So what is the truth?" I asked, and Luke smiled grimly.

"Another man asked that same question more than two thousand years ago. But he would not stay to hear the answer." The blue eyes caught mine, and held. I felt as if I couldn't have looked away, even if I'd wanted to. "I'd grown weary of Hell, Christa. Weary of the charge God had given me so many years ago. I asked for release, and He made a bargain with me."

I said nothing, but merely waited for him to go on.

"If I could love someone, and have them love me, then I would be free. I could live a mortal life, and pass into Heaven when my span of days on this earth was ended. That someone was you, of course."

At first I couldn't quite wrap my brain around the concept. How could the Devil not be the Devil anymore? Weren't there rules about that sort of thing? I realized then that of course God made the rules, and if He wanted to shatter them irrevocably, I supposed that was His prerogative. Still, I couldn't manage much more than a gasp of, "Me?"

Luke smiled. "You, Christa. God chose you, for reasons He of course kept to himself. Someone who on the surface seemed quite ordinary."

At first I felt a little offended—after all, who likes being called "ordinary"?—but then I realized he had said "on the surface." So I bit my lip and waited to see what he would say next.

"But God, being who He is, of course understood that you were far from ordinary, that you were in fact the one woman who could allow me to understand human love."

If the garden had seemed quiet before, now it sounded positively hushed. Even the birds had stopped their chatter in the trees. It was as if Luke and I were the only two beings in the entire world. Maybe for those few seconds we were.

He seemed not to notice the unnatural stillness, but continued, "The pain I experienced after you left the restaurant that night was unlike anything I had ever felt. At first I thought it was simply because I had seen my hopes of attaining Heaven dashed, and I was angry—angry that you, a mortal, had thwarted me so neatly. I went to confront God, to tell Him He had made a mistake and that love was an impossibility. To which He replied that of course it was, and that was what made it so perfect. I didn't want to listen to Him…and it took quite some time for me to understand what He'd been trying to tell me."

"Which was?" I asked.

"That I wasn't in pain because you'd taken away my dream of returning to Heaven," he replied. "I was in pain because I had lost *you*. Love is sometimes difficult to recognize when you have no frame of reference."

I waited, holding myself as still as the quiet garden that surrounded us. I was afraid to say or do anything to break the fragile thread his words had somehow woven between us two.

"What I want to say, Christa, is this…I love you."

The faint tingle that had passed through me after God touched my forehead was nothing to the wave of warmth that washed over me after I heard him say those words. I had hoped—I had dreamed—but I hadn't been sure. Not until now.

Believe, God had told me. Well, I certainly believed now.

I looked up at him, at the man I had come to love. If God had made a bargain with the Devil, then it was time I sealed it.

"I love you," I replied.

A tremor shook the ground beneath our feet. Luke reached out and drew me close against him, and I could hear his heart pounding beneath my ear. Several crows, possibly unnerved by the faint earthquake, exploded out of the trees above our heads, scolding and cackling at each other. The breeze picked up again, bringing with it the smell of the ocean and rain, even though the day was still dappled dark and light.

"What happened?" I asked at last.

"I'm free," Luke said in wondering tones. "I can feel it—I'm as mortal as you are."

"You don't seem any different," I replied, and he didn't. It was the same Luke who held me, whose heart beat against my cheek. The same man I had fallen in love with.

A semi-familiar voice intruded on the scene. "Did you feel that?"

I lifted my head to see Janice Wilkerson come striding into the garden in her high-heeled boots. She came to a dead stop as she saw me standing there in Luke's arms.

"Mr. Nicolini?" she asked. The last syllable came out as a sort of undignified squeak. Then again, probably the last thing she had expected to see was me in the arms of the man whose house she was trying to sell.

Somehow he managed to disentangle himself from me and shoot her a slightly apologetic smile. "Hello, Janice. It appears I won't be selling the house after all."

"You—what?" She looked from Luke to me and then back again, jaw waggling a bit. Probably she'd seen a lot in her real estate career, but it appeared this was a new twist even for her.

"I've decided to hold onto it," he replied. "I do regret wasting any of your time, though, so perhaps a compensation of half your usual broker's fee would help remedy the situation?"

On a place like this, that amount was probably double my annual salary. Not bad for about eighteen hours of work, a fact of which Ms. Wilkerson seemed immediately aware. The real estate agent smile snapped back into place, and she said, "Oh, of course, Mr. Nicolini. That's very generous of you."

"If I might have the key, then?" he inquired, extending a hand.

"Oh—certainly." She fished in her briefcase for something, then drew out a plain white envelope. With a nervous little laugh, she said, "I'm just glad I decided to put off the lockbox until last."

"Very fortunate," Luke agreed, and opened the envelope and withdrew the brass key it held. "Thank you, Janice, and enjoy the rest of your Saturday."

The dismissal was clear. She nodded, flashed a confused smile at me, and then fled. Probably she had left the stack of flyers in the kitchen, but they weren't good for much of anything except recycling at that point anyway.

"Now then," he said, and bent and kissed me.

This time I knew it was exactly right. I couldn't imagine feeling anyone else's lips touching mine ever again. How could I have been so stupid as to think Brad could ever replace Luke?

He pulled away then, and smiled wickedly. "I suppose I must forgive you that small indiscretion…especially since the poor man is feeling rather crushed at the moment."

"If I were a better person, I suppose I'd feel guilty," I remarked. "But as they say, karma's a bitch."

"Yes, she is," Luke agreed, and buried my mouth under his again.

We came up for air a few minutes later. All of my nerve endings were on fire, and I began to wonder if we'd be able to make it inside before we started tearing each other's clothes off. I for one was definitely ready to start making up for lost time. Still, I thought I'd better attempt to act like a rational human being.

"Can you afford that?" I asked, since I didn't know what else to say.

"Afford what?"

"Janice Wilkerson's fee."

He gave me a somewhat indulgent smile. "Of course. Let's just say that God has given me the ultimate golden handshake. You certainly don't need to worry about that sort of thing anymore."

I supposed an eternity of retirement benefits could start to add up, even though it was a little disconcerting to think that money would never be an issue again. "Oh," I said, since I couldn't come up with anything better.

"Let's go in, shall we?" Luke looked up toward the heavens; the blue overhead was being rapidly replaced by gray storm clouds.

I found I didn't mind—we could go into the house we would now share and spend the afternoon together…and all the days afterward.

Luke's fingers wrapped around mine. Warm, strong…*human*.

"So what happens next?" I asked.

His eyes were an echo of that last bit of blue sky. He smiled.

"The rest of our lives," he said.